D1311015

ACKNOWLEDGMENTS

I'd like to thank the early readers of *The Time Baroness*: Pat and Bill Josh Young, Susan Young-Freeman, Juliana Young, Bill Talen, Tara Hein-Phillips, Susan Izatt, Teresa Barile, Eric Johnsen, and Barbara Silkstone, all of whom offered me such encouragement, helpful critiques and edits. I'd especially like to thank my wonderful friend and editor, Kathlyn McGreevy, for helping to mold and shape *The Time Baroness* and for teaching me a thing or two about writing. Particular thanks to my dad, Bill Josh Young, for designing the beautiful book cover. Thanks as well to Lettie Lee and Mari Cronin of the Ann Elmo Agency in New York City for never losing faith. Special thanks to my son, Joshua David Ellis for being an inspiration in so many ways and primarily, thanks to my husband, Jonathan Ellis, reader, editor, constant support, technologically, emotionally and physically; he has continued to believe in me and my ideas and has always given me the space to live and breathe Art in an utterly creative atmosphere.

The Time Baroness

Georgina Young-Ellis

The Time Baroness
by
Georgina Young Ellis

Published by Leaping Tall Buildings Productions LLC
www.ltbprod.com

ISBN: 978-1463783044

1% of all profits from the sale of this book are donated to the
World Food Programme and/or *Heifer International*

 Leaping Tall Buildings Productions LLC

CONTENTS

The Time Baroness is dedicated to
Jonathan, Joshua, my parents,
my two sisters and my brother,
my nieces, nephews and extended family.

I adore you.

CHAPTER ONE

July 25, 2119—The lace tablecloth felt almost real beneath my fingers. Settings of fine china, sterling silverware and crystal goblets glimmered on the long table. I was wearing a burgundy gown in the Empire fashion—the fabric was stiff and chafed under the arms. The waistband of my underwear was too tight. I pulled at it, hoping no-one would see. My leg itched and I couldn't help but scratch it. I glanced at the hostess for clues about how to conduct myself in the formal setting. She was a woman several years my senior, wearing a silvery satin gown. The other guests seated around the table made small talk about the weather. One large-busted lady with pudgy hands asked me with a sneer about my journey from America. I tried to answer in the most appropriate ways, but she merely rolled her eyes and looked away. An elderly man with a hump on his back stared at me sullenly from under his bushy eyebrows without saying a word. A plain younger lady, dressed in lavender silk, snickered at my responses..

A glass of ruby wine sat before me on the table, beckoning. Though I was thirsty, I did not pick it up. Finally, a servant came from behind and ladled a greenish soup into the bowl at my place. I looked to my right. There were several spoons laid out and they all looked similar in size. I chose the one furthest from the bowl, and, after waiting for the hostess, began to eat. The soup was bland, but I was hungry and began to devour it. After a moment, I noticed the conversation had flagged and looked up to see the other guests staring at me, aghast. I dropped the spoon into my bowl and the room and the people all faded away.

I was left sitting in the black simulation room on a folding chair with a card table in front of me, on which there was a bowl of soup, and a glass of wine. Jake's voice boomed out of the darkness.

"Cassie! What was that?"

"I was hungry."

"It doesn't matter! If you're at a dinner party, you have to eat like you're barely interested in the food. You've got to make conversation between delicate bites, not down the meal like a football player!"

"I'm sorry. Can we start again?"

"We'll start from when the soup gets served."

I repeated the dinner party simulation five times before getting every detail correct.

******

"Doing a little shopping, Mom?"

Cassandra Reilly looked up and regarded her son fondly as he burst into her office. Above her desk, a holographic, brown velvet gown slowly rotated.

She laughed. "Yes, this one is nice. What do you think?"

"I have no opinion," he pushed his shaggy black hair out of his face.

"I think it will do. I shall have Shannon put it together for me and fit it, then that will make six dresses. They are quite lightweight for winter gowns; it's a miracle, I mean, *it is* a miracle women did not freeze to death. But, then, I will be wearing a heavy cloak and winter shoes, so there will be less to pack. I shall order more in London when I get there and have them sent down to Hampshire. But how long will it take?"

James opened his mouth to offer his opinion, but Cassandra cut him off. "Probably a couple of weeks." With a command she called up an array of shoes, gloves and bags on the display. "Women then did not have as many changes of clothes as we do now, six should be enough. Well, maybe one more for good measure."

"Mom, don't go crazy. Remember, you'll also be carrying nightclothes, underwear, and God knows what else women needed back then."

"They did not have heavy undergarments in 1820," Cassandra stated. "No corsets or bustles—I do not think I could deal with that."

"Yeah, but you also have to take a cosmetics case with all your potions and creams and stuff."

"Yes, you are right. I will just be carrying my luggage from the portal exit to the White Hart Inn, but it cannot be so much that I'm not able to handle it by myself."

"You used a contraction."

"Pardon?"

"You said, 'I'm' instead of 'I am.'"

"Oh, thank you."

"By the way, how did the inquest go?" James' dark eyes sparkled.

Cassandra chuckled. "It was not exactly an inquest. Just a ritual we have to go through with the Board of Trustees every year to make sure we have the funds for the next project."

"Which hopefully will be *my* journey."

"Yes, but you have to pick a time and place, and if you do not submit a proposal soon, you might get passed over. Suhan is next in line after you, you know."

"Yeah. Anyway, I came in here to tell you that we'll be ready to put Jake through the portal on January second, and as soon as he has all your details secure and he's back, you go."

"Excellent." Cassandra was now examining a holographic evening shawl.

"I wish I could go with him," James said suddenly.

She turned to him. "Why?"

"Because I want to make sure he gets everything right."

"Oh, please, Jake is an experienced time traveler. I trust him completely."

"Yeah, but I'm worried about you going for so long, and if I were there, at least I could be certain that he finds you the perfect house, in the perfect place—"

Cassandra flashed him a wry smile. "I have never known you to be so concerned about me. I think you just want in on the action."

"No, that's not true. I'm very concerned about you. You're going to be gone a long time, and you're going to be all on your own. I'll be worried about you."

"I appreciate that, sweetheart," she said, trying not to doubt his sincerity, "but the more we just focus on getting the details of my trip right in the here and now, the better off I shall be. Speaking of which, how is the coin duplication going?"

"Slowly. I still don't see why Jake can't just open your account with bills. Everyone used them then, especially in such large quantities."

"James, we have been over this. If we used bills, it would just be counterfeiting, and frankly, it would be a little harder to reproduce the look and feel of them as accurately as a gold coin, since we have almost no examples of the bills. But just like counterfeiting, introducing that many bills into the circulation that have no silver or gold to back them up would impact the economy negatively. Not hugely, and not for a while, but the last thing we want to do is cause any impact, negative or not."

"The good old Bank of England will sure be surprised when Jake walks in with a bag full of gold. I just hope he can get it safely from the portal exit to the White Hart, and then from there to the bank."

"It will be a challenge, but Jake can handle it. He is a strong man, and he does not have to carry many other things, like I do."

"Too bad they didn't have hover-luggage back then."

"Or at least luggage with wheels. Has Jake identified a realtor?"

"Mom, I'm sure they weren't called realtors, back then."

"Right you are—*purveyors of property*. Thank you.

"Well, the research shows that one of the most reputable 'purveyors of property' was Hacket and Smith, so Jake's going to try them first. And January's a good time to put a house up for rent."

"'Let' a house James, say 'let.' I have to get used to using the right words."

"Okay, 'let' a house. You're the one who has to say it, not me."

"I am practicing."

"I know. Anyway, everyone will be in town for 'the season,' as they say, including those who may have great property wealth, but little cash to speak of. It won't be hard to find the sort of family that's eager to let their estate, complete with furniture and all but their own personal servants for at least a year; especially if you're willing to pay well, which you are."

"Just like in *Persuasion*," mused Cassandra.

"Right," James said, rolling his eyes.

"Well, I know you do not understand, but that is the life I want to experience. I want to go, be a good little Hampshire tenant, live quietly in 1820 for a year, mingle as unobtrusively as possible in society, and just live life as closely as I can to how Jane Austen lived it. I will actually be there three years after her death; as you know, I will also be richer than she was, and I will not have my family about me like she did. I am older than she was when she died, and a widow (she never married), but I will be a single woman in more or less her class of society. I am just going to soak in Jane's countryside, her home, her England."

"Sounds fascinating."

"Well, you do not have to comprehend my reasons. I am just glad you are part of the team. You know the technical aspect almost better than I do, and that makes me feel safe."

"Could you just tell me one more time why you're not going a few years earlier so you can meet ol' Jane herself? I don't get it."

Cassandra sighed. "Because I do not want to…it is too…" She'd had trouble explaining this before. "I guess I do not want to intrude on her world. Meeting her is not the object; understanding her reality is."

"Whatever you say." James stood and ruffled the top of his mother's hair.

"Please refrain from doing that, James," she complained, "you know I do not like it." She rearranged her auburn curls.

"That's why I do it," he returned with a grin. "See ya later, mom." He bounded out the door.

She shook her head and went back to the hologram of a particularly adorable pair of evening slippers that were slowly twirling around in space above her desk.

******

Jan 1st, 2120—The first day of the New Year. I'm so excited about my upcoming journey, my stomach is churning, my mind is racing and I'm trying not to turn into a complete nervous wreck. Today I spent some time checking in on my townhouse in Boston with the virtual-cam, just to make sure everything's in good order there. I've been doing it every couple of weeks since we moved to our temporary lab in London, but I probably won't have time again before I go, so I wanted to really go over it thoroughly today.

As I virtually walked through the old townhouse, I realized how much I miss it: the place Franklin and I lived together so long, and where James was raised. I remember when we bought it; we couldn't believe our luck at finding a place that, though nearly three hundred years old, was large enough to accommodate the Steinway (which I also desperately miss). Going from room to room, I recalled so many memories, things that don't tend to occur to me when I'm there in person.

The place was spotless; I set it to self-clean once a week. The V-cam array doesn't extend out into the garden, so I couldn't check on it. I just have to trust that this gardener, who came so highly recommended, is taking as good care of it as I would.

The indoor plants all looked good; they're on their own watering systems, so that's not an issue. I have to remember to check with the neighbor to see how Meng the "merciless" cat is doing. He was so sweet to offer to keep her for more than a year.

Now I'm on my way to bed, so I can be at the lab in good time tomorrow for any last minute preparations for Jake's trip tomorrow night. I'll have another one to two weeks to make sure I'm ready, depending on how long it takes Jake to get everything set up for me. I'm excited and nervous for him too.

******

On the evening of Jake's departure, the entire team gathered in the crowded lab that had been constructed in a London alley. From the outside, it resembled a long rectangular metal box with a door at the front. It was essentially a glorified trailer. It took up every square inch of the alley, which dead-ended after about one hundred feet and was about eight feet wide, and situated just off Long Acre in Covent Garden. Three hundred years ago, it had existed in much the same way, but in the present it was used for the recycling waste of the buildings on either side. Professor Carver's team, temporarily displaced from MIT, had paid the building managers well to make other arrangements for the fourteen months or so that the lab would have to be in place. Passersby and residents of the area were curious about the strange edifice with many odd antennae, poles, and wires protruding from the roof; however, the team tried to keep its purpose a secret as much as possible, just to dissuade busybodies from disturbing them. Although the general population had known of Carver's discovery of time travel for many years, it wasn't helpful to have the curious snooping about.

The layout inside the lab was similar to an old-fashioned railroad apartment. The first room, just inside the front door, was a lounge area with sofas and coffee tables, music equipment, and a Virtual Reality Platform. Beyond that, there was a small kitchen and a bathroom. Behind the kitchen wall was the functioning part of the lab with computer panels and time calibrators. This was also where the pod was located, a vertical tube that could be accessed by a sliding door, resembling, in many ways, nothing more than a shower stall. Behind a final wall was a small sleeping area with an additional bathroom and working shower. The scientists would have to take turns manning the lab twenty-four hours a day for the entire length of Jake and Cassandra's journeys.

Jake stood ready in a brown waist coat and high-collared white shirt, slim, high-waisted trousers covering black boots, a double-breasted frock coat for warmth, and a tall, black hat on his head. In one hand he held a small satchel of extra clothing, in the other a bag filled with gold coins. It contained the equivalent of five thousand British pounds, which in 1820 could supply an entire family with a sumptuous living for years. The team had decided that Jake would use the name Jackson Taylor, rather than Jacob Hershowitz, to avoid the anti-Semitism common in Europe at that time, but physically, he would fit in just fine. He was stocky and short with pale skin, light brown, wavy hair, brown eyes, and an open, friendly face; he had been coached in the speech and mannerisms of the day and had participated in several of the VR simulations.

It was nine-thirty at night on Tuesday, January second. The team had calculated that Jake would actually emerge in 1820 on the fourth instead of the second, but at the same time in the evening. It would be cold and dark, and the streets would probably be mostly empty. Time-matter sensors in the lab could sense the warmth of living beings, and the size and approximate weight of life forms in the immediate vicinity of the portal exit at the back of the alley in 1820, the same location where the pod now resided. In order for Jake to return to 2120, he would have to return to the location of the portal exit in the alley. The scientist on duty would note the size and weight of the life form and make sure it exactly matched Jake's pre-recorded physical measurements before bringing him back. It all would happen in a matter of seconds.

As she looked at the heat sensor monitor, Cassandra noticed small flickers of light dart back and forth through the alley—cats and rats, by the size of them—but no humans. Another half hour ticked by. Jake was ready to go. If they waited much longer, the inn might be closed for the night. Jake stepped into the pod with his bags, and everyone stood ready at their stations. James was manning the travel mode. Cassandra double-checked that the functions were correctly set. All systems were ready to go. Jake waved enthusiastically, the pod door slid closed, the computer sounded a tone, the pod hummed, and within a second, he was gone.

CHAPTER TWO

It took Cassandra a moment to adjust to the enveloping darkness but Jake had warned her. Electricity made a huge difference to the lightness of a city. A faint flicker of firelight glowed in a few small windows of thick glass that shone onto the alleyway. She perceived a gas lamp softly glowing out on the street. She looked up. She could see a million stars—a peculiarly vivid night sky for London. She cleared her head; she had to hurry. It would be very dangerous for her to be caught alone in such an obscure place. She was carrying a knife in her cloak pocket, which she clutched. A second later, the cold hit her. She was not dressed for it. She let the knife fall back into her pocket, grabbed her two bags, and ran to the street. She knew to turn left; the inn was just one short block away. She passed only two or three people hurrying through the freezing night air. She arrived at the White Hart in a matter of minutes and breathed a sigh of relief. A doorman showed her in with a look of surprise, and immediately relieved her of her bags which were then passed off to the bellman.

"May I show ya the front desk, miss?" he asked, in a thick cockney accent. He looked her over thoroughly with protruding eyes.

"Yes, please," she replied, allowing herself to be led.

"Good evening, miss," said the innkeeper, who struggled to his feet from where he had been dozing in his chair, "May I help you?" He quickly smoothed his thinning hair.

"I am Mrs. Cassandra Franklin." she said to him. "My representative, Mr. Jackson Taylor was here several days ago arranging for my arrival. He said you would have a room available for me."

"Oh, yes, of course, Mrs. Franklin. He paid well to reserve you the best room in the inn. He predicted the date of your arrival quite accurately, and here you are!" He tapped on his registration book. "Good, very good. I am sure you are tired coming all that way from Portsmouth, not to mention the journey from America. How pleased we are to have you here! Can I set up a room for your maid as well?" he asked, craning to look around her.

"No," Cassandra said with a choke in her voice. "My maid, she…she did not survive the journey from America. I am quite alone."

"Oh dear heavens! We had no idea—so sorry, so very sorry," he exclaimed.

"If you please," replied Cassandra, dropping her eyelids, "I would like to simply retire for the evening; I am overcome."

"Yes, of course, at your service, ma'am. Charlie!" he called to the young bellman. "Get Betsy. Have her show Mrs. Franklin to her room immediately. Get the fire lit, bring her a warm basin of water; make sure she has the freshest linens, and a glass of wine. Hurry now, hurry! Are you hungry, Mrs. Franklin?"

"No, thank you," murmured Cassandra while dabbing at her eyes with a handkerchief. "You are too kind."

Charlie had not yet gone to fetch Betsy, but stood staring at the visitor. "Is it only the two bags, ma'am?" he uttered.

"Yes, I…I brought very little in the interest of—starting over, you know."

"No need to say another word, I'll fetch 'em upstairs in two shakes." He hurried off, leaving the bags in their place.

Cassandra and the innkeeper stood awkwardly alone for a moment. Cassandra sniffed the air. Something smelled like moldy cheese. Was it the innkeeper?

Betsy appeared and guided the visitor to her room. With the shock of being thrust into a world she could only before dream and read about, and the relief at having successfully arrived at her destination, Cassandra allowed herself to be fussed over by the maid. Charlie arrived with the bags and then retreated. Finally, locking herself in, she considered her first night in the world of 1820 England.

She gazed around the room, cheerfully lit by lamps and candles. The fire blazed in the hearth, but she now realized how she had always taken for granted the wonder of integrated heating. The gas that lit the lamps on the streets and the coal and wood that were used for heat were, by 2120, quaint remnants of a world that had once fought constantly over oil and almost driven itself to catastrophe by global warming with the use of fossil fuels. Now, at this moment, Cassandra was stunned by the inefficiency of fire. Her first order of business tomorrow would be to purchase heavier woolen undergarments and order sturdier gowns. Though Jake had warned her about the cold, he was a man who had the privilege of wearing pants and jackets and couldn't guess how much colder she would be.

The room was probably quite luxurious for an inn of the time, she decided. She took in each item. The curtains were heavy red velvet, faded with time and dusty at the top. The four poster bed, the principal piece of furniture in the room, had a thick headboard of dark wood, nicked in places, and was canopied with the same velvet curtains as the windows. At the foot was a large chest on which Charlie had placed her suitcase. There was a spindly writing desk and chair in a corner, an armoire against one wall with a crack running down one of the doors, a painted dresser against another with an oval mirror above it, and near the dresser, a pitcher of water, a glass and a basin on a small round table, covered with a yellowed lace doily. She looked down at a red print area rug at her feet that was worn, but clean. Something scuttled along the edge of the wall and caught her eye. A cockroach. She shuddered, and ran to her suitcase, extracting a tiny folded packet from a small cloth pouch containing many similar packets. She unfolded it and blew on the fine powder contained inside. It dispersed into the air, becoming invisible almost at once. The microfine insecticide went to work and in seconds the cockroach stopped dead. Cassandra breathed a sigh of relief knowing that all crawling creatures abiding in the room would now die as well (though the formula was totally harmless to humans), and none others would intrude for several days.

She lifted her cosmetics case onto the dresser and stopped for a moment to look in the mirror. How did she appear to these people, she wondered? Now that the trip was a reality, this question loomed larger than she ever thought it would. She'd been nervous about seeming out of place, but standing in front of the ancient mirror, that possibility took on a whole other level of importance.

Her image was soft in the lamplight. For one thing, she knew that no one would ever guess that she was anywhere close to her age. She could easily pass for thirty. In comparison, Betsy, who Cassandra imagined to actually be around thirty years old, was already missing teeth, her cheeks were hollow and her skin was lined. Cassandra smiled at herself. Her teeth were perfect, more perfect than those of ninety-nine percent of the people of any class that she would encounter during her stay—and white, too white. Well, she hadn't been willing to stain them; she'd have to make up some story about the miracle tooth powder in America if anyone commented. And her hair, even in the low light, shined. It had no gray, thanks to the years of taking herbal supplements, which allowed one's hair to continually grow any color one wanted, depending on the formula. Her blue/gray eyes had been treated by laser surgery to install

UV blockers and shade adjusters, which, like the sunglasses of decades ago, grew darker to shade the retina when exposed to the sun.

She turned her head from one side to the other and examined her face. Her skin was almost without wrinkles, sags or jowls, just a few laugh lines around the eyes (for good measure). She had collagen rebirth treatments to thank for that, as well as creams and pills that blocked sun damage and rebuilt cells. When she got really old, she figured, she could always rely on cosmetic adjustments to reverse the signs of aging. Of course, good health on the inside was a factor too.

She opened the cosmetics case. Inside were powdered concentrates of the various herbs and vitamins she relied on to maintain her health and youthfulness. They were all packaged to look like products of the day (things you could only buy in America, she would say). There were creams and lotions—more than enough for her year's stay.

Cassandra went back to her suitcase and removed her nightgown. She had insisted to Betsy that she unpack her own things; this was easier than worrying about what might arouse curiosity. She took off her gown and stiff undergarments, leaving on her bloomers, stockings, and chemise. (Shannon had insisted that she wear a lighter, shorter version of a corset, which she said the fashionable ladies wore at the time under their dressy clothes). She threw her nightgown over her thermal underthings, shivering. She quickly cleansed her face with her specially prepared creams and brushed her teeth with the sort of toothpowder and toothbrush that looked authentic to the time period but were, in fact, undetectably enhanced to perform up to modern standards. She was relieved not to have to take the time to remove make-up. Even though she'd had her eyelashes and eyebrows permanently dyed, and subtle, but permanent color applied to her lips, she was still used to wearing a little bit. Well, it's all natural for me from now on, she thought. Okay, not quite all natural.

Finally, she removed a vintage perfume bottle from her case. She removed the stopper, which extracted a little glass wand. Once she applied the lavender-scented liquid to her wrists it would work subcutaneously and she would be asleep within a minute. Time travel was upsetting to the body's natural rhythms, and though it was dark outside, her body had not adjusted to the time of day. This night was the zenith of nearly a lifetime's work. Anything could happen, anything could go wrong. She needed her wits about her and she needed sleep. She touched the cold wand of the sleep aid to her wrists, extinguished the candles, and climbed under the thick covers of the bed, confident that the bug powder had done its job. She snuggled in to get warm and noticed that the bed smelled of unidentifiable soap, of sheets still damp from the London air. Her heart was pounding with all that lay before her. But the sleep aid started doing its work, her heartbeat slowed, her breathing deepened, and she closed her eyes on the first few hours of her new life in Regency England.

******

In the morning she woke to a soft rap on the door.

"Come in!" she called from the warm bed.

A key turned in the lock as Cassandra peered out from under the covers. The cold in the room stung her face.

"Good morning, ma'am," declared Betsy as she entered. "I've come to light your fire and bring you some warm water for bathing. I could even arrange a tub for you if you please, after your long journey."

A bath sounded good but complicated. "I think I shall make do with the basin for now; thank-you, but perhaps later."

"Very well, ma'am." Cassandra watched Betsy stoke up the fire from the snug warmth of her bed. "Would you like me to open the curtains?"

"I shall do it, Betsy, thank you so much." She envied the thick fabric of the maid's dress.

Betsy hesitated. "Very well. And how about yer breakfast, ma'am. Shall I bring it up or would y' care to have it downstairs in the parlor?"

"I think I will take it up here," replied Cassandra; she wasn't quite ready to make small talk with the other guests. She considered it better to seem a little shy for now, and build up to the socializing in due time. She suddenly felt insecure about everything from her clothes to her mannerisms. She knew she was well studied and trained, but in spite of the help from all her coaches and the simulations, she knew she would eventually make mistakes.

"Very good, ma'am… if there is nothing else—"

"No Betsy, that will be all."

"Very well then, I will leave you to yerself, and I will have yer breakfast in about twenty minutes."

"Sounds wonderful, thank you."

Betsy's smile faded as she glanced around the room again. Cassandra just stared at her, at a loss for what else to say, until the woman finally gave a nod and backed out of the room.

"Sounds wonderful?" Cassandra repeated to herself. Is that something they would say? Think, Cassandra! Think before you speak, for God's sake!

She began to clean up as well as she could, as close to the fire as possible, and to dress in the warmest clothes she had brought. She had practiced getting in and out of the garments many times, and could manage it pretty well by now. Shannon designed both the inner and outer wear so that she could put it on without assistance, which was no small feat considering the complexity of the clothing that was worn by the upper class—and of course, it all must still appear completely authentic to anyone, such as a maid, who might come in contact with it. The gowns had flattering high waists and little need to be held in by girdles and corsets because the comfortable undergarments that Shannon had designed provided structure with stays and improved one's posture and bust line.

Cassandra finished dressing and turned to her hair. She had also practiced over and over winding it into a high pile of curls at the back of her head, using only the implements that would be available to her in 1820, and could do it quickly now. Just as she was finishing, Betsy appeared with the breakfast.

"Oh! Right elegant you are, ma'am, such a beauty, my goodness!" she exclaimed.

Cassandra blushed. "You are too kind, I am sure," she replied, feeling it was the correct response. She followed Betsy to the writing desk.

"Oh, not at all, ma'am, not at all," Betsy replied, setting the tray down. Her breath wafted over Cassandra, who quickly turned her head from the odor. But then the maid moved away and the delicious smell of the breakfast prevailed. Cassandra looked it over: eggs and ham, rolls and butter, tea with thick cream and honey, oatmeal porridge with dried fruit, a large slice of pale yellow cheese. She would never be able to eat it all.

"This looks delightful, Betsy, thank you."

"Will you be requiring anything else, ma'am?"

"No! Thank you. This is plenty."

"My pleasure, ma'am." The maid went out and closed the door.

First things first, Cassandra thought. She went to her case to extract a bottle of pills. The tablets would serve to regulate her digestion and protect against parasites or food or water-borne bacteria. She could not afford to get seriously ill; she had no way to call the team for help. They had supplied her with as many prophylactic and first aid substances as possible, but she could only carry so much. She had five-hundred of the digestive aids, more than enough for one day.

In addition to protecting her digestive tract, she had certain dietary concerns. Mostly, she could eat anything, but she wasn't used to caffeine, and the British tea was strong. Therefore, another tiny tablet, which she could carry with her and drop into her tea, would neutralize the effect of the stimulant. If someone wondered what she was putting in her cup, she would show the label, which read "Nerve Tablets for Ladies."

She also needed to be careful about her sugar intake. In 1820, fine pastries were made with the white sugar that her system was not used to handling. She had to be prepared to eat what was offered to her in the interest of politeness, but God knows she didn't need any hysterical episodes brought on by a blood-sugar crash.

Having fortified her system, she got set to explore the breakfast. The flavors were distinct and vivid, fresher than she'd ever tasted, though she was in the middle of London and people in her own world had access to the very freshest foods. The chickens were probably out in back of the inn laying the eggs, she thought. The ham was probably just recently smoked on a farm outside the city, the rolls baked moments ago in the inn's oven, the cream delivered every day from some nearby dairy farm, the tea, black as could be and thrillingly bitter. She ate more than she thought possible.

Breakfast finished, she looked over her planned schedule for the day. She had much to accomplish within eight hours. First she would post a note to the housekeeper in Hampshire, who was awaiting her arrival at her new home. She had brought a small writing set, the kind commonly used by a lady of her position, and, schooled in the flowery script that was nineteenth century handwriting, penned a quick note saying that she was in the country and expected to be down the next day. She could afford to pay anything it cost to get the message there in one day, and its destination was indeed an entire day's ride by horseback.

Her next task was clothes shopping. Jake had found a first-rate dressmaker nearby. She and Jake had walked there and back to the White Hart several times in the simulations they were able to create after he had returned from his advance journey. He had noted the names and addresses of the shops and businesses she would need, and the VR library had done a spectacular job of recreating those few blocks of old London with the information Jake had given them.

She was gathering up her cloak and gloves to go out, when she began to feel the need for the water closet. She had used the chamber pot in her room the night before and again that morning for urinating, but this urge, she had learned from her research, ought to, if at all possible, be deposited in the water closet down the hall. She stepped nervously into the hallway and peered around. All clear. She tiptoed down the hall and rapped on the door. No answer. She took a deep breath and opened the door. She was in luck, it flushed! It was rudimentary to be sure, but a crank on the side actually flushed it with water, though it didn't fill afterwards. Thank God, she thought, all right, here goes. She went in and latched the door——she could only hold her breath so long. She was forced to inhale at last. It wasn't so bad.

That done, she went back to her room, washed her hands in the basin, and put on her cloak, hood, and gloves. On the way out, she handed her letter to the desk clerk with the money for the post and a generous tip, and was assured it would go out that morning. She was carrying about ten British pounds in coins, divided between hidden pockets and her purse, to hold her over until she could get to the bank.

She stepped out the door of the inn into the street, and the stench hit her, a cross of human and animal excrement, rotting food, and shallow cemeteries. The simulations couldn't prepare her for this, and the night before, in her hurry, with the freezing temperatures, and the streets being so empty, she didn't notice it. But now the sun was warming the streets full of horses and carriages. She remembered that London, at this point, had a sewer system, but it essentially emptied into the Thames.

She set off for the dressmaker's, clutching a kerchief to her nose, but generally not attracting undue attention due to her hood and cloak, though it was odd for a woman of her obvious upper class to be out on the streets with no escort.

It was unbelievably cold, but she knew the way there and arrived quickly. Brown and Clark's it was called. She entered, lowered her hood, and was met with stares.

"Good morning," Cassandra smiled.

"Good morning, miss, how may I help you?" asked the proprietress.

"Yes, I…I am recently arrived from America and need some gowns and underthings. I am afraid I am ill prepared for the British climate. I hope you can help me."

"Oh, yes, of course," said the woman relaxing her gaze. Her face was pock-marked and she wore spectacles. Together they rifled through the bolts of fabric and reviewed dress patterns. Cassandra submitted to a fitting, and the shop owner essentially abandoned her other customers, though they didn't seem to mind, so fascinated were they with the striking American. The woman then found her some good woolen stockings, as well as heavier weight chemises and drawers. Cassandra's shoes were as fit for the weather as could be expected, as were her gloves and her cloak. She was beginning to feel she would be able to deal with the cold as long as it didn't get too much worse.

Paying the lady for her purchases, supplying her with the Hampshire address for their delivery and tipping her generously, Cassandra then hailed a hackney coach to take her the distance to the bank on Threadneedle Street. She carried only a small package containing her new undergarments. She would pay for the finished gowns when they were delivered to her.

When the cab stopped in front of the bank, Cassandra stepped out gingerly onto the muddy street and picked her way to the entrance of the enormous columned building, the original Bank of England. A doorman opened the heavy wooden doors, and looked down at her, lips pursed. Inside the bank, the air was only slightly warmer than the outside; a fire burned impotently in a great stone fireplace. The ceilings were too high, the granite walls and marble floors too unforgiving to allow themselves to be warmed. Before she could decide whom to approach, the bank manager hurried up to her as fast as his girth would allow, a frown creasing his flushed brow.

"Good morning, miss, is there something we can do for you?" he asked in a syrupy tone.

"Yes, I am, um, looking for a Mr. Howard," Cassandra said modestly. "I am Mrs. Cassandra Franklin."

"Oh, of course, Mrs. Franklin! Please forgive me. I am Mr. Howard." He suddenly stood up taller and tugged at his lapels. After all, this woman's legal representative had recently deposited several thousand pounds in his bank. "Right this way, madam. Please come into my office and we shall settle your business there."

"Thank you," she replied, and followed him into a large room with windows set high, a grand wooden desk with claw feet and two well-worn leather chairs, one on each side of the desk, all warmed somewhat more efficiently by a coal stove.

She withdrew two thousand pounds, more than enough to get her through the year. The full year's rent on the house had been paid by Jake, which included the salaries of all the servants. It was odd handling money, Cassandra thought. In the twenty-second century, skin-cell scanning was how one was identified to every bank-linked computer in nearly every shop or restaurant. She took the bills and coins and put them in her bag, enjoying the new feel of the money in her hand. She thanked Mr. Howard; he bowed deeply and offered his personal carriage and a bodyguard to escort her back to the inn. She gratefully accepted, and, once she arrived at her room, locked the money in the false bottom of her suitcase.

Jake had assured Cassandra that Sorrel Hall, as her new country home was called, had a fine piano, and he'd designated a music shop for her in London where she could buy sheet music. She'd brought none for fear of inadvertently exposing any composers who had not yet been published. So after a modest lunch alone in her room, she walked the few blocks to the shop, Jake's directions clutched in her hand. From halfway down the street she saw the sign Stockard's Music Shop. She entered the quiet store, dimly lit by half-burned candles and a small fire flickering in the corner hearth. The familiar smell of wood and old paper was tinged with pipe tobacco. Sheet music stores haven't changed in three hundred years, she thought.

The shopkeeper smiled at her. He was in his fifties, she guessed, with longish graying hair and warm brown eyes. His glance lingered on her for a moment; then he returned to closely examining a cello bow. She sighed with relief, knowing it was natural for a lady to be looking about in a music store.

Cassandra soon located Bach. The store had an admirable selection, and she chose several pieces that she had never tried to master. She then leafed through Beethoven; some of her favorite sonatas were there and some minor piano pieces. She browsed down the alphabet; there was plenty of Italian baroque, some of which she selected, but she didn't recognize too much else until she came to the H's where she found Handel and Hayden, some of which she had never seen before. She felt like a kid finding her Easter basket. Moving on, she located Mozart, and farther on Scarlatti, but no Schubert.

"Excuse me, you do not carry Schubert?"

"I am sorry, miss?" he looked up from his work.

"Schubert, Franz Schubert?"

"I am sorry, miss, I have never heard of him. Is he modern?"

"Yes, he is, quite modern. I heard him in Ger…Austria when I was there," she said, remembering that Germany, as such, did not yet exist, and neither did the works of Schubert. "But, I am being silly; his work cannot be known outside of that country yet."

"Do not trouble yourself, miss. Is there anything else I can help you find?"

"No," she replied, looking at the pile of music in her arms. Realizing that it would not all fit in her suitcase, she said, "let me narrow down my selections a little," and culling through her choices, she finally laid several pieces in front of him on the counter.

"Wonderful selections, miss. You must be quite a musician."

She smiled. "I do not think I am, but I love to play."

"That is all that matters, is it not? Where shall I have your package delivered?"

"The White Hart, Mrs. Cassandra Franklin."

He stopped for a moment, surprised, and studied her. "My pleasure, Mrs. Franklin, I will have them there shortly."

She paid him and then made the bold move to shake his hand. "You are Mr. Stockard?"

"Yes, I am, and it is delightful to make your acquaintance."

"The pleasure is mine," she replied.

"I hope to see you again."

"I am moving down to Hampshire tomorrow, but whenever I am in London, I shall visit your shop."

"I will look forward to it."

"Good afternoon," she said with a smile and stepped out into the waning daylight.

It was early, not yet four, but the days were short in London in winter, especially with the fog and overcast sky. She imagined it best to hurry back to the inn. Feeling confident of the way, she turned left out of the shop and walked past several storefronts until suddenly she felt disoriented. No, wait, she thought; she had come from the other way. She walked back and passed the shop again, continued to the end of the block, and turned left. Was it one or two blocks to Long Acre, she wondered. She couldn't remember, and the fog was closing in, making it difficult to see. She had heard about these fogs. They were much more severe than in modern London, due to so much smoke, mixed with the vapors off the river. She searched her pocket for Jake's directions but it was not there. She tried her handbag, but could not locate the slip of paper. Her jaw tightened. In spite of the fact that she had walked these same streets in the simulations, in reality, they did not look quite the same, and she now wasn't sure if she had gone one block or two. She couldn't see the street signs, nor even ten feet in front of her, and felt a twinge of anxiety. She continued on and nearly fell off a curb. This must be Long Acre, she thought. She could hear carriages passing in front and could just make out their looming shapes. The streets were starting to thin of people and vehicles. She turned right and walked for a few minutes, but it was getting darker and the fog was engulfing. She didn't know if she had passed the inn now. She looked for the overhead signs, but could see nothing. Maybe she had gone too far. She walked back to the corner, passing the occasional pedestrian who would appear suddenly out of the mist. She then walked carefully back in the direction she thought the White Hart to be, feeling along the walls for doorways. Her panic rose. What if I can't find it, she wondered. She could only dimly see the light of the gas lamps along the street. She kept walking; surely it couldn't be this far. She began to turn back, when all of a sudden someone grabbed her arm. She gasped and tried to wrench away, while feeling for the knife in her cloak pocket.

"Mrs. Franklin!" said a voice. The face came into focus.

"Mr. Stockard!" she cried with relief.

"I decided to bring your music myself," he said. "I think I must have given you quite a start."

"Oh yes," she said, her heart pounding. "I am so relieved to see you! I cannot find the inn."

"It is right here," he said, and in a few steps they were through the front of the door and inside.

"I am afraid I am not used to the fog." She touched her damp brow with the back of her gloved hand.

"It can be quite treacherous," he replied. "Sir," he called to the porter, "Help Mrs. Franklin to a chair and bring her a glass of wine."

"Oh, no, thank you," she said. "I think I will just go to my room. Thank you so much for your help. You are my hero today." She thought she detected a blush.

"I am just happy I arrived when I did. Miss," he called out to Betsy who had come over to see what the commotion was. "Will you please carry this package upstairs for Mrs. Franklin?"

"That will not be necessary," said Cassandra, "I shall take it. I really am fine now, I assure you. But thank you again."

"It was my pleasure," replied Mr. Stockard, smiling. "Goodnight then," he said, tipping his hat to her. "I hope we meet again."

"I hope so too," responded Cassandra graciously. "Goodnight." She smiled and shook his hand again. He opened the door and stepped briskly into the murky evening.

Cassandra ordered the wine in her room after all. If she was ever in need of a "soother" it was now. She told the porter she would have supper in the dining parlor in an hour. She didn't feel like spending the evening alone.

Her fire had been lit. She threw off her cloak and gloves and sank onto the bed. She looked over at the window; it was as if someone had hung a gray blanket outside. She sipped her wine and allowed its relaxing effect. Eventually she got up, lit some lamps and candles, and pored over her new music. Hunger finally led her to set it aside, and she wandered down to the front desk to have a coach ordered for nine in the morning to take her the forty miles to Hampshire the next day.

In the dining parlor, she was seated at a round table with four other guests, three men and a forlorn-looking young woman, thin and pale with light brown hair and large dark eyes in an oval face. During the course of the meal of leek soup, roast chicken and potatoes, boiled Brussels sprouts, fresh rolls and butter, cold ham and roast beef, dried fruit, cheese and cake, she chatted with the gentlemen. Each of them was a merchant of different sorts, in town for varying lengths of time to sell their wares.

Cassandra found it difficult to draw much information out of them because they were mostly curious about her. They wanted to know all about America and her reasons for travelling alone so far. Cassandra didn't reveal much except that she was born in Lyme Regis on the southern coast of England, and had moved to America with her parents when she was barely six years. She had married, had a son, and was eventually widowed. She'd longed to return to her homeland, and was going to Hampshire while her son studied at Harvard.

The young woman seated with them at the table had been staring at her.

"Do you mind if I ask where you are traveling to?" Cassandra said, turning to her. The merchants lost interest and began to talk among themselves.

The girl addressed her plate. "I am going to Kent, ma'am." Her light brown hair was pulled tightly into a bun, making her sharp cheekbones all the more prominent.

"I am Cassandra Franklin. Do you mind if I ask what takes you to Kent?"

"Pleased to make your acquaintance. My name is Rosalind Carr. I am going to be a governess, ma'am." Her response was barely audible.

"Oh!" said Cassandra. "How many children will you care for?"

"Four, ma'am."

"Girls or boys?"

"Three girls and a boy. The eldest girl is seven. The boy is the youngest; he is two."

"Ah." Cassandra felt inadequate in her response. Her questioning was not having the enlivening effect she had hoped.

"Have you met your employer?" She asked in a last effort.

"No," said Rosalind with a tremor in her voice. Her pointed chin began to quiver.

Cassandra gently touched her arm. "Oh, I am sure they are a lovely family."

"I am sure they are, ma'am." The young woman retrieved a hankie from her pocket and dabbed at her eyes. "Please excuse me," she said, pushing her half-eaten supper away. "I am terribly exhausted. I think I shall retire. Goodnight." She hurried out of the dining room.

Cassandra sighed and finished her meal in silence. The men finally took their leave to go smoke cigars, and, fatigued, Cassandra went upstairs to her room.

She pulled out her journal. It looked exactly like any lady's diary of that time, and though she'd begun practicing the archaic art of putting pen to paper a few months ago, the pages remained blank. There was a slim, golden bookmark attached with a clip to the book. Whenever she made an entry containing anachronistic information, she would run the bookmark over the page and her entry would disappear into the microscopic chips, residing both in the bookmark and the page. She dipped her pen into the inkwell.

January 15, 1820 – I met a young woman tonight, Rosalind, who is going to work as a nanny, obviously traveling alone, probably because there was no money for a maid or a companion. At least she has good lodgings, possibly paid for by the new employers so maybe they will be kind to her. The poor thing wasn't unattractive; I suppose she has a chance of meeting a man and marrying, but if her family is so impoverished that they had to send her off to be a governess, that means she doesn't have a dowry. I imagine she hasn't had any marriage prospects thus far.

It makes me think that perhaps my own invention of a life as a wealthy widow is unrealistic. Most of these women had no say over their destinies—so often their husbands' estates were left to surviving male relatives, whom their wives became dependent on. As the independent American, I am in an envious position.

At any rate, my year's experiment has begun. This will be a fascinating time, learning from a perspective that no other research on the time period could ever hope to reveal. My one day here has already proven so interesting, so challenging. I am elated at the prospect of what lies before me.

******

Cassandra wiped out the final two paragraphs of her entry with the bookmark. She stretched. The room was warm and cozy from the fire that had been maintained while she was at dinner. She went through her nighttime beauty routine and climbed into bed. She had brought a couple of reproduced books with her, some of the Gothic novels Miss Austen so loved to satirize, so that she'd have them on hand and wouldn't have to spend time in London searching for them. By the light of the candle, she read Ann Radcliffe's *The Mysteries of Udolpho* until she finally blew out the flame. As the complete darkness enveloped her, the thrill of the story remained. For a moment, in Cassandra's dreamlike wakefulness, fog swirled around a woman in a hooded cloak—the frail governess standing alone in the heath on the moors. In the next instant, without assistance from any potion, the time traveler fell into a deep sleep.

CHAPTER THREE

I n the morning, Cassandra rose early, stirred up the fire, began to dress and pack up her things. She felt disgusting from not having had a proper bath. Hopefully I don't smell too bad, she thought, God knows it's going to be hard to go a year without a shower.

At eight Betsy appeared with her breakfast. The coach arrived precisely an hour later, and within a few moments, she bid farewell to the White Hart. A footman guided her step into the black, polished carriage pulled by four horses.

She stared out the window as the coach rattled on the cobblestone streets, passing closely packed shops with residences above them. The steps were well swept, the hanging signs brightly painted, and smartly dressed patrons hurried along, clutching their cloaks. The coach headed south and soon they were following the river. The spires of Westminster Abbey rose in the cold morning sun and Cassandra peered around to identify which other major landmarks of London had not changed between then and three hundred years in the future. Big Ben was not yet part of the skyline, nor certainly the London Eye or Grant Tower, the tallest building in Europe since the year 2100. But the Houses of Parliament were there, and farther south across the river she could just make out the top of Lambeth Palace. Her view of the Thames was suddenly blocked by a high brick wall that continued on for some time; it gave her an uneasy feeling of confinement and she was relieved when it was behind them.

The smell of rot began to penetrate the closed windows of the carriage. The streets ceased to be cobblestone and grew muddy with the urine of horses. The houses became narrower, squeezed more tightly together, some leaning against each other for support. A butcher exited his shop and flung a bucket of blood into the street, barely missing the coach. Children in rags scurried through the streets and Cassandra feared they would be crushed by the wheels of the many rushing vehicles. Once the coach was beyond the city proper, she noticed the neighborhoods grew prosperous again with large stone homes surrounded by gardens, now winter bare. The horses climbed a bridge over the Thames and Cassandra watched boats glide under and out from the other side. The countryside opened before her and she was struck by the stillness of it. The road narrowed, fewer people were walking, some on horseback, some in carts and coaches, all bundled against the freezing air, the sun impotent in the bright blue sky.

What a different a world it was, she thought, without rapid-rail lines, highway systems, and ground vehicles. By the year 2075, when Cassandra was ten years old, the rapid-rail system in the United States had been completed. She thought fondly of it now as she rode in the jolting carriage with no warmth other than the scratchy wool blankets provided. The rail system was elevated high off the ground and ran noiselessly. The cars were comfortable and sunny with domed roofs of flexi-glass to allow for an optimum view. It could deliver Cassandra from Boston all the way across the country to her grandmother's in Portland, Oregon in only twenty-four hours.

How odd, she thought, to be riding for so many hours with literally nothing to do but look out the window since it was too bumpy to read, or write in a journal. When the driver stopped to let the horses rest and drink water from a half-frozen pond just off the main road, she stepped out to stretch her legs. She pulled her arms inside her cloak for warmth and meandered a ways out into a meadow, brown with dead grass. There were no birds in the bare trees, no wind blew, no houses were near, and there was no one else traveling on the road. The only sounds to be heard were the cajoling of the coachman as he unhitched the horses one by one and led them to the water, the light jingling of their bridles as they drank, an occasional soft whinny. It occurred to her that in her future world, one was always aware of the hum of civilization no matter where you were, even though relatively noiseless cars ran along grooved roads that provided the needed energy; the super-sonic jets that streaked through the skies were nearly silent, and in the cities, sleek, efficient subway trains whooshed quietly underneath. But here, outside of the major towns, the silence was absolute.

They were soon on their way again and as she rode and observed the countryside she realized that it was also strange to be seeing so few buildings. In her world, she thought with satisfaction, at least billboards were now forbidden in most countries, and power lines unnecessary, but progress marched ever onward and Cassandra knew there was hardly a place on earth anymore where it didn't leave its mark. In this world there was nothing to mar the vista of fields, woods, stone fences, and hedgerows, just an occasional farm or manor house and the small towns that they traveled through.

They rode into the Village of Selborne with a short row of shops along High Street. She pressed her forehead against the window as they passed the house she recognized from her research as the Wakes, large and rambling with peaked garrets and multiple chimneys jutting up into the darkening sky, surrounded by gardens that she imagined infused with color in the spring. Its previous owner, renowned naturalist

Gilbert White, had died two decades before, but was still considered the father of modern scientific documentation, meticulously journaling his thoughts and observations on the natural world.

Not long after they'd left Selborne behind, they turned onto a road surrounded on all sides by bare trees and shrubs, just wide enough for the coach to pass through. She was feeling nauseated from the ride and also hungry. She had the blankets wrapped around her tightly but her feet and face were frozen. She hoped it wouldn't be long now. Ten minutes later the coach passed between high evergreen hedges, and Cassandra felt it must be entry to the Sorrel Hall grounds. Moments later, the view opened out onto the vast browns, greens, and yellows of the gardens and parkland, and there was the house in the distance. It was set on a slight hill and flanked by a sentinel of oaks, their branches reaching up past the roof. Beyond the house, Cassandra could perceive a massive stretch of lawn and a silver glimmer of lake, and surrounding it, rolling hills and dense forests. A gazebo was off to the left, perched elegantly on a hill, and to the right, down a gentle slope at the edge of the woods, she spied a fairy tale cottage that could have been made of gingerbread, a ribbon of smoke rising from its chimney. The sun was setting and the world glowed in a soft, pink light.

Sorrel Hall was more beautiful than she ever imagined. It was two stories, built of pale yellow stone. Garrets on the two front corners and the peaked roof of the nursery in the center added a third story. Tall windows lined both levels, and on the two front, lower corners, bay windows jutted out from diminutive towers. Jake and Cassandra had considered, in the days between his return from 1820 and her own departure, driving down to Hampshire to see the grounds, as the manor was now an elite boarding school. She had decided against it, for she wanted to experience it in its original glory. She was grateful she had waited.

The coach pulled up to the front of the building, and the footman leapt off to open the carriage door and help her out. She flexed her stiff knees and stretched her back, then paid the driver and turned to face the house. The grand front doors opened, and the housekeeper stepped out, greeting Cassandra with a stony stare. She was a woman of about fifty, sturdy, and handsome, with strong bones, clear gray eyes, and steely hair pulled back neatly into a bun.

"Mrs. Franklin." the housekeeper stated without expression as Cassandra walked up the steps.

"You must be Mrs. Merriweather!" she replied, remembering the woman's name from Jake's notes.

"Yes. Welcome. Footman!" she commanded. "Bring that in here," and directed him to carry the luggage inside. Cassandra tipped him and then nervously stepped through the doorway. She pulled herself up straight and tried to feel like the mistress of the manor. The walls of the entryway were paneled in golden oak, and the floor was pale green marble, worn from a hundred years of use. There was a chandelier wrought of intricate ironwork and countless crystal teardrops suspended from the high ceiling. There were two small, marble-topped tables on either side of the door, and a few steps beyond, a large, elaborately carved, cedar armoire for coats. The entryway culminated in a grand stairway to the back of which, and on either side, were two sets of French doors, candlelight sparkling invitingly through the glass. On the left and right sides of the entryway were four more sets of French doors, the closer of which were delicately curtained in lace. Mrs. Merriweather led her through the first set of doors on the left.

"Please sit down if you care to; I shall order tea. Mary," she called to a short, plain-looking maid, "come take Mrs. Franklin's cloak."

"Thank you very much," Cassandra said to Mary, "but I shall keep my cloak for now." She clutched it against the chill of the interior. "I shall have tea in a while, but at the moment would very much like a glass of water." The maid scurried off to fetch it. "I should like to examine the house if you do not mind." Her tone was commanding and Mrs.

Merriweather nodded her assent. Cassandra then turned to admire the room she had just entered. Her nerves were getting the better of her, and she had to fight the urge to giggle as she beheld the beautiful space. It was not as formal as she had expected. The chairs and sofa were plump and newly upholstered in rich fabrics, with carved, marble-topped low tables of mottled gray placed conveniently about. The fire in the large fireplace was blazing—ineffectually. It reflected off a shining, wood parquet floor, scattered with Turkish carpets of vivid reds and rusts. The front of the room faced out onto the approach of the house, and through the many tall windows the countryside beyond could be seen in the waning light. There was a built-in seating area within the circular bay windows in the right front corner of the room. It was covered with velvet green cushions where, Cassandra imagined, she would lounge and enjoy the view from the gothic windows framing it.

She turned her attention to the grand piano, a Broadwood, one of the finest English pianos ever made, she well knew, situated near the front windows.

"I must take a moment to try the instrument," she said to Merriweather.

"Of course, ma'am."

Cassandra detected resentment in the woman's tone. Pretending not to notice, she sat down, opened the cover, and began to play a little minuet by Mozart. She had only meant to play a few measures to test the piano's quality, but once she began, she couldn't stop. She ended the last chord and glanced over at Mrs. Merriweather to see her face soften before she turned away.

Cassandra wondered how the housekeeper felt about the landowners. Jake had told her that the Collins had raised five children in the home; three of them married girls, and there were two boys. The parents had managed their finances badly, and the eldest son's debts from gambling were so great that they decided to move to Bath where they could live less expensively in a townhouse. The younger son was a parson, unmarried, and still lived in the rectory on the property about a mile away. Cassandra imagined that Mrs. Merriweather had been displeased about the family's decision to leave and turn over the house to a stranger.

She rose from the piano and asked if she could be shown the rest of the house; the housekeeper nodded her assent. "Though you will want to look it all over again in the light of the day," she commented, "I will take you through now, so that you can admire the rooms by lamplight."

She led Cassandra across the entry hall, through the opposite French doors and into a parlor, identical in dimensions to the one they had just left, but furnished with stiff, brocade chairs and sofas, spindly side tables and flowery rugs and draperies. Cassandra knew she would never use this room for herself. This was the parlor for receiving company, and it seemed cold and uncomfortable compared to the opposite room.

"The Collins much preferred the sitting room to this parlor," said Mrs. Merriweather.

"And so do I," replied Cassandra. "Though it is lovely," she added politely.

A glimmer of a smile flitted across the housekeeper's face. Mary arrived with the water and Cassandra drank it in a few great swallows then handed the glass back to the maid. The girl looked from the glass to Mrs. Merriweather, while Cassandra instantly regretted her action. The housekeeper nodded Mary away and turned to lead her new mistress back into the entry hall and through another set of doors into the dining room. Beyond it was the breakfast room with windows facing to the east. A door to the left led them into the warm kitchen, where the servants had gathered to eat. The kitchen was capacious, had a pump sink, a wide hearth hung with pots, copper pans lining the walls, and herbs and strings of garlic and onions dangling from the ceiling. Cassandra liked the look of it; she enjoyed cooking, but although she would be helping to plan the meals, she would not be expected to help prepare them.

Mrs. Merriweather introduced Cassandra to the assembled staff, at once on their feet upon her entering the kitchen. She nodded at them with a smile and they each nodded in return. As Mrs. Merriweather began to lead her back out again, Cassandra tapped her shoulder, and whispered to her that she required the water closet. The woman indicated a door off the kitchen, which Cassandra hastened to open. There she found a narrow hallway and the first door she opened revealed nothing but a wooden seat with a hole in it. With some difficulty she gathered up her cloak, petticoat and skirt, yanked down her drawers and sat. Cold radiated up from some unknowable source and she gasped. She finished peeing and looked around for something to wipe with. There were a pile of clean rags next to the seat, so she used one and deposited it in a bucket on the floor with others. The room stank and she hoped that the water closet she would be using on a regular basis would be more pleasant than this one, which she assumed was for the staff's use.

When she rejoined Mrs. Merriweather, the servants were all bent to their dinner and did not look up as Cassandra passed. She felt their embarrassment. She and the housekeeper continued out through the breakfast and dining rooms, through the entry hall, past the staircase and into the library. The room was old and comfortable, with the smell of paper and leather from the books lining every wall, and large, inviting leather chairs, slightly cracked with age. There was fire burning in a small fireplace on the north end of the room. The room was far warmer than the rest of the house and Cassandra found herself looking forward to perusing the bookshelves. Perhaps she would even find first-edition Jane Austens, she thought, and her heart leapt at the thought of reading her favorite author in England, just three years after her death.

Beyond the library was a small study with a heavy desk for writing and conducting business, and from that room a door opened onto the west side of the grounds. The housekeeper then led Cassandra back into the library and through a doorway to the left, into a long and echoing space which was the conservatory, with burning candles in sconces along the walls. The west and north ends of the room were lined from floor to ceiling with windows, looking out across the great lawn to the lake, barely visible now in the last few moments of daylight. The conservatory was sparsely furnished. Two chaise lounges were placed at either end of the room, flanked by small, wrought-iron end tables. A white spinet piano stood in one corner. There were plants growing vigorously in Grecian planters along the windows, and more French doors opened out onto a brick veranda.

"This room is used for balls and parties," said Merriweather, seeming to think an explanation was required, "Since it is so very spacious. The Collins girls enjoyed many dances here."

"It is absolutely enchanting!"

"I am pleased you like it," the woman replied blankly. "Shall we continue upstairs?" She led Cassandra on without waiting for consent. "I will show you two of the best rooms. Both have their own sitting areas. Of course, there are eight bedrooms altogether, but you may want to look those over in the morning. I cannot think you would like any of them more than the two that I shall show you now." It seemed more of a command than an observation.

"I am sure I can trust your judgment," Cassandra replied, and they went up the imposing marble staircase. On the second floor landing, portraits of ancestors stared in dark, murky palettes. She was grateful that Mrs. Merriweather forewent any historical explanations.

She followed the housekeeper to south side of the landing, and through a door into a sitting room, done up in creams and blues. Through narrow glass doors, the bedroom was revealed. The floors were of smooth wooden planks. A four poster bed dominated the space, graced with a cream-colored eyelet bedspread and curtains. Tall windows were curtained with a blue floral print. A fire welcomed her.

"Oh!" Cassandra cried, "I cannot imagine I should like any room better!" She removed her cloak and felt her body relax in the warmth of the space.

"No, I did not think so," replied Mrs. Merriweather. "This was Lady Collins' room; the other belonged to Sir Frederick. That one is more suited to a gentleman."

"Well, this is perfect," Cassandra decided.

"I am glad you like it, ma'am."

"May I ask you a favor, Mrs. Merriweather?"

"Anything you wish, Mrs. Franklin."

"I think I should like to take my supper here if you do not mind; I am tired and I would rather remain in my room for the night."

"Yes, of course, ma'am."

"And, finally, would it be terribly troublesome to ask for a bath to be drawn?"

"Would you like it after supper?"

"Yes, that would be lovely."

"I will have the tub brought up and filled for you then, when you are finished eating. In the meantime, I will send Mary to help you unpack."

"No, no, I would like to do it myself—I do not have much."

Disapproval flitted across the housekeeper's face. "I shall send the bags up then, and leave you to yourself. Supper in fifteen minutes."

"Yes, thank you," Cassandra replied. "And Mrs. Merriweather—I look forward to seeing more in the morning and to getting to know you better." She wasn't sure if it was the correct thing to say.

"Goodnight. If you need anything from me, pull this cord," she said indicating a red cord hanging on the wall. "The white one will bring Mary. She will be in charge of your supper and your bath."

"Very good," said Cassandra, "Good night."

With that Mrs. Merriweather went out and closed the door. Cassandra was left standing and looking about, feeling at once relieved and bewildered.

.

CHAPTER FOUR

January 30, 1820—I met a Lady Holcomb and her two teenage children today, and enjoyed their company very much. I visited just for a half an hour then returned home, played the piano, and read.

February 3, 1820—Lady Holcomb returned the visit and we talked for more than an hour and had tea. She has a sense of humor and is very talkative. I was obliged to tell the fabricated history of what drove me from the U.S. to be settled here in England. It was the first time I'd related it, and I think I was convincing.

After I returned home I did nothing but read and play the piano for the rest of the day. Mrs. Merriweather doesn't want my input on meals or the running of the household, and since I have no idea what to do in that area, I haven't tried to insist.

February 5, 1820—Met the Moores, a wealthy landowner, his wife, and two silly young daughters, who regaled me with their stories of disappointed love. It was very amusing. Then I told them my woeful story, and they were suitably horrified.

Afterward I came home, played the piano again, and read. There is no going outside for walks or other activities. It rains incessantly and is deathly cold.

February 20, 1820—Met the Charles family, an insufferably overbearing and pretentious mother, a distant husband, and a vapid daughter. Was bored to tears and though I told them my personal history, since they wanted to know, I didn't think they really cared. Well, the daughter seemed interested, but Lady Charles was more concerned with where I'd bought my gown. The husband only ate and then disappeared.

I came home, walked throughout the house three times trying to get some exercise, played the piano, and went to bed.

March 3, 1820—Met the Clarke family and entertained their pack of rambunctious children with stories and songs on the piano, which was fun. Avoided the long story, wasn't in the mood. Came home. Read. Played piano.

March 18, 1820—It's all more of the same. Getting together with the different families in the neighborhood, chatting awhile, coming home, doing nothing much of interest. I've been to some dinners and have thrown a few myself, but the conversation is always the same, and I tell that damned story endlessly. I'm starting to wonder why I thought this was going to be such a fascinating scientific exercise. I can't even muster up the interest to comment further.

March 25, 1820—The weather is dreadful and I'm going out of my mind. I miss my home in Boston, my son, my friends, and activity!

April 7, 1820—Last night I dreamt I was standing in a room with a single window; a gauzy curtain fluttered. When I saw my reflection in the full length mirror, I was only wearing my chemise and bloomers. I was being dressed by several maids whose faces I could not see. One pulled a dress down over my head, another yanked on the sleeves, while another one was buttoning up the back. The fourth immediately went to work on my hair. They weren't listening to my requests, but treating me as if I were a doll. Exasperated, I ordered them away and they fled in tears.

I woke up in a sweat, realizing that the dream bore a resemblance to a simulation sequence I had practiced with Shannon again and again. In reality, nothing so extreme has occurred in my dealings with Mary and the other servants. And that's just the problem. Nothing of interest has occurred. I'm crawling out of my skin with boredom. It's been three months since I arrived at Sorrel Hall and they've been three months of being cooped up inside this freezing cold house with nothing to do but go out in the cold to visit neighbors in their cold houses, and sit stiffly and reply graciously to their mundane observations on the cold *weather. Well, that's not entirely true; I do like Lady Holcomb, who lives nearby, and have made new friends with her, the Moores, and the Clarkes.*

I'm probably a better pianist now than ever, having little else to do for the last three months. Other than that, and the challenge of constantly striving to say and do the correct things, there are no balls, no handsome officers coming to town, no scandals—nothing that Miss Austen led me to believe I could expect. At least today there is some warm weather, so I can get out into the garden. This is not going at all like I thought it would.

CHAPTER FIVE

Cassandra flung open the western door that led out onto the flower garden. The cool, morning air of spring rushed in and blew her hair about her face. She brushed it away with a pang of guilt for not having allowed Mary to put it up. She simply hadn't had the patience. She grabbed her sunbonnet from the rack next to the door and slapped it on her head, glancing quickly in the mirror. What she saw was a fresh, pretty face with a few too many freckles and wild, reddish curls breaking out from under the bonnet. She decided it would have to do.

She marched across the damp lawn to the long, rectangular greenhouse; then hesitated before opening the glass door. The building was Mr. Merriweather's domain. He was the Head Gardner and not even Cassandra's own title of Mistress of Sorrel Hall could quite make her feel comfortable enough to intrude without invitation, though in the last two weeks, she'd talked her way in a handful of times to help him with some of the flowers and vegetables he'd started from seed. She took a breath and went in.

The old man, upright and slim with a shock of thick, white hair on his head was standing at a work table in brown wool trousers and a muslin shirt, transferring the flower seedlings into crates for Cassandra to plant in the garden. He snapped his head around to look at her as she entered.

She tried her most winning smile. "Good morning Mr. Merriweather!"

He turned back to his work and grunted.

"Are those for me?"

"Yes, ma'am. Got some young peony bushes, wallflowers, sweet williams "

"Oh, thank you!" She went to a tall, wooden cabinet, gray with age, and removed her gardening gloves, a spade and a few brown paper packages of seeds she'd bought in Selborne the week before. She returned to the gardener.

"Are they ready?"

"Yes ma'am," he croaked. She added her things to one of the boxes. "Let me carry it for you, now."

"No, no," Cassandra replied with purpose. "I can do it, please do not trouble yourself."

He frowned at her. "I shall bring out the shovel and the hoe then."

"Yes, thank you. I do appreciate your help."

"Yes ma'am."

Cassandra hefted the crate and turned to go, Mr. Merriweather following with the implements. They walked back across the grass, Cassandra more aware, now that he was behind her, of the dew moistening her hem and her tousled hair. She saw Mary waiting for them in the garden, bonnet slightly askew, holding a tray of lemonade, glasses, and biscuits. Cassandra smiled at her as they approached. Mary returned a self-conscious grin, her lips barely clearing her crooked front teeth.

"Please set down the tray there on the bench, Mary, and relax. I do not expect you to dig in the dirt with me."

"Whatever you desire, ma'am." Mary set the tray down with a rattle and plopped onto the bench. Cassandra winced. In the nearly three months she'd now been at Sorrel Hall, she still wasn't used to all the servants calling her that.

"Thank you, Mr. Merriweather," she said. "I know you have much to do with your day. I shall be quite well taken care of by Mary here."

"Ma'am," he began hesitantly. "I wish you would let me do the work. It is my job. A lady should not be performing such a dirty task."

"Sir, there is nothing in the world I would rather do. I cannot sit in that house one moment longer doing nothing of use. Please, allow me to work. I know what I am doing. I am used to tending my own garden in the States."

A flicker of approval passed over his face. "Very well, then." He turned and walked away.

Cassandra pulled on her gloves and crouched in the dirt with her plants. The sun rose in the sky as Mary drowsed in the shade and Cassandra worked, humming to herself. She was snipping away at a rosebush, trying to keep her hair and clothing from snagging on the thorns, when she heard the clopping of horses' hooves on the drive and glanced up to see a man approaching on horseback, so near that she wondered she had not heard him before. She was startled, recollecting that she was not presentable for visitors, especially men.

"Pardon me, miss!" he called. Mary jumped up from her seat, and for a moment, Cassandra wasn't sure if he was referring to her or her maid.

"Yes, can I help you?" Cassandra replied, and in the process of disentangling herself from the rosebush, stumbled over the shovel that was lying in front of her. Mary reached out to steady her mistress, grabbed the offending instrument, and hurried off to the greenhouse with it.

"I am so sorry to disturb you."

She tried to smooth her mass of curls.

"I seem to be lost." The man continued, "I am looking for Gatewick House, and I must have made a wrong turn." He sat tall in his saddle. A tan greatcoat fell to his knees, and sable riding boots covered trousers of the same hue. A broad, tan hat sat on his head, shading his features.

"It is very easy to overlook," she said. "The entrance is partially obscured by the shrubbery and is probably quite overgrown by now." She looked around for Mary, surprised to see that the girl had deserted her. "Are you thinking of buying it?"

"Well, really, I do not know, just looking, I suppose."

"It is a lovely place. Just go up to the road, turn right, and continue back about a mile. Look carefully on the left; you should see the drive."

Cassandra could see his eyes narrow, lingering on her face before he spoke.

"Thank you," he said after a moment. "So sorry to have disturbed you."

"It is not a bother," she replied. "Would you care to stop to eat? It must be nearly one."

He stammered, "That is very kind of you, miss, uh, madam, uh, I believe the housekeeper at Gatewick is expecting me; I had best be on my way. But, please excuse my rudeness; my name is Johnston, Mr. Benedict Johnston."

"Very nice to meet you," she said, smiling, "I am Mrs. Franklin."

"Are you the lady of the manor?"

"Yes, I am," she replied, following his glance over the muddy apron, her dirty hands, her gloves, tools, weeds, and empty plant crates strewn on the ground.

"Well," he said, raising his eyebrows, "perhaps we shall have the pleasure to meet again."

"That would be nice," she said simply.

He began to go but stopped. "May I ask where you are from?"

"America."

"Funny, I knew an American fellow once, he spoke nothing like you."

She paused and bit her lip. "He may have been from the southern region."

"Ah, that must be it. Good day." He turned his horse and rode away.

Cassandra looked around again for Mary and sighed. She gathered up her things and took them back to the greenhouse. Mr. Merriweather had gone.

After washing up, she went downstairs into the dining room and glanced at the elaborate place setting for one. It was positioned at the head of the table, her chair facing the tall, many-paned windows. Candles brightened the dark wood of the room. A slight servant with light blond hair, dressed in the house livery, stiffly walked over and pulled out Cassandra's chair. She nodded and sat down on its gold-brocade seat, resting her hands on the darkly stained wood of the armrests. She stared at the gilt-edged china that was covered with small, painted red roses, and at the three silver forks at her left, the two knives and two spoons at her right, and the spoon and small fork set above the plate. All the silver was embossed, amongst many curlicues, with the letter "C" for Collins. Above the knives were arranged three crystal goblets, and a small bread plate and knife awaited her use on the right. Such a fuss, she thought. How many times had she hinted to Mrs. Merriweather that she preferred to take her meals in the cheery breakfast room, no matter the time of day, whenever she wasn't out dining or entertaining at home, and that she could dispense with at least half of the dishware? Each time, the housekeeper had regarded her stonily with a tight smile and a nod.

Cassandra shoved the chair back out while the servant, who'd been standing rigidly against the wall, scurried to grab it. "Never mind, Thomas, you can relax," she said to the pale young man. She marched out of the room and into the kitchen where she found the Anna, the cook, ladling a green-colored soup into a tureen held by Mrs. Merriweather.

"Is that for me?" Cassandra asked Anna innocently.

"Yes, Mrs. Franklin," Mrs. Merriweather replied. The woman seemed to look right through her with slate-colored eyes.

"And all of this?" Her hand swept over platters of beef, potatoes, rolls, cheeses and sundry side dishes, resting on a massive, wooden table.

"Yes, Mrs. Franklin," replied Anna. Her hand was poised, holding the ladle over the bowl. Her face was flushed as red as her hair, and her blue eyes grew larger in her wide face.

"Anna, Mrs. Merriweather." Cassandra took a deep breath and made an effort to speak patiently. "We are expecting no luncheon guests."

"Yes, ma'am, that is true," said Mrs. Merriweather.

"But I can never eat all this food!"

Anna lowered the ladle into the soup pot on the stove. She looked at the housekeeper.

"Well, Mrs. Franklin," Mrs. Merriweather began, "It is proper to serve a luncheon befitting the mistress of the house. It is the way things are done."

"Yes, but," Cassandra said with a smile, "it is not how I want them done. Now then." She peeked into the tureen. "What is this?"

"Asparagus soup."

"Good. I will take a bowl of that. She went to look over the platters on the kitchen table. "I shall take a piece of the beef, a small helping of potatoes, some of …whatever this is; it looks good; a roll, and that is all."

The two women exchanged looks. "Very well, Mrs. Franklin," said Mrs. Merriweather with poise.

"Whatever is left over—well, I shall leave it to your imagination, Anna, for I do not presume to do your job for you, but I am sure the meat and potatoes would make a fine hash. Please make sure the servants enjoy as much of the food as they would like first. If there is still any left after that, I would like to see it delivered to one or more of the farmers."

"Yes, ma'am," Anna replied. Cassandra winked at her while Mrs. Merriweather was looking over the food. Anna grinned.

"Any salad greens yet from the greenhouse? I meant to ask your husband, Mrs. Merriweather."

"No, but in just a few more weeks, he says."

"Ugh! I can hardly survive much longer without a nice green salad!"

Anna and Mrs. Merriweather exchanged glances. Cassandra turned and walked back to the dining room and Thomas leapt to grab her chair. She smiled at him. A diminutive female servant walked in with the soup tureen and began ladling the steaming liquid into Cassandra's bowl, until her mistress held up a hand for her stop. "Lydia, when you have a chance, please remove these wine glasses and inform Mrs. Merriweather that I shall not be taking wine with lunch." The girl curtsied and left the room, rushing in a moment later to pluck the glasses from the table.

Cassandra began to eat, with nothing else to do but stare out the window and try to not be aware of Thomas' presence against the wall. She longed to be able to read a book while she took her meals.

After lunch, she submitted to Mary's fussing over her hair. She sat in her bedroom at the dressing table while her maid arranged her curls on the top of her head. She then chose a dark blue, silk gown for afternoon wear and allowed the maid to button it up the back and tie the ribbon that graced the seam under the bodice. When Mary finished with the bow, Cassandra made a step for the door.

"Wait, if you please, ma'am."

Cassandra sighed. She was anxious to get to her piano.

Mary walked around her mistress plucking at the dress, arranging the folds of the high-waisted gown so that they fell prettily into their proper place.

"Okay!" Cassandra blurted.

Mary jumped back. "Beg your pardon, ma'am?"

"I mean," Cassandra remembered that 'okay' was not an expression they would know. "That will do, Mary." She smiled to soften the command, patted the girl on the hand, and walked out of the room. Mary scurried after her.

"Mary, is there not something else that needs doing up here?"

"Um, no ma'am, now that the Collinses is no longer here, there is nothing needs doing."

"Very well, why do you not relax for a while? Take a nap."

"No, ma'am, if Mrs. Merriweather were ever to—"

"Very well, but I do not wish you to accompany me to my piano. I would like to have some time to myself while I play." She'd explained this to the girl a hundred times.

"Yes, ma'am."

She went to her instrument and settled herself down on the seat. She selected the music she was to play, ran her fingers through a few scales, then, clearing her mind, struck the tender opening notes of the first movement of a Beethoven sonata and became absorbed in the music.

Cassandra heard a sound behind her that made her clang a foul note. She turned and beheld Mary, brown eyes staring, her receding chin set in determination.

"Mrs. Franklin…"

Cassandra took a deep breath. "Yes?"

"Madam," the maid continued, "You have visitors. Lady Charles, Miss Charles, and a Miss Fairchild have come. I have shown them to the parlor."

"Oh, for heaven's sake," said Cassandra. "What could they want?"

"I am sorry, I do not know. Should I tell them you cannot be disturbed?"

"No, of course not," replied Cassandra, surrendering to a kinder tone. She got up and preceded the girl into the formal parlor. She did not dare entertain the regal Lady Charles in the inferior sitting room.

"Lady Charles! Miss Charles!" she exclaimed as she entered the room. "No, no, do not get up! To what do I owe the pleasure of this visit?"

"Good afternoon, Mrs. Franklin, we came to introduce you to my niece, Miss Fairchild, who is visiting from Birmingham. Say hello, Eunice."

Miss Fairchild whimpered, "Good afternoon."

"We have been telling Eunice about your fascinating life," said Lady Charles. "She has never met an American before." Eunice agreed by shaking her head. The girl looked upon Cassandra with awe.

The two young cousins presented quite a contrast to each other. Miss Charles, at eighteen, was bright-cheeked and the slightest bit plump. Her shining blond curls bounced around her face when she moved or spoke, and her blue eyes danced with youth. Miss Fairchild was thin and sallow. Cassandra guessed she was about a year her cousin's junior, but had yet to bloom. Her hair wasn't quite blond, rather an ashy light brown. Her eyes were also blue, but her pale lashes did not set them off. Her features weren't unpleasing, but she had little charm.

Lady Charles was the picture of her daughter, thirty years, about thirty pounds, and many gray hairs later. One could see that she had once been attractive, but now solely devoted herself to running the finest home in the county and marrying off her youngest daughter.

"Please, Mrs. Franklin," said Lady Charles. "Would you be so good as to recount to my niece the particulars of why you left America and came to reside in England? I could not remember all the details, and besides, it is so much more interesting coming from you. You have a way of saying things that is so very…I mean your manner is so—"

"I am honored that anyone would be so interested in my humble life," she offered, all smiles. Inwardly, she felt weary about recounting the story yet again. The emotional toll it took on her was considerable, though it was a necessary part of her creation of the character of Mrs. Cassandra Franklin. Before the journey, she had practiced the story numerous times in simulations and finally underwent hypnosis to key her in to the feelings she would need to talk about a painful past that never existed. Even the many acting classes she'd taken in school couldn't prepare her sufficiently.

"Oh, it is so much more exciting than anyone else's life that I know of," piped Miss Charles. "Mrs. Franklin related it to us upon our first meeting her," she continued, speaking solely to her cousin, "and I felt like I was listening to an adventure story!"

"You exaggerate, my dear." Lady Charles' gaze traveled over Cassandra's gown.

Cassandra glanced down at herself to see if anything was amiss. Mary came in with the tea and Cassandra served them all. When they were settled, she took a deep breath and commenced her story. Eunice leaned forward in anticipation.

Cassandra told how she'd left England with her mother and father and had gone to reside in America when she was a child of six, for reasons of her father's business. "My mother and I enjoyed a fashionable life in New York." She related. "My brother was born about two years after we settled there, and to me, he was a charming addition to our family."

"I did not know you had a brother, ma'am," said Miss Charles.

"Oh, maybe I have never mentioned him. At any rate, when I was eighteen, I became engaged to my husband, Zachary Franklin."

"Americans have such odd names!" exclaimed Miss Charles, then clapped her hand over her mouth.

Lady Charles glared at her daughter.

Cassandra laughed. "Let me see, where was I?"

"You had just become betrothed," the young woman offered.

"Oh, yes. So we were engaged and very happy, and soon we were married. Zachary was a printer of fine books and we set up house not far from my parents in a situation somewhat more modest, but very comfortable. A year after we were married, my son James was born."

"May I ask how old is James now?" ventured Miss Charles.

"He is nineteen, almost twenty."

Miss Charles and Eunice exchanged a look.

"My life was happy, but about three years ago, when James was sixteen, there was an outbreak of yellow fever in New York." 'Yellow fever' was the trigger word to drop Cassandra into a deeper emotional connection.

"Oh dear," peeped Eunice.

"Zachary insisted that James and I remove to my parents' summer home in the country, far from the closeness and contagion of the city. We did so at once, and Zachary told us that he would soon follow, but first had to wrap things up at his printing shop. Fearful for my son, we left."

"When may we meet your son, Mrs. Franklin?" Miss Charles broke in, the color in her cheeks high.

"Probably not for a great while," Cassandra replied, knowing that time would never come.

"My dear, do not interrupt," the girl's mother chided, her voice shrill.

Cassandra continued, her face somber. "My husband should have left with us; he died of yellow fever a few weeks later. I was devastated to have not been with him at the end." Her voice filled with emotion, "I should have nursed him myself, yet if I had stayed with him, I probably would have caught the disease myself."

"How horrible!" Eunice was bold enough to say.

"Well, needless to say, I felt my life was over, so much did I love my husband." The room was silent. A tear trickled down Cassandra's cheek and she caught it with a linen napkin. "My son and my close family were my only comfort. When the city was safe again, I returned to the home that I'd shared with my husband. It was a very sad time for me, but I made the best of it. Then day, I decided to finally set upon the task of cleaning out Zachary's desk." A shudder went through her body. "While doing so, I chanced upon bills of sale for five different slaves."

"How appalling!" exclaimed Eunice.

"It is simply barbaric," agreed Miss Charles.

"Surely you must have known, Mrs. Franklin, how could you not have?" asked Lady Charles.

"I assure you," said Cassandra, her eyes moist, "That I never had the slightest idea this was going on. I ran to my parents' house and showed my father the receipts. He confessed that he knew Zachery was dealing in human flesh but kept it from me in the interest of protecting my feelings. He knew, though I did not, that Zachery's printing business had not been doing well."

Lady Charles clucked.

"And so, I asked my father to remove Zachery's money from those horrible investments, and, not able to live any longer amongst the scenes of my former happiness, I took my dowry and the inheritance I had been promised and set sail to settle here in County Hampshire. It was a terrible ordeal, and I am trying to put it behind me." She closed her eyes and took another deep breath, repeating her grandmother's name, Chloë, three times to herself, a trick she had used during hypnosis to bring her back to the present. Her mind flooded with calm, and the emotions receded. She felt herself return fully to her surroundings.

"How astonishing," sighed Eunice. "It really is like what one reads about in books."

"I told you the story was fascinating," said Miss Charles to her cousin. "Are you not glad to have heard it directly from her?"

"Oh, yes," declared Eunice. "Mrs. Franklin," she continued, "I am amazed that you can have a son of nineteen, when you look scarcely above thirty yourself. My mother is thirty-five and she looks abominably old."

"Eunice!" cried Lady Charles, her nose in the air, "One does not discuss a lady's age! I am sure Mrs. Franklin is every bit as old as she says she is. I would not guess her a day over forty-five."

"I am thirty-eight," stated Cassandra.

"It is impossible," insisted Eunice.

"Perhaps the water in America has a youthful effect," said her cousin. "After all, Ponce de Leon went there in search of the fountain of youth."

"So he did," smiled Cassandra.

"Enough of that subject. Come, girls," sniffed Lady Charles. "Let us not keep dear Mrs. Franklin any longer. She has been most obliging."

"It is my pleasure," returned Cassandra.

"I am sorry to say," offered the lady, heaving herself up from the delicate chair on which she had been seated, "that we shall probably not be seeing you for some weeks. We are off to London in a few days to enjoy the rest of the spring season there. I do wish you could join us."

"Oh, that is a lovely invitation," replied Cassandra. "But after so many years in New York, I tend to now prefer the quiet life of the country." She coughed into the back of her hand.

"Yes, I understand. I much prefer the country as well, but Parliament is in session and my husband, Sir Robert, you know, has been there attending to the business of the government for over a month now. I know he misses us desperately."

"I am sure that he does," said Cassandra. "I wish you a safe journey and a delightful visit in town."

"Thank you," responded Lady Charles puffing out her chest. "We shall call on you the moment we return."

"I look forward to it," said Cassandra.

"Oh, and I do hope you will make use of the wisdom of our curate, Mr. Collins, now that the weather has warmed. I realize that the cold keeps many from Sunday service during the winter, but I admonish you not to neglect your religious instruction, Mrs. Franklin."

Cassandra raised her eyebrows. "I did not know that you were…that is…it had not occurred to me—"

"What, that a lady of my rank could benefit from a good sermon? Those of us who are well provided for, Mrs.

Franklin, must not forget our relationship with the Almighty. You know what they say, 'It is harder for a rich man to enter the kingdom of heaven, then for a camel to enter the eye of a needle,' or something like that."

Cassandra saw Miss Charles roll her eyes at her cousin, and Eunice smothered a snicker with her handkerchief.

"I shall certainly heed your advice," she told the lady.

"Yes, do not fall down in your religious duties as some of the others that you hobnob with have done. Mrs. Clarke, Mrs. Moore and her daughters, whom she ought to have married off well before now, and that Lady Holcomb. I cannot think of the last time I saw her at the parish church."

"Well, I shall not fail to follow your example."

"Mother—" Miss Charles prompted.

"Ah yes, we must be on our way. Good day, Mrs. Franklin!"

Her voice was beginning to grate on Cassandra's ears like the screech of a cat in heat.

"Good day." She led them to the entryway and Mary let them out.

Cassandra sighed and returned to her piano.

Around sunset, she was lounging in the window seat, watching a storm brewing in the west, *The Romance of the Forest* by Mrs. Radcliffe lying closed in her hand. Her gaze traveled out across the gentle rise and fall of the land—so different from the closeness of New York where, in reality, she'd grown up. Cassandra's family had spent summers at their home in the Hudson valley and she often considered that the landscape there was similar to that of England's, even though there was a difference between them in the quality of light and the severity of the angles. The English countryside had a more ancient quality, as if it had been worn and softened by so many more years of use.

In a flight of imagination, inspired by the black clouds roiling overhead and the torrent of rain that suddenly smacked the windows around her, she saw herself in her mind's eye as some interesting character in a book: the widow of Sorrel Hall, the expatriate looking for a home, the mysterious American. She began to feel a sense of purpose in being there..

CHAPTER SIX

*A*pril 17, 1820 – *While the weather was too cold for outdoor activity, I did yoga most mornings, and now continue to do it a couple of times a week. This morning, as I was lying on a blanket on the floor in my bloomers and chemise with my legs flung over my head, Mary walked in. I had forgot to lock the door. I leapt up as quickly as I could manage while Mary wildly apologized for not knocking, and I tried to explain how I'd been trying to work out a pain in my back. I think it's time I learned to ride a horse. I hear it is excellent exercise..*

******

Close to one o'clock Cassandra set off quickly on foot to cover the mile or so to the Holcomb cottage, which lay across the road from the grounds of Sorrel Hall and arrived there in less than twenty minutes. When Lady Holcomb's husband Sir Arthur died, his extensive parklands and most of his money had gone to their eldest son. In keeping with custom, the lady had moved into the cottage on the grounds. It was well-placed at the foot of low, green hills, near enough to a stream that Cassandra could hear it burbling as she approached. Built of stone, the house was two stories with a peaked roof of shingles. Blue shutters graced the many-paned windows that were numerous on the first story. On the second, the windows were framed by gabled dormers. Cassandra walked through a white gate, past a garden of yellow daffodils, pink tulips, purple pansies, and under a willow tree that shaded a carved stone bench. Before she reached the steps of the cottage, Lady Holcomb flung open the rounded, wooden door and dashed out to meet her.

"Cassandra!" The lady took her friend's arm. "How charming you look! What a lovely day it is, do not you think? Was the walk tiring? I have some delicious cakes and fresh watercress sandwiches. You will not mind a light repast at this time of day?"

"No, and no, the walk was not tiring in the least. What a beautiful gown! The blue matches your eyes perfectly." Inwardly, Cassandra observed that the dress masked the woman's heavy-set frame well.

Her friend patted her chestnut hair, streaked with grey. "Thank you, my dear."

"And I see your maid has discovered a flattering new hair style for you."

"Do you think so? You are most kind to say."

They stepped inside the cottage. Roses abounded everywhere: on the fabric of the chairs, sofa and curtains, in the pattern on the rug, on decorative plates situated on the fireplace mantle and in still life paintings on the rosebud wallpaper. A slim vase with one pink rosebud graced the oval-shaped marble table upon which sat a rose-themed tea set.

"Oh, my dear," said Lady Holcomb, once she was settled on the sofa, and the tea and delicacies had been delivered. Cassandra sat on an opposite chair. "Did you hear about the gentleman that purchased Gatewick House? He is to move in any day!"

"I think I met him," said Cassandra.

"You met him? How on earth?"

"He was lost the other day, and came by asking for directions. I was in the garden looking a fright."

"Oh no, I am sure you were not." She paused. "I heard he was a bachelor."

"Well, we did not discuss his marital status," said Cassandra, stirring one of her tiny pills into her tea.

"His marital status!" Lady Holcomb cackled. "You have such a way of putting things. So, what was he like?" She teetered on the edge of the flowery cushion.

"Well, I couldn't see his face very clearly under his hat, but he seemed about thirty-five or forty, very pleasant, but, you know, we did not get that familiar."

"Oh, Cassandra, really! You should visit him. You are just bold enough to do such a thing!"

"I am not!" cried Cassandra. "How would that appear, an old widow calling upon a gentleman? He will think I am looking to catch a husband."

"And are you not?" She laughed.

"Charlotte, I have told you a hundred times, I have no interest in remarrying! Why do I need a husband to tell me what to do? You, on the other hand—"

"Need someone to tell me what to do? I should say not. Besides, I am too old for him." Lady Holcomb lounged back into the sofa with her cup in her hand. "Well, anyway, if you have already met him, then it would not be improper for him to call on you, now would it, and I am sure he will, as soon as he gets settled. I shall ask Jeffrey to pay him a visit on our behalf and invite him to tea. I suppose Jane will consider him too old for her."

"Charlotte, he is at least twenty years older than Jane."

"Well, what difference does that make?" she laughed, "if he is handsome and he has money, which he obviously does."

"You are terrible," observed Cassandra.

"Really? Why? Here they are! Come, you two, say hello to Mrs. Franklin."

Her children sat to eat after greeting Cassandra.

"Have I told you," continued Charlotte, "that Jeffrey's assignment is expected to come into port by the end of the summer? He will then be off at sea for who knows how long! He is sure to be made a captain in no time."

"No, mother, it does not work like that!" He addressed Cassandra. "My mother seems to be an expert on naval matters." At eighteen he was tall, with dark brown hair, blue eyes, and a crooked, yet engaging smile.

Jane listened quietly as her mother and brother disputed his future. She had a round face with a little round chin, thick, light brown hair and warm brown eyes. Her dimples flashed as she turned her smile from her older brother to Cassandra.

Cassandra nodded and made brief comments as she ate and drank her tea. She had heard the same conversation more than once before. She lingered a respectable amount of time, and then made her excuses to leave.

"I know you want to rush home to your piano." Lady Holcomb said to her as they dallied in the entry way, waiting for the maid to fetch Cassandra's bonnet and shawl. "I have never known a grown woman to be so devoted to her instrument. I thought young ladies became accomplished in order to impress young men, and then they gave it all up when the demands of home and children pressed in upon them. Only a true *artiste* devotes themselves to an instrument all their lives. I declare you are an eccentric!"

"Yes, maybe I am," her friend admitted.

Lady Holcomb walked Cassandra out to the gate. The smell of wet earth filled the air, and the women breathed it in.

"Now, you must inform me at once if that Mr. Johnston calls on you," said the lady.

"And you must tell me if Jeffrey has the opportunity to meet him," replied Cassandra.

"Oh, you need not worry; you will be the first to know."

"Very well," laughed Cassandra, "good afternoon, my dear Charlotte."

"Good afternoon, my love!"

The two kissed good-bye and Cassandra walked briskly home in the mild afternoon sunlight.

******

Just before dinner the following Monday, she was perusing a London paper that she had picked up in Selborne over the weekend. A knock on the door announced a messenger. A card was presented, delivered from Mr. Benedict Johnston, asking for the honor of paying a call to Mrs. Cassandra Franklin. She replied with a note that the honor would be hers and that she would find the hour of eleven o'clock the next day a convenient time for a visit. Cassandra wondered if this call was a result of Lady Holcomb having shooed Jeffrey over to meet their new neighbor and that perhaps the boy had prodded him to call on Cassandra.

He arrived precisely on the hour. Mrs. Merriweather took the man's things and showed him into the sitting room where Cassandra was waiting for him, picturesquely arranged in the window seat holding *The Romance of the Forest*.

"Mr. Johnston," she pronounced, setting down the book, rising and going to him. "What a pleasure to see you again!"

She held out her hand which he took and bestowed with a brush of his lips. "The pleasure is mine."

Silence ensued.

"Did you ride? The weather is not pleasant."

"I did ride. I do not mind a little drizzle."

"The temperature has been remarkable until today."

"Very warm for this time of year."

"Indeed, very."

Now that Cassandra could observe him up close, without hat or riding cloak, she noticed that he had dark blond hair, peppered with gray, and bluish-green eyes that were framed with dark lashes. His features were defined, his jaw firm and his cheekbones prominent, though a slight asymmetry to his face made him just less than conventionally handsome. His skin was not pale, but almost olive, as if the spring sunshine had browned him. He was a few inches taller than her five and a half feet, and slim.

He gazed about with interest. "What a cheerful aspect this room has." He walked to the window seat and looked out. "A wonderful view in spite of the mist."

"Yes, I enjoy it immensely."

He continued to stroll around the room, touching objects and letting his hand linger. His fingers were long and he moved his arms slowly, as if engaged in a dance. He walked behind the sofa, running his hand along its back. "I appreciate a comfortable salon, where objects are placed for pleasure rather than style. Yet this room is ultimately very attractive."

Cassandra felt vindicated for having decided to receive him in the sitting room rather than the parlor as Mrs. Merriweather had strongly suggested. "Thank you, would you like to sit down?"

As she spoke, he spied the piano and immediately went to it. "This is an excellent instrument," he stated. "Do you play?"

"Yes, a little."

"May I look at your music?"

Before she could reply, he began to leaf through the stack she kept on top of the piano.

He smiled and his eyes crinkled at the edges. "Really, now, you must play more than a little if these are the pieces you have on hand."

She wanted to say that she played as well as most ladies, but stopped herself.

"Would you mind choosing a favorite to play for me?"

Cassandra was relieved. She was feeling shy around him, and playing would give her something to do. She chose a simple Bach prelude—she didn't want to appear to be showing off—and launched into it confidently.

When she was finished, Mr. Johnston stood silent for a moment. "Mrs. Franklin, you have been toying with me."

She opened her mouth to object but he cut her off. "Your musicianship is exceptional!"

"Thank you." Her heart beat faster.

"Please, I would not like to burden you, but would you mind playing something else for me? I have been so delighted by the piano music I hear of Ludwig van Beethoven and I see you have some sonatas here. Would it be too much to ask you to indulge me?"

She considered for a moment then spoke: "I usually do not perform such lengthy pieces for an audience. I find that most people say that they enjoy music, but their ability to sit and listen has its limits, though perhaps *you* are different."

"I could listen all day to the music of a performer such as yourself, but if it is really not too much, I will just request of you the one."

"Then I shall be delighted, but only if you sit down and relax over there, in the window seat."

He raised his eyebrows and took a step back, and for the hundredth time she made a mental note to try to express herself more delicately.

He obediently walked to his seat and arranged the pillows to suit him. She closed her eyes and let herself be still, then attacked the first dramatic chords of the "Pathetique" Sonata. She played effortlessly, flawlessly, all three movements, the temperamental first, the achingly beautiful second, the passionate third.

When she finished, his applause startled her. "Magnificent!" he exclaimed. He leapt to his feet and darted over to the piano. "I have not heard this piece performed often and certainly never as well! Congratulations on your playing, Mrs. Franklin, you are…I dare say you are a virtuoso!"

"My goodness, thank you." Cassandra looked down at her hands where they still fluttered at the keyboard.

"And Van Beethoven—he absolutely plumbs the depth of human emotion. Some call him a modernist, you know, as if it is a negative thing. But I find his music immensely stirring. I see that you must too." He stood by the instrument, looking at her expectantly, his eyes piercing.

She met his gaze. "There are no words to express how I feel about his work. When I hear his Ninth Symphony, for instance, I always think to myself that just that one masterpiece makes life on this earth worth living."

His brow furrowed. "His Ninth Symphony?"

"Yes, of course, the 'Choral.' You know, of course, you must be familiar…" her voice trailed off.

"I do not wish to contradict, but I believe he has only written eight."

Within a half of a second Cassandra mentally went though her music history but could not remember when Beethoven wrote the Ninth Symphony. Obviously sometime after 1820. "Oh the Eighth! Yes I meant the Eighth! Sheer ecstasy it is!"

"You called it the 'Choral?' There is no singing in it…"

"I misspoke. I sometimes feel lightheaded after I play, and I also feel myself becoming peckish. Let us call for some tea." She rose from her seat and went to ring the bell for Mary. The young woman stuck her head in the door immediately and Cassandra wondered how long she'd been hovering there, listening.

"Some tea if you please Mary, and some sandwiches."

"Yes ma'am." She shut the glass door with a bang and Cassandra shivered.

"Are you chilly, shall I light a fire?"

"Oh no, that is, I can call the servant—"

"No, please do not bother, I enjoy doing it."

Mr. Johnston set to work arranging kindling and wood from a bin near the fireplace and Cassandra settled back down at the piano bench. She picked up a piece of music by Carl Phillip Emmanuel Bach, and struck the opening notes.

By the time Mary returned with a tray of light fare, the fire was blazing. Cassandra finished her piece and went to sit with Mr. Johnston on the sofa in front of the hearth. They ate companionably and discussed their favorite *pre-1820s* composers. He mentioned that he played the violin and could manage at the piano as well. When they finished their tea, they took turns performing on her instrument. The rain increased as the afternoon wore on, and Cassandra invited him to dine with her to which he readily agreed.

They feasted on a fresh leg of roasted spring lamb from the Sorrel Hall pastures, with roasted potatoes, asparagus, wine from the cellar, Anna's freshly baked rolls, and a selection of Welsh, Irish, and English cheeses imported from around the region.

Before Mr. Johnston left, he extended to her an invitation to tea in the afternoon of the following day. She replied that she would be delighted to come, attended by her friend Lady Holcomb. He smiled, kissed her hand at the door, and rode away in the rain.

After he left, Cassandra sent off a note to Lady Holcomb informing her of the invitation. She then spent the evening reading in the library. She could hear the rain pounding on the windows and her mind meandered away from her book as she found herself wondering if Mr. Johnston had arrived home tolerably dry.

She finally realized that she was getting nowhere reading so she rose to call Mary to have her attend her to bed. Before she could ring the bell, a soft knock on the door told her that the girl had come already. Mary walked in and delivered to her mistress a note in reply from Lady Holcomb containing an enthusiastic affirmation for the morrow.

The next day Cassandra ordered the carriage to come for her at three o'clock, and then drove to Lady Holcomb's cottage. Cassandra would have preferred to walk, but it was a good mile to the lady's home and then two miles beyond to Mr. Johnston's property, and not only could she not expect her friend to walk so far, but a six-mile round trip walk when the weather was uncertain was even beyond Cassandra's hearty constitution. After all, she thought wryly, why not play the part of the grand lady for a change and arrive in style, rather than with her hair all disheveled and her hem and shoes muddied.

To approach Gatewick House, it was necessary to cross a wooden bridge that spanned a narrow moat. When the coach stopped before the entrance, Mr. Johnston was there to greet them and guided each out of the vehicle by their hands. Cassandra was the last to exit, watching with interest as his eyes lingered on Jane's pretty face. When he turned to offer Cassandra his hand, he smiled broadly.

The ladies stopped to take in the mansion. It was truly impressive, thought Cassandra, three stories of tan brick, with castle-like turrets along the flat roof and a broad, unornamented front, save for a carved, stone doorway. Green ivy covering the walls and framing the rows of many windows softened the overall effect, and the moat (Cassandra had never seen an actual moat before), choked with water lilies, encircled the entire structure.

Lady Holcomb and Jane gaped.

"Yes it is big for one person I grant you that!" Mr. Johnston laughed. "I bought it, you know, because I needed an escape from London!"

Lady Holcomb quickly recovered her capacity for speech. "Do you intend to spend more of your time now in the country, Mr. Johnston?"

He led them through the door where they beheld the white-marble floor of the entryway and were confronted with a double staircase which led to an open landing lined with portraits. Cassandra looked up at the two-storied ceiling, where afternoon light poured in from the windows above. "My parents live in town," Mr. Johnston was informing them, "as they always have, and I keep a townhouse there."

"Do you expect them to visit you in your new home soon?" Lady Holcomb inquired.

His smile faded and his jaw tightened. "No, probably not. I will see them when I next visit London." He turned and led them into a sitting room themed in blues, golds, and creams.

"Did you decorate yourself?" asked Cassandra.

"No, I am afraid not." His smiled returned. "Like most creatures of my sex, I am not adept in this area. Much of the furniture and décor was left by the former owners, a lovely older couple, Sir John and Lady Astor. You must have known them," he directed to Lady Holcomb.

"Yes!" she declared, "I did, but it has been many years since I have been in this house. They moved to town at least ten years ago, and rarely returned here, so I hardly recall what it looked like. They never had any children, poor things. They must have got lonely rolling around in this huge place."

"I am afraid," said Mr. Johnston, "that they both recently passed away, she within six months of him and so the house and land were sold."

"I am so sorry to hear that!" cried Lady Holcomb. "But I suppose they had got quite elderly."

"I suppose," replied Mr. Johnston, "I never met them. It was their nephew who sold the place. Apparently he has his own land, and had no need for it."

"You certainly did snatch the place up quickly, Mr. Johnston," quipped Lady Holcomb playfully.

"I, well…" He paused. "Sir John's nephew had no objection to moving quickly through the transaction; there was no reason for delay. When I saw the place, I knew it was for me, so I paid him and it became mine. It all happened within a few days."

"But Mr. Johnston," Lady Holcomb pressed, "surely a bachelor like you does not need all this space. How many bedrooms does it have?"

"Ten, madam," he replied. "I would be happy to show you them."

"Oh, no," Cassandra began, but Lady Holcomb cut her off.

"Of course we would love to see them! There is nothing I adore more than exploring these grand old houses. Now,

Mr. Johnston, as I was saying, why does a bachelor need so many rooms? Do you plan to entertain many visitors?"

"Not really," he replied. "But I do hope to marry and start a family soon. I cannot remain a bachelor forever."

Lady Holcomb looked at Cassandra, Cassandra looked at Jane, and Jane looked at her mother.

"Do you have a particular young lady in mind?" returned Lady Holcomb.

Jane blushed at her mother's forwardness, and Cassandra issued her friend a look. Mr. Johnston simply laughed good-naturedly. "No, ma'am, I do not."

Lady Holcomb let it go and the group continued to explore the house. Cassandra was impressed, even after the grandeur of Sorrel Hall. Each of the ten bedrooms was handsomely fitted up as if awaiting a family. There was a nursery and various sitting rooms as well as bedchambers on the upper floors.

"I do know that Lady Astor so wanted to have children," mused Lady Holcomb. "All this space merely to entertain nephews and nieces. It must have broken her heart."

Mr. Johnston did not reply to her observation but continued the tour, taking them back downstairs, through the ballroom and the informal and formal parlors where Cassandra noticed that the furniture was elegant, yet solid-looking, rather than the spindly French-inspired style that was currently the fashion. They continued through the library, study, dining room, billiard room and breakfast room, and Mr. Johnston continued to talk about his relocation, explaining that he had removed the Astor family portraits from the downstairs rooms and asked his sister to help him choose new wallpaper here and there, freshen up and modernize the curtains, cushions, and other decorations, choose china and cutlery, and hire the servants that the household would need, since it had been functioning with little more than a caretaker and a few maids for several years. This sister, his only one, a few years his elder, had gone back to London just two days before, where she lived with her husband and children, he said, apologizing that not all the work had been finished. But, he explained, he spent most of his time in the conservatory practicing his music, or the library, as he loved to read. The conservatory was where they finished the tour. It was at the back of the house and overlooked the shimmering moat and the shadowy woodland beyond. A large rug of a dark floral pattern intertwined with leaves and garlands covered the oak floor. The walls were paneled in the same golden wood. Tapers perched in candelabra on two low tables, next to which were situated armchairs cushioned in soft green brocade, all nestled near a rectangular piano. Next to it was a music stand, a sturdy wooden chair, and a green velvet-covered table upon which rested a violin case.

They strolled outside through the back doors of the conservatory so their host could acquaint them with the grounds. They found there an extensive rose garden and waited while Lady Holcomb ran about among the bushes, examining the newly formed buds and identifying each variety.

"I am afraid you are the expert, Lady Holcomb; I leave it to my gardener to tend the plants, though I enjoy how they look very much."

"Oh, you bachelors are all the same!" she exclaimed, and Cassandra wondered where her great knowledge of bachelors had suddenly come from.

They crossed the moat by another bridge.

Jane, mostly silent until now, commented: "I do so love a moat."

"Yes!" Mr. Johnston replied. He took the young woman's hand and helped her down the step at the end of the bridge.

They continued through a shrubbery garden, across a great expanse of lawn, and eventually came upon the stables.

"Now this is where my one of my great interest lies," said the gentleman, "with riding and hunting. I am now building up these stables, as the horses were not sold with the house."

They entered the wooden structure. Stacks of hay were piled about and bridles, saddles, and various tools hung neatly upon the walls. The pungent smell of manure hovered in the air. Mr. Johnston led them to a stall where Cassandra recognized the shimmering chestnut mare he had ridden twice to her house.

"Gloria," he said lovingly, and stroked the white star on the animal's nose. She whinnied softly. He took a handful of oats from a bag on the wall and fed them to her from his palm while the ladies watched. "Are you a great rider, Mrs. Franklin?"

Cassandra stammered. "Um, well, in America, ladies do not ride quite as much. In New York, I had not much opportunity—"

"Neither did I in London, though I tried to take Gloria out into the countryside as often as possible. Now that I am here in Hampshire, I ride every chance I get, that is, when I am not absorbed in my indoor pursuits. Do you ride, Miss Holcomb?"

"Yes, certainly," replied Jane. "My horse is at my brother's stable."

"Good. Well, that is a fine thing. Mrs. Franklin, there must be many worthy animals at Sorrel Hall. I venture to say you shall become a fine horse-woman soon if you put your mind to it."

There was a glimmer of amusement at the corner of his eyes and Cassandra wondered if he was making fun.

"Thank you for the suggestion," she said with an arch smile. "I think I shall do just that."

They left the stable and walked until they reached the summit of a small hill, where they could appreciate a broad sweep of the surrounding countryside. There was a chilly breeze, but as they stood for a moment in silence, the sun burst out from behind the clouds, showering them with its rays. Mr. Johnston spontaneously uttered a sigh of contentment, and almost to himself declared, "This is what my soul has always needed!"

Cassandra looked at him in wonder. Jane and her mother exchanged glances. Walking back to the house, Cassandra ventured a request of Mr. Johnston to play the violin for them. He politely declined, stating that he liked to play in the mornings, and besides, it was time for tea. Perhaps Mrs. Franklin or Miss Holcomb would do them the honor, after refreshments, of trying the piano.

By the time they entered the conservatory again, the candles had been lit. They reflected light off the golden walls and illuminated the pale wood of the piano. Cassandra deferred to Miss Holcomb for their musical entertainment, and Jane regaled them with some of the cursory pieces that young ladies were taught to perform in such circumstances. Afterward, Lady Holcomb applauded enthusiastically, and Cassandra and Mr. Johnston joined her, though with slightly less vigor.

Cassandra observed it was getting late. The ladies took their leave, and in the carriage Jane and Lady Holcomb chattered all the way to the cottage about Mr. Johnston's charm and the lovely house. Cassandra was only thinking about the violin and wondering how she could get him to play for her. She returned home anxious to spend time at her own instrument, and happily played until suppertime.

******

Cassandra determined upon waking the next morning that the weather looked promising, and so, after breakfast, she wandered out to the stables to find William, the stablemaster. It was the first time she'd ventured inside the space. Once there, inhaling the smells of horse and hay and oil and leather, she wondered why she'd never come before. The raftered ceiling was high, and the wide doors open at either end let the fresh breeze waft through. She wandered past stalls of horses that observed her with mild wonder. Finally she discovered William, a man of about fifty years, mostly bald, with a lined face, but a strong, stocky body, examining the hoof of a grey, dappled equine.

"Excuse me—" she began.

"Mrs. Franklin!" He stood and she detected a sharp odor of stale sweat and of clothes not recently washed. "I was wondering when I would get a visit from you."

"Well, I have decided that I need to learn to ride."

"I am sorry; my hearing is going a bit. Did you say you need to learn to ride?"

"Yes, I—in America—"

"Are you telling me they do not ride horses in the states? Those Americans!"

"Well, they do. It is just that I did not."

"Well, for heaven's sake, let us get you started!"

He led her back up past the stalls to one that contained a dark brown mare with a black silken mane and tail, and large, liquid brown eyes.

"This is Daisy. She is as gentle as they get, but she has some spirit as well."

He chose a saddle and fitted the horse with a bridle, then helped Cassandra on and led her outside into a ring. In less than an hour, she'd learned to turn the animal, stop her, and trot with ease. William grinned from ear to ear as he watched his student's first day's progress.

The subsequent few mornings she returned for lessons, and soon was riding very well. She and William went together on horseback around the parklands of Sorrel Hall, and it was during these rides that she began to form a plan. She hadn't heard from Mr. Johnston, and she couldn't invite him over if he didn't request an invitation, yet she desperately wanted to hear him play his violin.

She proposed to William that she go out for a solo ride, just around the environs of Sorrel Hall, over ground they had gone before, so she could test her abilities on her own. He reluctantly assented, and so she set off in the direction of Gatewick House, dressed unusually well for a morning ride. She cut across her own land, through a forested area to the road, so that William wouldn't know where she might be headed, and then stayed on the road until she was at Mr. Johnston's drive. She then continued on past the drive and entered the property through the woods, approaching the mansion unseen. When she was in sight of the moat, she stopped. The most achingly beautiful music was drifting to her across the breeze. It was an exquisite Bach violin sonata. She held her breath. Should she just remain still and listen, or should she make her presence known? But what would she say to him? She hadn't thought that part of the plan through. What she had wanted was to eavesdrop on his practice session. But now that she was there, she determined to go inside.

Suddenly, the barking of dogs caught her by surprise, and in a moment, the music stopped. As she was beginning to turn Daisy to go, two, small, playful shepherds bounded up, barking loudly. Daisy was spooked but was not flighty enough to rear up, so she pranced about nervously. Cassandra could not get her to turn and withdraw. The animal whinnied loudly, and soon the head gardener appeared, followed by Mr. Johnston.

"Mrs. Franklin!" Mr. Johnston called to her. "Whatever are you doing?"

"Oh dear," she said, trying to keep her wits. "I was lost. It was my first time out riding by myself, and I was here before I knew it."

The gardener called the dogs away, and the horse settled.

Mr. Johnston smiled. "Well, as long as you are here, you must come in for some refreshment and to calm your nerves."

Cassandra gratefully accepted. Her plan had worked better than she had hoped. He helped her down off the horse and took the animal by the reins. Soon a stable boy ran up and led the horse away. Mr. Johnston led Cassandra into the blue and gold parlor and asked her to make herself comfortable on the sofa while he ordered the maid to bring tea and toast. Soon they were laughing at her mishap.

"I am afraid I must have interrupted your practice," she finally admitted. "I heard you playing."

"You did? And what was your opinion?"

"Heavenly!" she replied. "Sir, I know that you prefer privacy when you play. I am the same. But I beg you to play something for me while I am here. It has been so long since I have heard any music but my own…and Miss Holcomb's the other day—"

"Yes, Miss Holcomb," he said. "Well, I only play for those whom I think would appreciate the music, and since I know you do, I would be honored to have you listen to me."

They went into the conservatory and Cassandra settled into one of the large green chairs. Mr. Johnston picked up his violin from the table near the piano, tuned it a little, and commenced the sonata he'd been playing before. She was immediately moved. His playing was perfection. How could a person of his social status, though, have been so well trained?

When finished, Mr. Johnson pulled another brocade chair near hers.

"You are wondering how I come to play as I do."

She nodded.

"Then I will ease your curiosity. I began playing at the age of five. My parents were entertaining their friends with a string quartet at our home. They often tried to impress others with their elegant taste, though really, they had very little appreciation of art of any kind."

Cassandra smiled in sympathy.

"I had crept down the stairs and was listening, and I was entranced with how the violin made a sound like it was singing. It went straight to my heart. The next day, I told my mother I wanted to play the violin, and, amused, she bought me a small one and hired a gentle old teacher to come once a week. I had a natural ability and learned rapidly. My father largely ignored my playing until I was about ten, and then he began to question a boy being so devoted to music. My sister played the piano, though not well, so my mother was particularly proud of me, and she insisted I continue regardless of Father's disapproval. He was really too busy with his business to take further notice, so my mother took it upon herself to engage the finest teachers in London."

"You were lucky that she was so devoted to your talent."

"Yes, I am grateful. It became a hobby of sorts for her. Anyway, when I was finished with my university education, she agreed to let me go and study with the masters in Vienna. When I became of age, and came into my money, I took my own house in London, and continued with my music, playing for friends and friends of friends in private salons. My father was unhappy that I didn't join him in his business, but he let me be. However, he did threaten to disinherit me if I became a professional, and so rather than incur his wrath and alienate myself from my family completely, I technically remain an amateur."

Cassandra wanted to ask what his father's business was, but thought it might be rude. "Do you compose?" she asked instead.

"I do. I have," he replied, "but not extensively, for I cannot publish. I do it to amuse myself and my ensemble."

"Is your ensemble in London?"

"Yes, they are all professionals and keep themselves busy playing for the opera and the theatre. Many of them are employed by the large London parishes and play at religious services. They are usually only available to play with me during the off-season. After all, musicians must play, and we prefer to play with other musicians. Of course, I am speaking of string musicians in particular, and the brass and woodwinds. Those of you who perform on the pianoforte are the true soloists."

"No, actually, I love to play duets, and I do love to *accompany*," she stated with a grin. "I do not always have to be the sun around which everything revolves."

He laughed. "Then perhaps you would like to accompany me now. I have been practicing a Bach sonata for violin and harpsichord with no accompaniment, waiting for the day when I would find an accomplished enough musician around Selborne. I think I may have found her."

"Well, I have never played it, but I shall try. You will have to pardon my fumbles."

"It is only you and me," he said, "It matters not." He held out his hand to her and led her to the piano. "It is not a harpsichord, but it is close enough. Here is the score."

They played it through, stopping and starting again twice, but once they found their mutual rhythm, the music flowed naturally. He was more familiar with the piece and was able to watch her as she played and adjust when needed to her tempo. She tuned into him with her ears and her heartbeat. She began to feel his urges toward crescendo or decrescendo. The mathematical logic of Bach united with their intuitive senses in a feeling of great fulfillment.

After the final notes of the piece sounded, Cassandra sat quietly at the piano, her eyes still resting on the music. Mr. Johnston took out a handkerchief and wiped his brow. They looked at each other. A smile formed at the corners of his eyes, and she could not suppress her delight.

"How immensely pleasing," Mr. Johnston noted.

"I could not be happier," remarked Cassandra.

"Will you stay to dinner?"

"I shall be honored."

******

Mr. Johnston rode back to Sorrel Hall alongside Cassandra. William had become frantic at her long absence (she had quite forgot about him) and had sent two stable boys out to look for her. Cassandra apologized profusely, and after Mr. Johnston explained how he'd discovered her lost, William seemed appeased.

From the stables, Mr. Johnston walked Cassandra to the house. "When can we meet again to play?" he asked.

Cassandra thought for a moment. "I think we should meet here, at Sorrel Hall. I am afraid—" She wasn't sure how to put it delicately. "That our playing together may seem a bit—"

"Unorthodox?"

She laughed. "Yes, unorthodox, that we are meeting to play at all. But if we do so at my home, at least my household staff and, perhaps our various neighbors, will not be as disapproving as they would of my going to a gentleman's house unescorted."

"Yes, I understand your thinking. When are you free next to meet?"

She briefly ran over her social calendar in her head, which was, thankfully, sparse.

"Saturday, I believe, would be perfect. You like to play in the morning, though I prefer the afternoon, but I would be happy to accommodate you—"

"I would not hear of such a thing. We can alternate mornings and afternoons. And we can communicate by messenger to arrange day to day."

"Yes, all right." Her heartbeat quickened.

"I will see you the day after tomorrow, then. Shall we say ten o'clock?"

"I look forward to it immensely."

"And I shall bring the Bach."

"Wonderful!"

"Goodnight, Mrs. Franklin." He took her hand and kissed it gently.

Her skin tingled. "Goodnight, Mr. Johnston." She turned and went into the house.

******

The next morning, she informed Mrs. Merriweather to expect Mr. Johnston on a regular basis as her musical partner and guest, her stomach churning as she did so. The housekeeper merely nodded in response as she inspected a silver serving spoon she had been polishing.

"Mrs. Merriweather, please tell me if what I propose is shocking," Cassandra ventured to say. "I am not familiar with the British etiquette concerning this sort of thing."

The woman looked at Cassandra directly, and after a moment spoke. "Well, I must admit that it is not the usual thing to do."

Cassandra steeled herself to form a rebuttal.

"However, you are a grown woman, Mrs. Franklin, independent, and with a grown-up son to boot. This is your house, and I should say you can make your own decisions and to blazes with anyone who does not like it." She set the spoon down firmly on the credenza, picked up a meat fork, and began rubbing it with resolve.

"Thank you, Mrs. Merriweather. I appreciate your open-mindedness."

The housekeeper looked up at her again. Cassandra gave a small, awkward bow, turned and walked away, wondering when she was going to stop saying bizarre things, but also marveling at the fact that Mrs. Merriweather was far more ahead of her time than the woman could possibly know..

CHAPTER SEVEN

M ay 10, 1820 – Things are becoming more interesting. Mr. Johnston and I have been meeting to play music together for about three weeks to, it seems, our mutual satisfaction. His company has certainly made my experiment much more pleasurable than it had been just those few short weeks ago. Amazing what a difference it makes throwing a man into the mix—not that I have any intentions of any sort. It's just nice to have his company..

******

Lady Holcomb was reclining in the sunlit window seat of Cassandra's sitting room, pouring cream into her tea. The two had been chatting for some minutes when she asked Cassandra if she would dine with them the coming Saturday. Cassandra replied that she was free and would be delighted.

"Good," said Lady Holcomb, "Because Mr. Johnston wishes it."

"Mr. Johnston?"

"Yes. I sent him a note yesterday, inviting him to dine with Jane, Jeffrey, and me, and he replied in the affirmative, and then, as a side note, inquired if Mrs. Franklin would be joining us. Of course, I was on the point of sending you an invitation, but I thought it was curious that he was so anxious for your company."

Cassandra blushed.

"Hmmm," the lady continued. "Your former protests about the gentleman are not so persuasive now."

"No, no! I do not know why he asked about me."

"Truly?"

"Truly." Cassandra's eyes flitted away from the gaze of her friend and wandered to the piano where a copy of the Bach sonata sat open on the music stand with an inscription in Mr. Johnston's hand. She'd memorized it. It read: *To Mrs. Franklin, your copy to practice and to enjoy. May your possession of it bring us both a great deal of musical pleasure. —Benedict Johnston.*

"Well, then, forgive me for being nosy," Lady Holcomb said. "I fear it is one of my faults." She took a sip of tea.

"You are too strict with yourself, my dear Charlotte. We all love a little gossip. It is just that in this case, there is nothing to tell."

******

It was raining on Saturday, so Cassandra ordered the carriage to take her to the cottage. When she arrived, Mr. Johnston was already there. He leapt up when she walked into the parlor and hurried over to take her hand. "Mrs. Franklin, how wonderful to see you again!"

"I am equally delighted," she returned. She let her hand linger in his, then remembered her friend and looked over to see Lady Holcomb and Jane sitting on the sofa, staring at them both.

Before another word could be spoken, Jeffrey bounded into the room, wet and red-cheeked. "Hello, Mr. Johnston!"

The gentleman let Cassandra's hand drop and reached out to shake Jeffrey's. "Hello, my boy, how are you doing?"

"Jeffrey!" his mother scolded, "What do you mean coming in here all wet and muddy? For goodness sake, go remove those boots and change your clothes!"

"I have been out hunting with my brother, sir," said the boy. "The manor house keeps an excellent stable and hounds. Upon my visit to you, I mentioned that you must join us one day and take advantage. I could not mean that more sincerely. We are going out tomorrow morning again, will you join us?"

Mr. Johnston glanced at Cassandra. They'd been scheduled to practice together in the morning. She gave the slightest nod of her head and smiled. He returned his gaze to Jeffrey. "I should like nothing better. Thank you for the invitation."

"Fine! Does nine o'clock suit you?"

"Perfectly."

"My brother's bitch has recently whelped eight gorgeous pups. The finest hunting hounds anywhere. Perhaps he would be willing to make you a gift—"

"Jeffrey!" screeched Lady Holcomb. "Will you please stop haranguing Mr. Johnston about hounds and hunting and go change your clothes!"

"Yes, mother," he grinned and bounded off.

"Goodness, what a troublesome boy," she said looking after him, her voice full of affection.

Once Jeffrey was dry and suitably coifed, the group sat down to dinner with Cassandra seated next to him, and Jane next to Mr. Johnston, who was diagonal from Cassandra. Lady Holcomb presided at the head. Talk proceeded along the lady's favorite topics of weather, neighbors, servants, roses, and gardening. Then, while Jeffrey and his mother returned to the subject of his impending naval career, Cassandra and Mr. Johnston fell into talk about music and composers. Jane was listening eagerly.

After dinner, Lady Holcomb suggested that Jane perform. The young woman leaned forward as she played without taking her eyes from her music book. The piece she'd chosen was not difficult by Cassandra's standards, but she executed it well. The American glanced at Mr. Johnston seated near her on a rose-pink chair. He was absorbed in watching the performer, smiling and nodding.

Next, Lady Holcomb asked Cassandra to oblige them on the instrument. She declined at first, but was urged so much by the lady and by Mr. Johnston that she finally assented, settling on a few simple pieces from her repertoire.

After the performance, the friends chatted until Cassandra excused herself. The weather was not improving, she noted, and she ought to get home. Mr. Johnston agreed, and so the party broke up in spite of the protests of the hostess. As he escorted Cassandra from the cottage door to her carriage under his umbrella, he had a chance to utter the words, "Tomorrow afternoon, then." She tilted her head in agreement and accepted his hand for the coach step.

******

With June almost halfway over, Cassandra rode out often on horseback around the countryside, accompanied by Jimmy, the Merriweather's great-nephew. He was a quiet boy of twelve years, not given to conversation, which suited Cassandra. On a particularly sunny Thursday, they had ridden to visit one of the farmers' wives that Cassandra was beginning to get to know well. The visit had lasted longer than Cassandra had planned, and now she was rushing back for an afternoon practice session with Benedict (as she now called Mr. Johnston), pressing Daisy to a slow cantor. Jimmy came up behind her, holding his own reins with one hand and munching an apple with the other. They had passed Gatewick House on the way and she found herself wishing she could just stop off there for practice rather than having to meet Benedict each time at Sorrel Hall. She hopped off in front of her stables and turned Daisy over to Jimmy.

She hurried into the sitting room while pulling off her bonnet. Benedict was sitting coolly in a chair, absorbed in a copy of *Tom Jones* that she'd left on a table. He looked up at her, amused. "This is a fascinating bit of fiction you have been partaking of."

Heat crept up over her neck and face. "Yes, it is not what I usually read, but I have been finding it…interesting."

He stared at her, eyes twinkling, lips pressed tightly to hide a smile. "Interesting? Is that what they call such things in the states?"

"You are making fun of me!" She went to him and playfully snatched the book from his hands, flinging it onto the table.

"I would *never* do such a thing."

"At any rate, I am sorry to be late." She turned her back on him, hoping the pink in her face would recede, and went to lay her bonnet on the mantle.

"It is of no importance. I was receiving a welcome education at the hands of Mr. Fielding."

She ignored his remark as she removed her gloves. "The ride back from MacIntosh Farm took longer than I imagined it would. It made me think that perhaps we could sometimes meet at Gatewick House to practice, rather than you always coming here."

"Would the neighborhood not be scandalized?"

"To blazes with them, as Mrs. Merriweather says!" She immediately regretted the outburst.

He lifted an eyebrow. "I see."

"I mean to say—"

"Oh no, quite perfectly said. And I agree with you. Meeting at Gatewick would suit me just fine."

"Oh good," she sighed with relief and moved toward the piano.

"Do you need a moment to refresh yourself before we begin?"

"No. I am most eager to start." She plunked herself down on the piano stool and positioned the music to her liking.

Benedict removed his violin from its case, which had been resting on the piano, and began to tune it. Cassandra arranged his music for him on the flat piano lid. It was the Bach Violin Sonata in G, the same they had been working on since they started playing together.

After the violin was tuned, she looked up at him and their eyes locked. Benedict tapped his foot to set the pace; Cassandra looked down at her music, took a breath, and began to play. It was a piece that required great precision.

The first movement flew at an incredible pace, and the concentration that was necessary from both musicians consumed them for the three and a half minutes. The second movement was slow and mournful, a brief interlude. Cassandra lifted her eyes from her music and found Benedict's. She felt herself connect with his emotions: sad, longing, hopeful. She sensed the barriers of formality drop away and in doing so, felt suddenly vulnerable. Then the movement ended and the connection shifted. The lengthy and complex Allegro permitted the musicians to only glance up from their music occasionally, smile, nod, check their tempo, and continue. Cassandra felt her heartbeat keeping time, racing with the exuberance of the bond she felt with her companion. Then came the Adagio, slow, though not sad, almost romantic. Cassandra closed her eyes, confident of the music, and as she played imagined a dance from the 18th century—two lovers, eyes locked, hands barely touching, stepping in sync, communicating with only a blush, a downcast glance, a shy smile, a searching look. The dancing couple resolved into her and Benedict. She opened her eyes and shook the image away. It was time to concentrate on the final movement: joyous, exalting. There was an exchange of power, one minute the violin took lead, the next the piano. It was a chase in Cassandra's mind, lovers racing through the woods, now hiding behind a tree, now jumping out to surprise, laughing, playful, hungry with desire. The movement culminated in a rousing finale. Benedict pulled out his handkerchief and mopped his brow. Cassandra stood, went to a table bearing a porcelain pitcher and glasses, and poured water for herself and Benedict. She took his glass to him and he drank without a word.

Finally he spoke. "Again?"

She nodded, took her seat, and the performance was repeated. This time they stopped and adjusted where necessary, playing over again one part or another until they were both satisfied. They then continued on to one of Benedict's favorite works of Mozart's, and when they'd played that piece three times through, Cassandra needed a break.

"Would you do me the honor of staying for dinner, Benedict? We shall have it early, I think. I had a late breakfast and seemed to have skipped lunch."

"Are you going to be serving one of those famous salads of yours, or will it be an actual meal?"

"I thought you enjoyed my salads!"

"Oh, very much!"

She had got in the habit of sometimes having nothing midday but fresh lettuce from the garden, sprinkled with roasted chicken and sheep's cheese, or whatever meats and vegetables were left over from the night before.

"Well, for your information," said Cassandra, "I do not know what Anna has planned for the meal, but let us go and annoy her. She so loves when I intrude on her kitchen sanctuary."

Benedict put his violin in its case, and the two of them tip-toed through the house, being careful to avoid Mrs. Merriweather or the other servants, until they arrived at the kitchen. Cassandra opened the door slightly and peaked in. Anna's back was to them as she stirred something in a pot over the fire. Two roasted partridges sat cooling on the table in the center of the room and a variety of raw vegetables lay nearby. A ribbon of steam rose from a pot of boiled potatoes. They could hear the clank of dishware in the distance, which meant Mrs. Merriweather was probably organizing dishes in the dining room. Lydia sat in a chair snapping peas into a bowl in her lap. When she saw Cassandra's face peering in through the door, she exclaimed, "Oh! Mrs. Franklin!" She leapt to her feet.

"Please, Lydia, sit down. Do not mind me."

Anna turned to observe the trespasser. "Hello, Mrs. Franklin," she said kindly. "What can I do for you?"

"May we come in? Mr. Johnston and I?"

"Oh yes, of course." She quickly wiped her hands on a towel.

The two entered the kitchen. Benedict looked about with interest. "I perceive this is quite a privilege you have allowed us, Anna. My own cook never lets me set foot in my kitchen," he said.

"Mrs. Franklin is always my honored guest," the woman replied smiling. Her eyes nearly disappeared into her red cheeks as she did so. "I have never known a lady so interested in cooking and such."

"Yes," Cassandra replied. "In America we participate much more in the preparation of meals for our families."

There was silence as the three others in the room stared at Cassandra.

"How odd," Anna remarked.

"I suppose. Anyway, we did not come merely to harass you," Cassandra continued. "I came to let you know that Mr. Johnston will be joining me for dinner and to ask you how soon we could eat. We are hungry." She breathed the wonderful aroma wafting about.

"Well, everything is nearly ready. The soup is done, and the fowl. Potatoes simply need mashing, and I was going to boil up these peas and put together a side salad for you as I know you like. Bread was baked this morning, and I have fresh butter churned."

"How heavenly," uttered Benedict. "I do not know if I can wait!"

"Well you must," Cassandra said, turning to him. "We do not want to rush Anna and her magic."

"Nonsense," Anna said, her cheeks rising even higher. "A half an hour should do it. Now, if you two would get on back to the parlor where you belong, I shall have Mary bring you some sherry and some newly cracked walnuts that I toasted to hold you over."

"Thank you, Anna, you are a saint!" Cassandra declared. She and Benedict turned to walk back to the sitting room and nearly ran into Mrs. Merriweather coming through the breakfast room door. The woman issued them a brisk curtsy as they passed and then hurried on.

The conversation over dinner ranged to deeper topics than usual. Benedict asked about her life in New England, and Cassandra found herself relating again the story she so often shared with her neighbors and acquaintances, though she omitted the information about her husband being involved in the slave trade. He listened thoughtfully. They lingered at the table, drinking wine and talking until the sun was nearly set.

******

Two days later, Cassandra went to Gatewick House, accompanied by Jimmy, and spent the morning there, while he lounged around the stable with the other boys. She and Benedict exchanged locations for their practice very nearly every day until Cassandra began to feel like she was neglecting her other friends and acquaintances in the interest of spending time with him.

At the end of June, the weather was hot and muggy. It was a Thursday, and Benedict was coming to Sorrel Hall that afternoon for a practice session. Cassandra had chosen her lightest gown, a diaphanous mist green. In her bedroom mirror, she admired how it clung around her legs and showed off their shape when she moved. She toyed with her shoes on the floor, slipping them on and off, but could not resign herself to keeping them on. Just the thought made her feel hotter. She finally kicked them aside and walked downstairs barefoot. Mary, coming up to help her fix her hair, stopped and gaped at her feet.

"Yes, Mary?" Cassandra asked pleasantly.

"I…was… just coming to help madam with her hair."

"No, I decided to do it myself this afternoon, do you like it?" It was halfway pulled up in back, with curls and tendrils falling past her shoulders. Cassandra laughed. "I daresay it will become the latest fashion!" She continued lightly down the stairs, amused at the thought that if she started a new trend, it could conceivably change the course of women's hairstyles forever.

She was walking into the sitting room just as Mrs. Merriweather was admitting Benedict. The two both stopped and regarded her, Benedict's eyes lingering on her neck and shoulders, and the housekeeper's pausing on her feet with a frown.

"Good afternoon, Mr. Johnston!"

He held the glass door open for her as she entered before him. "Good afternoon, Mrs. Franklin."

"Will you be requiring some refreshment, ma'am?" Mrs. Merriweather asked.

"Only water for me. Benedict? Could you do with a cup of coffee or tea?"

"Water will suit me fine. It is too warm for anything else."

Mrs. Merriweather nodded her head and retired.

Cassandra observed the sky from the window. "It looks as if it wants to rain."

"I wish it would. Perhaps it would not be so damned muggy if it did."

"You do not seem much in the mood to play."

"Perhaps I could listen to you for a while. I am feeling most lazy, and the ride over did not cure me of it."

"Of course." Cassandra sat down at the piano, selected a piece by Scarlatti, a fast-paced tune she hoped would energize him. He had taken off his jacket and lounged on the sofa in his shirt and trousers, boot-clad feet hanging off the edge. When finished, she noticed he was still unmoved. She began a light piece of Beethoven's, which inspired him sufficiently to rouse and join her in a sonata they had been working on by the same composer.

Mary came in with lemonade and sandwiches, and Cassandra and Benedict ate and talked little and did not resume practice for more than an hour. Benedict played, but without conviction. He finally set down his instrument and let her continue while he went back to the sofa. It had begun to drizzle, and the light from the windows shone softly through the mist.

She could feel his eyes on her as she played. Eventually, she forgot about him, completely lost in the music. After some time had passed, however, she became aware that he had gotten up from the sofa and approached the piano where he stood looking down at her. When she finished the piece, she raised her eyes to him. He reached out, took her hand, bent over, and kissed it. Then, gently, he pulled her to her feet, took her in his arms and kissed her. It was what she wanted—she suddenly knew it—and she returned the eagerness of his kiss. It was delicious and sweet, and as it grew more passionate, she became fully aware of the fact that it had been a long time since she'd been with a man. She pulled back from him and looked at him in wonder.

"Cassandra," he whispered. "I want you to marry me."

She gasped. "Oh my God." She sat back down on the piano seat.

He went to his knees. "Cassandra, I love you, more than I have ever loved anyone. I need to be with you forever. Please, please tell me you will be my wife."

"But what about Jane?"

"Jane?"

"Miss Holcomb."

"I do not understand."

"I thought that perhaps she—"

"Was of interest to me? Are you joking?"

"Well, why not? She is young and I am not."

"What are you talking about? To me you are the perfect woman in every way! I have no interest in Jane Holcomb."

"But, but," she went on, desperately reaching for a plausible reason for refusing him. "I cannot bear more children, and I know you want many, children that a young wife can give you."

"Cassandra, I thought that was what I wanted because that is what others wanted for me. I only want to have you as part of my life always. Your son can come and live with us. He can marry and fill the house with children. I do not care; I just want you."

Her mind raced. Did she love him? And what if she did? She certainly could not marry him. "Benedict, I do not know if I love you. I have not known you long."

"Yet I am certain of how much I love you. We have known each other long enough for me to know my heart completely."

"But I cannot marry you. It is too soon, too soon after my husband's death. I am just not ready, and I do not know when I will be."

He went pale, and moved to a nearby chair to sit down.

"But Benedict, I value our friendship very much, and I do not want to lose that."

"Our friendship? Is it no more than friendship to you?"

"Well, perhaps it is. But my future is uncertain. I may have to return to America for my son. I do not know yet."

"Then I will go with you," he said, brightening. "There is nothing to keep me here."

"Benedict, please, we must slow down. You must respect my widowhood. I do not know if I will ever marry again." This, she knew, was the truth.

He sat for a moment, thinking. "I understand. I understand that you do not wish to marry, though I hope to someday change your mind, but I do not want to lose you. If we must remain only as friends, then I choose that rather than nothing."

She remembered just then all the hours of boredom and frustration that she had experienced in the first few months of her experiment. She could not bear it again. "Maybe there is another choice." She watched hope bloom on his face. "Perhaps," she began slowly, "we could be lovers."

He blinked. "Are you proposing that you be my mistress?"

"Well, no," she said. "I do not think mistress is the word." Miss Austen hadn't prepared her for how to talk about physical intimacy. She stood up from the piano bench and walked to him. He instinctively rose as she did. "I mean I want to—"

He pulled her close. She looked up into his sea-colored eyes. He kissed her again, letting her feel the intensity of his emotions. "I am yours," he murmured simply, and they lost themselves in the kiss. Finally she began to be aware of the possibility of being seen by Mary or Mrs. Merriweather or any of the other servants, and gently pushed him away.

"We must be careful," she said, softly. "We must be thoughtful of my reputation and yours."

"Yes, of course," he said. He looked down at his trousers and quickly turned away. They both laughed.

"You must go," she said with a smile, "and when we next meet, we will plan how we can be alone together."

Cassandra," he said, looking at her tenderly, "are you sure this is how you want it?"

"Yes," she said. "I am a respectable woman, but I am a woman who has lived life and I know my mind. I hope your respect for me will not wane as a result of this."

"Never," he replied. "I could not admire you more, as a musician, as a lady, and as my dear friend."

Cassandra threw herself into his arms again. They embraced for a moment, and he took his leave.

Cassandra spent her evening walking from room to room without being able to focus on any particular activity. Every time she happened upon Mrs. Merriweather, the woman would eye her curiously, nod, and go about her way.

******

June 21, 1820—The hour is nine, much later than I usually sleep, but I am lazy this morning. I spent all night half dreaming, half wakefully thinking about yesterday. I have to ask myself, do I really want this man, or am I just infatuated with the idea of living out a story from some kind of romance novel? Or perhaps the summer solstice has infused me with a certain pagan wildness. Well, no matter what, next January I will go back to my life and out of Benedict's forever. I wonder if he will have had a change of heart since last night; perhaps my proposal was disgraceful after all.

******

There was a knock on the bedroom door. Cassandra quickly wiped the bookmark over the page and closed her journal.

"Come in, Mary."

The girl entered with a note. It was from Benedict, asking if she would do him the honor of paying him a visit that afternoon. She smiled to herself, and mentally congratulated him on his good thinking; their meetings always felt more private at Gatewick House.

She labored energetically in both the flower and vegetable gardens all morning, then ordered a bath to be started while she had lunch. As she ate, a brigade of servants hauled hot water up the back stairs to fill a copper tub in her room. This process took a good twenty minutes, and the whole ordeal made her feel guilty for bathing every other day. If she had her choice, she would just bathe in a tub in the kitchen where the water was pumped directly in and afterward drained into the vegetable garden. She would wash out her own underthings and gowns, but such a thing was unheard of, so she gave in to protocol. Her needs for cleanliness required much less of the servants than the Collins' large family had.

By two o'clock she was immersed in a lavender-scented bath. After a good soak, she dismissed Mary so that she could dress in private. She put on clean linens and a lightweight navy blue gown with white trim. She brushed her teeth, put on some simple white pearl earrings and short, tan boots, and arranged her hair in the style she had worn the day before. She scrutinized herself in the mirror and noted with satisfaction how the color of the dress complemented her dark red hair and gray-blue eyes.

She ordered the carriage to take her to Gatewick House rather than ride, since it threatened rain, and set off around three o'clock. Benedict was waiting for her when she arrived and handed her out of the coach with a wide grin on his face. She giggled and they hurried through the house to the conservatory. As soon as he closed the door behind him, he took her in his arms and kissed her deeply. He tasted like peppermint and cherries. She stood wrapped in his arms and he moved from kissing her mouth to her neck and shoulders. At last she gently pushed him away, struggling to catch her breath.

"You are so beautiful," he whispered.

Her knees went weak. "Benedict," she uttered, "let us sit down for a moment."

They moved to the sofa, and there he embraced her again, kissing her intensely.

"Wait, wait," she finally managed or say, "I am losing my mind! I want to know how we can be together. Please tell me if you have thought of anything."

"Yes, I have," he replied, "but it cannot be today."

She laughed. "I assumed it would not be. Tell me what you decided."

"Well, there is a little cottage about a half mile west of here, in the forest. It used to be one that the gamekeeper lived in, but since he died several years ago, it has remained empty. I have not yet hired a new gamekeeper, nor do I intend to for some time. But I will tell my housekeeper that I am looking for someone and I want to ready the cottage. I will have her send the servants there to clean it and put in a fresh feather mattress on the bed." At this, Cassandra blushed. "I will bring fresh linens myself when they are done, and only I will keep the keys. We can use it anytime we want to."

Just like *Lady Chatterley's Lover*! she almost cried, and then clamped her mouth shut. That book wouldn't be written for more than one hundred years. "It sounds perfect," she murmured. She thought for a moment, then added, "but I have to convince William to let me ride by myself so I can meet you there directly."

"Yes, it would not really do to have us leave here and disappear together into the woods for hours while your stable boy waits. I could just say I am going hunting, and you could say you are going for a ride, and there we would meet."

"But I could not be gone for more than two hours at the most. You know how anxious William gets."

Benedict sighed, and Cassandra stood up, pacing the room.

"This is ridiculous," she stated. "We are two adults, almost forty. I have a grown son, and we are worried about the opinion of our employees! They are not our parents. We should be able to sleep together in our own bedrooms if we want to!"

Benedict looked at her in shock. "Cassandra, what are you saying? If we want to be completely free to 'sleep together,' as you say, we must be husband and wife. Why not marry me then, if you want us to have no secrets from the servants?"

She bit her lip.

He continued, "You know that servants gossip. They talk to other servants at the market, and those servants let it slip to their mistresses, and soon the entire neighborhood knows. It may be inconvenient, but there is no choice. Unless, you will agree to marry me."

Her expression softened. "No. I still say no. But I will be firm with William. I will tell him that I am going directly to Gatewick House to play music with you and that I do not need an escort. I will simply tell him I am going by myself and that is that."

He chuckled. "You are quite determined, aren't you?"

She went and sat by him. "I see that you have lost no time in working things out either."

"I am on fire," he stated simply. "Nothing will stop me from being with you, married or not."

"I am glad," she said, and kissed him. "When will the cottage be ready?"

"In about a week," he replied.

"It will be the longest week of my life."

"You astonish me!" he said, pulling her close. "I have never met a woman like you. Are all American women like this, so...independent?"

"I do not think you were going to say independent."

"You know what I mean. It is as if you do not need a man to care for you. Neither do you care what others think. You know what you want. English women are not like that."

"American women are really not either," she told him. "I have just lived life and I know what I want, and also what I do not want. I think I *am* different from other women. I think that is why you like me."

"It is why I love you," he said, "and I cannot wait to be with you." He kissed her.

"All right, but for now we practice our music."

"Yes, we had better. If I cannot have you now, then give me my violin."

******

The next few days were occupied for both Cassandra and Benedict by other engagements. Lady Holcomb's son, Jeffrey, had invited Mr. Johnston to go hunting two days in a row, and Cassandra was busy paying visits to the neighbors she had been neglecting. Among them were Lady Charles, Miss Charles, and Eunice Fairchild, who had been back in Hampshire for three weeks, having spent most of spring in London.

Cassandra sat in Lady Charles' parlor during the obligatory visit, sipping tea from a translucent, pink china cup. Her mind wandered as the three other women chattered enthusiastically about London, the plays they had seen, the people they had met, and the balls they had attended. Her eyes rested on the pale blue brocade of the sofa just behind Eunice's shoulders. The girl was talking rapidly about something, but Cassandra was thinking of Benedict. Her gaze floated from a large painting on the wall of blue, pink, and yellow irises to a garish chandelier, dripping with crystal teardrops of pastel blues and pinks, then back down again to rest on two fragile looking, pink-upholstered chairs across the room, arranged on either side of a tiny table covered with a baby-blue satin cloth. A porcelain sculpture of a milkmaid flirting with her farm boy lover sat atop it, and held Cassandra's attention until she heard Miss Charles saying, "Oh, mother, we must have a ball and invite Mr. Johnston! I have heard so much about him, but we have not yet been introduced. I hear he is quite handsome."

"He is old," complained Eunice, "and I hear he is eccentric, a musician." The girls giggled.

Once she recovered herself, Miss Charles added, "Yes, but he is rich. You know him, do you not, Mrs. Franklin?"

Cassandra tried not to blush, but feared she was unsuccessful. "Yes," she replied. "I must admit, we are quite good friends. We enjoy playing music together."

"You play music together?" gaped Lady Charles. "How unusual!"

"Well," Cassandra ventured, "I suppose it is a little unusual, but it is an interest we share."

The three ladies stared at her. Cassandra suddenly felt her virtue to be in question. She understood that it was likely that Lady Charles and the girls had no precedent with which to compare it.

"Is there something you are not telling us, Mrs. Franklin?" said Lady Charles. "Is there a little romance here?"

"Oh, no. I assure you, I have no interest in marrying."

"Really? I suppose you can afford not to."

"Yes, financially, I have no concerns." The smile Cassandra had forced began to tire her.

Lady Charles hesitated. "It is just that it seems peculiar that you tumble about that large house of yours all by yourself, with no family, or no female companion. What is it that you do all day, other than play music with Mr. Johnston?"

Annoyance prickled Cassandra's scalp. "I garden, as you know. I visit my *friends*." She paused for a breath. "I read—"

"Personally," said Lady Charles, sharply, "I must have a bustle about me, or I am not happy. A big house should be filled with people: guests and family. It is most unseemly for a widow to be alone so much in the exclusive company of a *gentleman*."

"I didn't say—"

"Perhaps you *should* think of marrying!"

Cassandra reached out for her tea and took a large swallow. She set the delicate cup back in its saucer with a rattle.

"Again," she said calmly, "it really is not my intention."

"Then let me recommend that you desist in your entertaining of Mr. Johnston. It could easily be misconstrued."

"Thank you, Lady Charles," Cassandra said, looking down while heat rose in her chest. "I will certainly heed your valuable advice."

"Very well then." The lady paused. "After all, you know, people will talk."

Cassandra's pressed her fingertips to her temples for a split second.

"And as Christian people, we must ever be mindful of being examples to the lower classes. If we behave with impunity, then they will follow. This is how society disintegrates, you know."

Cassandra wondered if Lady Charles' moral scruples were adopted from her husband. "Yes, you are right; I must not let my love of music make me careless."

"Do tell us what news you hear from your son, Mrs. Franklin," Eunice broke in.

Cassandra was relieved to have the topic changed. She regained her composure and spent the rest of the visit making up inanities about James and his life at Harvard until she could escape.

On her way home in the open carriage, Cassandra breathed in the gentle, warm air and tried to clear her head.

What nerve that woman has, she thought, speaking to me as if I were a child! As if she has any right to tell me what to do!

Once she arrived at Sorrel Hall, all she wanted to do was to send Benedict a note and ask him to come to her so that she could forget the unpleasantness of her visit. Then she remembered he'd be engaged all day with Jeffrey Holcomb and felt a stab of jealousy, remembering that Jane was sure to be there. She reminded herself that she had no exclusive rights to the man; besides, he had sworn he had no interest in the younger woman. I'm being ridiculous, she thought. It shouldn't matter to me anyway. She shrugged the feelings away and called for a bath to soothe her nerves, then threw herself into her music for the rest of the afternoon.

The following day Cassandra had an appointment to visit with the Clarkes at their home, for she had not seen them for a month. There, all was ease, though not exactly relaxation, for Mrs. Clarke's several young children raced about the house continuously. The woman had neither time for, nor the interest in gossip, so Cassandra was safe from talk of Mr. Johnston. When the nanny finally herded the little ones off to the nursery for their lessons, the two ladies had the chance to chat about gardens, weather, child rearing, husbands, and America. Mrs. Clarke was always interested in hearing about Cassandra's life in the states, so Cassandra made things up just to entertain her. She learned from her friend that what she herself thought of as a simple, rural existence meant much more than lounging about the house with servants at her beck and call. Though the Clarkes were landed gentry, the large number of children reduced their ability to enjoy the luxuries that other wealthy families in the neighborhood took for granted. Mrs. Clarke mended her own children's clothing, supervised the house cleaning, laundry, and cooking, and the running of the dairy barn, for they kept cows. She also helped churned the butter and make the cheese. She tended the chickens and the vegetable garden because they only employed one gardener who could not handle all the work on the grounds himself. She also led the older children in their lessons, educating her girls and preparing the boys for the day when they would go off to boarding school. Cassandra ended her visit feeling tired at the mere thought of all Mrs. Clarke accomplished each and every day of her life, and also humbled. She realized, in comparison, how very spoiled and pampered she had become.

She arrived home that afternoon to find that Benedict had sent a note asking if he could see her. Lady Charles' words faded into the background of her mind. She decided resolutely that they would be discreet, but that she was not going to be denied the joy of being with him.

She decided to decline Benedict the invitation to come visit, however, enjoying the opportunity to tease him. She wrote a note that said she required him to practice his violin by himself for now, and that he would have to perfect the piece before he could see her. He replied by messenger about an hour later that he would be ready by Friday (she assumed he meant the cottage was ready) and would she be so kind as to meet him on the road at the entrance to Gatewick House at three o'clock?

By the time she was having her bath on Friday, the day was still lovely and bright. That morning she had spoken to William, graciously but firmly. She explained that she needn't have an escort any longer, that she was now an able horse-woman, and she thanked him for all his good care of her. His disapproval was evident in his silence.

At two-thirty, Cassandra joyfully set off on Daisy, a small satchel of dried meats, cheeses, and bread tied to the saddle, her bonnet firmly in place, her implanted lenses properly adjusted to the bright summer day. She was clean, lotioned, sunscreened, and in a light, rust-colored gown, as pretty as she'd ever felt.

When she arrived at the appointed meeting place, Benedict was there, waiting on his horse. They greeted each other cordially, and with minimum conversation rode across his grounds into the forest. Soon they were at the rustic cottage hidden in the trees. Benedict helped her down and secured the animals where they could eat and drink.

When he turned his attention to her, he untied her bonnet, removed it, and gazed at her in the dappled light of the forest.

"Take down your hair," he said. She did. Her dark red curls fell about her shoulders, shown off by the neckline of the dress. He put his hand under her hair, pulled her to him, and kissed her. Before she could respond with words, he took her by the hand and led her inside. The one-room cottage was spotlessly clean, with a heavy wooden table and two chairs in the center, a fireplace, small wood stove, a pump, basin, and sideboard. There was a dresser, a narrow armoire, a small desk and chair, and a large high bed against the far wall with a fluffy white, down coverlet.

"It is beautiful," she said.

"You are beautiful," he replied, never taking his eyes off of her. He took her bag from her and set it on the table. Then slowly, he began to undress her like a man who understood the complications of a woman's clothing. She reached out and took off his jacket and began to unbutton his shirt, admiring his slender body. He gently stopped her with one hand and continued to undress her until she stood before him in only her chemise and thin, knee-length bloomers. She felt vulnerable and delicious. He led her to the bed, and after she climbed on, quickly removed his own clothes and climbed on beside her. She was thrilled with his subtly sculpted muscles.

He removed her undergarments, gazed adoringly at her beautiful form, and ran his hands over her skin as if she were a marble statue. She responded instantly to his touch, and they became locked in an embrace, arms and legs entwined, touching, grasping, exploring each other.

Finally he entered her, and she cried out in relief and joy. He moved rhythmically until they could no longer contain themselves and finally reached a perfect, exquisite release.

They lay together, talking and touching, and then made love again.

Two hours had passed; the day had become overcast, and a gentle rain began to fall. The temptation to stay and light a fire, have supper, and sleep together all night was powerful, but she told him that she had to go. They dressed, shared a long kiss, then set off on their horses to the road where they parted.

CHAPTER EIGHT

The following morning, Cassandra sent a note asking Benedict to come for a music session that afternoon. They tried not to touch too much or kiss, unless they were sure they wouldn't be seen. Instead, they lost themselves in their music and, in a sense, felt satisfied. Before parting, he asked her when they could meet in the cottage again.

"I fear that more than once a week would raise suspicions," she reasoned.

"It is too little!" he cried. "I will never live another week if I cannot be with you."

"Well," she said, "perhaps Tuesday."

"Tuesdays and Fridays, then. Let those be our days together."

"And other days, when we are free, *you* come *here* to play because it would not look right for me to take the horse so often by myself."

"Agreed," he said, "and so I suppose we must be chaste and supplicant tomorrow, since it is Sunday. Shall we meet here again on Monday?"

"Yes. I will not make any engagements for the afternoon."

"Neither shall I," he said. He kissed her goodbye quickly, just before Mary walked into the room.

******

In church the next day, Cassandra tried to focus on the monotonous Mr. Collins, but it was warm inside the small stone building, and she was distracted by the smell of roses coming through the open door. Summer sounds outside, the buzzing of bees and hum of dragonflies, mixed with the droning of the sermon. She closed her eyes and imagined Benedict's lips on hers. She caught herself just before she dozed off, and gave her head a little shake. Mrs. MacIntosh, sitting across the aisle from Cassandra's pew near the front doors, gave her a sympathetic smirk and a wink.

Cassandra spent the rest of the service observing Lady Charles and her entourage seated in their box in the front, and noting with amusement the mother's efforts to keep her two young charges awake with jabs of her elbow, surreptitious coughs, and swats with her fan. When the service was over, Cassandra slipped out quickly so as to not have to make conversation with them.

Mrs. MacIntosh caught up with her at the churchyard gate, and the two ladies walked together across a flower-strewn meadow into Selborne, while Mrs. MacIntosh's children ran home, elated to be freed from their mother. The general store was the women's destination, for the farmer's wife to order five pounds of tea, and Cassandra to see if squash seeds were in.

Just as they were about to enter the shop, Cassandra heard her name called, and turned around to see Lady Charles, her daughter, and niece in tow, trundling up the street. The woman was sweating and looked annoyed. Her parasol bobbed over her head like the sail of a small ship as she hurried to overtake Cassandra.

"Run along girls," she said, waving the two away. "I will meet you at the milliners." The two young ladies happily ran off.

"Oh goodness, this infernal heat!" Lady Charles declared, dabbing at herself with a hankie. "How are you, my dear Mrs. Franklin?" she managed, out of breath. "I glimpsed you in church, but you hurried off afterward. Did you walk all the way here?"

"Yes, it was nothing."

"Oh, dear me, the walk is way beyond my capacity. The girls insisted on taking the barouche today, so I was exposed to the elements all the way. It is waiting for us by the teahouse, where we shall meet presently for refreshment. Will you not join us?"

"Thank you, I must return home directly after my errand." She waited for the lady to acknowledge her friend.

"And you do not mind walking so very far to Sorrel Hall?"

"Oh, no, I am enjoying the lovely day."

"Lovely? I cannot bear these blazing temperatures. But the girls both need new bonnets, and I could not deny them."

After a pause, Cassandra spoke. "Lady Charles, do you know Mrs. MacIntosh? They have a farm in the parish. Mrs. MacIntosh, Lady Charles."

"Nice to meet you," said the farmer's wife extending her hand.

Lady Charles ignored her. "Well, Mrs. Franklin, I had better go see what my girls are up to." And with a haughty snap of the head, Lady Charles turned away, leaving the two women staring after her.

"My goodness!" whispered Cassandra once the lady was out of earshot. "I am so sorry! I have never seen such rude behavior!"

"I have," replied Mrs. MacIntosh. "The fine ladies hereabouts have no time to hobnob with my class. I am quite used to it."

"It is appalling. She has no right to treat people like that."

"She thinks she does," Mrs. MacIntosh replied. "I would not worry yourself about it. I would, however, think about how your friendship with me reflects on you."

"I am not the least bit concerned about it."

Mrs. MacIntosh gave her a thoughtful look. "Well, I appreciate that, but it is not really how things are done, you know. Maybe it's because you are American."

"Maybe," said Cassandra. She was well aware of class distinctions, but didn't realize how deeply they ran.

"I am just saying, that most of your class are happy to give us their patronage, but only that, and nothing more. Do not worry about it. Your ways are different, that is all. I suppose they will all have to get used to it."

The two ladies went inside to make their purchases.

******

On Tuesday morning, it was pouring rain, and Cassandra had a feeling that her designated meeting with Ben would be foiled since she couldn't ride out on horseback. She felt disappointment wash over her. She couldn't wait to be in his bed again. She went down to breakfast, and was surprised to see that a note from him had already arrived.

Dear Mrs. Franklin,

I request the honor of your presence for dinner this afternoon at Gatewick House at four o'clock. A friend of mine has arrived, rather unexpectedly, from London, and will be staying with me for a few days. He is taking a summer tour of the region, and correctly assumed that I would not mind a visitor. I would like you to meet him, as he is musical. He has even brought his instrument in the hopes of our playing together. If I do not hear back from you, I shall assume you will attend.

Regards,

Mr. Benedict Johnston

******

At the appointed hour, she went in the carriage to Gatewick House as it was still raining heavily. The housekeeper took Cassandra's wrap as she came in the door and then led her into the parlor. Before her stood Mr.

Johnston, and, to her great surprise, Mr. Stockard from the music store in London.

"Mr. Stockard, my goodness!" she exclaimed.

"Hello, Mrs. Franklin," he said. He took her hand and kissed it. "It is an infinite pleasure to see you again."

"Mr. Johnston, you did not tell me you knew Mr. Stockard!"

"You did not tell me *you* knew him," he said coming forward to kiss her other hand.

Cassandra stood between the two men. "But," she said to Benedict, "I did not know you knew him."

"I think I can straighten it out," said Mr. Stockard, "Mr. Johnston and I are acquaintances from London, and he wrote to me a few weeks ago, telling me about his satisfaction with his new home and neighborhood. He said that he had met several delightful new people, among them, an American named Mrs. Cassandra Franklin."

"Yes," replied Benedict turning to Mr. Stockard. "But you did not respond to that letter, and so I did not know that you had met her in London last January. He did not tell me, until he arrived here yesterday, and then did not want me to mention his name in the invitation to you."

"I thought it would be good fun to surprise you, so I asked Mr. Johnston to invite you to dinner. I hoped that you would remember me."

"Do you not remember that you rescued me from the fog?"

"From the fog?" inquired Benedict.

"Yes, Mr. Stockard was my hero after I first arrived in London and got lost looking for my hotel. He was bringing me my delivery of sheet music and found me outside the White Hart Inn, looking for the entrance."

"I was only glad to have been of service," acknowledged Mr. Stockard with a bow.

"Well, the two of you have more of a history than I could have imagined," stated Benedict.

"I would not exactly call it a history," remarked Mr. Stockard.

"And yet, you had quite a distinct recollection of this customer that you only served once, six months ago," Benedict observed.

"Well, who would not remember the lovely Mrs. Franklin?"

"Of course." Benedict turned and walked toward the sofa near the fire. "But will you not come and sit down, Mrs. Franklin? There is no need for us all to remain standing there."

"You mentioned that Mrs. Franklin was a fine pianist, Mr. Johnston," said his visitor. "I do recall that she bought from me many complex pieces. You had said that perhaps we could play together. Are you game, Mrs. Franklin?"

"Let the lady catch her breath, my friend," said Benedict as he indicated a chair for her to sit on. "Tea, my lo....Mrs. Franklin?"

Cassandra started, and Mr. Johnston hurried to ring the bell without waiting for her to respond. Mr. Stockard looked from one to the other.

"What is it you play, Mr. Stockard?" Cassandra asked, trying to deflect Benedict's blunder.

"The cello," he replied, taking a seat across from her.

"Yes," said Benedict, returning to the sofa. "I thought we could make a trio. I have a lovely Haydn piece for cello, violin, and piano that Stockard and I have played before, and you could make the third on piano."

"I would be honored. When have you played together before?"

"In London," said Mr. Stockard. "When Mr. Johnston is free, he fills in for our chamber group. That is how we know each other. I have to say, Johnston has been missed there these past few months. I was a little disappointed that his letter did not say he was coming back to London any time soon."

"I see," replied Cassandra. "I feel you have been too modest about your status as a musician in London, Mr. Johnston."

"It is just a group of friends playing for friends," replied Benedict.

Mr. Stockard started to correct him, but the housekeeper walked into the parlor looking annoyed.

"Dinner is ready, sir. Were you ringing for tea?"

"Oh, no, if dinner is ready, we shall eat. Come," he indicated to the two others.

During the meal, the two men wanted Cassandra each to himself. Cassandra noted that they did not appear to be the closest of friends.

"How long are you staying here in Hampshire, Mr. Stockard?" she inquired.

"Well," he thought for a moment. "My schedule is flexible, but perhaps tomorrow I will move on to Winchester. It is my next stop."

"What areas of the country does your tour include?"

"I am ultimately making my way west to the Cornwall coast. I have never been there."

"Nor have I," said Cassandra with interest. "I have heard it is untamed and exotic."

"Yes," he replied enthusiastically, "the place of Arthurian legend."

"Oh, I would love to see it," she went on. "I wonder if I will have time while I—"

"While you what, Mrs. Franklin?" Benedict broke in.

"While the weather is nice."

"It is quite a long trip," remarked Benedict.

"Yes, you are right, maybe next spring."

Mr. Stockard stared at her strangely. She couldn't read this man. Why was he here? It almost seemed he had come on purpose to see her. At any rate, she could tell his presence was making Benedict uncomfortable.

They retired to the conservatory to play the Haydn. The three musicians fell into sync and were all smiling by the time they'd finished.

"I hope to see you again, someday, Mrs. Franklin," said Mr. Stockard, shaking her hand.

"Yes, that would be lovely," replied Cassandra, hesitantly.

"You will have to stop back by when you come through this part of the country, again, sir," offered Benedict. Cassandra thought he sounded insincere.

"Yes, perhaps I will!"

"Well, goodnight, gentlemen," said Cassandra at the door, a maid helping her with her things. She so wanted to kiss her lover.

He stepped out into the rain to help her into the carriage, holding an umbrella over their heads.

"I am sorry, my love," he murmured to her.

"Do not be silly. I had a lovely time. Mr. Stockard is a very nice fellow."

"He is, he is, no doubt."

"And we could not have met in the cottage today anyway, with the rain."

"That is true. I suppose I am disappointed about that, but it was not Stockard's fault."

"No indeed."

"Tomorrow for practice, then. Three o'clock?"

"I shall see you then."

He took her hand to help her into the carriage. "Have a good night, my love," he said to her, closing the door.

She did not think Mr. Stockard could see her through the carriage window with the rain and so she blew Benedict a kiss. As the carriage pulled away, she looked back to see the other man still standing in the doorway, looking at her as Benedict shook off his umbrella under the portico.

******

By the end of July, Benedict and Cassandra had been meeting for four weeks to make love or music, neglecting more and more the visits that were normally expected to be made to their society friends.

One day, Mrs. Merriweather took Cassandra aside. "Mrs. Franklin, I must have a word with you."

Cassandra's stomach jumped.

"You have told William and me that the two times a week you go out in the afternoons with the horse, you are going to Mr. Johnston's to play music, which I know you enjoy doing. However, the servants there say they have not seen you for ages. I am concerned; soon, more than the servants will be talking."

Cassandra took a deep breath. "The truth is, Mrs. Merriweather, that I have been riding out about the countryside by myself. Sometimes I just need to be alone. I stop and sit under a tree and read a book, or else I just sit by the stream and think. I know my ways seem strange, but in America, we are not so used to being followed about all the time. A lady can just venture out on her own, and I miss that. Sometimes I just need to not be around anybody. I like to go by horseback, so I can carry a little something to eat, a few books, and go wither I choose."

She thought that sounded convincing, but continued, "Frankly, I did think people were beginning to talk about Mr. Johnston and me. You should be relieved to know that though I say I am going to play music with him, I actually am not always doing so." Now, that was a little closer to the truth.

"Yes," said Mrs. Merriweather. "I am somewhat relieved. And you are correct. Though I do not really understand your ways, I am contented to know the truth."

Cassandra felt guilty about the lie. She knew she was playing a more and more dangerous game. All it would take is for the servants from each house to pay closer attention and realize that during the hours that she was going out, Mr. Johnston was also going out. She would have to talk to him about it.

But the next time they were together in the cottage, they were too wrapped up in the happiness of being together to worry about it. Their afternoons of lovemaking had become some of the most blissful moments that Cassandra could remember, and she treasured them as she knew Ben (as she now called him) did too.

She found herself surprised by his breadth of sexual knowledge. She had thought she'd have to teach him about "some of the things they did in America," but it seemed that he had already been well taught. On that particular afternoon, the weather was so hot that they had kicked the covers off the bed and were lolling about, sweaty and naked after a particularly rousing session of lovemaking. They had taken the chance to open the curtains, and what little breeze there was blew over them from the open windows. Cassandra lightly touched the soft hair on his chest and thought maybe he had dozed off. But then he lazily picked up her hand and kissed the tips of her fingers.

"So, Ben," she began, as he dipped her fingers deeper into his mouth, "how does a lifelong bachelor learn to be so proficient in pleasing a woman?"

He smiled without opening his eyes. "I have had many lovers."

"Really!" she said with surprise and reclaimed her hand.

"Yes." Now his eyes were open and he propped himself up on his elbow. "I spent many years studying violin with the masters in Europe, and the women abroad are much freer in the matters of love than the English women are."

"Hmm, this is interesting. Tell me more." She sat up in anticipation, pulled her knees to her chest, and draped the sheet loosely over them.

"Well, you know, I was around artists, mostly, and their world is different than the one we inhabit in this English society of ours. We both being artists understand that most people in this country don't relate to our way of thinking or doing things."

"Yes, I know what you mean."

"And then, once I settled back in London, I associated with musicians there, and through them, knew many actresses and singers. Like in Europe, their sense of propriety and morality is different in their particular class of society. I enjoyed myself with them, and they enjoyed me. I have never lacked for female company."

"My goodness," she managed.

"Does this make you jealous?"

"No, actually," she said, snuggling up to him. "Honestly, I am just surprised, and yet not, because you seemed so experienced."

"Did you think I paid for my experience?"

"Well," she admitted, "the thought did cross my mind."

"I have never paid for favors, I am happy to say."

Cassandra was relieved and intrigued. "Have you ever been engaged?"

"Yes, once, to a Viennese woman. She was a singer from a wealthy family, and very spoiled, but very beautiful, and I was in love with her voice. She had a terrible temper, though. I was lucky that I found out about it before the marriage took place. It was one reason I came back to England."

"What did your parents think of your marrying her?"

"They did not know. I never told them of the engagement. Fortunately, it was never necessary."

"They would not have approved?"

"No, but they do not approve of much that I do."

"I kind of got that impression."

"As a matter of fact, my father has been writing me lately, pushing me to get married."

"Oh."

"And he wants me to become serious, as he puts it, and join him in his business. He wants to pass it on to his son."

"What is his business?"

"He is a merchant, and he wants to expand into trading with the United States."

"Like everyone."

"I suppose. Does it bother you that my father is not of the gentry?"

"No, of course not, why would it?"

"Because my family has not always had money or a name."

"In America, we do not mind that sort of thing. I believe someone once said, 'In England every man you meet is some man's son; in America, he may be some man's father.'"

"I would like to meet the man who said that."

Who did say that? thought Cassandra. Oh, damn, it was Emerson, and I doubt he has said it yet. "I do not remember who said it," she murmured. "But it does not matter. Why will your father not let you live your own life? You have your own money, why does he care?"

"Well, I have my money, but not my inheritance. If I please him, I could have a lot more when he dies."

"And to please him, you would have to go into his business. Does he expect you to give up music?"

"I think he wants it very much. He is ashamed of me."

"Oh, that is horrible. I cannot believe how money drives a person's thinking and actions."

"Well, it is the way life is," he observed pragmatically.

"When I am here with you, I do not care about how life is, or what people think or say."

"I know, my love, but soon we may need to."

"Yes. Mrs. Merriweather told me the servants are talking."

"I know, which is why I want you to consider marrying me."

Cassandra was caught off guard again, and to avoid dealing with the situation further, she simply whispered, "I promise, I will consider it."

Ben looked up at the ceiling thoughtfully for a moment. Cassandra had a feeling something else was coming.

"My love," he ventured, "since we are speaking of that delicate subject of marriage, I have some curiosities of my own."

Cassandra felt a butterfly flit through her stomach. "Such as what?"

"About your husband," he said, looking at her directly. "You have never told me much about him, only that he was a printer and that he died of fever. I get the feeling from the tone of your voice when you speak of him, that you loved him very much, that he was a good man."

Cassandra looked down at the lace eyelet of the sheet. "He was," she said quietly.

"Tell me more."

She took a breath and thought of Franklin. She'd taken his first name as her last for the purposes of her time journey. Her married name, Reilly, was too Irish sounding, and her maiden name, Kephart, too German. Now, as she spoke of him, she'd have to be careful to separate fiction from reality; however, she couldn't help but describe the man she really had been married to and so in love with. She needed no hypnotic suggestion to bring on the deep emotion connected with him.

"He had dark, curly hair," she began with a faint smile, "but it was beginning to thin. He was also somewhat heavy set, but with a pleasing frame, and he was strong." Ben watched the emotions travel across her face. "He was from an Irish family originally, but his parents did not live into old age, and I had not many years with them. He was soft-spoken and patient, but could have a temper when riled. He rarely exhibited it to me, however. He was a good father to our son. He was playful and had a wonderful sense of humor. He made me laugh like no one else." She checked Ben's expression to make sure he wasn't uncomfortable, but he seemed to be listening intently, so she went on.

"He was not a musician, but he loved my music and could sit and listen to me play forever. He was rarely idle, though. He seemed to always have a book in his hand, usually something scientific, because he loved learning, and never stopped. He was compassionate and good to all people." In her description of her real husband, she forgot the callousness of the fictional man who supposedly invested in the slave trade. "I think that is what I loved most about him, his kindness. But he worked hard, too hard. Sometimes I think at the expense of time he could have been spending with his son, and definitely at the expense of his health. He left me too soon; that is all."

She fought back tears. Ben took her hand in his. He kissed her, and she began to give in to him. She would rather her thoughts of Franklin fade. She then noticed that the light coming from the window was dimming, and thought it better not to stir up their fire again. She disentangled herself, ducked under his arm, and hopped off the bed.

"Where are you going?"

"I am getting dressed."

"No, it is not so late." He stretched out enticingly on the bed.

"Yes, it is," she said, throwing a pillow at him that had fallen onto the floor. At that moment she glanced out the window and saw, through the trees, someone riding close by on horseback.

"Oh my goodness!" whispered Cassandra. "Someone is out there!"

"What?" he whispered back, "what do you mean?"

"Someone is out there on a horse. I cannot tell who it is."

"All right, we must be quiet, maybe they will go away."

Cassandra crept to the window and peaked around the curtain. The person had spotted the cottage and was now riding toward it.

"They are coming!"

"Be calm. Grab your clothes and get in the armoire. I will deal with them."

She did as he instructed while he threw his clothes on as fast as he could. There was a knock on the door. Cassandra heard Jeffrey Holcomb's voice outside the cottage.

"Hello? Mr. Johnston? Are you in there?"

There was silence other than Ben scuttling around for his clothes. Had they locked the door, she wondered in panic?

"Mr. Johnston?"

She heard the door slowly creak open, and then Ben's footsteps.

"Jeffrey!" she heard him say with feigned nonchalance. "What are you doing here?"

"Oh, I am sorry," replied Jeffrey, sounding mortified. "I did not know…I mean I was looking…they told me at your house that you had ridden out. As I was looking for you, I spotted this cottage, and the horses, and thought maybe you were here. I came to tell you that there are several brace of pheasant over on my brother's land and to ask if you wanted to come hunting." His voice had trailed off. She thought that he must be noticing the unmade bed. Did she have all her clothes? She couldn't tell in the cramped dark space.

"Yes, I—" replied Ben. "Well, you have discovered me, I see." He forced a laugh.

Cassandra rolled her eyes.

"Excuse me?" asked Jeffrey.

"Well, it is my secret hideaway," he said with another chuckle. "I come here sometimes to um, nap, or play music. Undisturbed, you know. No servants, no interruptions—"

"Oh, I am so sorry!" said Jeffrey with horror reflected in his voice.

"No, no, no! It is perfectly all right. So happy that you are here. I would love to go hunting. You are never a bother, Jeffrey, please do not feel so. Just let me get my boots on, here."

"Shall I wait outside?"

"No, no. Just a moment."

Goddammit, she thought. Why didn't he ask him to wait outside? Is he is just going to leave me here?

"All right, all set." She heard Ben say. "Hmm, let me see, do I have everything?"

"I noticed there were two horses outside," said Jeffrey innocently.

"Yes," replied Ben, fumbling for words. "That other one belongs to…Elliot, you know, my head gardener. He rode out here with me to look at some new seedlings. Decided to leave her here while he looked about so she could rest. He is around here somewhere. No need to wait for him. The mare will be fine. Let us go on."

"What about your violin?"

"I put it in the armoire for safekeeping. Come on, let us go."

"All…all right," said Jeffrey. "Are you not going to lock the door?"

"What? Lock the door? Oh, yes, yes, I had better."

She heard the key click in the lock. She waited until she heard their horses ride away and then pushed her way out of the armoire, fuming. "What is the matter with him?" she said to herself out loud. "He just locked me in here!" She thought, I guess he expects me to climb out the window, which is what I'll have to do! She got dressed hastily, but couldn't find her bonnet. Finally she saw it on one of the chairs and chastised herself for not having grabbed it before. She had no idea if Jeffrey had seen it. She made up the bed, took one more look around, and then clambered out the window ungracefully, landing with a thump on the ground. "Ow!" She brushed herself off and went to get her horse, which was placidly waiting. She asked herself, how could Ben not have thought of me? And I'm sure Jeffrey recognized my horse; he's certainly seen it more than once, and there's a lady's saddle on it! The man really doesn't think fast in a pinch, that's for sure.

As she rode home, she wondered if Ben had tried to explain the situation further. If Jeffrey recognized her horse, he must know that she was there in the cottage somewhere. What would he make of that? Would he tell his mother? She hoped not. He was an outgoing boy, but didn't seem like a gossip. Even if he didn't recognize the horse, he must have seen the lady's saddle, the rumpled bed, and possibly the bonnet. What would he think of Ben? Maybe he would admire his manliness and way with the ladies. Cassandra still didn't know enough about the mores of nineteenth-century men to be sure. She barely comprehended the modern man, much less those of three hundred years ago. She sighed. There was nothing she could do about it, but she was mad at Ben and hurt that he just left her there.

She arrived home looking disheveled, and mumbled something to William about having got caught in some tree branches while riding through the woods. He gave her a worried glance. She stole in through the study door and went quickly up to her room, passing only the cleaning maid. She desperately wanted a hot soak, but had already had a bath that day, and couldn't possibly order another. Oh, for the comforts of home, she thought, flopping onto her bed.

Later that evening, as she sat at the piano, a note arrived from Ben, and Mary brought it into the sitting room. Cassandra thanked her, waited for her to curtsey out of the room, and then sat down in the window seat with a candle to read it.

My love,

Please, please forgive me! I feel horrible for leaving you alone in the cottage. I was so flustered by Jeffrey's arrival that I could not think straight. I am sorry to say that I am not really a very good liar. I locked the door without thinking, and then realized you would have to climb out the window, and I was so worried that you would hurt yourself, or tear your lovely gown. Please assure me you got home all right. I will not sleep until I hear back from you. I did hunt with Jeffrey until sunset, but had no pleasure in it. I felt like such an idiot! He was a little quiet, and I realized, upon thinking about it, that your mare had a lady's saddle on it, and God only knows what he must have thought! I trust that he is an honorable man, and will not speak to anyone about it, but he must have known that I had a lady there. There is a certain unspoken law amongst gentlemen that we do not talk about such matters. I trust he will uphold it. I do not think he knows it was you, but so what if he does? I cannot imagine he would think any less of either of us. Besides, he is going into the navy soon, and will be away from the neighborhood for months, if not years, and during that time he will learn about life in a way he never has before. Once he is a man of the world, he will understand.

At any rate, please send a message back right away with my servant, assuring me you still love me. I told him not to leave without your reply.

Yours forever,
Benedict

******

Mary crept back into the room. "Ma'am?"

"Yes, Mary."

"Miss Anna said to tell you that Mr. Benedict Johnston has sent three nice pheasants, and would you like her to dress them for dinner tomorrow?"

"Yes, Mary. Tell her that would be lovely, and to expect a guest to be joining us." The girl curtseyed and turned to go. "Wait a moment, Mary, would please give a note to Mr. Johnston's man for me?"

"Certainly, ma'am."

Cassandra went to her little writing table, pulled out a delicate piece of note paper and an envelope, and wrote:

I love you, in spite of myself. Come to dinner tomorrow; we shall have pheasant.

She put the note in the envelope, sealed it with wax, and gave it to Mary.

CHAPTER NINE

J uly 31, 1820—Just getting back from being with Ben. I plan to have a quiet night tonight, just enjoy my thoughts about him. I now have a little less than six months here in 1820, less than six months with Ben. How my ideas about what I would be doing during my experiment here have changed! First, such disappointment in finding life so mundane; now, such exhilaration in this unexpected relationship. I no longer feel like a scientist—perhaps that is the most scientific thing about this experiment. I am not observing, as I thought I would be doing—I am living. Yet even this surprises me. I thought I would be able to maintain a certain objectivity, but being here I cannot help but be drawn into the lives of the people around me. And I cannot separate myself from surprisingly intense feelings about Ben..

At any rate, something seems to have gone awry with my intentions to experience a simple country life as it was lived in this century, since I've bent many of the customs and norms of this time to suit myself, but I suppose leeway must be given for the emotional foibles a human being brings to this sort of undertaking. I ultimately wonder what kind of impact I will have on the people of Selborne and its surrounding neighborhood. What impression will I leave? Is my experiment just a selfish one or do I intend to leave something good behind? Mrs. Clarke, Lady Holcomb, Mr. and Mrs. Merriweather, Mary and William, and so many others have been so kind to me. How can I say goodbye to them forever? I must do just that in six months time, and soon I should start preparing them by saying I've heard from James, that he needs me to return: the excuses I've planned to use all along. I don't believe Mary reads very well, so she probably doesn't look at the postmarks and such on my mail. If I say I've got a letter from James, she probably will not have noticed whether that is truly the case or not.

Cassandra wiped the page clean, closed her journal and went to the mirror to fix up her hair in preparation for an evening downstairs. As she finished her primping, she heard a carriage rumbling up the drive. She hastened to the window and peered out. An elegant coach pulled by four horses was approaching Sorrel Hall. It was not Lady Holcomb's, or Ben's, who usually came by horseback, or any other that she recognized. Besides, it was sunset, too late for unannounced visitors. She couldn't see the passenger in the carriage, couldn't imagine who it might be. She checked herself in the mirror one last time, and then hurried downstairs. As she arrived in the entryway, the bell was pulled, and Mrs. Merriweather preceded her to open the heavy doors. There, in front of Cassandra stood her son, grinning from ear to ear.

"James!" She took a step backward, and a wave of dizziness washed over her.

"Hello, Mother," he said in a British accent she'd never heard him use before. He was dressed to perfection in slim tan trousers, high boots, and a brown waistcoat, looking handsome and dapper and positively devilish.

"Oh my God!" said Cassandra, before she could keep the words from coming out of her mouth. She steadied herself, putting her hand against the armoire. "What are you doing here? I mean really, *what* are you doing *here?*"

"Mother," he said calmly, and indicated Mrs. Merriweather. "You haven't introduced me."

"Oh, oh, yes," she said, turning bright red. "Mrs. Merriweather, this is my son, James. He is just now, apparently, come from America with no notice whatsoever.

James, this is most peculiar, I must say, and most, most impetuous."

Mrs. Merriweather glanced at her, brow furrowed, and then at James. She readjusted her face to its usual polite mask and spoke to him. "It is delightful to meet you, sir. Your mother has told me much about you. But it seems that the two of you would probably like to have some privacy. Ma'am, why do you and your son not make yourselves comfortable in the sitting room? I will send your supper in there if you like, and get a fire started. I feel there is a chill. Shall I have your son's things sent up to the master's bedroom, next to yours?"

"Um, oh, certainly," said Cassandra still staring, stunned, at her son. Mrs. Merriweather took her by the arm and led them both into the sitting room; then she went out and closed the door behind them.

"James!" cried Cassandra, "what on earth?"

"Mom, it's okay, everything's okay. I just wanted to check on you. I was worried! We had no idea if you were dead or alive or what was going on. I was going crazy!"

"Dead or alive? I am perfectly fine! I could not be more pampered and coddled. James, I am a grown woman, and the risk of time travel, as you well know, is that you are on your own, whatever may happen. I am sure I would have made it back to the portal exit, even if something had gone really wrong."

"Well, you never know, Mom." He paused, and she knew that they were both thinking about Franklin. "I just couldn't stand it anymore, and I missed you!"

"Oh, sweetheart," she said, her anger dissipating. She went to hug him tightly, kissing his cheek, tears springing to her eyes. "I really am happy to see you."

"Thanks, and by the way, I have to say, wow, you look great!"

"Thank you, James," she replied, drying her eyes with a handkerchief. "But you cannot say 'wow.' From this moment, put that British accent back on, and use only the expressions that are used in this time period. I assume you have been properly trained." Her annoyance returned. "And, by the way, who approved this journey of yours, and how long are you staying?"

"Okay, first of all," he said, assuming his British accent, "of course they trained me, for about a month. It did take some persuading, but I convinced Professor Carver to let me come, because he was anxious about you too. However, I should probably stay quite a few weeks, or even months. After all, I did come all the way from America." He grinned. "I can't just turn around and go back."

"Right," she replied, a million things swimming around in her head, including Ben. "Come, let us sit down." She led him to the sofa. "All right, let us get everything straight. First of all, you are nineteen, not twenty-four, and I am thirty-eight, not—"

"I know, Mom," he interrupted, letting his accent slip.

"Call me mother, not mom!"

"Right, right. Mother."

"Let us see," continued Cassandra, "you are attending Harvard, but why are you here? What shall we tell people is the reason you have come?"

"Wow, you've really got the whole language thing down."

"James, you have to be serious about your speech!"

"So sorry, Mother."

"Right then, what is the story? How about, you broke off with your fiancée and were too heartbroken to stay in America any longer. You have decided to take a break in your studies—no wait—it is summertime. You will return in September to complete your studies, and you have compelled me to return a few months after, as you can no longer live without your mother by your side. That will give me the out I need next January."

"I can't live without my mother by my side? It sounds a little pathetic."

"Oh. Maybe so."

"Anyway, maybe I'll decide to stay longer," he said, breaking her train of thought.

"I do not think so, James."

"But Mother, now that I'm here, I should take advantage and learn from the experience, just like you're doing. I thought maybe I could use it for my PhD dissertation."

"Oh, so it was not just because you were worried about me, or you missed me; you had an ulterior motive! I know you, James. You were itching to do some time traveling yourself."

At that moment, a servant knocked, and they let him in to light the fire. Cassandra and her son spent the interim making small talk, James remarking on the fine furniture, the delightful view, the beautiful piano.

When they were alone again, Cassandra began, "I have been working thirty years to earn this privilege, James. Thirty years of research and hard work, and it would not take much for it to all blow up if one of us slips. This is a delicate situation. What did Professor Carver say about the length of your stay?"

"He said it was up to you."

"I see." She pondered the situation for a few moments. "By the way, how did you get yourself here from London? I assume you have money?"

"Yes, the team replicated some silver pounds for me. I have about two hundred."

"Oh, well that is more than most young English gentlemen have to spend in an entire year."

"I think it will last me."

"And the clothes?"

"Shannon made them, of course, but I'll probably have to buy more. I didn't bring very much."

"I should look over what you brought."

"Mother, the same experts who assembled your personal items did the same for me. Everything's authentic!"

Mary then rapped on the door bringing supper. She placed it on a low table in front of the sofa, staring so openly at James that she almost missed the table entirely.

"Mary," said Cassandra, "this is my son James, from America. James, this is Mary, my right arm. I would be lost without her."

"Oh, ma'am," said Mary, smiling and blushing simultaneously. "It is not true."

"Of course it is. Mary does everything for me."

"I only hope to be of service, ma'am," she murmured, staring down at her apron.

"Well, thank you for the dinner, Mary, it looks wonderful," said James.

"My pleasure, sir," she replied, stealing another glance at him before ducking out of the room.

Cassandra chuckled. "She only recently has got used to me and my odd ways. I do not know what she is going to think of you."

"She'll love me, because I'll be the perfect house guest. Now, what have we here?" He perused the tray of food.

Their supper consisted of roast chicken, sliced roast beef, ham, various cheeses, breads, local fruits, an assortment of pickled vegetables, sliced fresh tomatoes from the garden, wine, ale, and tea.

"Do you eat like this all the time?"

"This is nothing. It is a light supper. They have learned that when I am eating alone, to really tone it down, but when I have guests, it is five courses, more than you have ever seen in one place at a time."

"Wow—I mean, my goodness. How does one get enough exercise to burn all this off?" He piled food on his plate.

"Walk, ride…you had better get used to hunting, incidentally. I suppose you could go out rowing on the lake. I have not yet been. But there is no jogging, or weight lifting, that is for sure."

"I realize that."

"Let us get back to your story," Cassandra said as James dove into the food. "What was your fiancée's name? The young ladies around here will want to know."

"Young ladies?"

"Oh, yes. Anyway, what is her name?"

"Rebecca? That's a good American name."

"All right, Rebecca. What is her last name?"

"Um. Van, Van…derbilt?" He bit into a chicken leg.

"No."

"How about Van Riper? She's from an old Dutch family."

"Rebecca van Riper?"

"Why not?"

"Very well. How old is she?"

"Twenty-one."

"James, you are only nineteen, remember?"

"Oh yeah."

"James!"

"Mom, Mother, I promise I'll be fine. I reviewed your whole story; I know the background."

"But you just forgot how old you are supposed to be!"

"Just for a second. Okay, she's eighteen. And she's beautiful."

Cassandra chuckled.

"But she broke off with me because I'm not rich enough. That's simple." He sampled a hunk of cheese, then smeared butter onto a piece of bread.

"James, look around you, you are rich."

"But not rich enough for the Van Ripers, one of the wealthiest families in New York."

"In New England."

"In New England," he repeated.

"Well, all right, I guess that works. It is simple. And you are heartbroken. " Cassandra delicately placed some slices of meat and tomato on her plate.

"Yes, I'm heartbroken. So heartbroken that I'll need a lot of attention from the ladies to cheer me up."

"James, let us get something straight—"

"I'm kidding! I know, I really do! I cannot toy with affections or become involved in serious relationships. It's one of the primary rules of time travel, though I suspect that Jake may have broken it when he went to Renaissance Florence. I remember hearing a lot about a certain young Italian named Giuseppina."

"Really?" said Cassandra, blushing. She cut into a piece of meat and put it in her mouth, chewing it thoroughly as she stared at the fire.

"Mother, what?"

"Nothing."

"Mother, is there something you're not telling me?"

"No, no. It is just that…" She could never hide anything from her son; he could read her too well.

"Mother?"

"Oh dear, I do not know how to say this. I sort of have a boyfriend."

"You mean a boyfriend in 2120?"

"No."

"You have a boyfriend here?"

"Quiet!" hissed Cassandra.

"Mom, Mother! What were you thinking?"

"I could not help it! It is like he just fell out of the sky and into my quiet little life here. He moved into a manor house a couple of miles from here in April. He is a musician, James, a violinist, and he is so talented and worldly, and so different from other people of this time. He is open-minded and interesting and…really sexy."

"Oh, dear God, I really do not need to hear this."

"I am sorry, but I have not been able to tell anyone! I have been keeping it a secret, but it has not been easy. Everyone knows we are friends, but I think they may suspect more. We try to be very careful."

"Careful about what? No, I don't want to know. How old is he?"

"He is my age. I mean, he is the age I claim to be."

"You mean he's several years younger than you."

"Well, yes, but James, that age difference does not exist in the here and now. Everyone thought I was thirty, until I assured them I was thirty-eight."

"Yeah, thirty-eight."

"*That* is enough out of you." She picked up a piece of bread and nibbled it.

"Well, I see it's a good thing I came after all," remarked James. "Things are getting a little out of control." He wolfed his own bread in a few bites.

"Oh, really?" replied Cassandra. "And what do you intend to do about it?"

"Keep an eye on you, that's what," he said, chewing.

"I can handle myself, I assure you. I think I have managed to fit in quite well, in spite of the many challenges. You will see. Anyway, now that you are here, I really am so glad to see you, and I think it will be fun to have you around, as long as you behave yourself—"

James laughed. "I think you're the one who needs to behave herself."

More than he knows, she thought, and wondered if she would be able to keep up her rendezvous with Ben. She would have to send him a note in the morning, informing him of James' surprising arrival. She hoped they would get along, and had a sense they would.

Once mother and son had finished eating, she showed him around the house, which Mrs. Merriweather had lit up for them, and took him upstairs to his room. He was delighted with everything, and finally, before going to bed, asked if it were possible to have a bath.

"Oh, the servants will be thrilled," Cassandra said, "I just had one this afternoon. It is quite a lot of work."

"I know, I had one yesterday at the White Hart."

"Oh my goodness, the White Hart! How did you like it?"

"I loved it. The food was great."

"Isn't it? The food is one of the best things about being here; it is so fresh! Well, except when the meat goes bad."

"Ugh," James grunted.

"Did you remember to use the bug powder at the White Hart?"

"Absolutely, are you kidding me?"

"Good, but you will not need it here. How long were you in London?" she asked.

"Just the one night; I was anxious to get to you."

"You must be exhausted. I will order your bath, but you know, you cannot plan to bathe every day. Between me and you, we shall wear the servants out."

"It's weird to have servants."

"I know, but you will get used to them."

"Maybe I'll save them the effort of the bath and take to washing in the stream," he joked.

"That will be interesting. Well, my love, I will leave you to unpack, and I shall send up your bath. Mrs. Merriweather will bring you whatever else you might need. She thinks of everything."

James gave his mother an affectionate hug. "I'm so glad that you're okay. This is going to be fun."

"We shall see," she teased. She kissed him on his forehead.

******

In the morning, he came down to breakfast to join Cassandra, and once again he marveled at the array of foods. Anna was thrilled to have someone in the house with a large appetite, and she provided bacon, ham, poached eggs, fried potatoes, stewed tomatoes, smoked fish, hard and cream cheeses, sweet rolls, toast, porridge, jam, fresh butter and cream, milk, coffee, and tea, everything fresh from the nearby farms, and prepared moments before by her expert hands. On a plate in front of Cassandra were two slices of dark grain toast with butter, and one scrambled egg with wild mushrooms, gathered by Mr. Merriweather.

James piled up his plate. "This is incredible!" he uttered between bites. "I've never tasted anything like this. The flavors are absolutely vivid!"

"I know," Cassandra replied, "which is why I try not to eat too much of it; it is irresistible. Anna is a wonderful cook, and everything is fresher here than you and I have ever known." She tried to keep her voice down.

"And this house, Mother, I was exploring around upstairs. Eight bedrooms! And they're all beautiful. Then I noticed there's a garret above my room with a little stairway leading up to it. It seems like a great space for reading and stuff."

"You would think," observed Cassandra, "But it is bit hot now in the summer, and a bit cold in the winter. There is one above my room too. Did you go up to the nursery as well? It is quite comfortable because you can get a breeze through, or light a fire in the winter. It is so spacious and bright. The Collins children must have loved it."

"That's the family that owns this place, right?"

"Yes. Apparently they lived beyond their means. They are in Bath now."

"Oh, I want to go to Bath!" cried James, "It would be great to see it three hundred years—"

"James, shh!"

"I mean… I've never seen Bath."

"Right. I have been planning to go when the weather cools off a little. For now, though, you must prepare yourself to make the rounds of introductions. You will have to get to know all of the principle families in the neighborhood. They will be out of their minds to meet you."

"Are they going to be any fun, or will they be boring?"

"Some you will enjoy, and some will be boring. But you must endure them all at least once, just like I did. I have become quite good friends with many of them, and there are several young people closer to your age."

"Okay, I'll deal with it."

"Do not say okay," she reminded him. "After breakfast, I shall send off notes announcing your arrival and requesting visits. Then, how about you and I take a walk around the grounds so you can take it all in? It is so spectacular. Then we can talk more freely."

"Sounds good," he agreed, and applied himself to his breakfast, while Cassandra mused over how truly nice it was to be with her son.

An hour later, they met at the kitchen entrance so she could first show him the vegetable garden. They then wandered around behind the house to the great lawn and down to the lake. James noted with interest that the boathouse perched on the bank contained several rowboats with oars. After examining them, they headed west toward the woods and stream. It was a warm day, with an overcast sky. James expressed his appreciation of the peace and quiet, the lack of any sign of modern civilization, and the simple, soft, beauty of the English countryside. They continued walking.

"So, when am I going to meet this boyfriend?" he asked her.

"His name is Ben, Benedict Johnston. I sent a note off to him this morning. I am sure I shall hear from him soon. And what about your love life? Are you dating anyone?"

"Yeah, I met this girl in London, I mean, in 2120, of course."

"I figured."

"She's nice, but it's nothing serious."

"Hmm. And how is your music going? I imagine your band in Boston misses their lead aether-guitarist."

"Yeah, they do. I've been sitting in with these other guys sometimes on Saturday nights in Chelsea. They're pretty good. It's going to be hard to be here without my aether."

"That is why I am so glad to have a wonderful piano. And can you blame me for being drawn to someone that I can play music with? It is a dream come true! But besides that, he is kind and funny and sweet. You shall see."

They walked for more than an hour taking in the pleasure gardens on the west side of the house, including Cassandra's flower garden, and then meandered through the low hills off to the east, on down to the Merriweather's cottage. Coming back up to the house, they passed the stables, and Cassandra introduced James to William. The stablemaster complimented Cassandra's newly acquired horsemanship, and asked if James rode. He replied that he did, and Cassandra was suddenly grateful for the years of horseback riding lessons he'd taken near her parents' summer home.

As they were heading back in at the front of the house, they noticed a gentleman approaching by horse, and Cassandra recognized at once that it was Ben.

"Oh my goodness," said Cassandra, feeling flustered, "well, I guess the time has come for you to meet Ben."

"This is going to be interesting," said James.

"All right now, careful of your speech."

"Yes, Mother."

"Especially the contractions. I slip sometimes, which is easy to do."

"I shall be careful.

"Good."

"Good morning!" cried Ben from his horse, though it was now just noon.

"Good morning," replied Cassandra, "I see you got my note."

"Yes, I could not wait for permission. I had to come straightaway to see the apple of your eye."

"Well, here he is." She squeezed James' arm affectionately.

"Hello there!" said Ben. A stable boy came running to take the horse as Ben dismounted, and the two men shook hands.

"Ben, this is my son James Franklin; James, this is Mr. Benedict Johnston."

"I cannot tell you how pleased I am to meet you," said Ben.

"The pleasure is mine," replied James, smiling broadly.

Cassandra stood by nervously as Ben and James exchanged small talk about the house, the grounds, James' journey, and other generalities. Cassandra then motioned them into the house, and they entered the sitting room while Cassandra ordered some refreshment.

The two men seated themselves on the sofa and Cassandra went to sit across from them in a chair. Once the tea things were brought, she proceeded to serve them. Ben went on to inquire about the reason for James' sudden departure from America, and James related his story about the woman that jilted him with well-acted resentfulness. Ben was sympathetic, but they soon moved on to other topics. Ben wanted to know about Harvard, and since James' attending the school was an actual fact, rather than a just a part of his fictional history, he could describe it with vivid detail. He had to alter his personal time line, however, because in reality, he had just completed his masters' degree and was about to begin his doctoral studies. In non-reality, he was still, at the age of nineteen, working on his bachelor's degree in World History. He said he hoped to be a professor— it was one reason Rebecca van Riper had thrown him over—it was too lowly a profession. Cassandra thought that was a nice touch.

"Do you play an instrument, James?" Ben asked, glancing at the piano.

"Uh, well, I did study the piano, but I am afraid I no longer apply myself. That great talent belongs to my mother, of course."

"Yes," Ben replied. "She is exceptional." He nodded to Cassandra with a smile. She poured him another cup of tea, eyes downcast.

"I hear you play the violin, sir," said James. "I am looking forward to hearing you."

"Yes, it is one of my passions."

James urged him on. "You have been playing a long time?"

"Since I was a child."

"Which composers do you enjoy most?"

Cassandra watched her son carefully.

"Oh, I am a great fan of Bach. Your mother has also led me to be more of a follower of Beethoven's—and of course Mozart, Vivaldi—"

"I know mother loves Chopin—"

Cassandra let a teaspoon clatter onto the table. James looked at her.

"I am sorry, is that a composer?" Ben asked.

Cassandra raised an eyebrow to her son.

"An American one," answered James quickly. "I forgot that you would not know him."

"Ah, I did not know there were many renowned American composers. Mrs. Franklin, you have been hiding something from me." Ben had a twinkle in his eye.

"I did not bring any music with me from America," Cassandra demurred. "And I do not have anything by the Americans memorized. There are not many to speak of."

"Pity. Will you play something for us now? Anything you choose."

"I do not know if James is in the mood—"

"Of course, Mother! I have not heard you play for such a long time. I was raised on music, you know," he said to Ben. "It is, in a sense, a passion of mine as well."

"I am very gratified to hear that," Ben replied, patting him on the shoulder.

After she played, Cassandra invited Ben to stay to dinner. It was satisfying, she realized, to have the two men sit with her at the table and enjoy such easy conversation. Ben departed shortly after the meal. James went to nap in the window seat, and Cassandra curled up on the sofa with a book. She had begun to nod off when she heard the clatter of wheels on the drive.

Who on earth?—Cassandra could not complete her thought before Lady Holcomb and Jane were being ushered in by Mary. Cassandra received them graciously, but could not hide her surprise. Lady Holcomb offered her apologies, but stated that she could not stand on ceremony when something as momentous as the arrival of her dear friend's precious son had occurred. Cassandra knew that her curiosity had simply overcome her, and she made allowances for her good friend's impetuousness. She and James entertained the two women until late, and she could see that James was becoming weary. Still, he held up admirably, she thought, and for Jane's sake, added extra tragedy to the story of his split with the beautiful Rebecca van Riper. When they finally left, he kicked off his boots, slouched down on the sofa, and threw his legs onto the low table before it.

"This is exhausting! How do you do it?"

"I try to keep these kinds of visits to a minimum, even with the families I genuinely like. I usually pay or receive two or three visits a week, but when I first arrived it was every day for at least a month. It's wearing."

"I'm going to have to do this every day for a month?"

"Well, not all day, like today, but probably either morning or afternoon. I like to visit in the morning to get it over with, and from now on, I shall make sure every visit is scheduled, so we are not surprised. Today was an exception. But I am sorry to say, it goes with the territory, and you chose it. Having second thoughts about your stay?"

"No, no," he replied, "I'll put up with it. It's worth it to me to have this experience. By the way, that Jane wasn't too bad."

"Forget it, she just turned seventeen."

"She was looking me over pretty good."

"Oh, you would be a great match for her, but obviously that is not going to happen."

"No, she was a little insipid anyway. And what's with this "lady" thing? Why is your friend Lady Holcomb, but you're Mrs. Franklin. Why can't you be Lady Franklin?"

"Because I did not marry a baronet."

"What's a baronet?"

"You did not study this?"

"I was in a hurry."

"Well, a baronet is an inherited rank among commoners. In other words, if you are a baronet, you are called sir, but you are not nobility, and your wife is referred to as a lady."

"Is it like a baron?"

"Actually, it is a rank just below baron, but a baron is nobility."

"Can a woman be a baronet?"

"Usually a baronetcy can only be inherited by a man. A woman rarely inherits it. If she does, then she is called a baronetess, but they would refer to her as dame so-and-so."

"So, why didn't you choose to make yourself Lady Franklin or Dame Franklin?"

"Because the system was not used in America."

"And Ben isn't a baronet?"

"No, because his family is not old money. They are merchants, kind of nouveau-riche, which is somewhat frowned upon. He is not terribly proud of it."

"There's no way he can become a baronet?"

"Well, originally, the baronetcy was created by King James to raise money for the realm, and rich commoners could buy the rank. It is like being a knight, but not a knight of the garter, which is a special honor. However, I do not think you can buy a baronetcy any more; you would have to inherit it."

"If you married a baronet, would you be a baronetess?"

"No, I would only be a lady."

"Well, I think you look like a baroness or baronetess or lady or dame or whatever you want to call it, living in this unbelievable mansion with all these servants and stables and stable masters and head gardeners....I've never seen anything like it. So I'm going to start calling you Baroness Franklin, or maybe Baroness Cassandra. It sounds better than baronetess, and is more impressive than lady."

"You had better not," she said in a mock threat. "Now let me get back to my book."

"Fine. I'm going upstairs."

"Go on then, I'll see you in the morning."

The next day they received an invitation to call at Darrington, the mansion of Sir and Lady Charles, at the hour of two o'clock.

"Now James," Cassandra admonished as they rode along in the carriage under the overcast sky, "This visit is an important one. Not that making a good impression isn't always going to be vital in maintaining our illusion of normalcy, but Lady Charles has a sharper eye than most. I feel like she senses in me something inherently different and mistrusts me as a result."

"Maybe you're just being paranoid."

"I do not think so. You can judge for yourself."

"What's her daughter like?"

"Oh, she is nice enough, and her niece, Miss Fairchild, is a little goofy, but sweet. Oh, and remember, even if they use first names with each other, you have to refer to them as Miss Charles and Miss Fairchild, and they will call you Mr. Franklin."

"Really?"

"Yes."

"What if I forget?"

"You cannot forget. It will seem inappropriately intimate if you start referring to them by their first names so soon after meeting. As a matter of fact, you have to be very good friends or openly involved in a romantic relationship before you start using first names, and even then, it is not always done."

"It seems excessively formal."

"Well, maybe so, but I did not make the rules."

"What do I call the husband, is he Sir Charles?"

"No. He is Sir Robert Charles, or just Sir Robert. However, I do not think we will run into him today. I believe he is in London."

Cassandra had only met Sir Robert once, at a formal dinner party given in her honor back in March, and he had seemed distant and acted superior. As predicted, he was not around when Cassandra and her son arrived for James' grand introduction, conducted in Lady Charles's dignified parlor. Cassandra was worried that James was intimidated at first, but the giggles and glances from Miss Charles and her cousin soon put him in his element. In no time he was telling his heart-breaking tale, and the young ladies were appropriately outraged at the callousness of the cruel Miss van Riper. Lady Charles was all kind condescension toward her guests, and Cassandra began to feel that perhaps the lady was beginning to accept her after all.

She noticed James' attention drawn to the pretty face of Miss Charles, who at nineteen, considered herself ripe for romance, if not marriage. Cassandra knew that Lady Charles had been scouting for the perfect match for her daughter, and had not yet found anyone satisfactory. Cassandra was certain that the woman would never consider James. After all, he was an American with questionable heritage. And there was all this business of becoming a professor— Cassandra thought her son was safe from any designs the woman might have on him, but was not so sure about those of her daughter.

Before she knew it, Cassandra heard the word dancing mentioned, and the conversation quickly turned to talk of a ball. Beads of sweat sprang up on James' forehead, but the girls were thrilled with the idea and Lady Charles immediately took up the cause.

"Oh, a ball! Yes, how delightful; we must have it here! We have a very elegant ballroom, as you know, Mrs. Franklin, and we hardly ever use it. We shall invite the Clarkes, the Moores, the Holcombs, and that odd Mr. Johnston—" she said with a glance at Cassandra, "poor bachelor that he is. Oh, and the Whites, and—" her list went on and on.

Before the visit wound down, the date for the ball was set for a week from Saturday. The day being Sunday, there remained almost two weeks for Lady Charles to send out invitations and make all the preparations. Cassandra was glad that her house had not been volunteered. She hadn't the slightest idea how to prepare for the event, and she doubted she even had the correct thing to wear.

She did know how to dance, however, having studied period dancing extensively with experts when preparing for her trip, and now, looking over at James sitting somewhat uncomfortably in a stiff brocade chair, she figured that he probably had not. Thank God we have two weeks, she thought. Sure enough, as they returned home, a light rain falling on the carriage roof, James confessed that he had no clue how to dance according to the style of the early nineteenth century.

"Well, it is not easy," said Cassandra, "yet it does not take long to memorize the steps. The hard part is doing it with grace. I will have to teach you, and we had better get started today."

When they arrived home she sent a note off to Ben:

My dear,

I set a challenge before you. A ball has been arranged at Darrington, Saturday after next. My poor son has been devoted to studying, but not dancing and does not know a minuet from a quadrille. When you come on Monday for our practice, can you plan to stay and lend your expertise? I can teach him, but I shall need help!

Yours,

Cassandra

Mother and son spent the evening in the conservatory marching out the steps of the dances that were sure to be performed at the ball while she hummed the appropriate tunes.

Monday morning they visited with the Clarkes, and Monday afternoon Ben joined the Franklins at Sorrel Hall to play for them on the violin as they danced, and also to fill in the man's part of the dance wherever Cassandra's knowledge lacked. James was an able pupil and advanced quickly.

On Tuesday afternoon Cassandra abandoned James for her appointment with Ben at the gamekeeper's cottage, and returned home late in the afternoon. Ben surprised her that evening after supper by making an appearance just before eight o'clock to play the violin while she and James danced for an hour, perfecting the steps. Afterward, Ben and Cassandra played one of the Bach Violin Sonatas they'd been working on.

"The two of you are amazing together," James told her as she walked back into the sitting room after seeing Ben off at the door. He was lounging in a chair with his feet up on a velvet ottoman. "I think he's a great guy, but what will you do about him when you leave?"

She stood rearranging some flowers she'd placed in a vase on the mantel. "I have not exactly figured that out yet."

"I think he's in love with you."

"Yes, so he says."

"Geez, mother, that's a little cold. What, are you just going to leave him in the dust come January?"

"I do not know!" She plucked a wilting rose from the vase and tossed it into the fireplace. "I will just have to figure it all out when the time comes. Besides, anything could happen before I leave."

"What do you mean?"

"Well, relationships end for all kinds of reasons."

"You don't seem like you really care."

"Watch your contractions."

"You do not seem like you really care."

" 'As if' you really care."

"Mother! Stop correcting me!"

She went to the piano and began to straighten up the music books scattered over it. "Look, I like him a lot, but I view him as more of a distraction than anything else. I was dying of boredom before he came along, to be perfectly honest."

"Really? But this experience is what you always wanted."

"Yes, I thought so; I just thought it would be a lot...more...interesting. *Now* it has become interesting, I promise you that."

"So you just plan to break his heart? Isn't that, I mean *is that not* changing history?"

"I do not think so. I am not preventing him from doing anything, or leading him into any major decisions. Besides, time travelers take the chance with every interaction that they could change history. However, I do not think I am doing so."

Cassandra heard the sound of shuffling feet at the door and turned to see Mary standing there with a tray on which sat two glasses of wine. Mother and son exchanged glances.

"Yes, Mary?"

"Master Franklin ordered wine before bed—"

"Oh, of course, I shall take it; you may go." Cassandra took the glasses off the tray and stood holding them until Mary was out of hearing range.

"Do you think she heard what you said?" James asked his mother.

"I do not know. At any rate, she would not understand what I was talking about."

"True."

She went to hand one of the glasses of wine to James. "I am going to bed."

"Did you ever consider the possibility that Ben is supposed to meet and marry someone else?" James said, taking the glass.

"Like who?"

"What do you mean, like who? I do not know."

Cassandra considered Jane Holcomb's pretty face. "Well, if he is meant to do that, he will. I shall be gone in six months."

"Just be careful, mother."

"I will be. Do not worry. Goodnight." She turned to go.

"Goodnight." James replied softly.

CHAPTER TEN

*A*ugust 10, 1820—*It seems everyone in and around
Selborne is in mad preparation for the ball. Ladies are
rushing off to Basingstoke to buy gloves and fans and
slippers, things that are not readily available here. Charlotte even
dispatched a servant to London to find a particular handbag she'd
lusted after the last time she was there.*

*I'm having the wonderful Selborne seamstress, Miss Freeman,
make me a gown, as Mrs. Merriweather helped me determine I have
nothing in my wardrobe fit for a ball. Miss Freeman and I chose a
moss-green silk which she said would set off my hair. It is to be the
high-waisted fashion currently in vogue, the bodice embroidered with a
darker green silk thread of a floral design, sprinkled with tiny, glittering
beads. The short, capped sleeves will be slightly full, while the neckline
will fall just below the tops of my shoulders. The skirt will flow from
under the bust line to the floor, just allowing the shape of my leg to
show. I also plan to wear long, off-white, silk gloves to help cover the
freckles on my arms.*

*James and I decided that he did not have the appropriate formal
wear for a ball either, and anyway needs to augment his wardrobe and
linens if he's going to stay for a while (a point we have not yet settled).
And so we went to Brick and Son, the Selborne tailor, who crafted a
few pairs of slim trousers in black, brown, and grey, a short, black*

frock-coat, several high-collared white shirts, and some undergarments.
He will be the most dapper young gentleman in the neighborhood.

******

The Saturday of the ball arrived, hot and muggy. Cassandra woke late and after a light breakfast, still had not seen James. She wandered out behind the kitchen to gather ripe tomatoes from the garden when the sound of splashing caught her attention. She walked across the lawn toward the lake and glimpsed James' head popping up out of the water. He saw her and waved.

"Come swimming, Mother, the water is perfect!"

Cassandra laughed. "I have no bathing costume," she yelled to him, moving closer. "And what is that you are wearing?"

"My bathing costume! I ordered it from Basingstoke, and one for you too!" They arrived this morning. I left yours in my room since you were not awake. Go put it on! Come on!"

The sun was starting to beat down on her through the haze. "But my hair! And the ball tonight!"

"You have plenty of time to wash and dry it. Trust me, this will refresh you like nothing else."

"Very well!" She ran back to the house, up the rear stairs and found the garment lying on James' bed. She'd had some idea of what to expect, but when she saw it, her enthusiasm waned. It was a dress of grey wool, with long sleeves and a modest neckline. She picked it up. It was heavy. When she examined it, she saw there were weights in the bottom hem to keep the skirt from floating up. Tears stung behind her eyes for a moment. How could she enjoy a swim in a thing that made her feel hot just looking at it?

She threw the suit back on the bed and marched down the stairs and back out to the lake. James was splashing around in a black tank-top style, one-piece suit with legs that went about half-way down his thigh. She felt a pang of indignation that men could swim in practically nothing, while women had to be fully clothed.

Well, my house, my rules, she thought. She went into the boat house and stripped out of her pale yellow muslin gown. What remained was a chemise and bloomers. She walked out onto the short dock of the boathouse, and before anyone could see, jumped in. When her feet touched the bottom, the water was at her chest. The floor of the lake was sandy, and she could feel the reeds brushing against her legs. The water was clear and cool, kept that way by the stream that fed it from the north and that flowed out again to the south. She swam to James, several yards away. "This is wonderful!"

He laughed, bobbing up and down. "What happened to the bathing costume?"

"Are you kidding me? Did you feel how heavy that thing is? And it is wool for goodness sake!"

"Yes, it seemed completely impractical. On the other hand, are you sure you are being decent swimming in your underwear?"

"No, I am not sure, but regardless, I am still quite clothed. It is not easy to swim with all this fabric floating around me."

"I am sorry. I wish women had an easier time of it."

"Well, there is no changing the situation." She swam off, doing a back stroke.

The lake was large, and in her clinging undergarments she did not feel up to swimming the length of it, not knowing how deep it might get. But she and James enjoyed the water for the remainder of the morning. It was Mrs. Merriweather who finally drew them out. She came marching across the lawn with two large drying sheets draped over an arm. She set one on the grass and held the other open wide.

"Mrs. Franklin!" she called. "I think we ought to get you bathed so your hair can dry and you can be readied for this evening."

Cassandra felt chastised. "Yes, of course, I am coming," she called as she pulled herself out of the water, her bloomers and chemise plastered to her body. Mrs.

Merriweather hurried to the edge of the lake and quickly wrapped her mistress up.

"Thank you," said Cassandra.

Mrs. Merriweather said nothing, but pressed her lips tight. Cassandra thought she might be trying to hold back a smile.

"Could you just leave the towel on the lawn for me, Mrs. Merriweather?" James called.

"Yes sir," she replied. "Your bath will be ready in about a half an hour."

"Thank you!" He flipped backward into the water.

The two women hurried into the house and up the backstairs to Cassandra's bedroom, where she found that a bath had been drawn. Mary was waiting to attend to her. Her eyes grew wide as the towel fell off Cassandra, and she saw the wet undergarments sticking to her. The girl helped her peel them off and assisted her mistress into the warm water. She then gathered up the wet clothes and moved toward the door.

"Mary!"

The maid stopped.

"I left my yellow muslin in the boathouse," Cassandra said, "could you have someone fetch it?"

Mary suppressed a giggle. "Yes, ma'am." She hurried out with her bundle.

******

At eight twenty-five, the Franklin's carriage pulled up in front of the home of Sir and Lady Charles. Darrington blazed with light from its myriad windows. Cassandra and James were admitted at the door by a stately butler, and then a maid, ready to take away any wraps, though none had been carried on the warm night. Guests stood about, gawking at the ornate rooms and expensive furniture. Cassandra could hear a buzz of chatter from farther inside. She and James nodded and smiled at acquaintances as they made their way through the house, accompanied by a footman. Lady Charles rustled up to them in the main corridor, seemingly borne aloft by the many folds of her satin skirt. She sparkled with jewels—a large emerald brooch encircled with diamonds, diamond and pearl earrings, a necklace encrusted with sapphires, and even a diamond and emerald tiara to match the brooch.

"Mrs. Franklin, Mr. Franklin, where have you been?" the grand lady exclaimed. "We have been waiting for you!"

"You have?" Cassandra replied with surprise. She'd assumed that being fashionably late was a universal practice.

"Well, yes," Lady Charles said with some annoyance. "The ball could hardly begin without you, could it?"

James and Cassandra looked at each other.

"Never mind," she huffed. "I suppose I cannot expect you to do things the way we do them here. Well, come along, come along."

They allowed themselves to be led, Lady Charles marching in front of them with great purpose, and the footman bringing up the rear.

When they arrived at the entrance to the ballroom, Lady Charles stood to one side of Cassandra, and the footman stood to the side of James. The footman then stepped forward, capturing the attention of the crowd. "Mrs. Cassandra and Master James Franklin," he shouted above the din.

Everyone turned and then applauded resoundingly, startling the two guests. There were at least a hundred people in the high-ceilinged room. Two giant chandeliers hung down, lit with candles and sparkling crystal. The walls of the ballroom were painted with pastel images of ladies and gentlemen bedecked in the clothing of an era past, high white wigs on their heads. Cupids hovered above them while unicorns and satyrs gamboled about.

As the applause died down, the finely dressed people in the room stared at James and Cassandra as if expecting them to do something. Cassandra looked at her son, strikingly handsome with his father's dark features and winning smile, set off by a crisp white shirt with a dark red cravat tied at the throat. His tall, slim body was perfectly suited to the narrow cut of the black trousers and frock coat he sported. She quickly put her hand to her hair to make sure it was in place. Mary had helped her arrange a string of pearls in it, and she wore simple drop-pearl earrings and a long strand about her neck, which fell below the bodice of the gown. She'd thought that the green of the dress complemented her dark red hair, her blue eyes, and her pale skin well, but now that she was on display, she doubted everything about her appearance.

Her eyes quickly sought out Ben. He smiled broadly, and looked her up and down while nodding. She returned a panicked raise of her eyebrows that stirred him to action. He hurried forward to take her arm.

Lady Charles sharply clapped her hands together and called out in a shrill voice, "Let the dancing begin!"

The small orchestra struck up a minuet, while the crowd made way for Cassandra and Ben to lead the dance. They were followed by James with Miss Charles, then Jeffrey Holcomb with Eunice, and Jane with the Clarke's eldest boy, Edward. Cassandra passed Lady Holcomb as she went to take her place. Her friend was not smiling. Her eyebrows were raised quizzically and darted from Cassandra and Ben to Jane and her partner. Cassandra wondered if she'd hoped Ben would choose her daughter for the first dance. However, she knew it was appropriate to be honored in this way, as it was her first ball in the neighborhood. She merely nodded at Lady Holcomb and assumed her place opposite Ben. She was nervous; all eyes were upon her. She feared that she would make a mistake or that gossip would be raised that she was too old to dance, or too recently a widow, or that she was monopolizing a very eligible bachelor. But once the music began, they fell into step, and Ben's eyes made everything else fade away. They bowed and curtseyed and followed the tune, eyes locked, faces flushed.

After the first piece, she relinquished him, and looked on as he danced a set with Jane Holcomb. Cassandra went to stand next to the girl's mother, who greeted her with no smile, only a "Good evening." The woman's face softened, however, as she watched her lovely daughter glide through the dance with Ben. The couple moved gracefully together, speaking at intervals when the dance allowed. Cassandra wondered what they were talking about. When Ben exchanged partners for Eunice Fairchild for the next set, Lady Holcomb's mouth set again into a tight line. Cassandra ventured a sympathetic smile in her direction, relieved that it was not just she but anyone, other than Jane, who danced with Ben that seemed to upset her friend. They watched the two dance, Eunice giggling and missing steps. Finally, Lady Holcomb laced her arm through Cassandra's with an affectionate pat.

Cassandra noted that James and Miss Charles had not yet exchanged partners, and she hoped to be able to speak with her son at the break. They were too newly acquainted for such devotion to one another. The orchestra played on, and she was surprised to see herself approached by Jeffrey Holcomb who requested a dance. She glanced at Lady Holcomb, who nodded her approval. Cassandra stepped out onto the floor with him, feeling like his grandmother. If only anyone could guess my real age, she thought with horror. She caught James' eye, and he flashed her his evil grin. She smirked back and focused on the dance. Jeffrey was a fine dancer and a nice-looking young man, she decided. She tried to look anywhere but directly at him, gazing about the room at the other couples. But whenever she glanced at him, he would be looking at her in a penetrating way. He must know about her and Ben, she thought; in fact, she was sure he knew. She tried not to let herself become flustered, but only smiled benignly and concentrated on her steps.

As she danced, she spied Ben standing along the sidelines, chatting with Lady Holcomb, who seemed gratified to have his attention. Cassandra imagined that she was trying to pry some information out of him about their relationship.

Finally the musicians took a break and Cassandra made her way through the crowd to where James was now talking with Edward Clarke, along the way having to stop time and again to accept a compliment on her looks or those of her son's. She feared he would escape before she got to him.

She grabbed his arm. "James," she whispered as Ben began to lead her away to dance. "Do not only dance with Miss Charles. It is not correct." He responded with a thumbs up, not an appropriate gesture, she noted. But she was happy to see, as she took her place with Ben for a country dance, that James was approaching Jane Holcomb.

The couples took their turns galloping up and down a line, then twirled with their own partners, were claimed by another, twirled again, and skipped forward and back with a clap of the hands. The men performed a jig, and then the ladies did the same, and the whole thing was repeated again. Cassandra thought to sit down when the tune wound to a close, but Ben refused to relinquish her and they danced another reel.

"Enough!" she called to him, laughing, when the song ended. "You must let me catch my breath!"

"I shall," he returned, bowing. "But," he continued, close to her ear, "I will dance with no other lady tonight, but you." He kissed her hand, then wandered off to speak to friends in the crowd. As Cassandra watched him make his way through the throng, she scanned it for Lady Charles, wondering if the hostess approved of how her guests of honor were comporting themselves. All she could make out was the diamond tiara flashing in the candlelight as its owner dashed about.

A chime sounded, alerting the guests to retire to the dining hall for refreshment. As Cassandra made her way out of the ballroom with the rest of the multitude, Ben was suddenly beside her and grabbed her hand. He pulled her against the flow of the crowd out onto the veranda. He quietly closed the glass doors behind them and led her into the shadows.

"I cannot resist you tonight," he whispered, backing her up against the cool stone of the house. "You are dazzling." He kissed her long and sensuously, running his hands over her neck, her shoulders, across her breasts, and down to her slim waist.

She pulled away. "We must go in," she insisted. "We cannot be seen here."

"I know," he admitted, stepping away. "I am sorry. I had to have one kiss, just one. I could stand it no longer."

"Here is one more," she said, pulling him back to her and tenderly kissing him. "And now I am going. You wait a moment. I will say I needed some air."

She slid back in through the doors into the ballroom, empty now, except for the musicians, who sat in their places with food and drink. She wondered if there was a way to enter the dining room inconspicuously—perhaps there was more than one entrance. To her left she saw a paneled door, and decided to try it, thinking that it might lead her, through a circuitous route, into the dining room. Lady Charles had once given her a tour, but the place was so immense, she couldn't remember where the dining room lay in relation to the ballroom. She opened the paneled doors, and was immediately faced with a smoke-filled chamber, crowded with men sitting at tables with their cards, pipes, and drinks. She tried to back out without being seen, but everyone had turned to look at her.

Sir Robert called out to her in a booming voice, "Well, look, it is Mrs. Franklin, the famous American!" He was drunk, and there was something unpleasant about his tone. "Come on in m'lady. Will you not join us?"

"Oh, no, no," she replied, "I was just looking for—"

"Well you will not find the water closet here!" he guffawed.

Cassandra turned bright red. "No, I—"

Sir Robert rose and grabbed her by the arm. He was a big man, balding, with a red face, a turned up nose, and watery blue eyes.

"Come on, now," he slurred, "do not be so shy, say hello to the gentlemen." Some of them, equally drunk, were laughing. Others were looking about uncomfortably, reluctant to displease their host.

"No, thank you!" She twisted her arm to get free, but he held it tight.

"Come 'ere. You c'n have my have my seat," He pulled her to the table. "Or better yet, sit right here on my lap." He plopped in his chair, almost pulling her on top of him.

She wrenched away in time to avoid landing on him. "Sir! I will not be treated in such a manner. If you will now excuse me—" she hastened to the door, but he leapt after her, surprisingly quick for an overweight man in his forties. He grabbed her around the waist.

The self-defense training she'd undergone caused her to instinctively flex her knee, but before it could connect with Sir Robert's groin, Mr. Clarke was up and at her side in a moment. He extracted her from the other man's grip and stood to face him. "Sir, I think you have had too much to drink. Let Mrs. Franklin be on her way, or I am afraid there will be trouble between us."

Sir Robert stumbled backwards and growled. Cassandra ran out into the ballroom, shaking with fury. At that moment, Ben walked in from the veranda.

"Cassandra!" he cried, running to her. "Whatever is the matter? You are pale!"

"That horrible Sir Robert!" she said, struggling to keep her voice down. "He grabbed me! He was completely insolent! Whatever could make him think he could treat me in that way?"

Ben led her to a chair, while Mr. Clarke came bursting out of the card room.

"Mrs. Franklin, are you all right?" He was a tall, slender man, with thinning, wispy gray hair and a pleasant, intelligent face.

"Yes, yes," she said, regaining her calm. "Thank you so much!"

"Whatever happened?" asked Ben. He motioned for her to sit, but she ignored him.

"Sir Robert has had too much to drink," replied Mr. Clarke. "I have seen him get this way before. He loses his sense of propriety with the ladies."

"I suppose he thinks that because I have no husband, he has the liberty to treat me in such a disrespectful way!"

"I do not think so ma'am," said Mr. Clarke. "He has a reputation for acting inappropriately when he is drunk. I once had to rescue my wife from his familiarities while he was dancing with her at a party. His rudeness knows no limits when he is in that state."

"Well, maybe he would like to deal with me, this time," uttered Ben. He was red with anger.

"Mr. Johnston," said Cassandra, turning to him. "It is most kind of you to think of defending me, but it is not necessary. I think we had best leave well enough alone, now, and not ruin the evening for the others."

Ben wiped his face with his handkerchief.

"Mr. Clarke," she continued, "would you be so kind as to lead me to the dining room? I think a glass of wine would do me some good. Thank you again, Mr. Johnston, for your concern." She rose proudly and took Mr. Clarke's arm, yearning to throw herself into Ben's. Mr. Clarke delivered her into the dining room, and a few minutes later, Ben followed, loosening his cravat, his forehead damp with sweat.

She found James seated next to Miss Charles at a long table, saving a seat for her. She almost tipped her chair over as she pulled it out to sit. James leapt to his feet to assist her.

"Mother, is something the matter?"

"No, I am all right," she whispered. She watched Ben sullenly take a seat next to Jane Holcomb a few tables over. "I just need to eat something." A waiter swooped in with a plate for her, and she distracted herself by concentrating on the food. She looked over at the laughing Miss Charles. What an awful man to have for a father! She thought. You never really know what's going on inside someone else's home. There's so much formality and propriety on the outside, but behind closed doors…. She shuddered. She looked around for Lady Charles. The hostess was several tables away, chattering with some of the other ladies. She glanced in Cassandra's direction and gave her a polite nod and a smile.

People began to float toward the ballroom again. Cassandra felt a hand on her shoulder and looked around to find Ben standing next to her.

"Mrs. Franklin," he said, "I beg of you one more dance."

She looked up at him. He was not smiling. Once they took the dance floor, however, his face transformed to a look of pleasant disinterest.

He murmured to her as they took a step towards each other, obeying the dictates of the minuet, "I swear I will kill that bastard."

"No, you will not," she replied, calmly smiling.

"If you and I were engaged, I could challenge him to a duel."

"Then thank goodness we are not."

"But—"

The steps of the dance separated them. When they came together again, hands lightly touching as they turned in unison, she spoke. "I am all right. And now, my sweet, we must let the incident go. There is nothing else we can do."

"I resent a man like that, thinking he has so much power over others."

"It is disgusting, I agree. I will stay far away from him in the future."

"If he ever lays a hand on you again—"

"I know; you will kill him. But you shall have to beat me to it," she said with a charming smile. He laughed, and they didn't speak again until the dance ended. Cassandra then curtsied to her partner, and went to sit with the neighborhood matrons while Ben went in search of the billiard room.

The evening ended well after midnight, although Cassandra had been ready to leave earlier. Still, she was happy to indulge James as he danced. When the carriages were called and began to line up before the door, the Franklins' mysteriously appeared before the rest, and Cassandra suspected, gratefully, that Ben had had a hand in it.

As she and James rode home, she told him about her run in with Sir Robert. He was angry and, like Ben, threatened retaliation, but she was able to talk him out of it. James was, after all, less than keen about the idea of wielding a pistol in a life-and-death duel. In the end, they laughed at the thought and, through the soft August night, talked over the delights of the evening, all the way back to Sorrel Hall.

CHAPTER ELEVEN

Cassandra and James sifted through the invitations that were piled on the silver letter tray. Morning sunlight illuminated the remains of the breakfast that they'd pushed aside on the table to make room for the mail..

"You have got to be kidding me," grouched James as he opened the fifth invitation to dine.

"It has only been three days since the ball!" exclaimed Cassandra. "I guess you made quite a splash. Everyone wants to know you better now."

"Who are these people again?" asked James, holding out a card to his mother.

She took it and read it over. "Oh, this is from the Clarkes." She thought gratefully of the chivalrous man of the family. "They are very nice people. They have a lot of children—you should remember Edward, who was at the ball. I saw you talking to him."

He started at her blankly.

"He's got blond hair, freckles across his nose, a soft-spoken, but friendly young man."

"Ah, yes, Edward, capital fellow!"

Cassandra flashed him a wry grin. "There is also a daughter about sixteen, and lots of little ones."

"All right, give them a yes."

Cassandra took the card and placed it in a pile in front of her. "They are all yes, James. It would be rude to decline."

"Ugh! What about these people?" He held up another, and Cassandra took it from him.

"The Moores. They have two daughters in their early twenties, but they were not at the ball, so you have not met them. I heard they had colds that night. The invitation is for dinner a week Saturday."

"Are they, you know—"

"Attractive? I would not use that word, no. But I love to visit with them because they are the picture of young, silly English women and they amuse me to no end. Oh, what is this?" She picked up a pale pink envelope. "Ah, it is from Charlotte...Lady Holcomb."

"Jeffrey and Jane! I like them both a lot."

"Miss Holcomb, to you. Charlotte is asking us for tomorrow afternoon. I think we can do that after my practice with Ben."

Cassandra and James arrived at Lady Holcomb's cottage at four the next day. Their hostess saw to it that the young people were set up with lemonade and cake, then urged Cassandra outside to peruse her rose bushes.

"My dear Cassandra," she began as soon as they stepped into the garden. "Whatever could you mean dancing four sets with that Mr. Johnston? It was the most shocking display!"

"Was it?" replied Cassandra, examining a dark red rose. "I had no idea."

"But my love, you know how people will talk—everyone thinks you are engaged to him!"

Cassandra stood up straight. "They do?"

"Well, are you?"

"Charlotte, I have told you a hundred times that Mr. Johnston and I are only friends."

Lady Holcomb put a hand on her friend's arm. "Cassandra, you must tell me the truth. I have eyes, and I can see the way that man looks at you and you at him. Everyone could see, my dear. And if you believe that the two of you are just friends, then you are the only ones who believe it. Please, Cassandra, be honest with me. I know I have a reputation as a gossip, but I promise you, it will go no further than this rose garden."

Lady Holcomb led her to a stone bench in the shade. They sat down and Cassandra took a deep breath. "He has asked me to marry him," she said, "and I refused."

"Oh my goodness!" exclaimed Lady Holcomb. "Why will you not marry him?"

"Because I cannot. Not now, maybe someday, I do not know. I am not ready to be married again. Charlotte, you know how wounded I was by the death of my husband and the subsequent painful enlightenment about his business dealings. I am not ready to trust another man. I have not put it to Mr. Johnston in those words, but he understands that I have not yet been a widow two years, and it is too soon for me to think about marriage again, if ever. Also, James' future is uncertain, but I am determined that he will return to Harvard, and frankly, well, he may need me to go with him."

"You are thinking of leaving us?"

"I may have to."

"Oh, this is very distressing. Just when you have become such a necessary part of our little circle here."

"Yes, I know, I would hate to leave, but let us not think about it just yet, and please, please, do not say anything to anyone about it."

"I promise I will not."

Cassandra could imagine that her friend was mentally eliminating James as a prospect for her daughter's marriage. She was not as picky as Lady Charles, but Cassandra was certain that she would want her daughter and son-in-law to remain in England.

"Is your leaving another reason why you are refusing Mr. Johnston?"

"Well, not really, because he has offered to move to America."

"My!"

"But all talk of marriage must cease. I cannot think of it now, I simply cannot."

"Well, then, all the more reason for a possible scandal, Cassandra, if you know what I am saying. You and Mr. Johnston looked as if you could devour each other, to speak crudely, when you were dancing together."

Cassandra blushed. "Is it that obvious?"

"So you admit that you love him, then?"

Cassandra stared at her friend. "It is not accurate to say that I love him, but I do care for him. At any rate, I know how to practice restraint, and so when I say that Mr. Johnston and I are friends, I mean that we enjoy each other's company, we play music together, we laugh, we talk of our lives, and our pasts and our families, but that is all. We are platonic. It may be difficult, but we are."

"Just so you know, that is not how it appears to others. Be careful. Tongues are wagging. And I especially advise you to be wary of letting Lady Charles observe your behavior with the man. You are lucky that she was too distracted at the ball to notice how many times you danced with him and the flush of your cheek when he looked at you. If she thinks that something untoward is going on, she will waste no time in making things very unpleasant for you in this neighborhood."

"Yes, she let me know as much a few weeks ago."

"I would take her seriously if I were you."

"I thank you for your advice, Charlotte, and I will heed it." She thought to herself that she and Ben had been careless at the ball, and they must be more cautious now. She wondered if Jeffrey had said anything to his mother about the incident at the gamekeeper's cottage. If so, she admired Charlotte's tact for not mentioning it.

When she and Lady Holcomb returned to the house, they found Jane diligently pounding away at the piano, and Jeffrey and James loudly discussing hunting. Jeffrey had only one week before embarking upon his sailing career, he expressed to James, and he was anxious to do as much hunting as possible during that time. Cassandra stood in the doorway to listen as Lady Holcomb went to find a vase for the roses she'd picked.

James explained to Jeffrey that gentlemen did not hunt in America, that only wild men, or pioneers hunted, and then strictly for food or pelts, but not for sport. Cassandra knew this was not entirely true, noting that he hadn't done his research well on the subject. But as hunting (or even eating meat that was not humanely raised and killed) was a rarity in their reality of the future, she knew that such a sport would be difficult for her son to stomach.

Jeffrey then suggested that James stay the night and that they ride out together in the morning. James looked at his mother.

"Of course, my dear," she said, "I shall have a servant send over your riding clothes."

"Are you sure you can spare me?" She saw a twinge of panic in his eyes.

"Certainly." It gave her a small amount of satisfaction that he was getting more than he bargained for. "I would not dream of denying you the pleasure of hunting with Jeffrey."

"Thank you," he replied dryly.

Lady Holcomb came in to call them to dine at that moment, and they all followed her out of the room.

******

The following day Cassandra received a note from her son around noon, letting her know that the hunting was fine, though he had not had success with killing anything, and would she mind if he stayed the weekend. She happily replied that it was not a problem, and later that day escaped to the gameskeeper's cottage with Ben.

Monday morning James returned bubbling with talk of his weekend. While Cassandra pulled weeds in the flower garden, he lounged on the bench and regaled her with talk of the get-togethers that had taken place Saturday and Sunday night with Lady Charles' daughter and niece—one evening at the cottage, and the other at Darrington; of card games, impromptu dances, conversation and laughter.

"And by the way," he mentioned, "Bess suggested the idea of us hosting a garden party here soon."

"Who on earth is Bess?" inquired Cassandra throwing a handful of weeds into a pile.

"Lady Charles' daughter, you know, Elizabeth."

"I must say, in all this time, I never knew her first name. And you call her Bess? What did I tell you about that?"

"She insisted on it!"

"Then you must be getting to know her quite well."

"Oh, Mother, it is nothing like that."

Cassandra lifted an eyebrow. "Well, if 'Bess' has requested a garden party, then I suppose it must be. When would you like this event to take place?" She plucked at some errant blades of tall grass.

"How about the weekend after next?"

"That weekend is the Harvest Festival, we cannot do it then."

"Then the weekend after?"

"All right, that gives me time to prepare, and hopefully, the weather will still be warm enough. Saturday or Sunday?"

He took the time to think. "Saturday?"

"I am glad that you, or rather, 'Bess,' thought of this. I have not entertained on a large scale since I came, and I think it is about time I did. I will talk to Mrs. Merriweather and Anna right away, and get started sending invitations. Is it all right if I invite my boyfriend?" She threw the weeds several feet towards the pile. They landed near it.

"Yeah, as long as you tone it down. I thought you were going to start making out at the ball."

"Making out? James, you cannot use that expression."

"Really? I thought it was old-fashioned."

"Not old-fashioned enough. Besides, I do not know why everyone keeps saying that about me and Ben."

"Who else said it, for God's sake?"

"Charlotte. She knows he asked me to marry him, but I told her that I refused and that we are just platonic."

"So you lied."

"Well, I had to. Anyway," she giggled, "we did make out at the ball."

"Oh, Mother, really, I do not want to know that." He stood. "And there will be none of that sort of thing at the party." He walked to the weed pile.

"All right, but that goes for you too."

"I told you, Bess and I are just friends." With his boot, he nudged the stray weeds into place.

"Yes, of course," she said, "tell me about it."

******

The second Saturday of September all of the village and farming families gathered on the lawn of the Selborne parish church for the Harvest Festival. Mr. Collins, the parson, was there, greeting people as they arrived, peeking into picnic baskets and copper pots, exclaiming heartily at the foods that were arriving.

When the Franklin household pulled up in Mr. Merriweather's wagon with their own offerings from the harvest, Cassandra looked around and realized that the only society family in attendance besides her own was the Clarkes. She turned to Mrs. Merriweather as she was being helped from the wagon bench by her husband.

"Mrs. Merriweather," she whispered loudly. "Is it proper for us to be here? You did not say that the gentry did not attend these festivals."

Mrs. Merriweather observed her with the same perplexed furrow of the brow that she often wore when faced with Cassandra's lack of knowledge about suitable behavior.

"It is perfectly proper, Mrs. Franklin, or I should have objected to your desire to come. However, many of the nicer families do not attend for they do not wish to mingle with the farmers. The Collins family always made it a point to attend, though, as the patrons of the parish."

"I see."

James hopped out of the wagon and grabbed two large jugs of cider. He carried them to a table covered with food and began to make conversation with the people who were gathered near. His gregarious attitude gratified Cassandra. She looked about and realized that there was no need to feel out of place. She was friends with many of the farm families, as well as the village shop owners. With a smirk, she imagined the look on Lady Charles' face if she knew that Cassandra and her son were associating with the lower classes. All the more reason, she thought, to have a good time.

She helped unload the food from the wagon, and laid it out with the rest on the wooden tables that had been set up. She helped herself to a cup of cider and looked around for Ben. He'd said he was coming. She guessed that, as he had grown up in London and didn't know any more about country life and its traditions than she did.

She saw James looking about, probably expecting to find Elizabeth Charles, but soon he fell in with Edward Clarke and his many brothers and sisters, all of them vying for a chance to impress the American. Mrs. Clarke, a pudgy lady with dark curls under a white cap and sparkling dark eyes, threw up her hands at her unruly crew and hurried in Cassandra's direction. They sat together at one of the rough-hewn tables and were soon joined by some of the other women. One was Sarah Whitstone, a kind but overworked farmer's wife that Cassandra knew, with a lined face, a few missing teeth, and an abundance of children. There was also Clara MacIntosh, Mary Tottenham, and Marianne Overstreet, all with their myriad offspring in tow. Cassandra could not make out whose children were whose.

She looked upon the farm women with admiration, wondering how it was that they handled the work of the children and the household, the garden, the animals, the cooking, and so much else. She knew that even though they kept some servants, they still worked endless hours keeping up with all their tasks and educating their own children.

The village shopkeepers and their families had it a little easier, this she was sure, though they still worked, long hard hours. But at least their work was confined to the shop that was usually on the first floor of their home, and their income was consistent. The two groups were sitting apart at separate tables. Cassandra didn't know if it was because they considered themselves on a different social echelon or if it was just because they didn't have much in common with the farmers.

Mrs. MacIntosh, a tall, solidly built woman with sharp green eyes and a strong jaw, was asking Mrs. Whitstone about her health, and Cassandra listened eagerly, happy for the opportunity to learn about their lives. Mrs. Whitstone complained of nausea, swollen ankles, and another lost tooth, and Cassandra realized that she must be pregnant again, though it was impossible to tell how many months along she was under the many folds of her dress. That makes eight children, thought Cassandra, at least eight living children. She looked her over thoughtfully, trying to guess her age. Then Mrs. Overstreet, a petite woman with a heart-shaped face and blond, curling hair, commented that she thought Mrs. Whitstone had gone past her childbearing time. Mrs. Whitstone replied that she had thought so too. Although she was only thirty-eight, she had not borne a child for eight years, and she'd assumed she was indeed past her time.

Cassandra did not add much to the conversation. The ladies moved from the subject of childbirth to how best to assure that the chickens kept laying, to the quality of their servants, to the latest caper of one child or another. Cassandra had heard that Mrs. MacIntosh, Mrs. Tottenham, and Mrs. Whitstone had each lost at least one child. Mrs. Overstreet had a son that was considered slow, but no one seemed to think it was much out of the ordinary.

She saw that Ben had arrived, and was making his way around the party, greeting those he knew and chatting amiably. He came by her table to say hello, but then moved on to speak to James and the Merriweathers.

Soon it was time to slice the roast pig. The women helped serve the children and the men, and finally themselves. To Cassandra, the food seemed even more fresh and delicious than ever. She joined her own household to eat, at a table where Ben had also made himself at home.

After everyone ate, Mr. Overstreet tuned up a fiddle, and the dancing began. James did not know the country reels, so he sat on the sidelines, clapping and stomping time. Cassandra thought she could pick up the steps, but was reluctant to join in, even if Ben asked. She saw Mrs. Clarke get up and partner with her husband, the two of them laughing as they cavorted to the music. Ben finally jumped up and offered her his hand, and they were soon whirling about with the rest. It had grown dark, the evening lit only by a bonfire and torches. Cassandra felt freer under the mask of darkness to enjoy the dancing with her lover and no one seemed to be paying them any mind.

Before the evening was over, those remaining gathered around the fire to tell stories and sing songs. Everyone was drunk on wine and ale. Ben and Cassandra sat close, but did not test the limits of their momentary freedom. She was sad that she could not invite these people, who were now welcoming her with open arms, to her upcoming party. If she could design the experiment again, she might consider placing herself amongst this crowd. But she needed the independence that could only be bought with money.

******

The high society of Selborne Parish had been abuzz with news of the garden party at Sorrel Hall since the invitations had gone out nearly two weeks ago. The American was finally giving a party!

Though the day started out dreary and wet, by the time the guests were arriving at four o'clock, the sun had broken through, the air was tolerably warm, and the ground was beginning to dry. The servants rushed around drying off the outdoor furniture as the visitors poured through the front doors and out the back through the conservatory, onto the veranda and the great lawn beyond. Tea and light sandwiches were served on the veranda where tables and chairs awaited the ladies and gentleman who only wanted to relax and observe the festivities. The young children ran to play croquet, knocking the balls all about in spite of the efforts of their governesses to help guide them through the wickets. The older children played at badminton and cricket, and the young men and women wandered out and around the parkland.

Cassandra was standing at the top of the lawn, looking out over the scene before her, and observing her guests as they settled in. Glancing back toward the house, she spied Lady Holcomb exiting onto the veranda from the conservatory through the glass doors that were thrown open wide. She was dressed in a light, lilac-colored muslin gown, looking young and fresh. Cassandra herself had chosen an off-white, silky cotton with green trim, reminiscent of a Grecian toga.

"Cassandra!" Lady Holcomb called as she approached. "Thank goodness about the weather!"

"Yes," Cassandra replied when her friend reached her. "I was in a panic about it this morning, but I guess my little party was meant to be after all."

"Sorrel Hall has never looked more beautiful."

"Thank you, Charlotte, though I can hardly take the credit. My household staff is beyond compare."

"I agree; you are fortunate in that respect. Though I do quite well with my modest contingent, I think."

"Absolutely. Your home is always impeccable, and your table always beautiful and sumptuous."

"Sumptuous! My, there's a word. Listen, my dear, I have to tell you, I had a note from Lady Charles. She said to tell you that she would not be here today. She was not feeling herself, she said, but she is sending her daughter and niece in her stead."

As if on cue, the two young ladies sauntered out onto the veranda, and were immediately pounced upon by James, who seemed to have been keeping a lookout for them. The three young people scampered off together up the hill to the gazebo.

"Ah, I see they have arrived."

"Did Lady Charles say what was the matter?" asked Cassandra with as much concern as she could muster.

"Only that she was having an attack of nerves and was not up to such a crowd."

Cassandra sensed there was something Charlotte wasn't telling her.

"She was having an attack of nerves, or she was not feeling well?"

"Oh, I do not know, something like that, you know how she is. She also made apologies for Sir Robert, but of course, this kind of gathering is not really to his taste."

Cassandra felt herself bristle at hearing the name mentioned.

"Well, I am just happy that you are here, Charlotte, and that you have brought Jane. Where is she, by the way?"

Lady Holcomb looked around. "There." She pointed up at the gazebo. Jane had joined James and the other two young ladies, and Cassandra was certain that her son was gratified at being amongst the company of three such devoted admirers.

"I have to tell you though, Cassandra," continued Lady Holcomb, "I may not stay long myself. I am afraid I feel a headache coming on. Perhaps you would make sure Jane is properly escorted home when the time comes."

"Certainly," Cassandra replied. "But my dear Charlotte, come have a seat here at a table in the shade, let me get you a cool glass of lemonade. I am so sorry you are not feeling well either."

"Oh, thank you," said the lady, taking Cassandra's arm and allowing herself to be led to a small, wrought iron table on the veranda, where a servant awaited her. "But I think I would rather just have a cup of tea, if it is all the same to you."

"Of course," said Cassandra nodding to the servant who had overheard the request. She didn't think Lady Holcomb looked the least bit ill, but rather quite robust. She let the matter lie.

"Now, my dear, please do not fuss over me," Lady Holcomb uttered weakly. "You must mingle with your guests. Leave me here to sip my tea, and I am sure I shall be fine."

"Well, if you are certain."

"Absolutely. I do not want to distract you from your duties as hostess."

"I do need to say hello to Mrs. Moore."

"Do not give me another thought. I shall be right here. At least for a little while longer."

"All right, but do not leave until you say goodbye."

"Of course not," said Lady Holcomb, gently waving her away.

Cassandra was puzzled. Was she being shunned by Lady Charles, and was Lady Holcomb following her lead? It concerned her somewhat, but she had other things to think about. Most of the other guests had now arrived, and everyone had had a chance to eat and drink and look about as they pleased, and Cassandra had greeted them all in due fashion. Presently, she heard someone mention the lake, and soon the young people were filing down toward it from where they had been scattered about the grounds. They gathered by the boats and paired up.

Cassandra strolled down to the water to see how it would play out. Before long, James and Elizabeth Charles were skimming out across the water, followed by Jane and Edward. Jane laughed with excitement as Edward rowed dangerously close to James' boat, then steered away at the last minute before crashing into it.

Eunice looked forlorn, standing at the edge of the lake by herself, but then a handsome young man that Cassandra had seen at the ball, Thomas White, offered to take her out. She clapped her hands in acceptance. Cassandra observed that in the six months since Eunice had been with the Charles family, she had filled out. Her cheeks were pinker, and her eyes had more sparkle. Her life before coming to Hampshire had probably been spent breathing the sooty Birmingham air, Cassandra imagined, but four months in the country, and two amongst the fashionable environs of London, had made a difference. Though a year younger than her cousin, she was beginning to catch up with her in looks.

The boy who had asked Eunice to row was a nephew of Gilbert White and resided at the home were that famous scientist once lived. Though Cassandra continued to admire the Wakes, she was still not on familiar terms with the family and was happy to see that a representative thereof had accepted her invitation.

There were some brother and sister teams out on the boats, Cassandra noticed. The second and third eldest of the Clarkes went out together, as did that family's thirteen-year-old twin boys. The two Moore sisters were intrepidly rowing by themselves. At twenty-one and twenty-three, they were in danger of becoming spinsters. They were freckly and buck-toothed, gangly and giggly, and appeared to Cassandra somewhat empty headed. But their fortunes were large, so, although she felt a little sorry for them, she figured that a couple of desperate gentlemen would eventually snatch them up.

Some of the other adults came down to watch the water sport, including Ben, who had arrived late. He smiled at Cassandra, but didn't approach her. He waved to someone out on the water, and Cassandra looked to see who it was. Jane Holcomb waved back, a pretty smile on her face, cheeks flushed pink in spite of the shade of her bonnet.

Edward looked over his shoulder and saw the object of Jane's salutation, then turning back, gave the boat a rock with his hips. Jane squealed and Cassandra wondered how deep the lake was where they were, way out in the middle. She had a moment of panic. If it were deep, and the boat toppled over, Jane's skirts would drag her down, and she doubted if the girl knew how to swim. The Clarke twins, Randall and Ralph, saw their brother's antics and began to rock their boat as well.

The twins' boat tipped over with a splash. Cassandra ran to the edge of the lake, ready to rip off her dress and dive in. But the next second, the two carrot-tops popped up, splashing each other and laughing, shoulder-deep in the water. Cassandra sighed in relief, knowing that the water was shallow. The ladies in the boats shrieked to get away from the splashing, so the gentlemen rowed in closer to get them wet, while Mrs. Clarke stood on the shore and shouted angrily to the boys to come in and dry off. They ignored her as everyone else stood by laughing.

As the sun went down, the air cooled and the guests started to drift inside. The Clarke twins had been sent home to bed, but the other guests were dry enough to stay. Supper was served at seven in the dining room, but the visitors scattered about the house to eat, as the dining room only sat sixteen. On the side table, laid out like a buffet, was more of the bounty of the harvest: roasted wild turkey, venison, mutton, ham, freshly caught, baked trout, meat pies, boiled new potatoes sautéed in butter and garden herbs, baked noodles in a casserole, tomato and cucumber salad, mashed butternut squash, plates of cheeses and breads, fruits and nuts from the orchards, and a three-tiered vanilla cake garnished with fresh peaches—all served with the utmost style and elegance. There were the best wines from the cellar, part of Cassandra's rental agreement with the Collins, and home-brewed ale.

There was a call for music, and Cassandra was in the mood to oblige. The guests gathered in the sitting room while Cassandra entertained them with some popular tunes on the piano. Soon toes were tapping, and James suggested a dance in earnest. There was a small spinet piano in the conservatory for just such occasions, with a stack of sheet music for dancing. Everyone convened in the large room, and the servants moved the sparse furniture to the walls while the young people paired off. Cassandra launched into a favorite country dance, and James led the way with Elizabeth. These dances he now knew well enough. Everyone was stepping, jumping, clapping, bowing, linking arms and hands—all the variations of the familiar dances. Cassandra played with enthusiasm, delighted to see her son and all his friends having such a wonderful time. She thought that he probably had never imagined such simple, uncomplicated fun could be had, and honestly didn't know when she'd last seen him so happy. She glanced around for Ben, but he was nowhere to be seen.

After she had played another few dances, she heard a small commotion and realized that Ben was standing by the spinet, taking his violin out of its case. He must have sent a servant for it. A crowd was gathering round, so she finished up her song and looked up at him in wonder.

"I thought I would accompany you," he said with a smile. There was clapping all around, and the dancers formed sets again. They began another country dance, suddenly made all the livelier by what could only be called fiddling in the style of Mr. Overstreet. Cassandra had never heard Ben play like this, and she laughed in delight. They performed more pieces until Cassandra was finally worn out. Ben then took the music over on his own, fiddling to shouts of enjoyment, and applause.

When the dancers had also tired, Ben treated them to a final piece, a beautiful and haunting solo violin concerto by Vivaldi that she had never heard him play before. The guests were entranced, and when he was done, they all realized that the evening had reached its conclusion, and slowly took their leave as each carriage came round to collect its family. As

Ben departed, he gazed into Cassandra's eyes and kissed her hand. She felt there had been a breakthrough. They had played together in public, and it was accepted. And he was accepted as a musician in Selborne Society.

******

September 12, 1820 – Well the party went off perfectly without a hitch. The last of the stragglers have finally gone, the Charles girls among them with Jane, whom they gave a ride home in their carriage. I realized as they were leaving that Lady Holcomb left without saying goodbye as she had promised. When Jane came to bid me farewell and thank me for the evening, I asked her to send her regards to her mother and tell her I hoped she was feeling better. The girl flushed, and stammered and said she would, then was whisked out the door by her friends before I had the chance to say anything more. It was odd behavior and it makes me uncomfortable. Did Charlotte not want to be here? What on earth is going on with that woman?

CHAPTER TWELVE

O *ctober 5, 1820—The harvest is still underway throughout the county, and the smell of smoked meats and freshly cut hay hover in the air. I am outside on the veranda, looking out over the landscape of changing leaves in the bright afternoon light. I am so charmed by the loveliness of the season I can hardly bear it. I remember that long ago, at my parents' Hudson Valley home, autumn brought these feelings, of skies so blue they shimmered, of a cozy sweater after the shorts and t-shirts of summer, of going to pick pumpkins at the local farm, the smell of leaves burning, climbing on haystacks, staying inside with my mother to bake. When did I lose that awareness that the change of season was special and sacred?.*

I am seeking refuge, at the moment, from the busy Selborne social calendar that is in full swing. James is out for a ride with his new group of friends, having thrown himself into the fall activities wholeheartedly. It seems every the day he is out on horseback either by himself or with friends in a curricle to visit some interesting site or another. He has befriended Edward Clarke and Thomas White and sometimes they go hunting together and joke about James' bad luck with a kill (they have decided that Americans just weren't born to hunt). Nearly every evening he has a card party, supper, or impromptu dance to attend.

I join occasionally in the events and outings that include the older people, but I prefer my quiet nights, usually spent with Ben—he will be here soon for an evening of music and dinner. Often we just talk or read to each other by the fire, or go for walks under the moonlight. I am beginning to see how this companionship could easily turn into a life together. I cannot think about the inevitable a few months off. I realize now that his is not the only heart that will be breaking.

******

As if on cue, Ben came walking through the doors of the conservatory. Cassandra hurriedly shut her journal and rose to meet him. They walked back through the house, Cassandra detouring into the office where she could deposit the journal in the desk under lock and key. She then met him at the front door and they proceeded out onto a section of the grounds where she wanted to show him a cluster of mushrooms and get his opinion on whether or not they were edible. They had bent down near a birch tree and were examining the fungi, when they perceived the rattle of a carriage. They looked up to see Lady Holcomb's approaching at a clip. They were easily within view of the drive and stood up with a start. Cassandra moved away, hoping they hadn't been seen conferring so closely together. The carriage slowed—she was too late. It rolled to a stop, and the footman hopped down to help Lady Holcomb descend. Her face appeared stern as she waved to Cassandra, more a beckoning than a greeting. Cassandra and Ben hurried over to her, and Ben took the lady by the arm as they walked to the house.

"I am here to tell you," she said to Cassandra after they had exchanged greetings, "That the young people: your son, my daughter, Miss Charles, Miss Fairchild, and Mr. Clarke, have been eagerly discussing a plan to travel to Bath for a fortnight. This is usually the season when Lady Charles goes, and I often partake of the waters there for a few weeks in the autumn myself. She and I spoke yesterday, and we thought it was a good scheme. What do you think? We insist upon having you as a part of the group."

Her tone seemed to have shifted from the easy pleasantness of just a few weeks ago. There was something of Lady Charles' imperiousness in it.

"Well," Cassandra began, "it has been a great desire of mine to see Bath, and I would love to take advantage of the opportunity. I am honored by the invitation." She was aware of how formal she sounded. "And what about Mr. Johnston here," she ventured, "Is he included in the invitation?"

"Of course, if he should wish it," Lady Holcomb said, turning her head with a forced smile to acknowledge him.

"I will certainly consider the invitation, thank you," returned Ben pleasantly.

They were nearly at the entrance to Sorrel Hall, and Ben detached himself from Lady Holcomb's arm. "Let me leave you here, if you do not mind. I have some business I must attend to at home. I am sure you would enjoy a chat alone together."

Cassandra nodded her farewell to him. He took Lady Holcomb's hand and kissed it gallantly, and when the lady's head was turned, winked at Cassandra. Her heart sank as she watched him walk away to the stables.

Cassandra led Lady Holcomb into the sitting room and rang for Mary to take their wraps and bring in the tea things. She and her friend took two chairs by the fire.

"Charlotte," she said simply, "will you please tell me what is going on?"

"Why, whatever do you mean, Cassandra?" The lady fluttered her handkerchief around her neck. "You startle me with that terribly direct manner of yours."

"You do know what I mean. Your attitude toward me has changed as of late. You seem cold and disapproving, not like the warm and friendly Charlotte Holcomb that I have come to love so much."

"My dear, there certainly has been no intention on my part of seeming distant. But Lady Charles has lately been sharing with me her opinion of you and your friend Mr. Johnston, and, well, I have to say, I see her point."

Cassandra struggled to hold in her anger. "And what exactly is that opinion?"

"She thinks you are scandalous, to put it mildly. You and I spoke of this after the ball, but I had not yet known of her disapprobation. She has had me over to tea twice or thrice in the last few weeks, and the subject of your behavior always comes up. I told you that tongues would wag, and so they are. And yet you do not seem to have paid my advice any mind. I saw the two of you hobnobbing there under the tree a few moments ago. You seem as if you are encouraging the poor man, though you tell me you have no desire to marry him."

"I understand your concern, Charlotte. But frankly, I do not see how it is any business of Lady Charles' what I do or do not do. She does not like me; I do not think she ever has, and she is looking for reasons to turn my friends against me, though I do not know why."

"It is her way, I suppose, to be rather strong in her opinions," responded Lady Holcomb. "But you cannot simply dismiss her. She has a great deal of influence in this neighborhood."

Cassandra sighed. "Charlotte, if I have offended you with my behavior, than I apologize. I do not care what Lady Charles thinks, but I do care if my friendship with you jeopardizes your standing in the neighborhood. In light of that, I appreciate that you still want me to go to Bath with you, and that you would allow Mr. Johnston to join us."

"Well, Lady Charles realized that we could not very well invite James without you, and as for Mr. Johnston, I suppose she cannot stop him. I, myself, could not imagine making the trip without you. I still very much consider you my dear friend."

"I promise that I will be the picture of propriety in Bath. You will not have reason to regret the invitation. I am just so sorry that I have caused you any pain or alarm."

"Oh, my love, I could not stay angry with you." She clasped Cassandra's hands in hers. "Not that I was exactly angry, but Lady Charles' words were having such an effect on me! She is very persuasive, you know."

By now Mary had come and gone with the tea service and a tray of diminutive sandwiches and sweets, and the ladies took a moment to enjoy them.

Cassandra dove into the subject again. "If you do not mind, Charlotte, would you tell me just what it is that Lady Charles does say about me?"

Her friend's face colored. "You know, just that—well, she thinks you are too…different."

"That is all? She thinks I am different?"

"That is not exactly how she puts it. She thinks there is something wrong in your manner and your actions. It is not just how you are with Mr. Johnston. She says that there is something very unusual about you, and that she does not trust you."

"Does she think I am a spy for the U.S. government?"

"Oh my goodness! Oh, Cassandra, I see that you are joking. No, I guess if it is anything, she would say that in an earlier era she might suspect you of being a…oh, I do not know, it is just that you are flouting moral convention terribly. She finds it distinctly non-Christian."

Cassandra wondered what word Charlotte could not bring herself to say. "Non-Christian? I am sure she says that I am a loose woman."

"Well, no, not exactly that, but she says that she thinks you have enchanted the people of the neighborhood, Mr. Johnston included, to all love you. That they are all under your spell—the farmer's wives, the shopkeepers, everybody."

Cassandra saw clearly the situation now. "Does she think I am some kind of sorceress?"

"Oh, that is putting it in very strong terms."

"What do you mean? Does she actually perceive me as having unnatural powers?"

"Yes, if she were to iterate it that clearly, I believe she would say that."

"Are we not past the time of such superstitions?"

"Of course we are!"

"And James?"

"She says that James is innocent in it all. That she is sorry for him to have such a mother."

Cassandra felt the blood rise to her face.

Lady Holcomb hurried on. "Let us not continue to discuss it, my dear. It does not matter anyway. I am sorry for repeating her rantings. Let her think what she will. I know the kind of person, and mother, you really are. I am sorry for having let her influence me."

Cassandra was having difficulty seeing how she could spend a vacation in Bath with the woman who saw her essentially as an evil, unfit mother. She absentmindedly arranged the sugar bowl and creamer on the tea tray.

"It is fine, Charlotte," she finally said with a shaky smile. "I will begin to make plans for Bath, and you shall see. We will have a fine time together, and perhaps I will even turn Lady Charles' opinion of me around."

"If anyone can do it, you can," the lady replied.

"Now, do tell me what you hear of Jeffrey. Have you received any mail from the ship yet?"

An hour or so after Lady Holcomb left, Ben returned. The couple ensconced themselves in the sitting room, playing music until James returned late. And then, as if in defiance of what she'd learned that day, Cassandra walked her lover out to the stables and kissed him goodbye under the moonlight.

******

It was finally decided that the group traveling to Bath, including the Holcombs, the Charleses, Edward Clarke and Ben, along with James and Cassandra, would plan to stay for at least two weeks. The season was under way there, and Cassandra was dying to experience the place that Jane Austen wrote about with such piercing insight.

Edward and James planned to leave on horseback a few days ahead to secure rooms. The Charles family had their own townhouse in Bath and pointedly did not offer to have

Cassandra and James stay with them. However, a few days before the trip, Lady Charles threw a dinner party for all those planning to go so that they could discuss what to see and do there. Cassandra was mortified to find that Sir Robert was in attendance, for she had been informed he would not be joining them in Bath. He sat sulkily in his seat, ate his dinner, and excused himself to go smoke as soon as he could. He made a point to avoid Cassandra's eyes, and she did the same. Lady Charles was not unpleasant, but obviously cooler to Cassandra than she was to the others.

Cassandra had been seated as far as possible from Ben; next to him sat Jane Holcomb. Cassandra was determined to be engaged in conversation with Edward, seated to her left, and not notice when Jane laughed at something that Ben said, or to let him see that she was looking in his direction at all.

James was directly across the table from his mother, Elizabeth Charles seated closely by his side. Cassandra thought she perceived Lady Charles looking fondly at the couple from the head of the table. She definitely noticed Elizabeth gazing dreamily at James. He was doing his best to seem detached, but she could see that he was weakening dangerously under the young woman's charms. Cassandra knew that Lady Charles was just that kind of indulgent mother, who, if her daughter wanted something badly enough, would be hard pressed to deny her. She imagined the lady must think that if she could just get rid of his mother, the son, with a hefty inheritance, wouldn't be such a bad match for her daughter after all.

The situation was made all the more obvious when Lady Charles invited the young people to stay for cards. Then there was confusion about who would go home in which carriage. Ben offered his to Lady Holcomb and Cassandra so that James could have his mother's to go home in later. Lady Charles decreed that Edward and Jane would be driven to their respective homes in her own vehicle.

Ben rode on the outside seat with the driver until they had deposited Lady Holcomb at the cottage. Then, once out of sight, they stopped, and he climbed into the carriage with Cassandra.

"Are you angry with me, my love?" he immediately asked.

"No. Why?"

"Because you did not look at me all evening."

"I am surprised you noticed." Cassandra did not like the jealous tone in her own voice.

"What are you saying?"

"Nothing. I am being silly."

"Please tell me."

"No, it is not worth bringing up."

"Is it because I was talking with Jane Holcomb?"

"It is…only because you seemed so happy to talk with Jane Holcomb."

"I had no choice. She was my dinner partner."

"And yet you were so engaging with her, so very charming."

"She is nothing to me. She is a girl."

"A pretty one, at that." Cassandra's eyes began to sting and she cursed herself for becoming emotional.

"I cannot believe you are jealous of her. She is less than nothing compared to you. You are the love of my life, Cassandra! I would do anything for you, go anywhere, risk anything. Do you not understand that?"

Cassandra turned her head to him, surprised at the vehemence in his voice. "No, perhaps I did not."

He looked out his window. "Surely you must know that by now."

She looked out her own but said nothing. The moon shone full in the sky and lit the ground like daylight. They turned into the drive of Sorrel Hall.

"Cassandra," he said after several moments. "I have been very patient. I will continue to be patient. But I want you to know that this love affair of ours is not a game to me. The only logical conclusion is marriage. I will wait for you as long as I have to wait, but I will not accept any less than you becoming my wife."

She looked at her gloved hands. The carriage rattled to a stop in front of the house. Ben flung the door open and leapt out, then came around and opened the door for her, offering his hand. His expression was severe. As she stepped down, he said, "I will see you in Bath."

She nodded and hurried into the house, fighting back tears.

******

After James and Edward left for Bath, the remaining members of the party departed within a few days, each on their own schedule. Cassandra offered her carriage to Lady Holcomb and Jane; the Charles group came the next day. She had not heard from Ben, but knew was planning to bring his phaeton to use in and around Bath when he finally did come.

When Cassandra arrived with the Holcombs on the tenth of October, James was waiting for them in front of the hotel. When she stepped out of the carriage to behold the Royal Crescent, the perfect semi-circle of four-story townhouses, all attached and uniform of which their hotel was a part, she marveled that three hundred years in the future, it would not have changed at all. The Crescent overlooked a handsome park, one of the favorite gathering places of the townspeople on fine days, and on the afternoon of their arrival, it was alive with ladies and gentlemen strolling in the sunshine.

As the Holcombs arranged to have their luggage taken to the suite above the Franklins', James led his mother to the third floor to inspect their own rooms. He opened the door for her onto a small foyer with golden yellow walls and a diminutive chandelier hanging from the ceiling. To the left was a circular space with four doors positioned around it. These were the entrances to the two bedrooms, the water closet, and bathing room. James led his mother through the farthest door to the right, where Cassandra found a perfectly feminine room: a four poster bed with white lace covers and bed curtains, a white vanity and wrought iron chair, and a painted white dresser and armoire.

Her luggage was brought up, accompanied by one of the hotel maids assigned to their suite. Cassandra directed the luggage to her room and left instructions for the maid to begin to unpack. She and James then continued with their tour. He led her back through the foyer to a large parlor, sunny, with tall windows that overlooked the Crescent. The furniture consisted of a pale green, satin sofa and two armchairs to match, with curved, carved legs and arms. There was a grey marble coffee table in the center of the seating area. Another grouping of stiff-backed chairs huddled around a card table. Cassandra's eyes settled on the finely carved, rectangular piano of golden oak, occupying a position just before the parlor windows. She went to it and ran her hands over the keys.

"It's perfect," she whispered.

"I knew you'd like it," replied James.

Moving towards the dining room, she stopped in front of the gold-framed mirror hanging over the fireplace mantle to arrange a stray hair; then touched the cool green-veined marble that made up the mantle and front-piece. The double doors connecting the dining room to the parlor were now open wide, creating a feeling of spaciousness between the two rooms. In the dining room was a smaller fireplace. The walls were painted a robin's egg blue, and on the ceiling were murals of angels and clouds. Cassandra looked up at them and smiled.

She went to dress for the evening, donning a white, silk gown with a low neck and capped sleeves and a slight train. She added long gloves, drop earrings, a fan, and a warm silk and woolen shawl patterned in red and purple flowers, with long purple fringe. She met James in the parlor, he wearing the same suit of clothing he had for the Darrington ball, only with a blue cravat instead of red. They ate a light repast in the dining room, then descended to find the Holcombs waiting for them in the lobby.

The theater they attended on their first night in Bath was a grand venue with many tiers of seats and boxes for the upper class. The entire party had been invited to join Lady Charles and her two girls in a box situated on the second level above the ground floor, so near the stage Cassandra felt she could almost reach down and touch the top of the actors' heads. Once the play started, Shakespeare's *Twelfth Night*, she and James looked around at the audience who would not quiet their loud whispering conversations. Though Cassandra knew that a night at the theater was more a chance to see and be seen then to take in the offering, she found it very distracting.

She felt bad for her son, and kept looking over to catch his eye. This was an experience of a lifetime, and it was hard to take in because of the chatter. Although the actors spoke their lines in a stilted and overblown style, Cassandra felt that, as was true throughout history, the British had a grasp on Shakespeare that actors of other nationalities could never really master. More than once Lady Holcomb tried to engage Cassandra in talk about a woman's gown in the box across the way, but the American merely smiled at her friend and turned her head back to the stage. She watched James rebuff the attempts at conversation by both Elizabeth and Jane, who were seated on either side of him, with only a friendly nod. At the end of the performance, she and James burst into wild applause, and it took the rest of the audience a few moments to catch up to their level of enthusiasm.

In the mornings, they attended the Pump Room, a cavernous space fitted with columns and arches, a great chandelier hanging from the center of the high ceiling, and walls painted in soothing pastels. This is where the Bath high society assembled. At one end of the room the healing waters, hot and sulfurous, were distributed in cups by an attendant. At another, an orchestra played. Cassandra and James met their friends there, and were soon introduced to many more of the Holcombs' and Charles' acquaintances. By the end of their first week, Ben had still not arrived.

******

October 17, 1820—I recall a simulation I did as I prepared for my journey, of the public bathing experience in Bath. The men and women sat together in the great Roman bath, speaking little. The men all wore brown, linen suits, the women brown jackets and petticoats, slightly different than the bathing costume James bought for me in Bathingstoke. I was wearing one of these outfits, getting ready to submerge myself, looking around at the room of rough, stone walls, etched with worn-down carvings of suns and other Roman symbols, taking in the high, arched ceiling. I had difficulty summoning up the desire to get wet and hesitated before stepping in. The clothes felt like they would be heavy and clingy. Some of the people in the water looked up at me curiously. The warm, moist air swirled around me, and I knew I would only get hotter as I stood there. I moved to the steps and descended into the murky water. Once in, almost up to my chest, the warmth of it was, indeed, quite relaxing. The fabric alternately clung and billowed away from my body. Bowls of pomanders and sweet oils floated on the water, but didn't make much of a dent in the sulfurous odor of the place. It didn't take long for me to feel like I'd had enough. How long should I stay in, I wondered? It was not only boring, but not exactly what I long for in a spa experience.

As the people all faded away, and the ancient Roman bath turned into the black simulation room, I became miraculously dry. I removed the porous sensory mask covering my entire head, and, looking down, now saw only the sensory jump suit I was wearing. Since I had such a vivid simulation of the experience, I now actually have no desire to get into that icky looking water in real life. James says he's going to give it a try—I say, have fun.

******

In the evenings, the group from Selborne usually attended the Upper Rooms for dancing. The ballroom was a vast hall with tall ceilings, windows on the second story, and no less than five crystal chandeliers. On those evenings Cassandra found herself appealed to by many partners but took no pleasure in the dancing, always looking around the room, hoping for Ben to suddenly appear.

The night of the eighteenth, Cassandra was dancing with an officer of the navy who was in town with his regiment. He'd been introduced to her by Lady Holcomb. He was a tall man, with dark hair, graying at the temples. His face was weathered, but Cassandra found his dark complexion handsome. His features were chiseled, his teeth straight and white. They spoke about Jeffrey as they danced; the man, Captain Wayne, had known him during the young man's training. Another couple came into view and Cassandra immediately saw that it was Ben dancing with Jane. She almost missed a step. He glanced at her, then looked away. Cassandra got through the end of the dance, making only the cursory responses to Captain Wayne's remarks. She curtsied and hurried to grab her cloak from the coat room. In moments, she felt a touch on her shoulder and looked around. Ben stood before her. He put his hand on her wrist.

"Wait, Cassandra," he whispered.

"What is the meaning of your behavior, Ben?" She said in a low voice as people milled around them. "I do not understand. Why have you waited so long to come to Bath? Why have you not at least written?"

"I was angry because you will not marry me."

She sighed, frustrated.

"Come." He tipped the coat check man, took her cloak, and wrapped it around her shoulders. They moved through the crowd and out onto the street. They walked through the plaza towards Bath Abbey, not speaking until they were in the shadows of the great church.

"If you cannot accept that marriage is not in my immediate future, then we have nothing else to say to each other." She felt a choke in her voice.

"I do not want to be estranged from you. I have been in agony. I will not press you, Cassandra, I promise. I was going to wait for you to come crawling back to me, but seeing you dancing with that man threw me into fits of jealousy." He took her in his arms.

"You have me," she whispered. They kissed hungrily, their bodies pressed closely. "Enough." She finally said, pushing him away. "We cannot be seen like this. Tomorrow night there is a private concert at the home of Lady Rochester's, a friend of Lady Charles—"

"Yes, an invitation came to my parents' townhouse where I am staying."

"So I will see you then."

"I love you, my angel."

She kissed him lightly on the cheek. "Good night."

******

The concert the next evening was of operatic songs performed by a large soprano with bright, blond hair and waggling upper arms. Cassandra and Ben were seated far apart, but spent the majority of the evening stealing glances across the room. Cassandra thought it would never end. But once the singing was finished and they'd all partaken in wine and sweets, the crowd began to file out of the stuffy parlor. As Cassandra passed near Ben, he took her elbow and drew her aside, a look of excitement sparkling in his eye.

"Mrs. Franklin," he began, "I think that before we leave Bath, you and I should put on a musical performance at my place."

"What?" she exclaimed, then dropped her voice. "And expose our collaboration to public scrutiny?"

"We did as much at Sorrel Hall when we played at your garden party."

"But that was just the neighborhood, and Lady Charles was not even there."

"You do not think word got back to her about that?"

The lady in question was moving near them just then, her eyes firmly fixed in their direction. Cassandra instinctively moved a step away from Ben and lowered her gaze. They waited until she passed by.

"Let us do it, why not?" he pressed. "It will be a formal evening, with a dinner included. And only our close acquaintance—nothing public. Let us show these people what we are together. They think we are lovers, perhaps; let us show them this other, very precious part of our relationship."

"I do not know." Cassandra glanced across the room and nodded to Lady Holcomb who was gathering her wrap.

"We have been practicing together so long," Ben continued, ignoring all others in the room, "we must have some outcome for it all."

"But we have not played together for nearly two weeks!"

"Then we had better get to practicing."

Cassandra looked at him, thinking, then smiled softly with her eyes. "Yes. Let us do it!"

"Capital!" he cried and people turned to look in their direction. He lowered his voice and went on excitedly "We have all but perfected the two Bach Violin Sonatas for Harpsichord, and Beethoven's Sonata Number Five. Let us do one of the Bach and also the Beethoven and it will add up to around an hour of music, perfect for an evening soiree, and then dinner!"

"Yes, yes," she quieted him further with a tap of her fan on his shoulder. "But let us plan it tomorrow when we meet to practice. Enough talk now, people are looking."

"Of course, yes." He bowed and moved away. Cassandra caught up with James, and took the arm that wasn't escorting Elizabeth Charles.

******

The following day was Monday; five days remained of their stay in Bath. The Franklins and most of the others would return to Hampshire on Saturday. Only the Charleses were planning to stay on for several more weeks, much to the disappointment of James and Elizabeth. Friday they were all planning to ride out to the countryside to picnic along the Avon River since the mid-October weather had, so far, been temperate, the days sunny.

Cassandra and Ben set the evening of their concert for Thursday and immediately sent invitations out to their circle. Cassandra received a reply from Lady Charles that same day, refusing the invitation, on grounds that she was occupied elsewhere that evening. On Wednesday, a curt apology arrived from the lady with news that her other plans had been canceled, and that she would indeed attend the concert. Cassandra assumed pressure had been put on her by not only the daughter and niece, who wanted to be anywhere James was, but by their circle of friends in general, who were all abuzz over the upcoming event.

On Thursday evening at seven o'clock, everyone was assembled in the grand parlor of Ben's parents' townhouse on George Street. His parents were in London, and he was occupying the place alone. His mother had been the decorator, and gilt ornamentation shone from the moldings of all the walls and ceilings, and framed the paintings of fine ladies and gentlemen cavorting in pastoral scenes. Gold adorned a great crystal chandelier dangling from the high ceiling. The sofas and chairs were covered in satin brocade in dark pinks and wines. Bronze and marble statuettes of Grecian ladies posed on pedestals about the room.

The guests were transfixed by the grandeur. After champagne and hors d'ourvres were served, they settled into the seats arranged near the instruments. Cassandra sat down at the gold-encrusted piano, and Ben took a moment to tune up his violin.

They began with the Bach piece, playing fluidly, yet precisely. When the Bach concluded, the audience applauded heartily. Ben and Cassandra took a moment to gather themselves, and then launched into the Beethoven Sonata. At the beginning, the piece shifted its focus from violin to piano. When one stood out, the other accompanied, weaving focus back and forth between the two instruments, and then joining in equal strength. In the first movement, the arpeggios on the piano were difficult, and Cassandra concentrated deeply. There was great power in the piece. As they played, Cassandra was aware of how perfectly it reflected their relationship. Fiery at one moment, sweet the next, passionate and then contemplative.

The second movement was even sweeter, sublimely tender. The musicians smiled at each other as they played. In the third movement the music frolicked—it was for this movement, and the last, that it was called the Spring Sonata.

When it concluded, the musicians happily spent, the assembly leapt to their feet, all except Lady Charles, who feigned exhaustion and sat waving a large fan in front of her face. Cassandra and Ben took a modest bow, and there were shaking of hands and congratulations. They all filed into the dining room for a dinner served by many attendants.

******

Although the sky threatened rain the morning of their trip to the countryside, no one was willing to let it be thwarted. The servants packed up carriages and curricles with food and tableware, and the Charleses, the Franklins, the Holcombs, and Edward Clarke set out around ten o'clock, dressed warmly, but with anticipation of a pleasant day. They drove north along the river for about an hour until they found an idyllic spot with clusters of trees, rambling low hills, and inviting meadows. While servants unpacked the picnic, the others went to explore. James and Elizabeth immediately struck out on their own. They seemed to Cassandra to be dejected in contrast to last night's merriment. She worried for James. He had gotten too attached.

She and Ben had no such luxury to wander off alone together. They were forced to keep company with Ladies Charles and Holcomb, while Jane, Eunice, and Edward formed their own expedition. The two young women took each of Edward's arms as they strolled off toward the river. While Eunice looked about at the scenery, Cassandra noticed that Edward and Jane continuously stole glances at each other. She smiled to herself.

She longed to walk briskly up a nearby incline and continue among the rolling hills for exercise. But the other two ladies began a slow amble down a slope toward a meadow, and Cassandra had no choice but to join them.

Ben, ever the gentleman, obliged the slower pace without objection, engaging cheerfully in any topic of conversation the women entertained.

Cassandra relaxed into the moment and took in the bright oranges and golds of the leaves on the birches, poplars, and maples abundant in the area. They had gained some vivid color during the past two weeks. Even under the overcast sky, they were striking, Cassandra thought, more so than she could remember seeing in her future world. Could it be, she thought, that everything here in this time is actually more intense than it will be three hundred years from now? Her thoughts wandered to the party the night before, the pleasure of performing with Ben. She tried to ignore the longing ache in her body at not having been in bed with him since before they'd left Selborne. In Bath, the quarters were too close, their movements too monitored.

The young people convened back at the picnic area where the food had been laid out; the others joined them, and all arranged themselves on blankets for the lunch of cold fowl, meats and cheeses, breads, pickled vegetables, apples, nuts, and sweets. James, Elizabeth, Jane, Eunice, and Edward dispersed once more for a final look at what may not have been explored.

Cassandra saw Elizabeth and James break away from their friends, running off around the side of a hill and out of sight. She noticed Lady Charles' lips tighten, watching the young people go.

"My Lady," she began, hoping to distract her, "do not you think the leaves are strikingly vivid?"

"I suppose," the woman responded, adjusting a pillow under her posterior. "Every year is the same to me, but if you say so."

"It is just that, well, I think they are more so here than in the States. I do not remember seeing such yellows and oranges."

"Well it does not surprise me. This is England after all!"

"What do we all say to a walk down there by the river, as long as the ground is not too damp?" she suggested.

"Yes, good idea," said Lady Holcomb rising to her feet, "I could use some exercise."

Ben leapt to assist her, and Cassandra stood up on her own, smoothing out her overcoat.

"I think I have had enough walking," complained Lady Charles. "Will no one stay here to keep me company?" Ben, Charlotte, and Cassandra hesitated, looking from one to the other.

Suddenly, there was a shout, a girl's piercing cry of alarm, and everyone looked in the direction of where James and Elizabeth had disappeared to. The shriek came again, louder.

Lady Charles scrambled to her feet. "Elizabeth!" she cried.

Ben and Edward were already running toward the sound, and the ladies moved as quickly as their gowns would allow. Elizabeth soon came racing around from behind the hillock, shrieking and sobbing. Ben got to her first and tried to hold her, but she broke away and ran to her mother in hysterics.

"Evil" she cried, "It is evil. I…I cannot…do not let it near me!" She was almost unintelligible. James appeared a moment later, running after her, calling her name, but Elizabeth clasped onto her mother crying, "No, no! Send him away! He is evil!"

"My God, James," said Ben, going quickly to him, "what did you do?"

"Nothing!" cried James, "I didn't harm her! I did nothing!"

"James!" said Cassandra in distress, "what happened? What is going on?" She had a sudden, sinking fear.

"Mother," he gasped, running up to her. "I must speak to you—only you."

"Oh my God, what is it?"

"Tell us, Elizabeth," interjected Lady Charles. "Tell us what happened."

"No!" cried James.

"Tell us this minute!" commanded Lady Charles.

"He has something. Something evil; it is something of the devil!"

"What on earth?" Lady Charles asked in horror. "Did you touch her?"

"No! Of course not. I can't—" uttered James, "I can't. Mother—" His face was stark white.

"Please," said Cassandra, "please, let me talk to him for a moment; let me determine—"

"No!" shouted Lady Charles, "I want an explanation. I demand an explanation right now!"

"For goodness sake," remarked Lady Holcomb, trying to calm the situation. "Whatever it is, it cannot be so bad."

Jane and Eunice clung to each other, and Edward's freckles stood out as the color faded from his face.

Cassandra turned to Ben pleadingly, "Ben, I must speak to him—"

"Tell us now!" shrieked Lady Charles, "or I will have him arrested!" A rather ridiculous thing to say, Cassandra thought with irritation, as there was no-one around but their own party.

"Cassandra," said Ben gently, "I think it best if the young man explains himself."

"There is no explanation! It is a terrible, terrible thing!" screamed Elizabeth. Lady Charles held her close, stroking her brow.

"Calm down, everyone," said Ben. "Why do you not explain to me what happened, son," he said kindly to James. "I am sure it is nothing."

Cassandra remained frozen. She feared the worst. Slowly James reached into his pocket and pulled out his hand to reveal a small, black, metallic object, one-eighth of an inch thick, and one inch square. In the middle was a small circle. Cassandra gasped reflexively. Everyone leaned in to see, except Elizabeth who turned away and sobbed into her mother's bosom.

"What is it?" asked Edward.

"It is nothing!" said James.

Ben looked at Cassandra, who felt as if she were going to faint. "Cassandra, do you know what it is?"

"I, um—"

"She does not know!" James blurted out.

"Well, what is it?" pressed Ben.

"Touch the circle!" cried Elizabeth. "You shall see; it is enchanted!"

They all looked at each other, except for Cassandra, who stared fixedly at the object in James's hand. Ben slowly reached out his hand and tentatively touched the circle. Everyone stepped back. Nothing happened. "Press it!" Elizabeth insisted, "press it hard!"

Ben pressed it harder and then jumped as if he had received an electrical shock. He looked all around wildly, his eyes frightened. Then he began to bat at the air, and shake his head. "What is it?" he cried. "Who is that? I do not see them. What is happening?" James pressed the button again and Ben relaxed somewhat but still trembled.

"What! What?" exclaimed Lady Charles.

"Some kind of music!" declared Ben. "Music in the air, but, but something like fairy music, strange singing, and an instrument. I do not know. I do not know what it was or where it came from!"

"There was no music," scoffed Lady Charles, "what do you mean?"

"There was!" cried Ben, "there was! Music all around me."

"It is true, mother," cried Elizabeth, "you push that circle and music comes into your head, horrible, terrible music. It is magic!"

"May I try?" asked Edward, stepping slowly forward.

James shrugged in resignation and held out the contraption. Edward took it and pressed the circle and, like Ben, looked around wildly in panic at first. But after a few moments, he began to accept what he was hearing and stared ahead in amazement. "It sounds like your voice, James," he said loudly, "like you have been enchanted!"

"Yes, yes!" screamed Elizabeth, "it is him, he told me it was him singing, but he is standing here in front of us, silent. How can he be singing and not singing? And such horrible music, it is not fairy music, but devil music!"

"Edward," interrupted Jane, "can you hear me?"

"Yes," replied Edward, "just fine, but this music is all around me!"

"How can it be?" asked Jane. She grasped Eunice's arm more tightly.

"It is James' voice," added Ben. "You are right, Edward, I thought the voice sounded very familiar. I do not understand," he said looking from James to Cassandra. "What does this mean?"

James hung his head, and Cassandra opened her mouth to speak, but could say nothing.

Edward gingerly pressed the circle on the object and handed it back to James.

"What is it, James? Tell us," he said.

"I cannot explain it, exactly," he replied slowly.

"He said it was a wondrous invention from America!" Elizabeth declared. "He said that it could capture music. He said that he wrote a song, and he wanted me to hear it, that he also played a strange kind of American instrument, and that the tiny box captured the song for others to hear. But no kind of human could make music like that! And how can it be in such a tiny thing!" She began to sob anew. "I am scared, mother, take me away from him!"

"Cassandra, what do you know of this?" pressed Lady Holcomb.

"Nothing!" exclaimed James fiercely, "I told you; she does not know anything about it. It was something recently invented in America. She does not know about it!"

Cassandra shot him a look to shut him up.

Lady Charles turned to Cassandra, "I am reporting this to the authorities, Mrs. Franklin. I do not know what that thing is, but as far as I am concerned, it must be some kind of dangerous alchemy. I do not know what the two of you have been up to over there in America, but it is something decidedly wicked. I knew there was something wrong about you, Cassandra. I knew you could not be trusted. And I am horribly disappointed in you, James. How dare you to have toyed with the affections of my daughter. You will both be sorry you ever set foot in our neighborhood!"

With that she grabbed the hands of Elizabeth and Eunice. "Come, girls, we are going back to town." She turned as if to go, but as if on second thought, suddenly reached back and snatched the device from James' hand. Inadvertently, she pressed the button, and the music filled her head.

"Aaaahhh!" she screamed. "Make it stop! Make it stop!" She threw it on the ground and James dove for it, but Lady Holcomb stepped on it to prevent him from taking it back. The pressure of her foot turned the music off. She gave James an imperious look, and he moved away from the player. She extracted a handkerchief from her pocket, and delicately used it to pick up the object, then held it out to Lady Charles, who regarded it with horror.

"I will not be responsible for this thing," Lady Holcomb said to Lady Charles. "If you want to take it to the police, that is your business. I will not be a part of persecuting my friends." She turned to Cassandra. "Or those whom I *thought* to be my friends."

"Very well," replied Lady Charles. She shakily held out the small, satin handbag that was attached with a ribbon to her dress, and Lady Holcomb dropped it in.

"What are you doing?" demanded James, "give it back to me!"

"Do not speak to me like that, young man," declared Lady Charles, holding the bag warily, yet firmly. "As much as I do not want to touch this thing, I am keeping it safe in case you try to do away with it, and deny ever having it. I want proof."

"Proof of what, Lady Charles?" said Ben, having recovered somewhat. "You do not know what this object is or if it is connected to alchemy."

"Maybe not, but I *do* know that is not of God. Maybe the farmers are right to believe in fairies and superstitions. I am taking this dangerous object to the authorities, and we shall let them judge. Now get away from me!"

Cassandra, Ben, James, and even Edward made attempts to reason with her. But she re-gathered her young ladies, ordered her servants to pack up her things, and departed with them regally in her carriage with Elizabeth trembling at her side and Eunice following behind.

Lady Holcomb grabbed Jane by the hand, and made her way to Cassandra's carriage, casting her a final look of disappointment. "Come, Edward," she ordered, "you may ride with us."

Edward gave James an apologetic look, but obediently followed.

A cold drizzle began to fall and the remaining three looked at each other in confusion.

"Well," Ben said to James. "I do not know what that thing is, but if she takes it to the authorities, there will be trouble. We are long past the days of witch hunts, but if you do not have a rational explanation for the thing, you may very well be questioned by the police. I will use all the power of my family's attorneys to assist you, but this situation may be serious. Now let us go back to town. I expect to have a thorough explanation there."

The attendants were asked to pack up the remaining picnic, and the three rode back to Bath silently in the Johnston family carriage, followed by the servants' wagon.

Cassandra sat with tears rolling down her cheeks, and Ben seemed angry. She couldn't imagine what would happen. She was furious with James, who sat, pale, staring out the window. Cassandra was astounded that he had brought the thing, much less shown it to the girl. Of course she knew what it was. Everyone she knew had a PAL, a Personalized

Audio Link, including herself, but couldn't think how to explain the device to Ben.

When they arrived, Cassandra told Ben that she needed to be alone with James, that she would see him in the morning, and that she would try to explain things after she talked to James. He reluctantly agreed.

******

The moment she closed the door to her suite, she whirled around to face her son. "What on earth possessed you? You know the most sacred rule is to bring nothing, *nothing* that cannot be exactly replicated to match the objects of the time!"

"But Mom, I can't live without my music!"

"That is the deal when you travel, and you know it! You should not have come if you could not keep it!"

He looked down, then spoke calmly. "You should understand. You have your piano; you can play the music you love anytime. I can't."

"But why show it to Elizabeth?"

"I do not know," he said slowly. "I like her. I wanted to show her something wonderful, something that would open her eyes. I wanted her to hear a song that I wrote, so that she would...remember me."

"Oh, James, the girl is silly. How did you think she would react, with intellectual curiosity? Or did you think she would fawn over you like you were a rock star? That device is something that these people cannot, in their wildest dreams, conceive of. They can only call it evil or sorcery, or perhaps see it as some kind of hoax. It cannot exist for them any other way. What are we going to say? How are we going to explain it? And most importantly, how are we going to get it back? We cannot leave that thing here."

"Mom, maybe I should just get out of here." There was fear in his eyes. "I could go and get the first coach I can find to London. Then I can easily get to the portal exit and just disappear. They'll think I hopped a boat to America."

"Yes, that's it!" she said pacing. "You must go now. Pack a small case with just a few things. You may have to find an inn for the night. I will come with you and help you make arrangements, and then we will get you on the next coach to London."

"No, wait! That's no good! I cannot just leave you hear to deal with it. They will tie you to it. You won't be able to convince them that you do not know what it is."

"I can convince them," she insisted. "I will just say that you must have been practicing some strange alchemy in America, that I knew nothing about it."

"You will be the mother of a—I don't know, heretic or sorcerer or something. That's not a good position to be in. I cannot leave you like that; they'll burn you at the stake!"

"No, they will not. They have not burned witches in England for a couple of centuries at least. You are thinking of the Salem witch trials."

"Yeah, but they might make an exception in your case and decide to do it anyway. And they'll still have the player! No, I cannot leave; we have to get it back."

After hours of conversation, they grew exhausted and determined to decide on a solution in the morning. There was a knock on the front door of the suite. James and Cassandra went hesitantly to open it. Three constables stood there with the hotel manager. One of the constables held a small leather pouch. They all looked shaken.

"James Franklin?" the sergeant inquired.

"I am he," said James with a tremble in his voice.

"You are under arrest. Come with us."

"What are you arresting him for?" Cassandra demanded.

The sergeant put on a righteous look. "For possession of a dangerous and subversive object."

Mother and son exchanged a look.

"May I go with him?"

"No, ma'am," said the sergeant, "but you may come and visit him in the morning."

"Where are you taking him?"

"To the jailhouse. Do not worry; he shall be treated civilly. But the day after tomorrow, he will be sent to London for trial. Things may not be so comfortable there."

"Oh, dear God," gasped Cassandra.

"It's all right, Mother," said James faintly, turning pale. "It will be all right."

"Oh, James!" she sobbed into her hands. "How could this be happening?"

"It will be all right, Mother," he whispered again.

"I'm going to get Ben," she called through her tears as they took her son down the stairs. "He will know what to do." She grabbed her coat, and ran out into the rain

CHAPTER THIRTEEN

O ct. 19, 1820—The jailhouse wasn't as bad as I'd feared. However, as soon as I arrived this morning, I "dusted" for bugs, surreptitiously leaning through the bars to blow the powder which I'd smuggled in my glove. My poor darling had already received his fair share of insect bites from the mattress, but the constables seem to be treating him well enough—they did not object to the food that I brought him. They all seem skittish around him and did not hesitate to inform me that the device was locked away in the jailhouse safe. I presumed from their pale faces and nervous expressions that they'd pressed the button in their curiosity and received the shock of their lives. I am trying to imagine what exactly Lady Charles said about it, and if she prompted them to try it for themselves. If anyone is a witch, it is that dreadful woman. I rue the day that we got ourselves mixed up with her and her family.

I'm about to return to the jailhouse now to meet Ben again and see what news he has from his lawyers.

******

On the jailhouse steps, Ben detained Cassandra there so they could talk in private. "I have sent notice to my attorneys in London to await instructions there about a delicate case I am bringing them."

"Thank you, my darl—"

He held up his hand. "I am willing to do everything in my power to help you and your son, but—" He turned away from her and looked up the street, folding his arms in front of his chest. His face was strained, his lips tightly set.

"Ben." She touched his elbow and he half turned back to her. "Listen to me." She lowered her voice to a whisper. "I do not know how the thing works, only that in America, there had been rumors of scientists or alchemists, I do not know what you would call them, experimenting with strange ideas."

He regarded her uneasily, and she wondered if she was making matters worse.

"Enough," he said. "Best not to speak more of it now."

They went inside and he told James about getting legal counsel, but cautioned him to say nothing, to him or anyone else in the presence of the police, about the object.

That evening in her suite, Cassandra sent a note off to Lady Holcomb, by way of the maid, not having the courage to go upstairs and look her friend in the face. In it, she apologized as best she could for whatever discomfort she had put the lady and her daughter through, and asked her to pass those sentiments on to Edward Clarke. She told her that James was being taken to London, but that she was sure they'd have the whole "misunderstanding" straightened out soon, and that she hoped to see her back in Hampshire before too long.

A quarter of an hour later, the maid returned with a reply.

Mrs. Franklin,

Lady Charles is still extremely upset about the incident and Elizabeth so hysterical that a doctor was finally called in. I just want to warn you that Lady Charles is planning to write to Sir Robert at Parliament to see if he can influence the proceedings against your son. I received the impression that the family may abandon their lengthy stay in Bath so that they can go to London and be present at the trial as witnesses.

Jane, Edward, and I are removing to Hampshire very shortly and are in a great rush to organize our things so you will forgive me for not stopping by to bid you farewell.

I wish you and your son good luck,
Lady Charlotte Holcomb

Cassandra sat, holding the letter in her hand, tears running down her cheeks. Her friends were abandoning them. Her fear for James rose up through her throat and spilled out in sobs. She felt utterly alone and could only think of one thing, to get to London, to the portal exit.

Early the following morning, James was transported to London. The chief constable allowed the Franklins to ride together in their own coach, a privilege befitting their class, yet accompanied by four guards on horseback. Ben rode behind in his phaeton.

The trip to London was a full day. When they arrived, the coach was directed to the police station where James would stay one night. In the morning, he would be taken to Millbank prison. Cassandra tearfully said goodbye to him, promising to be there in the morning for his transport, and slipped him a tiny packet of bug powder for the night, which he pocketed.

Ben led Cassandra to one of the finest hotels in London, and saw to it that she was ensconced with all her luggage and a hired personal maid. He then went to the townhouse he kept in the city.

Was this the time, she wondered, staring blankly out the hotel window, to try to use the portal exit? No. There was nothing they could do tonight. She knew that when she went back through the portal, several hours of planning would be required to find a solution to the dilemma they were in, and she had to be there for James tomorrow when he was taken to Millbank. She would have to plan her trip to the portal exit for when she could get there unseen and not be missed, possibly for a full day.

In the morning, Cassandra arrived at the central London police station where James was held, ready to accompany him on his move to the prison, but they would not allow her to go along, instructing her instead to arrive three hours hence, after he had been properly processed. Cassandra did as instructed and discovered upon her approach to the prison, driving down the same road she'd taken when she left London the January before, that the long expanse of brick wall that had made her feel so uneasy then was the exterior wall of the massive complex. The intimidating fortress of brick and iron, practically new with parts still under construction, was situated in the southern part of London, along the Thames near Vauxhall Bridge. Cassandra knew from her research that according to the progressive nineteenth-century British penal philosophy, prisoners were separated into sections of the facility according to their class, and each prisoner had to have their own cell to avoid negatively influencing each other.

Her carriage deposited her at the entrance, where she was met by a guard and taken inside, through a series of anterooms, and asked to sign her name. She had her purse briefly checked, as well as the satchel she had brought containing James' clothes and personal effects. She was then led across an eerily empty courtyard, through another building, across another courtyard, and into yet another building and through various hallways and up and down stairs until finally arriving at James' cell. She knew she would never be able to find her way in or out again without an escort.

She was relieved to find that James had been taken to the highest stratum of the prison class level and provided with a relatively comfortable, clean cell. In it, there was a narrow bed, a small desk and chair, a small round table with two chairs to accommodate visitors, and a narrow dresser for clothing, above which hung a mirror. There was also a cabinet for the chamber pot. He'd been informed that once a week the gentlemen prisoners were allowed a bath. The rest of the time they washed with a pitcher and basin on a stand. Cassandra appreciated how irksome this would be for James, given his penchant for bathing. Once a day the prison barber came in to shave the gentlemen prisoners, and once every two weeks they received a haircut.

Cassandra had brought some of the bug powder to James, stored in a pocket of her dress, and she promised to bring back with her the next day several books and a supply of appetizing foods. James informed her that the food they had given him that morning wasn't too bad, and there was an abundance of it. He had no fear of starving, but welcomed whatever she might bring. Cassandra had proof of what he told her when they served her and her son a midday meal of roast beef, potatoes, bread, butter, ale, apples and cheese that was surprisingly palatable.

An hour later, Ben and his team of barristers arrived for a conference. The three lawyers had been allowed to examine the evidence and now huddled together on the edge of the bed, wearing white wigs and black robes—looking like nervous vultures. First they asked James to explain to them, as plainly as he could, what the device was and how it worked. During lunch, Cassandra and James had tried to nail down some conceivable explanation. The best they could come up with was that James worked with an American inventor at Harvard, a fellow student. He was a genius, almost mad. He had figured out how to make an alloy of metals found in the American soil that actually magnetized music. It drew music into the tiny box, and the heat of your finger touching it released the music, but only into the head of the person who pressed the button. It was not witchcraft, but science. The strange instrument they heard (James' aether-guitar), he explained, was a Native American instrument, given to him by an Indian he had once met. (The PAL was currently programmed by James to play only the one song over and over, a love song he'd once written to a girlfriend and recorded. He could easily command it by voice to play any of the hundreds of thousands of songs, simms, virtual reality movies, and games. The central button, a manual feature, wasn't even necessary, but James hadn't showed the voice feature to Elizabeth, figuring it would be too incomprehensible for her.)

Once James had finished with his explanation, the barristers stared at him blankly. They promptly excused themselves, saying they were going to begin working on the case. Cassandra kissed James goodbye and left with Ben. He had ridden to Millbank with the barristers and so accompanied Cassandra back in her carriage. The ride into the center of the city took about a half an hour. They rode together silently. Cassandra didn't know what to say. She couldn't tell if Ben had believed the story or not.

When they were nearing her hotel, Ben turned to her and quietly asked if she would agree to have dinner with him. She timidly assented. He directed the driver to take them to a small pub he knew of. They found a table toward the back of the room near the fire. The place was clean, the wooden tables freshly scrubbed, and the plank floor recently swept. The ceiling was low, plastered, and whitewashed. A plump, middle-aged woman with a friendly smile, a neat bun, and a spotless, sky-blue apron took their order of meat pies, roasted squash, and two pints of stout ale. After a few moments of strained silence, concentrating on their drink, Ben reached out and grasped Cassandra's hand. Cassandra looked up at him and her eyes filled with tears.

"My darling," he said to her, leaning close. "Do not cry; I am so sorry for my abominable behavior."

"You have every right," replied Cassandra. "You should not have to be involved in this awful situation."

"Just tell me," he said, "that you did not know about the device and I shall be satisfied."

"All I knew," she said as sincerely as possible, "is that James had begun working on something with this friend he speaks of. Though James is a history major, he has always been interested in the scientific world. Before I left America, he confided in me that they were working on this miraculous device. I told him to be careful—that people would associate such a thing with alchemy or worse, but he said they would not show it to anyone. That is all I know. I do not know if the thing really works as he says it does. I have no idea. I am truly baffled by it myself—"

"That is all I needed to hear, my love. Do not worry; we will get through this. It will be all right, you shall see."

"But how do you know?" she pleaded. "I cannot imagine that a judge will believe his story. It is, frankly, unbelievable, even to me. What will they do to him?"

"Well—" he said uncertainly.

"They will not hang him, will they?" she cried in terror.

"Oh, no, my love," he assured her. "That punishment is reserved for thieves and murderers. We are much more rational about these things than Americans are."

"Oh," she sighed in relief. "Well, what will they do? Sentence him to prison for years?"

"I do not know, really." He examined the back of his hand. "But do not worry. My attorneys are very good; they will think of something."

Cassandra remained unconvinced. "Ben, there is something I need to tell you. Before leaving Bath, I received a note from Lady Holcomb, informing me that Lady Charles was planning to come to London with Elizabeth so that they can serve as witnesses for the prosecution. They may already be here. She also said that they plan to get Sir Robert to try to use his influence in Parliament to sway the case."

"Really! Well I would not worry too much about Sir Robert. He is a big blowhard, and not taken very seriously in government. I am sure he tells his wife otherwise, though, and she believes him since she is totally ignorant of the affairs of state. However, having those two women offer themselves as witnesses would be very bad indeed. It could mean the death knell for James."

"The death knell?" she shrieked. Other patrons of the pub turned to look at them.

"No, no, no, terrible choice of words! I am sorry. I only meant that the prosecution would certainly win."

"Good God," Cassandra whispered.

"Tomorrow morning, however, I will inform my attorneys about this bit of information. They must know of it in preparing the case."

"Yes, of course," she said, not really listening. She could now only focus on the portal exit, on getting the device, and getting James home somehow.

They finished their meal, both deep in thought. Finally, Ben leaned across the table and kissed her. "I have missed being with you," he said.

"Yes," she replied, "I wish we had never left Selborne." Although, she thought, James probably would have screwed up anyway, as long as Elizabeth Charles had been around.

"Still," he continued, "we must not do anything that might be construed as improper while this trial is underway, or it could hurt James even more. We must continue to seem like friends only...or mostly." He kissed her again.

"You are right." she said, "perhaps we should go. I am exhausted, and I want to get up tomorrow and go back to see James. I do not want him to be lonely."

"I will be there with you as much as I can," he said and squeezed her hand.

In the enclosed carriage, Ben attacked Cassandra with kisses. His affection was a comfort to her, but her resolve to get to the portal exit took precedence over all other thoughts. After dropping Ben at his townhouse, she instructed the driver to go around to Covent Garden so she could take a look down the alley where the portal resided. The street was dark; the street lamps provided little light. As the carriage rattled past the alleyway, dim lights from the thick windows of the buildings on either side were enough for her to make out the shapes of people huddled in the dark. Between the shapes, she could see a tiny fire glowing. It would not do. She could not confront vagrants on her own. Perhaps if she tried to go in the daytime.

The next morning at the prison, she, James, and Ben were informed by the head barrister that the trial was set for two weeks from that day, which was a Tuesday. James assured his mother that he was reasonably comfortable, though bored, and Cassandra vowed to be there every day to keep him company. He seemed calm; Cassandra thought he trusted that the lawyers would be successful. She did not tell him what she was planning.

She left just after noon, complaining of a headache and sore throat. Ben stayed, his violin in tow, to keep James company and help pass the hours.

When she arrived at the hotel, the clerk peeked at her from the top of a newspaper he was reading. The headline screamed: AMERICAN ALCHEMIST TERRIFIES HAMPSHIRE RESIDENTS. Cassandra stopped in her tracks and approached the clerk.

"Could I borrow that paper?" she asked with as much superiority as she could muster. The clerk mutely nodded and handed it over, pulling back his hand abruptly when it accidentally touched hers.

She took the paper and hurried to her suite to read it. The article claimed that a strange object was found on the perpetrator, which conjured music out of thin air with the purpose of driving mad anyone who touched it.

```
James Franklin, student at
Harvard University in
Massachusetts, allegedly
attempted to bewitch the daughter
of prominent Parliament member,
Sir Robert Charles, last week
during an outing near Bath.
The victim's mother commented:
'We were shocked, I tell you,
absolutely shocked, that this
young man, who seemed so polite
and good-natured, would in fact
be harboring evil in the form of
this horrible thing, which poured
a terrible kind of hideous fairy
music into my daughter's lovely
```

```
head. He practically admitted
that he was trying to enchant her
to come away with him to America,
where he was planning to ensconce
her in his sorcerer's lair, never
to return her to England or her
family. I know how overpowering
the spell was. He forced the
music into my head as well, and I
was almost overcome—almost
permanently driven mad, as was
his intention—but fortunately, I
have a strong will and was able
to fight it off."
The mother of the accused, a Mrs.
Cassandra Franklin currently
residing in Hampshire, our
sources tell us, was unavailable
for comment.
```

"How do they know whether I'm unavailable for comment?" Cassandra threw the paper down in disgust. This was terrible, she thought despondently with her head in her hands. If this was the kind of thing that Lady Charles was planning to say in court, they were lost. Even worse, if the beautiful Elizabeth agreed to give her version of the story, however warped that might be, the judge would not be able to resist her. Add to that Sir Robert's connection, and whatever clout he might carry (regardless of Ben's indications otherwise), and there would simply be no defense. She and James were nobodies in England, especially compared to the Charles family. Not to mention the fact that the prosecution would definitely produce the object for evidence. The public would be terrified. She had to act now.

She threw on her cloak and hurried down the marble staircase of the hotel to the lobby. As she approached the first floor, she heard someone mention her name.

"I am sorry, sir," the desk clerk was saying, "I am not at liberty to divulge that information."

Both the clerk and the man he was speaking to glanced up to see her descend the last few stairs.

"Mr. Stockard!" she cried.

"Mrs. Franklin!" he replied. "You are just the person I was looking for!"

"I am? Why, how did you know where to find me?"

"I, um—" he glanced at the clerk. "It is a long story. But you will be glad to know that this fine gentleman would not be persuaded to admit that you were staying here."

"It is my job to protect the privacy of our guests, sir," the man said defensively, "even if—"

"And a fine job you did," Mr. Stockard said, cutting him off with a wan smile. "You should be commended."

Mr. Stockard turned to Cassandra. "I have a carriage waiting outside. Would you care to accompany me back to my shop? I have something pressing to speak to you about."

Cassandra was baffled. What pressing business could the man possibly have with her? Something concerning sheet music? No, it must be about James, or perhaps Ben. Her heart began to pound. She opened her mouth to speak.

"It would be better," Mr. Stockard said, "if we could speak privately."

"Very well then, let us go."

They stepped into the coach. "Mr. Stockard," Cassandra began, "I do not understand. Why were you looking for me?"

The coach lurched and began to traverse the ten or so blocks to the music shop.

"It concerns this business in the papers about you and your son."

"And what have you to do with it?" she said. She wondered if she should ask the coachman to stop. She didn't need this man prying into her affairs.

"Nothing. I only want to talk to you."

"How did you know where to find me?"

218

"Because of the article. I knew you were here in London, so I went to the White Hart and asked if you were staying there, and they said you were not. I simply tried the better hotels, inquiring after you in each one. I said I was your brother, and it was a family emergency. It did not take me long."

"I still do not understand why you were looking for me."

He hesitated, looking into her eyes for a moment. "I only thought that maybe I could help you."

The coach stopped in front of the music store, and the driver came around to open the door.

Cassandra and Mr. Stockard stepped out, and he unlocked the door of the shop. Cassandra took a deep breath as she walked inside. There was that same familiar and welcoming smell, that enveloping calm.

"Come," he said to her, "sit down." He motioned to one of the well-worn chairs that were scattered about the shop. "Let me get you some tea. Please, relax a minute." She started to object, but he was already gone to the back of the shop and in a moment returned with tea and pastries. She realized she was hungry, so she sat down impatiently and bit into a scone. He pulled up a chair and gazed at her intently. After a moment, he said, "The audio link, is it an R-10 model?"

Her jaw dropped in astonishment, and, struggling not to choke on her scone, quickly grabbed for her tea, knocking it to the floor.

Just as quickly, her host casually tossed a napkin over the spill. "Nicholas Stockard, time traveler," he said, holding out his hand to her and smiling mischievously.

She swallowed. "What? But—" She numbly shook his hand and stared at him in disbelief. "But, who is your team? When did you come here?"

"I am independently funded, you might say."

"Why have I not ever heard of you?"

"Our organization is private. We do not publish our work. We were just within reach of the breakthrough, back in 2090, when Carver beat us to it. We were disappointed, but we kept at it and accomplished it a year later."

"I did not know anyone else was traveling," she said. "Professor Carver owns all the rights to the invention."

"That is why we did it in secret," he said, but hurriedly added, "besides, our process is slightly different, so we are not technically infringing on his patents. Anyway, my team is now defunct. There is no competition with Carver anymore, at least as far as I know."

"But wait a minute," she said suddenly. "Why are you here—with this shop?"

"I came back to this time to live."

"Your team does not maintain a portal exit for you?"

"No. I told you, there is no team anymore."

"But, did you not ever plan to leave?"

"No," he answered, shifting in his chair. "I had my reasons for wanting to stay. My whole life I have been in love with the nineteenth century. I chose the pre-Victorian era to avoid getting caught up in the industrial revolution. I am set here. I have a house in the country where I go periodically, as well as one in town. I have been happy, mostly."

"How long have you been here?"

"Ten years."

"You are joking!"

"No, I thought I was in it for life. But the day you came into my shop, I realized that another traveler had arrived, and I started thinking about hitching a ride home. I just did not know how I would find you again, until Johnston wrote me and mentioned your name. I could not believe the coincidence, and I was determined to get down to Hampshire to see you."

"But how did you know I was a time traveler?"

"When I saw you back in January, I thought you looked familiar. Of course I had seen pictures of you in the scientific publications with Carver's team, and was familiar with the members' names. Then you said your name was Cassandra, and you used your husband, Franklin Reilly's, first name as your last. I remember reading about his work. What did he think of you and your son making this trip, by the way?"

"He passed away more than five years ago."

"I am sorry. I had no idea."

"Do not worry yourself."

There was a pause. He pressed on. "A couple of other clues gave you away. Your white teeth, your accent, and... your mention of Schubert."

"Yes, I remember that blunder."

"Well, no harm done."

"You must think we are a bunch of idiots, James bringing that damned thing, and then exposing it! He was not even supposed to be here; he came to check on me, so he said. He really just wanted in on the action."

"But what possessed him to show the music player to someone?"

"He was trying to impress a girl," said Cassandra glumly.

Mr. Stockard laughed. "That figures."

"I did not know what to make of you when you suddenly dropped in on Mr. Johnston, and we dined together that day at Gatewick House. I felt like there was something strange about you, Nicholas. May I call you Nicholas?"

"Nick."

"Nick, the timing is perfect. You are here and I need your help."

"I will do anything I can."

"James is going to trial in two weeks. The defense is almost nonexistent. The lawyers have no idea what to do or say, and there are of course witnesses—I am afraid he will be sentenced to that place forever!"

"They will most likely send him to Australia," stated Nick.

"Oh my God!" she cried.

"Yes, it is their new system. They only keep prisoners around for three months or so after sentencing; then they send them off as indentured servants. Eventually, they can work off their debt to society and become free men. Not the truly violent, of course, but anyone else who is sentenced for a very long term, which your son may be."

"Dear God, what will we do?" she exclaimed, now truly in a panic. "I was just on my way to my portal exit, when I saw you at the hotel. If it is clear, I will go back through and try to and get some help."

"You have an exit nearby?"

"Yes, just a few blocks away."

"Then there is only one thing to do. We must get the device and get your son out of prison and to the exit, right away."

"How?"

"Getting James out will be tough, but getting the device will be tougher. You do need to go back to 2120 and get some help from your team. They will have ideas and the tools to implement them. However, James' life takes precedence over getting the player back. If we have to leave it, we will, though it would best not to."

"I should say."

"All right, we must get you through the exit. Are you ready?"

"Yes, absolutely."

"Good. Now let me see, what kinds of things would be helpful for James' escape?" he asked himself. "I am thinking of a laser saw, the smaller the better, and whatever else you think of that may be of help, but only if it can be well hidden or disguised. You may have to be gone overnight, but no longer."

She suddenly thought of Ben. "Um, Mr. Johnston may be looking for me tonight," she said with a blush.

"Are you involved with him, if you do not mind my asking?"

"Um, yes, well, kind of. I mean, yes, I am."

"Cassandra!" he said teasingly, "One of the first rules of time travel—"

"I know, I know, it is just that he might panic if he thinks I am missing."

"I knew something was going on between you two."

"We can talk about that another time. Let us deal with this right now."

"All right, here," he said handing her some note paper and a quill, "write him a note. Say you are too sick to see him or something, and I will drop it by your hotel and leave it with the front desk. You can make something up to explain later."

"Perfect! I already mentioned this morning that I did not feel well." Cassandra wrote the note out, then she and Nick walked to Covent Garden to the location of the portal exit. It was almost dark. A few beggars were still loitering about at the back of the alley. The pungent smells of London wafted through the air.

"I will cause a distraction, and you go," he said. "Let us decide to meet back here at seven AM. In other words, I will be here to make sure the coast is clear, and you have got thirteen hours to get anything you think will be helpful. But remember: Do not bring anything that cannot be easily concealed. All we need is to be caught with another inexplicable object. Also, do not bring anyone back with you. It is too risky to involve anyone else, and there is not time to prepare them. Ready?"

"Yes," she said steadily.

"All right, then." He stalked boldly into the alleyway. "You there!" he called to the vagrants. They were startled. "Clear out, now, be gone, private property, come on, move along!" He was so forceful that the beggars immediately scurried out of the alley, grumbling as they went. Cassandra ran to the back of the alley, and after a moment, disappeared.

Blackness. She felt the familiar dizziness—vertigo, like the world was dropping out from under her. She felt the need to grab onto something, that she was falling, falling, but there was nothing to hold onto. Then she was being pulled and lifted, hurtled forward. It was like being in a speeding train but with no seat or floor or walls about her. Her training reminded her to take deep breaths, keep her eyes closed, and stay focused on her heartbeat, which was pounding in her chest. On the inside of her eyelids, she could perceive the bright lights of eons flashing past. It was ill advised to look; the swirling lights could further disorient you. She felt sweat break out on her brow. Then nausea. Breathe, breathe, she told herself. It will be over soon. Traveling farther into the past meant that the journey through the portal took longer, and she had only traveled this far once before, after all. The journey took about a minute in all, though to her it felt much longer. If I can just keep from throwing up, she thought.

CHAPTER FOURTEEN

Jake was on duty to monitor the other end of the portal. He had just finished a meal of fish and chips and had begun to doze off. Suddenly, lights flashed and alarms sounded, alerting him that there was an exact match to Cassandra's proportions.

He roused himself at once. "Hey!" he yelled to the other team members lounging around at the front of the lab. "It's Cassandra!"

He activated the travel mode, and in seconds the pod was humming. Her form appeared one minute later. As the opaque door slid open, they all ran to help her out.

"Quiet, quiet!" yelled Jake. "Someone transmit to Professor Carver! Cassandra, my God, what's happened? Are you all right?"

"James…" she stammered.

"Where's James? Is he okay?"

"He has been arrested!" she managed to blurt out.

"Oh, no!" responded Jake. "Come on, come sit down. Do you need something to eat? Someone get her some water!"

Jake led her over to a sofa and sat her down, while handing her the glass.

"Listen, I am in a hurry. I have a lot to tell you and we have a lot to do, and we have until exactly seven tomorrow morning."

Jake glanced at his watch. It was just past six in the evening. "Okay, go. We'll get to work, and when Professor Carver gets here, we'll fill him in so he can see if we missed anything."

Cassandra laid out the situation fully. Though everyone was shocked that James had brought the music player, no one was surprised he had used it to impress a woman. There was amazement all around that a time traveler was already living in the nineteenth century, and Cassandra briefly related Nick's background as far as she knew it. She explained to them that she and Nick planned to break James out of prison and that they also had to think of a way to dispose of the music player.

"The prison is divided into class sections, and the guards of the section for the upper class are more lax than the others," Cassandra continued. "We just have to get to him, get him out and back to the portal exit before being caught. Nick is coming back with him, by the way."

"He is? For good?" asked Jake.

"So he says."

"What about you?"

Cassandra hesitated, "I do not know. I do not think so, I mean, I want to finish my year out and I have some loose ends. But let us not worry about that now. I shall figure it out. We need to think about what else might be useful in getting James out of the prison undetected, but we also need to focus on eliminating the device."

The scientists put their heads together to confer, and decided that they first needed to see the layout of the prison. Jake spoke his request into his console, and in a moment the team was able to gather around a miniature hologram of Millbank. It was six stories high and resembled a wagon wheel. There was a guard post in the middle of a central courtyard, surrounded by a pentagon-shaped building.

Attached to the center pentagon by corridors were six other pentagons, each with its own courtyard and center guard post. A twelve-foot wall surrounded the entire structure.

His cell should be approximately here," said Cassandra, pointing to a window on the second story of the back left pentagon. "He is definitely on an outer wall, here at the back. It is the area of lowest security."

"This thing is impressive," said Jake looking at the model with awe. "You're going to have to determine exactly which window it is from the outside."

"Right," she said, "I can figure that out the next time I go visit him."

"Okay then, you're going to need a ladder."

"A nanofiber ladder would be best," Cassandra stated. "At least fifteen feet long. Inactivated, it will be tiny and easy to carry. It will just look like a ball of yarn."

"I'll put in a transmit," said Suhan, a small, slim female scientist of Turkish descent.

Cassandra went on. "Nick mentioned that we would need a laser saw, and another thing that would be helpful is lightweight black clothing, including night vision hoods."

Jake shook his head. "You're going back with a lot of gadgets. What'll you do if you get caught?"

Cassandra looked up at him. "If we are well prepared, we will not get caught."

"You have a point. Someone get a hold of Shannon and have her start whipping up the black period clothing and tell her to get the fabric for the hoods as well." He turned to a young team member named Simon. "Do you know anything about that molecular dissolution compound that the World Space Organization was working on a few years ago?"

"Not a lot," Simon replied, "but I'll find out." He pushed his curly, white-blond hair out of the way and activated the button resting in his ear with a turn of his wrist.

"I was thinking," Jake continued, returning his attention to Cassandra, "that if you had some of that compound, you could use it to simply *evaporate* things, like the saw and the ladder in case you're apprehended. I don't know exactly how the stuff works, or even how to use it, so that it doesn't dissolve everything it comes in contact with. We'll need to find out."

"About the saw," said Suhan, wandering over from the corner where she'd been talking on her transmit. "I was thinking. Rather than slicing the bars, which would freak people out once they saw the results of the laser saw, how about using a V-FOG?" Her intelligent black eyes flashed.

"A what?" said Cassandra.

A Variable Frequency Oscillation Generator. It's what was used several years back to dislocate telephone poles from their bases easily, when so many countries were getting rid of them. I spent time overseeing some of those construction projects."

"But I don't understand—"

"You can attach it to the glass of the prison window and it will shatter it within seconds. Then, you can attach it to the bars and it will shake them loose from the cement. When the authorities discover the breakout, they will puzzle that the bars could be pulled loose, but it will seem more explainable than if they've been cut cleanly and perfectly. No device that existed back then could do that."

"Excellent idea," said Jake. "How big are they?"

"Oh, they vary in size according to need. You could get a very small one for this. It just looks like a black box to the untrained eye."

"Can you try to drum one up?" he asked.

"On it." She quickly pulled her long, black hair back into a ponytail with a band from around her wrist and activated her transmit again.

At that moment Professor Carver strode in with a calm that belied the desperate situation. He had been filled in via transmit.

"Cassie, my dear!" he called out as he entered the lab. His considerable height gave him a commanding presence. She stood and moved toward him, taking in the comforting warmth of his brown eyes, his milk chocolate skin subtly creased with age, the gray of the close cut hair around his temples. He clasped her hands and held her at arm's length. "Look at you!" he cried, "you look like you just stepped out of a nineteenth century painting. Living in the past seems to agree with you."

She smiled warmly and hugged him. "Oh, Elton, it is so good to see you." Tears formed in her eyes.

"Now, now, we'll figure this out. That's what we do." He glanced appreciatively at the image of Millbank prison hovering over the coffee table in the lab's lounge area. "Simon's been in communication with me moment to moment with breakdowns on your progress, and it all sounds good so far. I'm going to start working on getting rid of the device. All right," he said removing his jacket and rolling up his sleeves. "I need the exact mineral and chemical components of that music player. It must be the precise make and model that James possesses."

One of the scientists leapt to a computer station and within seconds, the information the professor requested was hovering in the air for him to examine. "Great, I'll work on this. You all go back to figuring out how to get that boy out of prison."

Cassandra exhaled, feeling like she had been holding her breath for days. She realized that she was starting to feel that she had some control over the situation. After two hours, the team of scientists had rounded up the V-FOG and the ladder. Shannon had arrived and was furiously working on the clothes, with the proportions she had on file of Cassandra and James, and approximating those of Nick, based on Cassandra's description of him.

The other scientists were dispersed about, transmitting and discussing other possibilities. Cassandra was still gazing at the virtual reality prison, catching snatches of conversation from the others, her own ideas percolating. She got up from the lounge sofa and approached Jake where he sat at the computer with Professor Carver.

"Jake, I just thought of something," she said to him. "What about a sound blocking machine. Like musicians use to keep from disturbing their neighbors? I have one by my bed in Boston. It can be set to block sounds either from coming into or going out from around a thirty foot radius. They are available at any techtronics store, and they are tiny. I think it could be really useful. We can activate it when we go over the wall. No one will hear anything even when we shake loose the bars."

"Good," responded Jake, "Suhan! Can you arrange for that? The smallest one available."

"No problem!" replied Suhan.

"And how about this," Jake continued. "Do you have any of your sleep formula left?"

"Yes, why?"

"It's applied like perfume, right? If you touch it to your skin, it enters the bloodstream quickly. If you brought it along, and someone caught you, you'd just touch them with the wand, and they'd be asleep in minutes—eight hours worth," he declared with a smirk.

"Oh my goodness, you are right! I have plenty left! I hardly ever use it."

"Perfect!"

"Okay, everyone, listen," announced Professor Carver. "I have the exact magnetic match to the elements contained in the R-20 PAL. We're going to use the dissolution compound that Jake was talking about and add the magnetic elements that will find and attach themselves to the player, and only the player. One of you will have to get into the vicinity of the R-20," he said to Cassandra, "and spray the compound into the air. The microscopic particles will find it, wherever it is, and dissolve it completely."

"That is amazing," she said. "How close will we have to be?"

"I don't know yet, we'll have to test it."

"Simon! How long 'til we have that compound?" Jake bellowed.

"It'll be here in an hour."

"What time is it?" Professor Carver said to himself, checking his watch. "Almost nine. That won't give us a lot of time, so let's make sure we have everything else we need ready to go, including a perfume atomizer. The particular magnetic elements and a neutral liquid base to contain them can be easily assembled at the main lab...Yoshi!" The tall, wiry scientist came rushing over to the Professor. "Here take these specs to the lab. I want you back here with that compound within an hour."

"Yessir!"

"I'm also going to need one of the R-20 PALs. Does anyone have one?"

Every member of the team pulled one of the devices out of his or her pocket. Professor Carver laughed. "Good. We may need more than one guinea pig."

All of the necessary items and compounds had been assembled for the professor to begin working on the spray. The rope ladder, the V-FOG, the sound blocking machine, and the base form of the dissolving liquid in an authentic looking dropper bottle, so they could dispose of all the gadgets if necessary, had been deposited into a small satchel. Shannon was almost finished with the clothes and the hoods.

A wide array of fast food had been brought in so they could all remain energized while working. It all tasted incredibly strange to Cassandra's altered palate. It was as if it had no real flavor. She didn't say it out loud, but she couldn't believe that the team members would eat the kind of junk food that she normally wouldn't have touched, even in 2120. She had never realized that it so little resembled real food. She felt herself becoming anxious to return to the past that now felt like home.

The minutes ticked by. Close to midnight, Professor Carver turned to Cassandra from the adjustments he was making on the spray. It wasn't yet working to his satisfaction.

"Cassie, I think I'm getting close with this stuff. Don't worry; it'll be ready on time. Why don't you go in the back and lie down? You need to get a little rest. There's nothing more you can do right now."

She suddenly realized she was exhausted. "Well, all right."

"We'll wake you up in plenty of time," he assured her.

Shannon came over and sat down next to her, her full lips pressed firmly together, her square jaw set, and her dark eyes exuding concern. She breathed deeply through her nose and then spoke. "You know Cass, I have one of the gowns here you didn't take before. Why don't you take a shower and change into it when you wake up. It'll make you feel better."

Yoshi, Simon, and Suhan glanced hopefully in Cassandra's direction. She realized that her standards of cleanliness no longer matched those of the twenty-second century. She hadn't had a bath in three days, and she had worn her gown more than a few times without washing it. It occurred to her that she really didn't notice body odor any more.

"Good idea," she said to Shannon, "I do not even remember what it feels like to have a shower." She went into the back room, undressed to her underwear, and lay down on the cot. She thought she was too anxious to sleep, but when there was a gentle knock on the door, it was already six AM. Shannon peeked in.

"Everything's ready, Cass. You might want to shower quickly so the Professor can go over everything one more time. Here's your gown." It was a shimmering brown taffeta, a little formal for the occasion, but it was clean. Shannon also handed her a clean set of underclothing.

"Thank you," Cassandra said to her.

She walked into the small bathroom, peeled off her underthings and pushed a button in the modest shower stall. She appreciated as never before the technology which sent a perfectly modulated stream of hot water flowing over her body, followed by a gentle cleanser mixed into the water, followed by plain water again, followed by hot air to perfectly dry her skin, hair and the shower stall itself. She thought, I wonder if I shall ever take this for granted again.

When she entered the main room of the lab, she received smiles of approval. She looked around the room to see six or seven R-20 players in various degrees of dissolution lying about.

"We finally got it!" declared Professor Carver. "Watch this." He aimed a blue glass atomizer in the direction of one of the partially dissolved players twenty feet away. He sprayed a substance into the air, which invisibly traveled across the room. The half-dissolved player then broke up completely into tiny particles and floated away like dust.

"Fantastic!" exclaimed Cassandra.

"Why don't you eat a little breakfast, Cassie, while we double check your bags?"

She nibbled on an unappetizing muffin while she went through the check with the team. The atomizer was added to the satchel with the other items, and another small bag was filled with the black clothing and hoods.

"Remember," said Professor Carver, "you've got to get within twenty feet of the player for the magnetic molecules to find it. I know that will be tricky, but it's the best we could do."

"Do not worry," said Cassandra, "we will figure out how to get close to it." She glanced at the time display hovering above the computer panel. "It is time. I cannot begin to thank you all for everything. I have never been so grateful to work with this team."

"Don't mention it," said Jake.

She threw her cloak over her shoulders and grabbed the satchels. "Hopefully, you will be seeing James and Nick very shortly. I will send a message back with them letting you know what I am going to do, but if all goes well, you will see me again in January."

"Okay, we'll be ready for whatever happens. Good luck!" Professor Carver gave her a kiss on the cheek, and she stepped into the module. The coordinates had already been set. Simon activated the travel mode, the machine hummed, and she was gone.

CHAPTER FIFTEEN

When she emerged from the portal exit, Cassandra could just perceive Nick through the fog, standing at the end of the alley by the street, keeping a lookout.

"Nick!" she called to him softly. He ran back to her and took the bags out of her hands.

"Thank God," he said, and then stopped and stared at her for a moment.

"What?" She asked, alarmed.

"You look great!" he said, "and you smell amazing."

"It's called a shower, and a clean change of clothes."

"Lucky you. I can hardly remember what it is like to have a shower."

"It was incredible. Anyway, let's get out of here."

They walked quickly to Nick's store and locked the door behind them. Cassandra showed Nick the things she had brought. He was thrilled with her success, and truly impressed by the ingenuity of her team.

"Yes, they are absolutely top notch," Cassandra remarked. They then fell to discussing their plan. They decided that she would visit James that morning to inform him of the plan. That very evening after midnight, they'd break him out.

"Cassandra, you are going to have to wait with the carriage. There is no point in both of us going in. It will be much less conspicuous if just one of us goes in to get him. I think I am the better candidate. I mean, I am not trying to be sexist, but do you not agree it is more of a man's job?"

"I think you are probably stronger and quicker if that is what you mean."

"Good," he said.

"But I do not know how to drive a carriage," she worried.

"You do not have to drive it, just hold the horses there. If anyone threatening approaches you, put them to sleep. We should both have some of the elixir on us. Also, we shall situate you far enough away so that you will not seem suspicious."

"But not too far."

"Agreed."

Once all of the details were worked out, Cassandra went back to her hotel to send a note to Ben. There was one waiting there from him, a worried missive, wondering if she was all right. She replied:

My Dearest Ben,

I am so sorry to have caused you concern. I am indeed, quite ill—worse than before. I am determined to go briefly to see James this morning, and then must stay in and should not receive visitors—I especially do not want to infect you. I will send word the moment I am on the mend for I loathe to be without you so long.

Yours,

Cassandra

That sent, she changed into a simpler dress and had herself driven out to Millbank. She and James whispered in French to not be understood by the guards and other prisoners (they both knew enough to communicate basically – Virtual Enhanced Learning Environments in many languages were part of all time travelers' training). She told him about their plan and about the dissolving mist for the player. He was excited and scared. James was also concerned how she would get to the device. The lawyers had told them it was still kept at the central police station quite near Covent Garden. She'd have to go there, she said, but not until he was safely through the portal exit. She told him to expect them around three in the morning and snuck his pocket watch to him to keep track of the time.

She went to the window, which was about shoulder height, to determine exactly where his cell was situated. She looked up and noticed a flagpole, sticking out from the roof of the building, flying the Union Jack. His window was five down and three to the left of the pole. They'd have to get it right. She told him to tie a white cloth to the bars, which were set just inside a pane of glass. It would not be seen from the guard's station, but Nick would be able to detect it when he got close enough. Then she kissed her son goodbye and left.

She went back to the hotel to rest. When she got there, there was a little bouquet of autumn flowers waiting for her from Ben with a get well wish. God, he's sweet, she thought. I may never find another one like him. But now wasn't the time to think about it. She was able to sleep for a few hours, eat some supper, and calm herself at the piano.

A knock sounded on her suite door two full hours before she expected Nick. Her maid went to answer it, and in a moment came into the parlor to announce the visitor.

"A Sir Frederick Collins is here to see you, ma'am."

Cassandra was dumbstruck. Sir Frederick Collins? she thought. The Baronet of Sorrel Hall? It couldn't be!

"Please, show him in," Cassandra replied,

A moment later, a short, stout man with spectacles and a smattering of wispy gray and black hair stood before her. He had moved into the room with great purpose and importance, but the moment he registered Cassandra's face, he stopped as if uncertain how to proceed. "G-good evening, Mrs. Franklin," he stammered. "I am Sir Frederick Collins, it is a pleasure to make your acquaintance."

Cassandra was infinitely surprised to finally be meeting the Baronet so unexpectedly, but she composed herself and moved forward with all the grace she could muster, extending her hand to him and smiling. "Sir Frederick! What an immense honor it is to meet you face to face. Please, won't you sit down?" She gestured to a small divan by the fire.

"Um, yes, thank you," he said, not taking his eyes off of her.

"Would you care for a sherry?" she offered.

"Um, no, no, that will not be necessary, I am here, well, rather, that is…I am here on business."

"Sir Frederick," she began, feeling as if perhaps the purpose of his visit was not going to be to her liking, and hoping to distract him. "Before you share the reason for your honoring me this meeting, let me say that I could not be more in debt to you for allowing me to inhabit, truly, one of the most beautiful and elegant homes I have ever in my life been privileged to see. Sorrel Hall has been a veritable heaven to me. Yes, absolute heaven. From the moment I arrived there last January, I have felt that living there was like having my own little piece of paradise. Your and Lady Collins' exquisite taste in décor, your painstaking upkeep of the house and property, your expert staff, have been a joy to my existence each and every day. How can I ever thank you for agreeing to let me reside there this past year?"

The man opened his mouth to speak, closed it, thought for a moment and took a breath. "Well! My goodness. I am so happy that everything has met so much with your approval."

"Beyond that," Cassandra gushed, "Really, beyond that."

"I see, well, um—" He was still staring at her, transfixed. "I only came to say that—"

"Sir Frederick, are you sure I cannot offer you that sherry?"

"Oh," he chuckled nervously, "Maybe after all—"

Cassandra leapt up and rang a bell. "Oh good, I am so glad. On a chilly night like this, there is nothing like it to warm the spirit."

The maid entered. "Regina, could you please bring Sir Frederick a glass of the finest sherry?"

"Yes, ma'am," she replied, and scurried off.

"Now, my dear sir," Cassandra smiled warmly, "won't you please tell me what brings you here this evening?" She sat back in the chair opposite him.

"Well, I…yes." He cleared his throat and lifted his chin. "I, that is, my wife, that is, *we* are anxious over this business with your son, to be quite frank."

Cassandra's look turned to one of eager concern. "Oh, yes," she said. "I am sure you have read of it in the papers. I am so very distressed, as you might imagine. Of course, the whole thing is simply a misunderstanding. You know, in America, things are very different. There are many mysteries as yet unsolved, stemming from the native peoples and their ways."

She rose and walked back and forth before the fire, aware that he was observing her figure as she did so. "I am afraid that my son was curious and got mixed up with those who were experimenting with certain objects and theories. I really do not understand it myself." She went to sit dangerously close to him on the divan and gazed into his eyes. "But I am sure it will be all straightened out in the trial. I know that Lady Charles is a reasonable person, as we all are, and this whole matter will be laid to rest."

"I do c-certainly hope so," he managed to spit out, "because my wife is concerned about our good name, and that of Sorrel Hall, being connected with a scandal, you know."

"Of course. But we are all educated, rational people. Sometimes there is the seemingly inexplicable, but in the end, there is always a logical reason for everything."

Regina came in with the sherry, and Sir Frederick took it from her and slugged down a large gulp.

Cassandra lowered her eyes. "I guess this is a good time to tell you, that I will not be requiring the use of Sorrel Hall after January, but I hope that you will be good enough to let me finish out my year's lease as our attorneys agreed upon. And, as a gesture of good will, I would like to now offer you an additional half-year's rental payment, for your kindness and understanding in this matter. This has been a difficult time for me, and knowing that I have Sorrel Hall to return to when this whole mess is over, is of infinite comfort. I hope you will not refuse me. I feel it is the least I can do for you and Lady Collins, since you have already been so very generous with me." She looked up at him again, deeply into his eyes.

His mouth fell open. "Why, thank you, Mrs. Franklin, that is a most exceptional offer. I am sure my wife will be pleased."

"Very good, then." Cassandra rose. Nick was expected at ten, and she wanted this man gone. "When shall I have the money delivered to you?"

"Whenever it is convenient, I mean, really it is no rush, you know. I am in London for another two weeks on some other business."

"All right then," said Cassandra smiling, "you shall have it in a day or two." She gently took his arm and began walking him toward the parlor door. She leaned in close to him so he could breathe the mild perfume of her soap. He was shorter than her, so his eyes were positioned to easily take in her modest cleavage.

"Thank you so much for this delightful visit," she said. "It has done my heart good to finally meet the man to whom I owe so much of my happiness at Sorrel Hall. I do hope we have the opportunity to meet again."

"Yes, I hope so too," he breathed, looking directly at her breasts. "It has been a delight."

She let go of his arm and offered him her hand to kiss. "If you do not mind," she said, "please leave your address with the clerk downstairs."

"Oh, yes, yes," he said, and he placed a slobbery kiss on her hand.

"By the way," she couldn't help but ask, "how on earth did you know where to find me?"

"Oh, you know," he mumbled. "My attorneys, they have their, ahem, ways."

"Of course," she laughed. "Well good evening." She smiled enchantingly as she slowly closed the door on him, he looking her up and down one last time. She heard Regina helping him with his things, and finally, the outer door closed.

She wiped her hand on her dress. She was not pleased with herself for the disgusting display of feminine wiles, but the performance had been necessary. And of course, the mention of the attorneys and the few hundred pounds didn't hurt either. She took a deep breath. She needed to focus on what lay ahead. She shivered at what she knew she and Nick had to do.

Nick arrived on time, and they spent a couple of hours going over and over the plan. Finally, Cassandra realized there was a snag. What was she going to do with the horses after Nick and James went through the portal exit? But Nick had thought about it. It required Cassandra driving the carriage a few blocks to his store. He had already alerted his shop boy, who was slightly slow-witted, that a lady would bring the horses to the shop early in the morning and ring the bell, and that he was to take the horses and carriage to the stable house. The boy would not ask her any questions. They decided that they would leave for Millbank early, so she could practice driving on the empty streets.

Nick left the hotel around midnight, taking his set of black clothes with him. Cassandra pretended to go to bed, so Regina wouldn't think anything was strange and would go to sleep herself.

At one-thirty, she dressed in her black gown, grabbed her sleep potion, and added it to the satchel of necessities. She crept out of the suite, downstairs, and past the dozing desk clerk. Nick was waiting for her a little ways up the block with his small, enclosed carriage, pulled by only two horses. He was sitting up on the driver's bench and Cassandra climbed on to join him.

Once out of the center of the city, he stopped the carriage and she took the reins. After ten minutes or so, she got the hang of starting, stopping, and turning well enough so she thought she could handle it alone. Nick drove the rest of the way and parked in a humble neighborhood within sight of the prison, but where the carriage could not be seen by the guards. They hugged each other for luck. Nick put on his hood, took the satchel, which now also contained the clothing for James, and headed toward the prison. They were already on the same side of the facility as James' cell.

First Nick extracted the sound blocking machine, activated it, and put it back in the satchel where it would continue to obscure all sound for twenty feet. He used the setting that allowed for no one outside of the radius to hear his actions or speech, though *he* was able to hear both within and without that same radius. As he approached the outer wall of Millbank, he removed the balled-up ladder and grasped a bud on two ends of string, letting the small sphere drop to the ground and unroll. He held it at arm's length, pinched the buds, and the string instantly sprang into an impossibly skinny ladder of fifteen feet, stiff and unbendable. Nick placed it against the wall and began to climb. Though the rungs were only a half an inch wide, they were strong as iron and tacky to the touch. He was on top of the wall in a moment, satchel in hand. He deactivated the ladder, pulled it up, activated it again on the other side of the wall, and climbed down, finally reinstating it to the satchel.

Staying low, he crept up to the building, keeping the flagpole in sight. It was a dark night, and he had to assume the guards were asleep. They had lanterns at their posts, but the feeble candlelight only penetrated a few feet. Once up against the building, and being careful to avoid the first floor windows, he looked up to locate James'. He counted five down and three over from the flag pole, which glimmered faintly at the top of the building. There was just enough starlight to dimly reflect on it and the windows of the prison.

He activated the ladder again and climbed up. The white rag was tied to the bar. He rapped quietly on the window, and James came up to it and waved. Nick motioned him to move back from the window. Secure that his actions couldn't be detected by ear, he removed the V-FOG, attached it to the glass, where it stuck by suction, and activated it by pressing a tiny switch on the side. Within a few seconds, the glass began to vibrate violently. Nick backed a few rungs down and turned his face away. The glass shattered with a pop and glass rained over him. He heard the V-FOG clatter down the ladder and reached out to catch it. He then scurried back up and attached it to the bars with a wire fastener. He activated it again, and again he moved down and out of the way. This time, the shaking created a great grinding noise. The bars fell out of the window in one piece as he swung around to the back of the ladder just in time to avoid being hit. They landed on the ground with thud and the V-FOG deactivated itself. He scrambled back up, threw the black clothing in to James and motioned him to hurry. James put the clothes on over what he was wearing and donned the hood.

"Grab the sheets off your bed!" whispered Nick.

"What? Why?" replied James.

"Just do it!"

James pulled off the rough cotton sheets and, standing on a chair, stuffed them out the window. Nick threw them to the ground. The only thing James took from his cell was his journal and his pocket watch, which he snatched up and stuffed into his shirt. He then clambered out the window, while Nick climbed down the ladder before him.

Just as they reached the ground, Nick put out his hand to stop James. A guard was coming around the side of the building on his rounds, lantern swinging. They stood still, but it was clear that he would collide with them if he didn't see them first. Nick reached in the satchel and pulled out a bottle of sleep elixir. The guard moved to within the sound-proofed area and spotted two black-clad figures, hovering before him like phantoms. Horror stricken, he shouted with alarm, and blew hard on his whistle, though it was unheard by anyone. As he stood uselessly blowing, Nick ran up to him, grabbed his arm, and touched him on his exposed wrist with the sleep elixir. The guard tried to wrench away, but James went to Nick's aid, and they both wrestled the large man to the ground, James kicking over the lantern to extinguish it.

The guard struggled wildly, but not for long. His strength soon began to ebb and within two minutes was fast asleep. Nick grabbed up the sheets and quickly tied them together. He nodded at James, and they ran across the yard to the wall. They easily scaled the ladder up one side and down the other. Nick left the bundle of sheets at the bottom of the wall. James cocked his head inquisitively.

"Let them figure it out," Nick whispered. "At least they can imagine that you used them in some way to get over the wall."

The two men then continued noiselessly to the carriage, where Cassandra sat shivering with cold and anxiety. The men removed their hoods, and Nick helped Cassandra down off the bench and into the coach with her son.

Nick drove while Cassandra sat inside with James, clinging to him and weeping for joy. James was tense, worried that they wouldn't get to the portal exit before they were apprehended. But the streets were bare. It would probably be past daybreak before anyone noticed the sleeping guard or looked in on James' cell. They left the sound blocker engaged until they were well into the center of town.

Once they approached the area around Covent Garden, the wheels began rattling away on the cobblestone streets. Nick pulled up in front of the alleyway. Cassandra and James could just make out, through the carriage windows, the sleeping figures of some ragged men at the far end of the alley. There was the faintest light in the sky.

Nick came around to open the door. He was holding a cello case by the handle.

"What is that?" asked Cassandra.

"My cello."

"I know it is a—"

"I could not leave it behind, so I stuck it in the luggage compartment of the carriage. It is the only thing I am taking back with me."

"Of course," she smiled.

"Hurry now," he said, turning to James. "We have to be careful, though, not to wake the beggars."

"Good-bye, my sweetheart," said Cassandra and clasped her son in her arms.

"Mom, I am so sorry—" he began.

"Shhh," she replied, "I love you so much. You are my boy, and nothing else matters. I am glad we experienced this together."

He hugged and kissed her. "Mom, be careful. Promise me you will be careful. Are you sure you will be all right?"

"Yes. I am going to the police station now. I will just pretend to be an addled woman. You will have to trust, until you see me on January twelfth, that I will be fine. I have Ben to take care of me."

"But you promise you will come back? You will not stay here for love, will you?"

"I promise, James. Nothing is more important than you."

He gave her a wide grin. Nick coughed, looking at the ground, then urged James toward the exit. "Good-bye, Cassandra," he said. They embraced. "Oh, wait!" He took the atomizer out of his satchel. "Do not forget this!"

"Oh my God!" she whispered.

"We have everything else in the bag. I shall be waiting for you to return too," he said fondly. "Maybe I will join the team if they will have me."

"I do not think there is any doubt that they would welcome you." She kissed him on the cheek and he beamed like a schoolboy. "Good-bye," she said. "I shall see you soon. Go!"

The two men crept to the end of the alleyway, carefully avoiding the vagrants, and in seconds, first James, then moments later, Nick, with his cello, disappeared.

Cassandra had to finish the job. She climbed back onto the carriage, and, following Nick's instructions, managed to maneuver the horses a few blocks to the music shop. There was a *Closed* sign on the door. Cassandra imagined that people would wonder about the quiet music seller so mysteriously disappearing the same day as James Franklin. He had told the shop boy in advance that he was leaving, and he had left a letter for him, knowing that the young man's caring mother was just literate enough to understand it. It said, without great explanation, that he had gone back to America. It contained enough money to keep the boy and his family comfortable their whole life. He'd explained to Cassandra that he didn't want to raise suspicions by closing out his bank account, but he had hurriedly left instructions with his attorney the morning before to sell off his property, including the store, pay all his servants a ten-year advance in salary, and give the remainder of the money to charity. He'd sealed the instructions and asked them to open it if they didn't hear from him in a week.

When Cassandra got to the music store and rang the bell, the shop boy appeared, looking sleepy. Cassandra turned the horses and carriage over to him, tipped him, and hurried off to the police station on foot, clutching the atomizer in one hand. She was becoming numb from the cold, but she pressed on. After ten minutes, she arrived at the station. She took a deep breath, flung open the doors, and ran inside.

"Where is the sergeant?" she cried, "I must see the sergeant! There has been a breakout at the prison! Get the sergeant!"

The drowsy station sprang into action, and, as several constables tried to subdue the hysterical lady, the sergeant was summoned. She refused to speak to anyone but him. Rather than sitting quietly in a chair, she leapt up and walked nervously about the station house, muttering something about a strange smell and spraying her atomizer into the air.

Once the sergeant arrived, she insisted on seeing him alone in his office. She looked around the cramped space until she noticed the safe in the corner. She sprayed the atomizer in its direction, knowing the submicroscopic particles would travel inside the safe to where the player must reside.

"Madam, please!" said the sergeant, "would y' stop that? What on earth's the matter?"

"I had a dream!" she shrieked.

"You woke me out of bed and called me here for a dream?"

"Yes, I dreamt that my son, James Franklin, had broken out of prison and was making his way to Ireland. I am desperately worried about him! I fear I will never see him again! Please find him!" She buried her head on the desk and pretended to sob.

"James Franklin? Oh, that sorcerer fellow. We have that witchy thing of his right here in the safe. You are his mother, ay?"

"Yes, yes," she sobbed, "and he is gone! I just know it, gone!"

"Now, now, ma'am, don't you worry. He is safe at Millbank. No one has ever broke outta there. You just go on home now. Gibson!" he called to a constable. "Get Mrs. Franklin a cab, will ya?" Turning back to her he said, "He will be fine. You go home and rest now. Go on."

Cassandra complied, whimpering and mumbling to herself. The cab arrived and the sergeant ushered her out, shaking his head. She went back to her hotel, wondering if she'd had success, and if her performance would help to avoid implicating her in the escape. She fell fast asleep.

Around noon Regina came to summon her. A constable was at the door. Cassandra was escorted back to the police station, where she was informed that James had indeed escaped from Millbank and could not be found. The guard who witnessed the escape thought he'd seen two men, but couldn't be sure because he'd passed out. At this news Cassandra launched into an even greater performance, outdoing the last, weeping real tears, screaming and flailing about and shrieking about her dream. The sergeant then tried to question her to see if there was any reason to suspect her, but could find none, and so dismissed her. No one had bothered to look inside the safe.

CHAPTER SIXTEEN

Cassandra left the police station and hurried through the chilly damp air, her thoughts racing. She passed a man handing out political pamphlets and absentmindedly took one from him. Glancing down at the paper, she formed an idea.

She arrived at her hotel and ensconced herself in her bedroom. Observing that the fire in the grate was cold, she plucked out a bit of coal and scrawled a note over the print in thick, dark letters. She then took a hack chaise to Ben's townhouse, preparing herself to continue the performance. As soon as she was shown into the parlor, she burst into tears.

"He is gone!"

"What? Who?" Ben strode across the room to her and took her by the shoulders.

"James! He has escaped!" She wrung her hands and moved away so as not to look him in the eye.

"Cassandra what are you talking about! No one could escape from that place!"

"I have just been to the police station," she said walking to the fireplace and pulling a handkerchief out of her handbag. "They said the bars had been pulled loose, the glass shattered, and he used a sheet to get over the wall!" She wiped at her eyes.

"I do not understand! How could James have pulled those bars out?"

"I do not know! Oh, I must sit down." She dropped down onto a divan as if in a swoon. "Perhaps the cement that anchored them was old."

"But the prison is practically brand new!" He went and stood over her.

"Well, perhaps the construction is shoddy. Anyway, there is something you must see. Look!" She held out the pamphlet to him. He took it and read out loud:

Mother,

I have escaped. I am on a boat on the Thames. By the time you read this, I will be on my way to America. I have bartered to work for my passage. Do not worry.

James

"A street urchin stopped me on my way to the hotel as I was on my way back from the police station. He was wearing James' pocket watch—payment, I assume, for the delivery. Oh, dear heavens," she wailed. "What if he is caught? Or what if something happens to him on the passage! I may never see him again!"

"This is extraordinary!" exclaimed Ben. "We have only to hope he will not be apprehended before the vessel gets beyond the channel. We must hope that the authorities do not think to detain and search ships for a few days. It depends on the swiftness of their thinking, their determination, and the resources at hand."

"I see." Cassandra sniffled.

Ben rang the bell for a servant, then threw the pamphlet in the fire. "Best to destroy this."

"Of course."

The servant entered, and Ben ordered brandy. He looked at Cassandra. "I know it is early, but I think we could use it."

"My darling, I think this means I should go back to America myself. Right away. I must go to my son."

"Yes, of course," Ben replied, taking a chair across from her. "But, my love—"

"On the other hand," she added quickly, "If I hasten to leave the country, it would look suspicious, as if I knew he was going back to America. Perhaps I had better wait, resume my life, fulfill my year's lease at Sorrel Hall, and go when this has all blown over."

"Yes, Cassandra, yes, you are right. But…you have to know that if you go, I shall go with you."

"Oh, my love, let us not speak of that yet. Right now, we must deal with the situation at hand."

The servant entered the room with a decanter of brandy and two glasses, and Ben poured them. Cassandra sipped the strong, sweet liquid and let it melt down her throat. Ben moved to sit with her on the divan, picked up her hand, and began to stroke it.

She regarded him thoughtfully. "Although I have been cleared by the police, what will the papers say? By tomorrow morning I am sure they will be full of news of James' escape, and I will be hounded. Perhaps even by the Charleses themselves. I should not leave the country, but perhaps I should leave London for awhile—somewhere remote. Not back to Hampshire."

"Yes, certainly," he responded with concern. "It would be best to get out of London. Right away, even. But where will you go?"

She thought while she sipped her brandy. "Well, I have always wanted to visit Dorsetshire, the county of my birth, and the town of Lyme Regis, where my mother was born."

Ben cleared his throat. "What do you think of me going with you?"

She tried not to smile. "Really? You could go?"

"Of course, why not?" He drew closer to her on the divan. "Can you imagine, just the two of us, alone in a place where no one would know us?"

She shivered with the anticipation of it. "No, I can hardly conceive of it. All the more reason. Can we leave tomorrow?

I will have no problem packing my things up on short notice. I want to get out of this town." She set down her glass. "Oh, Ben, my poor James! Do you really think he will be all right?"

"I think he is quite an intelligent and resourceful young man, far more so than I ever imagined, if he could manage to escape from Millbank."

"Yes, even I, who think he is the brightest young person on earth, would never have thought he could have the courage and the ingenuity to do such a thing. If he can be so brave, I must be brave for him as well. I must believe that he will return to America in one piece. I must have faith in my boy."

"I agree. But I do think we should leave London immediately. Can you be ready by morning?"

"Yes. I do not have much to arrange." She rose, and then a thought stopped her. "Ben, what do your parents know of this situation? Do they know of your association with me? With my name all over the paper, and then you suddenly leaving town—"

"No." He stopped her. "I have never mentioned you to them, which I hope you will not take amiss. I do not want them to know about my personal affairs. They do not know I am in London and I have admonished my attorneys not to tell them. Therefore, all the better that I go with haste."

Cassandra went to her hotel to pack. At nine the next morning she breakfasted, then sent a missive to her bank, ordering them to pay the additional six months rent to Sir Frederick. Ben came at ten, bringing Cassandra's coach and four from the nearby stable house to carry them the more than one hundred miles to the Dorsetshire coast.

The first day of their journey, they passed through Hampshire within just a few miles of Selborne. They stayed in Winchester overnight, though in separate rooms. They took the opportunity that evening, just after sunset, to walk around the city by lamplight, passing by the famous Winchester Cathedral. Cassandra knew that this was the burial place of Jane Austen, but the Cathedral was closed for the night, and they could not go inside.

The next day they pressed on to Lyme Regis. It was well past dark by the time they were descending the narrow road through the town that led to the waterfront. Ben had the name of an inn that had been recommended to him by a friend, and, as it was the off-season for visiting the seaside, they hoped there would be a room. When they arrived at the small inn, nestled just at the edge of the road, they presented themselves as Mr. and Mrs. Johnston.

The proprietor was a short, stout man with a bald head and a large, bulbous nose. "Sorry to say," he informed them, "I have got no rooms at such late notice, just a li'l cottage a bit down the hill that I sometimes rent." He looked the two guests up and down. "It might suit ye, if y'were staying more than a night or two, 'cause normally I would charge a higher rate for it, but if yer in town for a while, I can knock down the price." Ben began to speak but the innkeeper cut him off. "In the summer, families sometimes take it, as it is bigger than a room; it includes a wood stove for heatin' and cookin', if yer so inclined, a basin and pump. It is very private, and has a nice view o' the Cobb. Would y' like to see it?"

Ben and Cassandra grinned at each other. "Yes, we would," Ben replied.

They followed the innkeeper down a steep hillside of stone steps sloping toward the sea. The man opened the door with a skeleton key. Cassandra gasped when she beheld the spacious room of plank floors, a raftered ceiling, rough-hewn furniture, and windows of thick-paned glass, white lace curtains hanging daintily from pegs. "It is charming!"

"Yes!" said Ben at once, spying the bed in the corner topped with white feather quilts and pillows. "We will take it, for two weeks." He paid the innkeeper.

"Sir," Cassandra stopped him on his way out the door. "Is it too late to order a bath?" Ben raised his eyebrows, and she winked at him.

"No, problem, none at all, think nothing of it, have it down in two shakes of a lamb's tail. Something like a half an hour, I should say." With that the innkeeper bowed out the door.

When he was gone, Ben grabbed Cassandra in his arms and pulled her close. "I want you now," he whispered. "I do not want to wait for a bath."

"Nonsense," she teased. "We shall have a bite to eat as well."

When two servants came in with the wooden tub, she asked if the innkeeper could also send down some cold meat, cheese, and bread. A maid appeared soon afterward with an appetizing supper, and they ate at the thick wooden table as the bath was filled with hot water and a fire was lit in the stone fireplace.

When the final bucket had been added, Cassandra thanked the servants, tipped them well, and asked that they wait 'til morning to return to fetch the tub.

"Oh, and please do not disturb us in the morning," she requested. "We will light the fire ourselves. We have had a long day today, and will probably want to sleep late."

"As you wish, ma'am," replied the last maid who curtsied out of the room.

In the firelight, Cassandra turned to Ben, and slowly, as he watched, began to undress. He observed her hungrily. When she had finished, she stood glimmering, naked before him.

"Why don't you join me?" she said to him, stepping gingerly into the hot water. She sank down into it. Ben began to remove his clothes. She thrilled to see his slim, muscled body before her again, and made room for him in the tub as he eased into it opposite her. He gazed at her, taking in her delicate breasts just submerged below the water, her hair floating on top like seaweed, her gleaming shoulders.

She wrapped her long legs around him and they languidly kissed. His hands traveled over her slippery body, as did hers on his, finding him erect. She lowered herself onto him, tightening her legs behind his back, and they slowly moved together in a gentle rhythm. After several minutes he gasped, "Let us get into bed."

"One minute," she responded.

She reached for the soap on a stool nearby, and smoothed it over his body and her own. Laughing, she dunked under the water and washed her hair, then did the same to him. The night was cold, and in spite of the fire, the water was cooling fast. The air was chilly on their wet bodies. They reached for the drying sheets that lay close and quickly dried off. They ran to the bed and jumped under the clean bed sheets and thick covers.

"This is what I have been waiting for," growled Ben as he covered her body with kisses, ending with her mouth, and thrusting his tongue deep inside. She responded with all the passion and longing that she had stored up since they had last been together in Hampshire. All of the anguish, fear, and frustration of the last month she let go of now as she buried her face in his shoulders and felt his strong arms around her, his hands caressing her. Finally he entered her and moved on top of her with all of his long-restrained urgency. Her release was immediate and then seemed like it would never end. He soon erupted into complete ecstasy, and then collapsed beside her. They did not speak, but only kissed. She then simply curled up in his arms and they fell asleep, for the whole night, the first since their relationship began.

In the morning, they made love again, taking their time, knowing that for once, their time was practically limitless. When they were satisfied, Ben dressed and walked up to the inn to ask that breakfast be brought to the room. In the meantime, Cassandra dressed in a simple, warm woolen gown, appropriate for a day of exploring along the coast.

After breakfast, the couple decided to start with a stroll on the Cobb. The day was sunny and brisk, and Cassandra donned her cloak. Her heartbeat quickened as they approached the famous stone jetty from the beach. They mounted narrow steps that took them the twelve feet up onto its walkway. She then linked her arm into Ben's, and they followed the inner curve of the structure the few hundred feet that it jutted out into the English Channel. Waves lashed the outer ledge, making it slippery, an abrupt plunge to the sharp rocks below. On the opposite side, the water was calm, fishing boats anchored nearby and protected from the violent sea.

Cassandra felt justified that she had waited to visit this place until her time journey, so she could have the experience of seeing it unchanged by modern progress. They stood quietly at the end of the Cobb, taking in the view, the green-gray ocean, the distant blue silhouette of the Isle of Wight, and the cliffs along the Dorset shore.

"It reminds one of Persuasion, does it not?" offered Ben.

"I am sorry?" Cassandra responded, startled.

"Persuasion," he repeated, "Miss Austen's Persuasion. You know, when Louisa Musgrove jumps down off the Cobb right over there, and Captain Wentworth fails to catch her."

Cassandra could not speak.

"Have you not read it?" he said. "Oh, you must borrow mine. I have a copy at Gatewick House. It is as wonderful as her other works. Oh no, but of course you would not have heard of her; they are probably not available in America yet. Her last two were only published two years ago."

"Yes, yes, I have read them, all of her books," she finally broke in. "They are at the library at Sorrel Hall. I was just surprised that you had read them. Most men do not—" She was going to say that most men don't read Jane Austen because she had never in actuality met one who had read her and admitted to liking her other than her beloved Franklin.

Ben cut her off. "Most men do not read novels? Nonsense. Men read novels. They just do not admit it. We love a good story, just like women. We do not only read financial reports and historical biographies."

Cassandra laughed with delight. "Why have we never spoken of her books before?"

"I would suppose because we were too busy," he grinned, pulling her close and kissing her.

******

November 1st, 1820 – How is it possible that I have found a man with whom I can discuss Austen as if she's just popped up on the New York Times Bestseller list? I suppose I've rather systematically avoided discussing literature with anyone, subconsciously fearful that I would give myself away, but Austen is my main reason for this visit. She's been like a sacred secret hidden away in my heart, and now here we are wandering around Lyme Regis, this amazing seventh-century fishing village, sharing our favorite moments and characters in her novels. Perhaps Ben's loving her work is partly a British thing, maybe partly a result of living in Austen's day and understanding so clearly what she was writing about. I think I understand her more intimately now as well. I've always related to her from a woman's perspective, and treasured her observations on human nature, her humor and satire, her passion and her uncanny sense of romance. But now I understand her place and time.

******

For the next two weeks, Cassandra and Ben clambered through the forests and along the cliffs around Lyme Regis. They visited neighboring towns, including Broadwindsor, where she, in her fictional history, had been born. She was able to say in all truthfulness that she did not remember it.

During those days together, they made love again and again, rambled on the beach, talked of music and books, and since she had no piano, Ben played for her at night. She had to remind herself to express anguish over James now and then, but inwardly, she felt light-hearted.

Toward the middle of November, they made the day's ride back to Selborne, and Cassandra left Ben off at Gatewick house. She had kept Mrs. Merriweather generally informed about the events of the past several weeks by post, without going into much detail. She knew that the news of James' arrest and escape had long preceded her by way of Lady Holcomb and the others who had returned to Selborne. As far as Cassandra knew, Lady Charles was still in

London, or had returned to Bath, which was for the best; she had no desire to mix with her.

She was anxious as the great front doors to Sorrel Hall opened. The housekeeper stood primly at the door, her face unreadable. In the most recent missive to her, Cassandra had written that she had gone to visit the county of her birth to have some time for quiet contemplation and that she would return from there in a little more than a fortnight.

The woman greeted her mistress in her usual manner, formal and detached, and sent Cassandra's bags upstairs, after which she inquired if she were hungry. Cassandra replied that she was, and so Mrs. Merriweather had a meal prepared while Cassandra changed out of her travelling clothes.

When she went down to the dining room and saw the dishes organized in front of the lonesome looking chair, she realized she could not bear to sit there all by herself and eat in solitude. She decided to flout convention and asked Mrs. Merriweather if she could eat in the kitchen where she, Mr. Merriweather and Anna were having their meal alone, the other servants enjoying their Sunday evening off.

The housekeeper slightly raised an eyebrow and replied, "Of course, Mrs. Franklin." Cassandra grabbed what she wanted off the table and Mrs. Merriweather took the rest.

Mr. Merriweather leapt to his feet when she entered, and Anna rose to tend to her, but she motioned them back down after she'd set her plates on the table. The housekeeper followed her into the room.

"I hope you do not mind if I impose on you," Cassandra said to them, feeling soothed at the warmth of the room and the wonderful smells. "But I need to be around familiar faces." She sat. "These last few weeks have been very trying."

Mr. Merriweather and Anna assented with nods. Mrs. Merriweather spoke: "Your comfort is our primary concern, Mrs. Franklin."

"Thank you so much," Cassandra replied and fell to eating as the others followed her lead. After a few minutes silence, she broached a question. "Would you mind telling me what you've heard from the neighbors?"

The three servants looked at each other. "We do not listen to idle gossip, ma'am," said Mr. Merriweather.

His wife continued. "James is a good boy, as you know better than anyone. He probably just had some… curiosity is all. If you ask me, it was a lot made out of nothing."

"We only hope he is safe and sound," Anna piped up, "and will be in the bosom of his native land soon."

Cassandra wondered if they would be so supportive had they seen the device themselves. "Thank you so much," she said. "I was worried that you would be uncomfortable with me living here after such an uproar."

"Well, Mrs. Franklin, firstly, that is not for us to judge," said Mrs. Merriweather.

Cassandra began to speak, but the housekeeper continued, looking at her directly. "Secondly, you have been a kind and thoughtful mistress to us all. We have a great fondness for you, if I am not being too familiar by saying so."

Cassandra shook her head.

"If you cannot find support and comfort here in your own house, with your own servants, then where can you find it? We are glad you are home, and that is all."

Tears filled Cassandra's eyes, but she blinked them back and smiled. "Thank you," she whispered.

They finished the meal with small talk about the state of the gardens and other local news about the farmers and the neighborhood. Cassandra finally told them that James' escape meant that she would have to plan to return to America herself come January.

"We are sorry to hear that," Mrs. Merriweather said. "We will miss you greatly." Mr. Merriweather coughed and took a gulp of cider. Anna dabbed at her eyes with her napkin.

"As will I, so very much." She rose and excused herself and went to her piano to play.

Mrs. Merriweather had already prepared her a bath by the time Cassandra was ready to retire. Cassandra had a long, luxurious soak in front of the fire in her bedroom. It made her think of Ben, whom she missed already, and now that she was back at Sorrel Hall, she realized she missed James terribly as well. She had somewhat less than two months to remain in Hampshire, and she feared it would be lonely without James and the constant presence of Ben. She also did not know how her friends in the neighborhood perceived her now, and if they would accept her invitations to visit. Well, she decided, it was all something to worry about in the morning. She put on the fresh nightclothes the housekeeper had left out for her, climbed into her clean, cozy bed, picked up the copy of *Mansfield Park* that she had left on her nightstand several weeks ago, and started rereading it for the tenth time.

CHAPTER SEVENTEEN

*W*ednesday, November 18, 1820 – I am so happy to be back in Hampshire! Though Lyme was incredible, for so many obvious reasons, this place has truly come to feel like my home. A few bright leaves still cling to some of the trees, and we are still getting squash from the garden, pumpkins, butternut and acorn, to be specific. Mr. Merriweather says that we can grow lettuce and even keep some tomatoes going in the greenhouse for a little while longer. But if December is harsh, those vegetables will not respond, even in the warmer environment.

Although life here has returned to the quiet pace that it had before James came, I no longer find it dull in any way. Part of that, of course, has to do with Ben, who is so much a part of my life; so much, that I do not want to give him up. I never thought that he would ensconce himself so deeply in my heart. I want to stay here with him; I want to be this woman of the nineteenth century that I have created, even though it is just an illusion.

I don't really care much if I am accepted back into Selborne "high society," although I have sent off the customary notes requesting the visits that I know are expected now that I've returned to the neighborhood. We shall see what they bring.

******

Cassandra's note to Lady Holcomb requesting an invitation to the cottage was met with a curt reply that the Holcombs were otherwise engaged. Cassandra was more pained than she expected to be, but not surprised. A visit to the Clarke family produced little more than lukewarm enthusiasm. Mrs. Clarke had heard the description of the device from Edward, but she did not allude to it during the course of Cassandra's visit. The conversation remained distantly polite and stiff.

Edward sat with them silently for a while, but when his mother left to see about one of the little ones, he cautiously asked Cassandra about James's fate. She only replied that she had not heard from him since the mysterious escape (all of which they'd read about in the London papers) and that she was anxiously awaiting word. Edward asked her to have him write, but Cassandra simply replied that it would probably be unwise for James to reveal his whereabouts. She said she would let him know as soon as she heard anything.

She concluded her visit with the Clarkes with a sense that their old intimacy had disintegrated, even though the ever-gallant Mr. Clarke had popped into the parlor with a few warm words of greeting for her.

Several days later, she went to visit Mrs. Moore. She and her two awkward daughters were even more fascinated with her, it seemed, than before, and they enjoyed a lively conversation together. However, Cassandra left feeling like her circle of friends and acquaintances had significantly diminished.

Her time with Ben naturally expanded as her time with others decreased. They no longer worried about when and where they met when they played music together. They went on walks and horseback rides together whenever the weather was less than biting, and their afternoons in the cottage were only hampered if the weather forbade them to ride.

Cassandra also spent more time now with the farmers' wives whose company she had always enjoyed. The gossip that reached them about James had been vague, and anyway, they were grateful for her patronage. They always pressed on Cassandra their jars of homemade jams and pickles, cheeses, or dried herbs. She always made sure she brought many more gifts for them than she came away with.

On one such visit, she was sitting in the warm kitchen of her friend Mrs. MacIntosh, sharing with her some oat muffins that Cassandra had made herself that morning. She had also brought a fine ham that was now stored in the farm's cellar.

One of Mrs. MacIntosh's three sons came running in, knocking over an empty laundry bucket in the process.

"Freddy!" cried Mrs. MacIntosh. "Will you please be careful? There is no need to run about like a pig on the loose!"

"Mama," exclaimed Freddy, out of breath, "Jamie's come from Mrs. Whitstone's. He says it is his mum's time and she called for you! He said to hurry!"

"Oh, dear," responded Mrs. MacIntosh, "the babe is early." She jumped into action. "Freddy, go get me my black bag and fetch my sewing scissors from the table in the parlor and put them in it. And call Susan in here right away!"

The boy ran off, and she began rummaging in her cupboards, pulling out bundles and jars of dried herbs.

"Clara, what can I do to help," asked Cassandra, a tremor in her voice. "May I come with you?"

The tall, sturdy woman turned and considered her friend for a moment, no doubt taking in the fine clothing Cassandra was wearing, and the smooth hands that had never known a day's serious toil.

"What do you know about delivering babies?" she asked briskly.

"Well, I have had one," answered Cassandra. What she wished she could say was, as a PhD, a scientist, and a woman of three hundred years in the future, she probably knew more about the biology of a woman's body and methods of sanitation than Mrs. MacIntosh. She actually had even trained once in emergency childbirth assistance, as part of the required first aid course that every high school student in the U.S. took part in. But that was a long time ago, as was the birth of her son, which was totally natural, though completely painless, thanks to the miracles of modern medicine. She had to admit to herself, she knew nothing about delivering a baby in the circumstances she was about to face.

The farmer's wife offered a wry grin, and the lines around her eyes crinkled. "I could certainly use another pair of hands, if you do not mind getting that gown of yours messy."

"Do not be silly," was all Cassandra could think to say.

"All right then," said the Mrs. MacIntosh throwing her a clean muslin apron. "Put this on and let us go." Cassandra could see respect glimmer in the woman's eyes.

Freddy came running back in with a small black leather satchel for his mother that resembled an old-fashioned doctor's bag, his older sister Susan at his side.

"The scissors are in there?" his mother asked.

"Yes, ma'am."

"Susan, you are in charge. I do not know how long I will be gone. You will have leftovers for supper; Edith will take care of that. Make sure the little ones are in bed on time, and go to bed yourself if I am not home before ten o'clock."

"Yes, Mama," Susan said, her pale blue eyes large in her thin face. She looked to be about sixteen and had, of course, gone through this with her mother several times.

"All right, Mrs. Franklin, let us go." They threw on their outer garments and went outside to face a bitter wind that had blown up.

"We can take my horse," Cassandra said, not knowing if Mrs. MacIntosh had access to one herself. The woman hesitated. "Yes," insisted Cassandra, "she is strong. She can carry us." They ran to the stable and had a young farm hand throw off the saddle and replace it with a blanket. The ladies than clambered on one after another with the help of an overturned bucket.

It was a mile to the Whitstone's farm, but with the horse at a gentle canter, they were there in ten minutes. When they approached the low, rambling farmhouse, they could hear the woman's screams within. Several children ran to the door, white-faced and scared.

"Heaven help us," whispered Mrs. MacIntosh under her breath.

She and Cassandra leapt down off the horse, and one of the older boys came to take it and put it in the barn. They hurried into the house, and the oldest daughter took them to her mother's room. Before they entered, Mrs. MacIntosh turned to the young woman.

"Is there scalding water on the stove?"

The girl nodded speechlessly, her large brown eyes brimming with tears.

"And plenty of clean rags?"

"I will fetch them," she said and ran off.

"Martha," she called after her, "make sure I have two basins of hot water and a bar of lye soap as well."

"Yes, ma'am," came the answer from down the hall.

Cassandra was skeptical about the cleanliness of the rags and the implements they were about to use. She knew nothing could have been sanitized properly. She looked about the shabby farmhouse. It could hardly be called clean.

Mrs. MacIntosh glanced at her, took a breath, and opened the door.

Mrs. Whitstone lay sweating and writhing on the bed, a young maid beside her, trembling.

"It is all right, dear," Mrs. MacIntosh said to her. "We are here now. You go help Martha with the rags and the hot water. Then stand there by the door. Whenever I say, you be ready to fetch some more, do you hear?"

"Yes, ma'am," the maid said. She jumped up and flew out of the room.

"Sarah," she said, turning to Mrs. Whitstone . With a soothing voice she continued. "Sarah, we are here to help. Mrs. Franklin has come with me."

Mrs. Whitstone opened her eyes and looked glassily at them. "Something is wrong," she croaked with her parched throat. "It is early."

"I know," replied Mrs. MacIntosh. "It will be all right. Cassandra," she said, using the familiarity of her given name for the first time. "Take this herb to the kitchen and make a cup of strong tea with it. Hurry." She handed her a small bundle of dried plant from her bag and Cassandra rushed out. The water in the kitchen was hot, so she soon had the tea ready in the cup. She then pumped out a cup of ice cold water from the kitchen sink and ran back to the bedroom with both. The basins of hot water, the soap, and the rags had also been delivered.

"Good," said Mrs. MacIntosh softly. Mrs. Whitstone was beginning to moan. Another contraction was coming. The moan heightened until it was a scream that brought tears to Cassandra's eyes. She wondered how such suffering could exist. It made her realize how idyllic her world really was.

When the contraction was done, Cassandra took a small rag, dipped it in the cold water, and pressed it to the woman's lips. She sucked at it gratefully.

"Good!" said Mrs. MacIntosh again. "Now she needs to sip some of this tea." She held it up to Mrs. Whitstone's lips and helped her drink it. She gagged, but her friend urged her on. The next contraction came on again sooner than the last and with even more force. When it was through, Mrs. MacIntosh gave her more tea, and the woman seemed to relax.

"All right," she said to Cassandra, "hold her hand. Sarah, we are going to check the baby."

The patient nodded, her eyes half-closed.

Mrs. MacIntosh dipped her hands in one basin of hot water, washed them with the lye soap, rinsed them in another and wiped them, then lifted up her friend's skirts and gently put one hand inside to feel for the baby. Mrs. Whitstone gasped. It only took a moment and then she was done. She withdrew her hand and looked at Cassandra.

"What, what?" croaked Sarah.

"It is breach." She replied.

"Oh no," cried Sarah.

Cassandra drew in her breath.

"We have got to get it out, Sarah," she told her. "All this struggling you are doing will not help. It will just kill you. We need brandy," she said to Cassandra.

"I will get it!" yelled Martha's from behind the door.

Another contraction came, and Sarah screamed. Martha appeared at the door with the glass of brandy, tears streaming down her face.

"It will be all right," Cassandra whispered to her and closed the door.

They gave Sarah the glass and made her drink it down in spite of her protests. Cassandra was terrified at the prospect of their trying to pull the baby, legs first, from its mother with no other painkiller. She had a small stock of powerful pain and germ killers at Sorrel Hall, but she knew, even if she could get to them in time, it would not be right to use them.

They waited for the next contraction. Cassandra took Sarah's hand, Mrs. MacIntosh cleaned her hands again, and then she reached inside. Sarah screamed like she was being tortured to death. Cassandra sobbed, holding onto her, trying to keep her still so Mrs. MacIntosh could do her work. Mrs. MacIntosh was sweating and grunting, trying to grasp the slippery child. Blood gushed out and Cassandra, who always considered herself strong, thought she was going to faint.

"Caroline!" shouted Mrs. MacIntosh to the maid. "Get in here!" The young woman came running in, terror written on her face. "Wipe away this blood! I have to be able to see." The maid did as she was told, too frightened not to. Cassandra could see Mrs. MacIntosh struggling with all her might to pull out the child, and then mercifully, Sarah fainted. The baby finally came out with a slosh of blood, Mrs. MacIntosh grasping its tiny legs. It was indeed tiny, which made it possible to get it out at all, but it was not living. Cassandra could see that at once. It was blue, and its spine looked bent. She leapt to help Caroline mop up the copious blood while Mrs. MacIntosh cut the umbilical cord and wrapped the dead, premature baby in a rag.

Slowly and methodically, the women cleaned the bed and the floor, stripped Sarah of her clothes, diapered her with clean, soft strips of fabric, and replaced her clothing with an old, but clean nightgown. They covered the blood-soaked mattress with an old blanket, though it would have to be thrown away. Sarah was still unconscious, but breathing regularly. There was no sign of fever.

Mr. Whitstone came from the fields where he had been working and mutely took the baby in his arms to bury it under a tree in back of the farmhouse. It wasn't the first baby he'd had to bury, and they couldn't afford to have it interred in the churchyard. He then came back in and gently carried his wife to a clean bed in another bedroom where she'd have to stay until a new mattress could be made for their marriage bed.

There was nothing more for Cassandra and Mrs. MacIntosh to do. The children were all in the kitchen now, eating their supper quietly.

As Cassandra and Mrs. MacIntosh rode back to her farm, Clara spoke quietly. "It is a blessing, you know. The little one would not have been normal, and they did not need another mouth to feed."

Cassandra nodded in front of her on the horse. She left Mrs. MacIntosh at her door, both of them too tired and hungry for any lengthy parting, and got herself home through the dark, shivering with shock and cold.

William, Mrs. Merriweather, Mr. Merriweather, Mary, and Anna were all frantic for her return. They only knew she had gone to the MacIntosh's farm, and William was just on the point of setting off to find her when she returned. When she told them what had happened, they all fussed around her, making her warm and comfortable and seeing that she had something good to eat.

The next day, Cassandra had an expensive new mattress ordered for the Whitstones from the furniture maker in Basingstoke and went back to see Sarah in the carriage, bringing as much food as she could without seeming overbearing. She also brought some nightgowns and linens that she gathered from around Sorrel Hall and, against the ethics of time travel, a powerful painkilling tablet and an antibiotic, both nano-programmed to continue to work until the recipient's body no longer required it. When she went in to see Sarah, the woman was almost delirious from the pain of having the baby pulled from her. Cassandra knew she must be terribly torn, but hoped all her internal organs were intact. There was nothing anyone could do if they weren't.

As soon as Cassandra was alone with her, she surreptitiously dissolved the pills in a cup of tea, helped Sarah drink it, and left with hardly a word.

******

Tuesday, December 1st, 1880 – I received word today from the Whitstone farm that Sarah has made a miraculous recovery. Martha sent a note saying that her mother's pain abated just a day after the delivery, and that now, a week later, she is sitting up in bed, eating and drinking with good color in her face, doing needlework, and should be up on her feet any day now. She says she knows God must have done what He, in his infinite wisdom, knows to be best.

They thanked me for the mattress and the gifts. I only hope to do more for them. As there is so much abundance from my lands that I don't have need of, the Whitstones will be the recipients of it, at least until their mother can go back to her usual duties.

CHAPTER EIGHTEEN

Cassandra was savoring the final few weeks of her time in1820. When the last leaf had fallen from the trees and all the color had faded from the landscape, she began to admire the contrasts of browns and grays, light and shadow, the stark shapes of the bare trees, and the sharp brightness of the stars that could be seen from her bedroom window. She knew she would never see the earth like this again.

Another opportunity to time travel would be unlikely. She had to give way to the others waiting their turns. She knew she would never again experience the quiet that was so complete, the air that was so pure, the flavors that were so clean, and the absolute simplicity of daily life. She now reveled in the slow passage of time that allowed her to sit and read a book for hours, to play the piano uninterrupted as long as she liked, to just sit by a window and watch the shadows move across the earth, to walk and hear nothing, nothing but the birds and the wind and the sound of her own footsteps.

Christmas was approaching, and the poignancy of having to say goodbye to her nineteenth-century life started to blend with the loneliness of not having her family and friends around her during the traditional preparations of the season. But she, Mrs. Merriweather, and Anna kept busy putting together festive baskets of food and sweets for the laborers of the neighborhood. Cassandra went to Selborne and over to Basingstoke to purchase gifts of fabric, gloves, scarves, and other necessities for the members of her own household, and little luxury items, such as powders and fragrances, to send to all her society friends, former or not. She made sure to include little toys and packages of candy for the children, books and jewelry for the young ladies, and hunting knives for the young men.

One afternoon a messenger arrived at Sorrel Hall from Darrington with a package for Cassandra. Mary brought it in to the sitting room where her mistress was hanging fresh holly garlands above the windows.

"Who is it from, Mary?" she asked from the chair she was standing on as she reached up to the top of the window.

"It is from Lady Charles," she replied. "It is your package, returned."

Cassandra hopped down off of the chair. "Thank you, Mary." Cassandra took the accompanying note and sat down on her chair to read it as Mary left the room, leaving the package on a table.

The letter began abruptly:

Mrs. Franklin,

I am returning the package you sent, which may be indication enough of my feelings toward you, but I feel compelled to explain them further, and so I shall seize this opportunity to do so. I must tell you that I disapprove heartily of your continued presence in our neighborhood. I was shocked to return from Bath last week and find that you had the audacity to show your face here again after the disgrace your family brought upon us all. You should be ashamed that your son was not man enough to stand trial for his crimes, but instead, fled away like the guilty rogue that he is. I was equally disappointed that you were not held responsible in his stead. Rather, you insinuated yourself back into our society as if nothing had happened. I hope you do not think you will ever be back in my good graces. To the contrary, I shall never again consider you a friend.

In addition, and for your edification, my husband has personally taken it upon himself to push for the reinstatement of England's strict anti-witchcraft laws to protect the citizens from such evil and sorcery as you and your son have inflicted upon us. He is making this his new cause in Parliament.

Incidentally, he recently told me how you tried to seduce him at the ball at Darrington. I am sure that these are the tactics you and your son were using to ensnare your victims. To think that my Elizabeth almost succumbed to your son's wiles!

In short, I reject you and your ways and hope to never see you darken my path again.

With Disdain,

Lady Katherine Elizabeth Smythe Charles

Cassandra sat stunned for a moment at the vindictiveness of the letter. She felt anger seething up within her. She got up and paced around the room, trying to decide how, or if, she should respond. But after a few moments' reflection, she realized that she must simply let it all go. Mrs. Charles's fears were fictional, whether she realized it or not. Let her have her disdain, she thought. It affects me not at all. I will be gone soon anyway. Maybe she'll even think I left as a result of her, and she can triumph at that. Cassandra went to toss the letter into the fire, then thought better of it. She'd keep it for scientific documentation. She tucked it into her skirt pocket and called Mary back into the room. Her only real fear was that if Sir Robert had success with his campaign for re-instating the witchcraft laws, people might needlessly suffer, and history might be changed. She prayed Ben was right about his ineffectiveness as a politician.

"Please, Mary, have Mrs. Merriweather change the name and address on the package. I would like it sent instead to Sarah Whitstone." She thought about the contents. They were expensive, lovely niceties, not like the practical items she had already sent the Whitstone family as a Christmas offering. She went to her desk and dashed off a note.

Dear Sarah,

I hope you like these little trinkets. A mother so rarely gets to enjoy nice things; I thought you would like to have them just for yourself.

Merry Christmas,

Cassandra Franklin

******

December 16, 1820 – Mr. Merriweather and I went out today to cut down a Christmas tree. He keeps a special stand of evergreens just for this purpose, and every year when he cuts one down, he plants two or three more. We chose a tall one; it must be about ten feet high, and beautifully shaped. It is a fir—such graceful bows and silvery-green color. We brought the hay cart for the purpose and rode with plenty of blankets piled on our laps. After he cut it, we struggled to lift the tree on the cart, just the two of us, laughing and falling. It was surprising to see him so merry; he usually is such a taciturn man. On the way back, he shared with me a little of his Christmas cheer, a pint of brandy hidden in his coat!

With the aid of some of the servants, we finally got the tree in the house and placed it, standing in a regal spot in my sitting room, between the fireplace and the bay windows. It adds such splendor to the room. Mrs. Merriweather brought out the decorations that the Collins family left behind, and everyone in the household, including Ben, who had come for the occasion, helped decorate it. I told them of the American tradition of stringing popcorn and cranberries for ornaments. Anna popped the corn, and we tried to get it strung on the tree before eating it all. We had no cranberries, so we used dried crabapples instead. The tree is now gorgeous, and I think everyone in Sorrel Hall is enjoying it.

******

A week before Christmas, Ben told Cassandra he had a surprise for her. He told her to be prepared the following day to take a short trip and to dress warmly. His coach arrived for her at nine. He told her it was only a short drive; they weren't going beyond the borders of Hampshire County. They passed the time with him teasing her with words and kisses, but she tried to keep her eyes on the landscape as it rolled by out the window.

She saw a small sign announcing their entrance into the village of Steventon, and she shrieked with delight.

"It is Jane Austen's birthplace! We are going to see where she grew up, her family home!"

"How do you know?" He uttered in surprise. He couldn't know that three hundred years after the author's death, biography after biography had been written about her.

"Someone in London mentioned it to me when I said I was moving to Hampshire."

"Oh," he said, a little deflated.

"Yes," she continued, "this person said they knew her family somewhat. It was just a passing conversation."

"Well, I am just surprised because not many people know much about her, other than the titles of her books. It took me some real investigating to find out about this place. I do not think we should go inside and disturb her brother, who still lives there. But I thought you would like to see the village and the parsonage where she grew up from the outside at least."

The village was simply a row of a few cottages without shop or inn. The parsonage where Jane was born and raised was a few hundred feet past it. Once they arrived there, they had the driver take them beyond the property so as not to seem obtrusive. The coachman alighted, helped them from the carriage, and began tending to the horses.

Ben and Cassandra walked past the front of the parsonage looking around at the scenery as if they were only out on a country stroll. The house was a simple structure of two stories with a peaked roof and included various outbuildings beyond. Behind it was farmland, which rose gently for some distance. There were chickens meandering about, a large fallow vegetable garden, and the sound of cows lowing from inside a great, grey barn. A thin column of smoke rose from in back of the main house.

Cassandra knew for certain that this parsonage did not survive into the future, actually, not too many more years at all. This was a very special opportunity to see it, for this little

274

village was mostly obliterated by 2120. She happened to know that only the thirteenth-century church remained and a small marker at the site of the parsonage. Steventon wasn't even on most maps of Britain or mentioned in tourist guidebooks.

She could have made this trip easily from London the few times she had visited England in her life, but had studiously stayed away from "Jane Austen country," as she called it, because she knew if she ever got a chance to time travel, Hampshire was where she would come.

The sound of a door banging startled them, but they saw no one emerge from the front of the house. Cassandra was overcome with an intense curiosity to explore the situation and possibly spy upon one of her heroine's relatives.

"Mr. Johnston!" cried the coachman just then. "Better come have a look at this!"

Ben jogged back up the road, while Cassandra remained. A moment later Ben called out, "This one has a pebble stuck in her hoof! You go on; we need to get it out."

Cassandra nodded to him and took a deep breath. Summoning up her courage, she walked around the side of the building. Behind the house, a woman stood bent over a small trash fire, her face hidden by the hood of her cloak. She held some papers in her hand, and one by one, she was throwing them into the fire. Cassandra walked boldly up to the wooden gate that led into the yard, and the woman turned to look at her. Cassandra gasped. It was the same face that she knew so well from the few surviving portraits of Jane Austen: the oval face, the large, dark eyes, the thin lips, and the straight, slender nose. Her heart pounded.

"Hello," the lady called out in a friendly tone. "May I help you?"

"I was just looking for—" Cassandra froze. What was she looking for?

"My father?"

"I, I, I am an admirer of—"

"Oh my aunt!" declared the young woman. "I am sorry. She passed away three years ago."

"Yes, I am aware," said Cassandra breathing more steadily now.

"Please, come in," the niece said.

Cassandra opened the gate and walked towards her. "I do not mean to disturb you; I only wanted to have a glance at where your aunt once lived. You must get a lot of visitors by here."

"Not really, only a very few since she passed." said the niece.

"Oh!" responded Cassandra with surprise. "Well, allow me to introduce myself. I am Mrs. Franklin of Sorrel Hall, near Selborne."

"Nice to meet you. I am Miss Austen."

Cassandra's heart fluttered. She could barely believe she was speaking to one of Jane Austen's very relatives, and looking into eyes that were so like the author's.

"Forgive me if I do not shake your hand," the niece continued. "Mine are covered with dust and soot."

Cassandra glanced down at the papers the young woman held. They appeared to be handwritten epistles of some kind.

The historian in her was piqued with curiosity. "What is it you are burning there, if you don't mind me asking?"

"Just some family letters," the girl replied. Cassandra's heart jumped. "My father hoards them ridiculously, and my mother insisted that we rid the house of the lion's share."

"Are, are they—" Cassandra stammered. "Are any of them your Aunt Jane's?"

"Oh, certainly," she replied. "She wrote endless letters. No one could ever read them all." She carelessly threw the remainder of her papers into the fire and Cassandra shrieked.

"No! Wait!" She made a grab at the few that were still floating down toward the flames.

"Mrs. Franklin, really!" cried Miss Austen.

"I am sorry. I am sorry," said Cassandra, gasping and clinging to the singed papers. "It is just that—" tears sprang to her eyes at the thought of all the family history, all the possible insight about the great author that had just gone up in smoke. "I just adore her writing so."

"Do you mind?" asked Miss Austen archly, holding out her hand.

Cassandra reluctantly turned them over to her.

The girl examined the letters. "This one is from my Aunt Jane to her sister. If you'd like to have it, it really makes no difference to me."

"Oh, thank you, thank you!" Cassandra cried, taking the letter from her and gazing at it adoringly.

Miss Austen stared at Cassandra. "You are welcome," the niece replied, "and now, if you don't mind, it is quite cold and I have other work to do."

"Of course, I am so sorry to have disturbed you. Just one last thing."

The young woman looked at her.

"Please, do not burn any more of her letters. They might turn out to be of great value some day."

Miss Austen turned the letters over in her hand as if this thought had never occurred to her. "Certainly," she replied, humoring her guest. "Good day." She then turned and hurried into the house, clutching the remaining papers tightly.

Cassandra ran back out the gate, harboring her precious prize. She stopped at the corner of the house and carefully put it into her bag. She'd read it later. She decided not to tell Ben about it; she wouldn't be able to explain to him the breadth of its significance. She then calmly walked up the road to meet him.

"What happened?" he asked, as she approached.

"I met Jane's niece! She was quite pleasant, but we only chatted for a moment. I did not want to keep her."

"Very nice." He remarked. "I am glad you got to meet someone from her family. Shall we go look at the church?"

"Yes, let us," she replied. She was aware of the letter in her bag as if it weighed a hundred pounds.

They went on to see the old church where Jane had listened to her father's sermons every Sunday. It was simple and quiet and very cold—not a degree warmer than the frigid air outside, so they didn't linger. It was too cold to walk around any longer, so they had the coachman drive them a mile or so further into Basingstoke, where they ate lunch at a pub.

There they made their plans for Christmas. They'd both received a few other invitations, but neither wanted to do anything but spend the time together. That settled, they finished up their meal and drove back to Selborne, Ben dropping her at Sorrel Hall a little before sunset.

Upon entering the house, she deposited her cloak with Mary, only uttering a few brief words, and then rushed upstairs to her room. She closed the door, sat down in a chair by the fire, and carefully withdrew the relic from her purse.

"My dearest Cassandra," it began. She nearly fell off her chair. Then she recalled that Jane's sister was also named Cassandra and she laughed out loud. The letter was a rambling discussion of Jane's neighbors' reaction to the recent publication of *Pride and Prejudice*, including the author's own critique of the novel. "…The work is rather too light & bright & sparkling: -it wants shade;-it wants to be stretched out here & there with a long chapter…" Cassandra read with fascination. She couldn't believe she was holding in her hand the same paper that Jane had touched, beholding the actual ink from her pen. She had seen some of Austen's preserved letters under glass, had even had access to some that were not available for public perusal, due to her historian's status. But this, this was her own personal treasure, and she would bring it back into the future with her, whether it was appropriate to do so or not. After reading it over several times, she finally tucked it into her journal for safekeeping.

She went down to greet Mrs. Merriweather and have supper.

******

Dec. 21, 1820—Ben and I haven't seen each other for a week. I've been busy putting together last-minute gifts for the farmers and all the servants, not bothering to wait for Boxing Day.

It was hard to decide what to get him, but finally I did. I have never played for him my most beloved music—that of the one composer I adore over all, one who was born before 1820—1805, in fact, but could not yet have composed the piece that I want him to hear. In another ten years, he will likely hear of Felix Mendelssohn, and probably even play his music, but he will probably never hear of his sister, Fanny. I'm going to play for him one of the most beautiful pieces of music ever written. It's called "Farewell to Rome (Abschied von Rom)," and Fanny Mendelssohn-Hensel wrote it after spending the happiest time of her life, six months in Rome with her husband and son, amongst artists and musicians that valued her for her own accomplishments, rather than for those of her brother. When she had to leave, she knew she'd likely never return, and she was devastated. For me, it reflects the joy of some of my happiest moments here Hampshire, mixed with the bitterness of leaving.

It's daring to play this piece that is from later than this time—I'm also transcribing the music on beautiful parchment to give to him and I'll make him vow never to show it to anyone. Am I crazy to do this? Yes, I suppose. But I'm feeling conflicted at the moment, trying to figure out how to say goodbye to him.

******

They agreed to exchange presents on Christmas Eve. Ben arrived at Sorrel Hall at three o'clock for an early dinner. The light was already fading. Cassandra had lit candles all throughout the entry hall, dining hall, and sitting room, as well as fires in each room. She had decorated the doorways and windows with freshly cut greenery, and the house smelled of spicy pine.

They enjoyed a private dinner together, just the two of them, sitting across the center of the great dining table from each other. Cassandra had all his favorite foods and desserts prepared, and they feasted and drank some of the best wines from the cellar. They retired into the sitting room to play together all the Christmas music they knew and had each been practicing for the occasion. They invited all the household in to listen and drink rum punch, and ended the evening with a rousing singing of carols. Cassandra had given the servants the next day off (though she knew Mrs. Merriweather wouldn't comply). When it was late, and everyone else in the house had gone to bed, Cassandra and Ben exchanged gifts.

She played *Farewell to Rome* for him, expressing all of her pent up feelings through the music. She knew the piece by heart—it had long been her friend—but she had never experienced the totality of its yearning until that moment. She was in tears when she finished, and looked over at Ben. He was silent, a look of astonishment on his face.

She picked up the leaves of parchment, tied with a ribbon, and went to join him on the sofa. Placing it on her lap, she said, "This piece is by someone whose name I cannot say. It is not me, to be sure, but it is a woman who wrote it. To protect her anonymity, I cannot tell you who it is."

"It is extraordinary!" he gasped. "The harmonies are…so surprising, the cadences, so unusual. It is filled with emotion, so full—it is not quite like Beethoven, not like anything I have heard!"

"I know," she replied, beaming. "It is one of my favorite pieces."

"You must tell me who wrote it."

"I cannot," she said, "but here," she gave him the parchment. "This is for you to play whenever you choose, for I know that you are able at the piano. But you must promise me that you will never play it for, or show it to anyone. Do you promise you will never share it with anyone?"

"I promise, but it is so mysterious!"

"It will have to remain so," she smiled.

He glanced at the title of the piece, and then looked at her. He reached into his pocket. "I want to give you your gift." He removed a small box and handed it to her. She opened it. Inside was a gold ring with a single ruby of about half a carat in an intricate filigree setting.

"Oh, Ben!"

He leaned close to her. "The ruby is for the color of your hair, and the color of our passion."

She covered him with kisses.

"Wait, wait!" he said, pulling away slightly. "Look at the inside."

There was an inscription. It read in the tiniest letters, 'Marry Me.'

"Ben—" she whispered.

"The time has come."

She looked up at him. "I am leaving soon."

"Then marry me first and we will go together."

She lowered her gaze and stared at the ring. He took it from her and placed it on her finger.

"Do not answer me now," he said. "Let us enjoy our Christmas without the burden of making great decisions. By tomorrow night, will you give me your answer?"

"Yes," she replied, her eyes still lowered so he would not see the tears brimming in them. "I will."

Outside it had begun to snow. They banked the fires, blew out the candles, and crept quietly upstairs. There in her bed, they made love until the early morning. Before falling asleep, Ben stole out into the adjoining bedroom. Cassandra lay awake in the darkness after he left, twisting the ring on her finger. She wondered what would happen if she stayed.

******

By mid-morning, there were several inches of snow on the ground. They slept in late, then met downstairs, where Mrs. Merriweather was stirring and had prepared a large Christmas breakfast, in spite of Cassandra's instructions to take the day off. The housekeeper raised an eyebrow when Ben walked into the breakfast room, but when he grinned broadly and wished her a Happy Christmas, she cracked a smile and returned the greeting warmly.

The other servants had made their way to church through the snow, but around noon, they came stomping back into the kitchen. Cassandra told them their presents were under the tree, and she and Ben enjoyed their delight as they all gathered in the sitting room, by the fire that Ben had lit, to open and exclaim over their gifts.

A knock sounded at the great door, and Cassandra went to answer it. It was a messenger from Gatewick House with a note for Ben. Cassandra took it to him, and he went pale when he read it.

"What is it?" she whispered.

"My parents," he replied, looking up at her. "They have come."

"Without notice?"

"Yes," he said, distraught. "I must go. They arrived last night and were surprised not to find me there." He went out to the entryway to put on his great cloak, his hat, gloves and boots, and Cassandra followed him, bringing the parchment of music, which she placed inside his jacket.

"I will send a note back as soon as I have a moment," he said to her, "and let you know the reason for their sudden appearance."

"Perhaps they just want to spend Christmas with you," she said hopefully.

He looked at her, his face grim. "Not likely." He pulled her close and kissed her. "I love you," he said. "You shall hear from me soon."

"I love you, too," she said, realizing it was the first time she had said it. His face lit with joy. "Cassandra, does this mean... can I tell my parents?"

"No!"

He pulled back from her, startled.

"No," she said more softly. "I have not made a decision. But the fact is that I do love you. I have loved you for a long time. Say nothing to your parents. I must have a little more time."

"I live for your answer. Happy Christmas, my love." He smiled and went out.

Cassandra spent the rest of the day quietly. She played the piano at length, then went to the window seat with a book, but found herself doing little more than looking out at the snow—the first snowfall of the season. Her ring caught a reflection of candlelight and flashed. Cassandra gazed at it. Thoughts whirled in her head. What if I stayed? What if I married him, moved into Gatewick House? I could go to London, go through the portal, and tell them. James could come visit me. No. He is wanted by the authorities here. Then I could go into the future sometimes to see him. No. They could not keep the portal maintained indefinitely. I would have to choose. James or Ben. My life there or here.

******

All of the servants had gone to homes of friends or relatives for Christmas dinner, or to the Merriweather's cottage, where they and Anna were preparing their own meal. Ben and Cassandra had planned to prepare dinner together, but now she was alone in the house, trying to buoy her spirits as best she could. As night fell, she nibbled some leftovers from the pantry and finally made herself an omelet.

Just before seven, a knock came at the door, and she ran to answer it. It was a messenger from the Clarkes, delivering to her a gift of books by Maria Edgeworth, a thoughtful and expensive present. She thought of the other niceties she had received in the last few days: a crocheted shawl from the Moore girls, a muff from the Merriweather's, made from a fox that Mr. Merriweather had caught trying to get into the chicken coop, a delicate, embroidered lace handkerchief from Anna, and some French soaps and powders sent from the Holcombs, an obligatory response to the gifts she had sent to them.

She went into the sitting room, took a chair by the fire, and settled in with one of the books. After a time, there was another knock and she was at the door in moments. This time, a messenger from Gatewick House placed a note in her hand. She invited him in to warm in the kitchen while she read it.

My love,

My father has taken it into his head to come, this blessed Christmas day, to express his displeasure with me. To put it concisely, he wants me to quit my music and go into business with him. He has told me that if I refuse, he will disinherit me. I am in a terrible state. I have the money I received when I came of age, but it is running low. I feel I may have no choice but to succumb to his wishes. Pray for me; I am despondent. He and my mother are staying indefinitely. My father does not approve of my life and wants to 'put me in order,' as he says. I cannot see you for a few days, but I will come the moment I can get away. Send no note back; only know that I adore you.

Yours, Benedict.

Cassandra sat down with the missive in her hand, trying to take in all the implications of the situation. After several moments, she roused herself, went to the kitchen, and told the messenger there was no reply. She spent another hour with her book. She played "Farewell to Rome" for herself, thinking of Ben. She then went up to bed and before falling asleep, read Jane's letter again for comfort.

CHAPTER NINETEEN

*D*ecember 28, 1820 – *The days since Christmas have dragged by. It has continued to snow off and on (unusual for this part of the country, but most welcomed by me), and the landscape is beautiful. I put on my sturdiest boots and warmest cloak and went out in it several times over the last few days to walk and meditate on the pure, pure white. It is simply untouched. There are rabbit and deer tracks, even some fox, but not a footstep from a human being other than my own..*

I feel like a lone wolf when I wander about in the snow, looking for something, I don't know what. Unlike the wolf, or maybe just like him, I find peace in the quiet stillness. Then I go indoors and that peacefulness becomes replaced by restlessness. I have trouble concentrating on a book, even on the piano.

I will force myself to go to church this morning and listen to Mr. Collins drone on, for it will be good to get out and see others. I have heard that the Charles family retired to London until after the New Year, so I will be safe from encountering that evil creature.

I have only two weeks before I'm scheduled to return. I have not made a decision, but I'm continuing to organize my things and take care of final details around the house.

******

The snow ended just before New Year's Eve, but it continued cold and gray. The snow from Christmas and the few days after remained on the ground, and not many travelers were inclined to brave the roads.

Cassandra was surprised to hear a loud knock on the door around four o'clock. It was answered by Mary, who ushered Ben into the sitting room. After the girl had closed the doors, Cassandra ran to his arms and he kissed her deeply. She looked at his face—it appeared weary and haggard. She led him to the sofa and ordered some tea and wine. They made small talk as Mary bustled about bringing in the tea tray with a special warm, spiced wine that Anna had concocted. Cassandra poured a glass for Ben, and he sipped it gratefully. Cassandra was quiet, letting him gather his thoughts.

Finally he began with a sigh, "My love, never have I been so plagued. My mother and father find fault with everything in my household and in my life. That is why I have not invited you. They are merciless, and I cannot subject you. I could bear them if I knew they would soon go and leave me in peace. Yet my father is pressing me beyond reason to join his business. He is getting old, he says, and wants the business to carry on, and of course my mother supports this, for she is used to the money. I have played no music since they arrived—I have no peace of mind."

"My darling, I am so sorry!"

"The tragedy is that I feel I must give in to their wishes. I need his money; my inheritance would be enormous. I do not have the strength of character to be a starving musician. Frankly, I am not good with business, but I suppose I will learn. I will play my violin when I am alone, but nowhere else, never for friends, never with an ensemble. He forbids it. He wants me to sell Gatewick House and come back to London. I will go to work in his offices, doing, I know not what—his bidding, I suppose."

"Sell Gatewick House? But is not that your decision to make?"

"Unfortunately, it is not mine," he said with pain in his voice. "My parents paid for the house. I convinced them that I could focus on settling down and finding a wife if I had a nice, big home in the country. Really, I just wanted to get away from life in the city, where they were constantly hovering about. But, in fact, I did entertain a hope that as a bachelor moving into a grand country mansion I would attract the single women of the neighborhood. If I had to marry, I thought, I wanted to find a sweet, simple girl."

He gave Cassandra a sad smile, and she was conscious of the irony of his falling in love with her instead. "Didn't Miss Austen have something to say about a single man of a certain income, necessarily being in want of a wife?" he asked with tired humor.

"I believe so," Cassandra responded and paused. "But how is this possible? How can you give up what you love so much? At this time in life to not be able to be your own man!"

"I have no choice," he said with finality.

"Of course you do," she replied. "Money is not everything. It is nothing compared to your love of music. That is your life, it is who you are!"

"You can say that," he said bitterly, "you are independent and no one is your master. Now I must live a life devoted to my parents' whims until they die. It could be twenty years, for God's sake! But if you marry me—"

"You would be free of this burden," she remarked, a chill running down her spine.

"Yes," he whispered.

She took a deep breath. "You never told me what your father's business is."

"He is in the sugar trade with Jamaica," he said flatly.

Her blood turned from cold to ice. The sugar plantations fueled the slave trade. Sugar made rum, rum was a hugely important commodity, and the plantations could not be run without slaves. These industries were completely dependent on each other. To be in the sugar trade meant, directly or indirectly, one was involved in the slave trade.

"You cannot do it," she said firmly. "You can say what you want about my financially independent perspective, but you cannot participate in that business. To trade sugar means to trade slaves. You must know that."

He turned away from her, his face red. "I am not sure of that—"

"Yes, you are!" she cried. "Do not tell me that. You know your father must be involved with slavery. How could you be a part of that?"

"Cassandra, you cannot know—"

"I do! My husband bought and sold slaves," she said tearfully, now believing her own false history. "I never told you. I found out after he died."

"Dear God."

It all seemed suddenly too real.

"Cassandra," he continued, "if you do not marry me, I will have no choice but to do that terrible work. You can save me from such a fate!"

She regarded him with disdain. "If I am the only thing standing between you and participation in such atrocities, you are not the man I thought you were. I have my answer for you, Ben, and it is no. I am leaving soon, and I am leaving alone."

"Cassandra" he uttered, now in tears. "Please reconsider. Please let me go with you."

She was moved by his anguish and took his hand. "I am sorry, but I cannot feel the same way about you if you would even consider such work. However, you must live your life and do what you have to do. I must go back to my son. I will always love you, but we can never see each other again."

She let go his hand and took off the ring. "Please, take this," she said, putting it into his palm. "I am leaving for London to settle my business affairs as soon as I have everything in order here. Then I am off to Portsmouth and America, so let us say goodbye now. But Benedict," she continued, taking his hand again and speaking adamantly, "Listen to me. As a person who has seen the horror and the ravages that slavery inflicts on individuals and on a nation, I beseech you to act with your conscience. That is all I have to say to you."

"Please, Cassandra."

"Good-bye, Benedict." She stood and walked away from him to the window, tears streaming down her face. She heard his footsteps, then the sitting room door closed behind him.

Moments later, she felt the thud of the great doors of Sorrel Hall.

******

January 1st, 1821 – The first day of the New Year. I have been at Sorrel Hall almost a full year, and now, it is time for me to return home. Today, I am not celebrating the New Year, and neither am I mourning the loss of the old. Within my soul I am celebrating the experiences I have had this last year, both good and bad, and I am trying to anticipate what the future will have to offer me. There are certainly many people I shall be joyous to see again, my darling son primary among them.

I won't be able to take back much of the clothing and various other items I've acquired here, because I'd have to carry it all to the portal exit from the White Hart Inn. But I do intend to bring some things with me, and am glad there is no taboo about bringing souvenirs from the past to the future as there is the other way around, bringing modern items into the past. The only possible exception to this is Jane's letter because it is something that would not have otherwise existed in the future if I had not saved it from the fire. The other things, such as the Christmas gifts I received, will simply be relics, my mementos: authentic artifacts from a time I can never return to.

I have given many of my clothes away to my friends among the farmers' wives, who were thrilled to have such finery. I also gave away undergarments, gloves, slippers, and other necessities to Mary, Anna, and the other female servants. I knew Mrs. Merriweather would accept no charity, but the others heartily appreciated the lovely things. And, from the excess cash I still keep hidden in the false bottom of my suitcase, I've made up envelopes of bonuses for all the servants who've been under my employ.

Mary wondered at my taking so few things on my journey to America, but I simply assured her that the fashions were different there and that I only need a few things for the boat. I will bring back much of my music, but some of it I sent to Jane Holcomb to encourage her playing. I also decided to bring back some of the food given to me by the farmers' wives, so I can have it for awhile to remember the special flavors of the era.

I do all of this with a heavy heart. I am sad beyond words.

******

Cassandra hurriedly paid the obligatory parting visits, traveling by carriage over the frozen ground to all who would receive her, to say farewell and make her excuses for her sudden departure. She had originally anticipated returning to the portal on January twelfth to make her journey exactly one year, but now didn't see the point in waiting. She was dejected and the weather was dreary. She decided she would need until the sixth to finish getting ready, and she would leave for London then.

The day before her departure, she was in her bedroom packing up a few last things when she heard a horse's footsteps approaching the house. She looked out and saw Ben dismounting and walking up to the door. She had left strict instructions with the servants that she did not wish to speak with him if he should decide to try and see her again, so she wasn't surprised to see him turn and go, after a moment at the door. Cassandra flung herself on the bed and sobbed.

That evening she spent with Mrs. Merriweather. She talked about Ben, trying to make sense of what happened, though not explaining everything. Mrs. Merriweather was practical in her responses, and Cassandra found comfort in them. The housekeeper did express her sorrow at seeing her mistress go, and it was hard for Cassandra to say she would write, knowing that the woman would never receive a letter from her.

Before bed, Mary helped her mistress pack and organize her last few things. The time traveler then went to sleep for the final time at Sorrel Hall.

******

Mary stood at the front doors watching while the coachman loaded Cassandra's two bags into the carriage. Mr. and Mrs. Merriweather, Anna, William, Thomas, Lydia, and all the other servants had said their goodbyes in the entryway. Anna's eyes were red, William seemed to be clearing his throat excessively, and Mrs. Merriweather had extracted a handkerchief and was holding it at the ready while her husband busily stuffed tobacco into his pipe without looking up. Cassandra paused in the doorway, clutching her handbag.

"Well, good-bye." The words caught in her throat. She took a step toward the carriage.

"Ma'am, wait a moment," said Mary. "I shall see you into the carriage." She took her mistress' arm, and they walked out into the chilly morning air. "I have one thing to ask you before you go, if you do not mind."

"Yes, Mary. Anything."

"What is a time traveler?"

Cassandra stopped. She looked at her closely. "Why do you ask me this?"

"Because I heard you call yourself that when Master Franklin was here. Before you go on your journey, I felt I had to ask you, as I may never see you again."

With a feeling of panic Cassandra recalled the conversation that Mary had overheard in the sitting room the past summer. "Well, it is—" She searched for an explanation. "It is a person who…who travels without thought to time or schedule. A person who is free to come and go without worry about when they arrive or leave, like James himself did when he came here from America."

"You are going back to find him, is that true?"

"Yes, Mary, I am."

"And did he change history?"

"Do you know what that means?"

"No, I am afraid not, but I heard you say it."

Cassandra glanced at the house and the servants gathered in the doorway. She and Mary were at the carriage, and the coachman was waiting to hand her in. She held up a finger to him to wait and he moved away.

"What I meant was that sometimes our own actions change the story of our lives in a way we never anticipated. My coming here, I believe, changed the course of my life, and James' life was certainly changed."

The young woman nodded slowly. "I think I understand. For instance, because I know you and how you love to read, I have begun to learn. Anna is teaching me."

"Oh Mary!" She embraced the startled girl. "That makes me very happy." She released her after a moment and took a step back.

"Thank you, ma'am." Mary smiled, her eyes downcast.

"Good-bye." Tears welled in Cassandra's eyes.

"Good-bye," Mary whispered.

Cassandra waved to the household staff, and they waved back, Mrs. Merriweather applying the handkerchief to her eyes.

When a person visits a place, Cassandra thought as she rode away, soaking in every sight, there is always the hope of returning. When a person visits a time, saying good-bye is permanent.

She asked to be taken to the White Hart. There, she was well remembered by Betsy and the rest of the staff. She decided she would wrap up her business in one day. After a night's rest in her former room, she went to the bank to close her account. The Bank of England was sorry to lose her money, most of which still remained untouched. It would be a blow to the institution, but the handsome fee they extracted for such a large withdrawal softened it somewhat. Getting names and addresses of some of London's orphanages from Mr. Howard at the bank, she hired a hack chaise to carry her to them, one by one. She divided the sum of her remaining wealth, a little less than three thousand pounds, among five of the neediest.

Her final chore was to visit the office of Ben's barristers. She paid them to keep an eye on the orphanages and see that they used the money for the direct benefit of the children. She knew that such a charitable action might be changing history, but she hoped it would be for the better. She had considered leaving money in Ben's bank account to free him from the tyranny of his father, but she decided that to do it could be radically altering history. He had his own decisions to make.

Finally, back at the White Hart, she gathered her bags, and headed down the hotel stairs with them. A young man and woman passed her in the entryway, and Cassandra stopped, recognizing the woman. It was Rosalind Carr, the girl who had been on her way to become a governess, the one Cassandra had met the night she'd eaten in the dining room. Rosalind didn't notice her —her eyes were only for the man. Cassandra spied a wedding ring flashing on her finger and smiled to herself. That story had ended far better than she had predicted.

She was suddenly startled by the bellman rushing up to her. "Mrs. Franklin! Please let me take your bags!" He moved to grab them from her hands, but she held on firmly.

"No, thank you, Charlie. I am only going a short distance and will handle them myself."

Charlie looked around helplessly at the desk clerk who was on his feet in a moment. "No! No! Let us order you a carriage, Mrs. Franklin, I insist!"

The doorman went out to whistle for a hack chaise.

"No!" Cassandra screeched. The three men froze in their tracks. She modulated her voice and continued. "I am going only a few blocks to a friend's house, who will assist me on my way to Portsmouth. I need the walk to clear my head. Please, let me be."

"If you say so, Mrs. Franklin," uttered the desk clerk.

"I do. But thank you for your efforts. Good evening." Cassandra straightened her back, hefted her bags, and marched out the door.

"Good evening, Mrs. Franklin!" called the clerk after her as Charlie shrugged and moved away, and the doorman slunk back in. "Please come again!"

It was around four o'clock; the sky was almost dark, and the fog had set in. She scurried the short distance to the alleyway and peeked around the corner. It thankfully was empty—too cold even for vagrants. She ran to the end of the alley, and in seconds disappeared.

CHAPTER TWENTY

Before Cassandra could focus her sight on anything, she heard James' voice.

"Mom!"

The pod door slid open, and he grabbed her in his arms, hugging her tightly. "Oh, Mom, I can't tell you how glad...I'm so happy! We were so worried—"

Over his shoulder, she saw Nick Stockard standing, wiping tears away and smiling.

Professor Carver's voice boomed. "Cassie! Oh, Cassie we knew you'd make it!" He was beside her in a moment, stealing her away from James and giving her one of his enveloping hugs. "It's so good to see you!"

Next it was Jake's turn, then Shannon's, and then Simon's. Most of the team was there to witness her return. Nick hung back, letting her greet her friends. Finally she went to him. They looked at each other for a moment, and then she threw her arms around him and embraced him warmly. "I knew you'd be okay," he whispered.

"We weren't sure when you'd be back, Mom, even though the twelfth was the target date. We didn't even know *if* you'd be back!"

Cassandra grasped her son's arm. "I told you nothing would keep me from getting back."

"I know," he breathed.

"Actually, we made a pool," laughed Jake.

"What!"

"Yeah," he continued, "we made bets on which day and time you'd return, and I won! Or at least I was the closest."

"I refrained, Cassandra," remarked Nick good-naturedly.

"As did I, Cassie," added Professor Carver. "Most un-scientific!" Everyone laughed. "Come, let's sit you down."

They all crowded into the lounge area and sat around Cassandra, James closest to her on the small couch.

"Seriously, Cass," said Shannon. "We were really worried. You could have gone to prison in James' stead. We were trying not to imagine the worst, but—"

Cassandra quickly related the tale of her performance in the police station and how she managed to disintegrate the music player and divorce herself from any suspicion. She also told how she faked the note from James so that Ben would be convinced of his escape.

"Incredible!" gasped Simon.

"Pretty quick thinking, Cass," said Jake, "though I have to confess that I did ask Elton's permission to go back and check on you."

"Yeah, me too," added Nick sheepishly.

"But I said no, as I know you would have wanted," Professor Carver remarked. "We all know the dangers of time travel; we all know what we might be in for when we go, and that we're responsible for our own safety."

"I appreciate everyone's concern, but I also appreciate that you trusted me, Elton." She squeezed her boss's hand as they locked eyes.

"You are a brilliant scientist and a resourceful woman, Cassie," he replied. "However, I can't tell you how relieved we are to have you back with us again."

"Thank you." She beamed at her colleagues.

She remained in the lab with the team for several hours. All of the items she carried and her clothes had to be specially sanitized in case they contained any disease or parasite. This was routine. The scientists ran tests on the food she'd brought along to see if it was safe to take out of the lab, while she went into the shower and washed with special cleanser. She put on her own clothes that were waiting for her on this occasion. She was pleased to see they still fit. Then she was required to stand under a high-intensity ray, which further purged her of any ancient biological threats.

No one could leave the lab, now that they'd touched her, until they also stepped under the sanitizer for decontamination. The air in the lab was tested for airborne viruses.

While going through the sanitation process, she left her bags to the mercy of the scientists as they removed everything for scrutiny. When she emerged from the final phase of the process into the lounge area of the lab, James was waiting for her with a peculiar look on his face.

"What?" she asked in alarm.

"I found this in your suitcase," he said, holding open a small velvet box with the ring from Ben inside.

"How on earth?" she uttered in surprise. "How did it get in there?" Then she remembered that Ben must have met Mary at the front door of Sorrel Hall, and that later that day the girl had been arranging things in her suitcase. He must have given it to her and she slipped it in among Cassandra's clothes. She smiled to herself.

"I will explain it later," she said to James, "just keep it safe. There's something else, you will be interested in seeing." She went to where her things were scattered about on the examination table and extracted her journal from the pile. The scientists huddled in with anticipation. She opened the journal and carefully removed the letter.

"What is it?" Shannon was the first to ask.

"It's a letter from Jane Austen to her sister."

There were exclamations all around, and she looked at Professor Carver out of the corner of her eye.

"How did you get it, Cassie?" he inquired.

She told the story and when she was through, the general consensus was that she'd done the right thing in preserving it.

"Well, I would say," offered Carver, "that if this is an item for your personal collection, there's no harm done. But I would hesitate to publish it with your other documentation."

Cassandra agreed to defer to his judgment, and then let the letter be carefully decontaminated.

******

After returning from any time journey, there was always a certain period of debriefing, especially in Cassandra's case as she had been gone so long. The shock of stepping out into the modern day world could be great, so she spent the night in the lab, and went out early in the morning, before the hub of the city of London was at its peak. Nevertheless, the noise was hard on her ears, and the general stimulation intense.

She went with Professor Carver, James, and Nick, who was now officially a member of the team, to her Bloomsbury apartment to continue the debriefing. She would remain there, venturing out little by little, until she felt assimilated enough to fly home to Boston and resume her normal life.

Debriefing a time traveler was a matter of asking questions and getting the person to sort out past from present. Since Cassandra's journey had been a long one, it took more time than usual. But Cassandra was resilient, and she responded well. Between the sessions with the three of her colleagues, she watched the VV (virtual vision) and reacquainted herself with modern culture. She tuned into the news of the day via sens-net and tried to focus on the here and now in as many ways as possible.

When Professor Carver was confident that her debriefing was complete, he gave her the okay to return to the U.S. She did not want to remain in England long. Even three hundred years in the future, there was too much there that reminded her of the past. It was time to be the objective scientist. Within two weeks of her return to the twenty-second century, she was back at her Boston townhouse.

Now she had to get on with the second phase of her project, which was to record it. This phase was already partly accomplished as a result of her journaling. By swiping the pages she had neglected to erase during her journey, she was able to record its entirety in the database. As she read them over again, she verbally recorded her additional comments and observations.

Phase three of her experiment was analysis, and then finally, she would publish. Analyzing her experience meant she would be researching the records of the lives of the people she had come in contact with throughout her visit, determining if she had had any effect on the outcome of those lives. The research itself was not difficult. All historical dates ever recorded about deaths, births, marriages and other information of public interest had, over time, been computerized from church records, family histories, ship logs, and other sources. Within the last one hundred and fifty years, information that was already on computers had then been added to the database so that one could enter the name and the approximate time and country, and get all the possible matches in an instant.

Both Nick and James were highly interested in working with Cassandra on this particular phase of the project. Nick had expressed that he wasn't ready to publish yet. He had ten years of experiences to officially record, though, like any good scientist, he had kept a journal. He had spent almost two months debriefing with Professor Carver's team and needed a break from thinking about his own experience, so he was in no hurry to begin his work. He would also eventually look up the people whose lives he touched, but he wanted to help Cassandra first.

She, of course, was most curious to know about the outcome of Ben's life, but decided to save him for last. She was anxious about what the result would be. She was finding it difficult to adjust to the fact that he was long dead. Instead, she felt like she was just recovering from a recent heartbreak.

The three scientists gathered in the study of Cassandra's townhouse on an afternoon in February to begin the research. James wanted to know about Elizabeth Charles, so they started there. It turned out that in 1821 she married a man named Sir Richard Thorpe. The fact that he had a title indicated that he might have been somewhat older than her at the time of their marriage, so they looked up his birth record, and indeed, he was ten years older than she. The only other reference to her in history was that in delivering her first child, in 1822, both mother and baby perished. This was a sad realization for James.

Lady Charles did not live much longer than her daughter. She died in 1823, but Sir Robert remained a prominent member of Parliament until his death in 1835. He never remarried, and they saw no evidence that he'd had any success re-instating an anti-witchcraft law. Cassandra breathed a sigh of relief.

Next they entered the name Eunice Fairchild. Here was a happy surprise. Eunice married Jeffrey Holcomb in 1825. He had great success in his military career, and by 1840 was an admiral in the British Navy. They had four children, all of whom lived into adulthood.

Cassandra's heart was in her throat as they looked up Jane Holcomb, wondering if she would see Ben's name connected with hers. An irrational jealousy overcame her. But once the information was called up, she was pleasantly surprised to find that Jane married Edward Clarke in 1824. Cassandra chuckled. Lady Holcomb couldn't have been too pleased about the match. Edward took his orders as a clergyman in 1821 in a parish near Selborne. Cassandra figured that his inheritance was probably rather small, as would be his income as a preacher. But since Jane had a decent dowry, they probably scraped by, in spite of the fact that they had eight children. Six of them survived into adulthood. Lady Holcomb died in 1830.

The two Moore girls, surprisingly, both married baronets and both remained childless.

Mr. and Mrs. Merriweather stayed on at Sorrel Hall until their deaths at the ages of seventy and seventy-five, respectively. As Cassandra went to look for Mary's records, she realized that, try as she might, she could not recall the girl's last name. "I can't believe I never asked," she said out loud.

"She might have ended up doing something notable," James remarked. "Since she apparently educated herself. "

"We will never know," said Cassandra, sadly.

They found that the Collins did not return to Sorrel Hall. It was sold to Eunice and Jeffery Holcomb in 1831, and Cassandra was glad to know that it had fallen into good hands.

Finally they were ready to search Ben's history. Cassandra began to chew on her pinky nail, and Nick cleared his throat and ran his fingers through his hair. She smiled at him, and he reached out and squeezed her hand. James went down to the kitchen to get a bottle of wine and poured out a glass for each of them when he returned. Gratefully accepting the wine from her son, Cassandra took a hearty sip and then spoke the words, "Benedict Johnston, circa 1821, England." The computer responded immediately, and projected the information.

There was a record of a Benedict Johnston who set sail for America from Portsmouth on board the Crescent in July of 1821. The ship docked at New York harbor two months later.

Cassandra was stunned. "He left his father!"

"Don't jump to conclusions, Mom," warned James. "Maybe he went to the U.S. on his father's business. Let's see if his name shows up in any transactions."

However, the next record of Benedict Johnston in the U.S. was a marriage to a Sarah Williams in 1823. Cassandra sharply took in a breath. The name Benedict Johnston then turned up in 1826 on a list of musicians for a concert with the Grand Symphony Orchestra as first violinist. Cassandra's heart was racing now.

She decided to look up Sarah Williams. Her father was an Anglican minister at the Church of All Angels in New York City. His name was Jeremiah Williams, and there were a couple of newspaper articles at the time mentioning him as a fervent abolitionist. Sarah and Benedict were married in his church. The records noted that they had three children together, Cassandra, Jeremiah and James. The two boys had families of their own, but Cassandra Johnston did not.

Now Cassandra was weeping, and James and Nick looked at each other, unsure what to do. Nobody spoke. All she could think was that, yes, she had changed history, though she hadn't meant to. She had led Ben to happiness, for so it seemed. He had rejected work that would have made him a party to slavery, and instead had gone in search of a new life. For all she knew, he had gone in search of her. But instead, he found Sarah Williams and became a father and a successful musician. Where were his descendents today, she wondered? Maybe she would meet them someday.

James went to get his mother a glass of water and, as he left the room, subtly gestured to Nick, who gathered Cassandra in his arms, gently rocking her. She cried on his shoulder until she was spent. James returned with the glass of water and lightly stroked her hair until she looked up at him. There was no doubt now of the impact of their visit.

Still, there was one more thing both she and James had to consider in their research. Cassandra took his hand and pulled him back down into his chair.

"James," she began, taking a breath to clear her thoughts, "have you looked up your own name yet in the records since you've been back?"

"Yeah," he replied. "I had to. I was dying to see what the newspapers said about my escape." He grinned at Nick.

"It's serious, James!" his mother admonished him. "Fortunately, it doesn't look like their knowledge of the event adversely affected any of our acquaintances. Quite the contrary, as a matter of fact, but I want to know if you had an impact otherwise—in London, or on the poor police captain, for instance."

"No, Mom, not that I can see. Here, I'll show you." He called up his name in conjunction with the year 1820, and there was the article that Cassandra had read in the Times while in London, and several others after the escape—all very sensational. The mystery was marveled at in the papers for two weeks after the event. But the three scientists noted with interest that the police never revealed the disappearance of the music device, probably they were too embarrassed.

Both James and Nick had read the irate letter from Lady Charles that Cassandra kept for her documentation, and Cassandra began to think about it now more than she had for some time. "You know," she remarked, "I feel I'm coming to a conclusion about the success of my experiment, and it's not a positive one."

"What?" Nick and James both exclaimed, overlapping. "What are you talking about?"

"Well," she continued calmly. "First of all, I...we," she glanced at James, "obviously affected the past and altered history."

"Well, yeah, somewhat," admitted James.

"But for me, more personally, the issue is that I was not successful in fitting in with the people and ways of the time, and therein, I feel I failed in my experiment."

"What do you mean?" exclaimed her son. "You were loved my many people, accepted as a friend by many, you made someone fall in love with you." He glanced at Nick. "You were valued by the lower class as a wonderful patron. How is that not success?"

"I appreciate what you're saying, James, but people still regarded me as an outsider, in particular Lady Charles. For all her faults, she was really the most perceptive. She knew there was something inherently different about me—something more than being an American. She thought it was something… well, paranormal, for lack of a better word. She was right—I was from the future, for God's sake. And because of my oddness, I alienated her."

"Mom, I was the one who did the damage. I was the one who brought the PAL. If anyone sabotaged your experiment, it was me."

"My love," she replied, "I will not let you feel guilty about that. This was my experiment, and I take the responsibility for it. The fact that I failed to properly fit in stirred Lady Charles' ire before you even arrived. Not to even mention the fact that Nick here knew I was a time traveler, practically from the moment I walked through his door."

"Well, now, that's different," chimed Nick. "I was able to recognize the signs of a time traveler because I am one."

"Look, don't get me wrong," continued Cassandra. "It goes without saying that a failed experiment is just as valuable as a successful one. I learned something here for scientists to benefit from in the future."

"Of course," Nick agreed. To James he said, "You and I have yet to analyze the success or failure of our journeys."

"Well, mine was pretty much analyzed right here today," James said.

"Yes, but you still need to combine your perspective with the result," added his mother.

Feeling emotionally weary, they decided to quit for the day. James took his leave to go spend time with some of his friends. Nick asked Cassandra if she'd like to get some dinner, and she realized she was starving. They went to a good seafood restaurant nearby that she knew of, for that was the food she had missed the most during her time in the past—fresh shellfish didn't make it much farther than the port towns in those days.

Cassandra was exhausted from thinking about her own time travel experience, so as they sipped their wine and waited for their food in the candle-lit bistro. She decided it was finally a good time to ask Nick why he had once made the decision to journey to nineteenth-century England, presumably to stay forever. She didn't need to ask, for before she could inquire, he began the conversation himself.

"You asked me once why I had traveled to old England and stayed so long. I think it's time to give you an answer."

"I would love to know," she replied, "but I didn't want to pry."

"Well, it's not a happy story, nor one I like telling. But I want you to know my reasons." He picked up a piece of bread and put it on his plate. "Back in the 2080s, I formed a chronology team of my own. I had just completed my PhD at MIT, studying under Carver."

"Really!"

"Yeah. It was when he was still teaching, before he had a team. I admired him immensely. But he was too slow for me, too cautious. I was young, you know, still in my twenties, and I thought I knew everything."

"I know someone like that," she said, chuckling.

"Yes, exactly. And to make matters worse, I was heir to a huge fortune. My parents are among the wealthiest people in the world, I'm somewhat embarrassed to say."

Cassandra thought for a moment. "Stockard…wait a minute not *the* Stockards."

"Yes," he laughed, "*the* Stockards"

"Goodness," she murmured raising her eyebrow.

"Wealth, combined with youth, made me cockier than I deserved to be. I gathered around me several brilliant scientists and built a laboratory of state-of-the-art equipment, and we rushed to beat Carver to the breakthrough."

"He beat you, though."

"Yes, he did. But as I told you before, we weren't far behind, with just enough of a difference in our methods so that we couldn't be accused of stealing from him. It didn't really matter, because each person on our team had signed a nondisclosure agreement, and we didn't plan on telling anyone what we were doing anyway. We just didn't want to be under the scrutiny of the scientific community. As it turns out, we should have been more cautious."

"What happened?" Cassandra asked with trepidation.

"Well, first of all, I fell in love with and married one of my colleagues. Her name was Nagla Sumeria."

"That doesn't seem so bad."

"No, no, it was wonderful, she was wonderful—"

Nick looked down; Cassandra took a sip of water.

"Anyway, we took the same precautions as Carver, tested and retested the machine, but I was anxious to start traveling. I was the first one to make a trip. It was just a brief one, back to the 1920s to check out jazz clubs in Harlem. It was successful, so we started planning longer ones. My wife was of Egyptian descent and wanted to go to ancient Egypt, but just for a short stay, just to get a taste of it, because it was a very volatile time. I was against it, but she eventually persuaded me. My problem was that I couldn't go with her to help keep her safe. As you know, time travel is usually done solo, but there was no way I would send a woman back to that time period alone. However, as a white man, I just simply could not go. Nobody existed there who looked like me; I would stand out like a phantom."

He buttered his bread, took a bite, and chewed it. "So another scientist on the team, an African American fellow, offered to go. Using anthropological and archeological studies, we determined that they both looked enough like the ancient Egyptians to get by without undue notice. Well, we were wrong." Nick took a gulp of wine. "We set up the portal exit on the outskirts of Alexandria, using ancient maps to assure that it was in a remote area. But when they walked into the city, looking like travelers, they were soon seized and thrown in jail. Apparently they were of the wrong race to be seen together as man and woman. We had taken so much care with the costumes, the hair and jewelry, and all the other details, but we just didn't know enough about the cultural taboos."

"Oh my God, what happened?" asked Cassandra.

"They killed my wife."

"Oh no!" cried Cassandra.

"Yes, and they sentenced our friend Rodney to slavery."

Just then the waiter came and delivered their salads. They both sat staring at them.

"Fortunately, Rodney was able to escape within just a couple of days and made it back to the portal exit. We could not recover Nagla's body, though. I don't even know what they did with her."

"Oh, Nick, I…oh, dear God. I'm so, so sorry. It's, it's just beyond comprehension."

"Yeah," he said sorrowfully, picking at his salad. "At the time, I just wanted to kill myself. I felt fully responsible for her death. I scrapped my work, and the team went their separate ways. I just stumbled around through life for awhile and then decided that I couldn't live in a world anymore that reminded me of her. So I gathered enough of the team back together to help me set up a temporary lab and one-way portal exit. I left for nineteenth-century England with a huge wad of money and my eighteenth-century cello. All I wanted around me was music, so I opened up the shop and played now and then at salons and private concerts. I kept a low profile."

They sat silently for a few minutes, mechanically eating their salads.

"Why did you choose that time period in England?" Cassandra finally ventured.

"Because it was easy for me to fit in there. And there was no upheaval in the country. Actually, England was still fighting Napoleon, but I already knew the outcome. I liked the time period; most of my favorite music was written before 1810—a baroque fan." He smiled. "I tried not to get involved with people's lives. I had a few friends, some devoted servants. I thought I was happy. And then you walked in, and I had to suddenly reassess why I was there and what I was doing with my life."

"Did you really know right away that I was a time traveler?"

"Pretty much. You were just so different. People must have really noticed you everywhere you went."

"Yeah, they did. But as soon as I said I was American, they assumed that was it."

"Well, it's not like people in the past ran around thinking that people were visiting from the future."

"No, just you. Nick," she said, pushing her salad away, "it's horrible about your wife. I can't imagine! And when I think how close I came to having James shipped off irretrievably to nineteenth-century Australia !" She shuddered.

"It's riskier than we think. We're scientists. We think we've got it all under control. But," he said thoughtfully, having a drink of wine, "it's been a long time since Nagla's death. I've had enough time to deal with it, and I'm ready to move on with my life."

She was staring down at the ruby ring on her finger. She glanced up at him and smiled. "You know I'll always be in your debt for rescuing my son."

"The debt is mine. You rescued *me*. I couldn't tell you this before, but that day we spent together at Benedict's house really stayed with me. I couldn't stop thinking about you after that, and not just because I knew you were a time traveler."

She caught the significance in his eyes. At that moment, the waiter appeared with their lobsters. They dove into them wholeheartedly, cracking the shells, pulling out the meat, dipping it in the melted butter, and savoring the rich flavor.

They happily ate for several minutes, commenting only on the food and the wine. Nick spoke again. "I was wondering if you would mind telling me about how Franklin died."

Cassandra looked up from her food with a start.

Nick continued, "I almost asked James, but it just didn't seem appropriate. It thought I'd wait and see if you were willing to tell me."

Cassandra stared at the hull of lobster on her plate.

"I'm sorry," he said hurriedly. "I'm being nosy. Let's talk about something else."

"No," she said with hesitation. "I want to tell you."

Nick sat quietly, his wine in his hand.

"He traveled into the future," she stated simply.

"Oh," said Nick with understanding.

"He did it against Professor Carver's wishes and without his permission. Without mine, either. He snuck into the lab one night, eight years ago, set the coordinates himself for two years into the future, went, and came right back, having preset the travel mode to receive him. He felt sure that he'd only go into the lab of the future, not even step out of the portal, and return immediately. He did. He told me about it afterwards, and I was angry, but, frankly, curious myself."

"I certainly would have been," Nick commented.

"But as we now know," she continued, "traveling into the future disrupts the body's DNA at a cellular level. At that time, we hadn't seen the results in the test dummies, because it took a couple of years for the mutations to develop. But not long after Franklin took the trip, the test dummies showed signs of cellular degeneration. Our scientists, as well as a team of doctors, tried and tried to find the cure before Franklin developed them, but they had no success. They kept him out of pain, but that was all they could do."

"God, I'm—" Nick began.

"It's okay," Cassandra replied without conviction.

"Did you think about, you know, traveling back to before he did it to try to stop him? I know I considered it with Nagla."

"Of course, of course," she said vehemently, "but I didn't do it for the same reason you didn't."

"Once you make the decision to travel, into the past or future, you're stuck with the results. If you try to undo what you've done, you could set up a chain reaction."

"You don't know anymore what was meant to be and what you created. Whatever you do during your time travel, you live with the results."

"Which is why we're so careful," he said quietly.

"Why we try to be. We almost blew it in James' case."

"Yeah, but that was a little different. The outcome wasn't established. We had to take the chance to remove him from that situation."

"We did break some rules, but for me there wasn't a choice. He is my son."

"I can't tell you how I struggled with the decision not to go back a few weeks into the past and dissuade Nagla from taking the trip."

They both sat for a few minutes staring at the flame of the candle in the middle of the table.

A tear rolled down Cassandra's cheek and Nick caught it with his finger.

"I'm so sorry about Franklin." He whispered.

"Let's not talk about it anymore." She mustered a smile. "I'm as past it as I'll ever be, which is to say, I'll never be past it, but, like you, I've moved on."

They talked about their experiences they had during their time in England, food from the era, inconveniences, and comparisons to the twenty-second century. They were finally able to laugh, and Cassandra found herself thinking that she had not enjoyed herself like this since her time with Ben. She looked down at the ring again, and thought that, really, maybe she shouldn't wear it after all. Maybe if she ever found one of Ben's descendents, she would give it to them instead. It was time to move on from him as well.

Nick interrupted her thoughts. "Thinking about Ben?"

"No," she smiled, "not really. I was just thinking that it's time to let go of other things too. Ben is long dead, isn't he?" She took off the ring and plopped it into her purse.

Nick chuckled. "I'm afraid so." He called the waiter over, and they both ordered some strong English tea. As the waiter cleared the table, she noticed the label on a pat of butter that had been sitting there in a dish. It said 'Whitstone's.'

"Wait a minute," she said just before he whisked it away. "Can I see that?" The waiter put down the dish and walked away to get their tea. Cassandra picked up the pat of butter and looked at it closely. She read aloud the label, "Whitstone's Dairy, Hampshire, England."

"What?" asked Nick.

"Nothing. Should I know this brand?"

"What are you talking about? Of course. Whitstone's is a household name all over the world."

"Right." She was confused. Could it be that her giving Sarah Whitstone the antibiotics not only saved her life, but made her farm successful in a way it never would have been otherwise? She couldn't possibly know. If she had changed history, making Whitstone's a household word, the paradox would be that Whitstone's butter wouldn't have existed before she went on her time journey, and yet once she did go and saved Sarah's life, the diary farm would have begun being successful from that time forward, and always would have been a household name. She shook her head to clear it.

"Never mind," she said. "I'll explain it another time."

"Okay, well then, there's something I've been meaning to ask you."

"What is it?"

"Well, I know you wanted to time travel to the nineteenth century to experience life as Jane Austen lived it, but I've been wondering why you chose the year 1820. Why not go five years earlier and meet her yourself, when she was at the height of her creativity?"

"Do you know a lot about her?"

"Not exactly, but living in London for that particular decade, her books were popular. I couldn't avoid them."

Cassandra gave him a look of mock disapproval. "I considered going earlier, but then I thought that meeting her would probably be a letdown. She was shy and didn't move much outside her circle. She saved her wit and humor for those she knew best. She never enjoyed meeting strangers, and I would have had to work hard to get into her private world. Then, what if I changed it? I mean, not to flatter myself, but what if my meeting her changed even one word of one book. What if I knocked on the door while she was writing the moment of Emma's romantic revelation about Mr. Knightly and I caused her to lose her train of thought? No, I couldn't do it. So I chose a few years after her death, so that her world would scarcely have changed, but she was no longer in it."

"That's a beautifully scientific, and shockingly romantic reason." Nick had a sparkle in his eye.

"I did manage to get that letter though, didn't I?"

"Yes, I have to admit, that was well done. Do you think you'll ever time travel again?"

"I doubt it. Time to let others have their chance. I have a lot of work to do in the here and now."

"Me too," said Nick. "It's been nice helping you."

"Maybe you'd let me help you with your research," she offered.

"I'd love that. But you know, I'm also hoping that we could spend time together."

"We could play music together," she said.

"I'd really like that."

She studied his face. It was a nice one, she admitted. Handsome, just a little quirky. He was athletic and slim. She had been trying not to think of him as anything other than a friend, but now realized that she was free to do so, since it was becoming obvious that he had more than just friendly feelings for her.

He reached across the table and took her hand and gently kissed it. In the quaint atmosphere of the restaurant that had probably been there for two hundred years, drinking tea, and looking into Nick's eyes as he held her hand, Cassandra could almost feel herself transported back in time to old England again. But in that moment she realized that going forward was all she wanted to do. The past slipped into the past where it belonged, and before her, the future stretched out. Perhaps, she thought, she'd even found someone to travel it with.

ABOUT THE AUTHOR

Georgina lives in New York City with her family of artists. She has been an actress for most of her life, is a member of the Screen Actors Guild, and still does film work when not writing novels. She is also a feature writer and film/theater reviewer for various publications.

Watch for the second novel in The Time Mistress Series, *The Time Goddess*, in which Dr. Cassandra Reilly travels to pre-Civil War New York City and is thrown into a world of slave catchers, abolitionists and unexpected passion.